SONG

OF

BLOOD

&

STONE

EARTHSINGER CHRONICLES
BOOK ONE

SONG

OF

BLOOD

&

STONE

EARTHSINGER CHRONICLES
BOOK ONE

L. PENELOPE

ST. MARTIN'S PRESS ❧ NEW YORK

www.stmartins.com

Designed by Steven Seighman

Illustrations by David Curtis Studio

The Library of Congress Cataloging-in-Publication Data is available upon request.

ISBN 978-1-250-14807-0 (hardcover)
ISBN 978-1-250-14808-7 (ebook)

Our books may be purchased in bulk for promotional, educational, or business use. Please contact your local bookseller or the Macmillan Corporate and Premium Sales Department at 1-800-221-7945, extension 5442, or by email at MacmillanSpecialMarkets@macmillan.com.

First Edition: May 2018

10 9 8 7 6 5 4 3 2 1

For my father, who wanted me to live a happy life

SONG

OF

BLOOD

&

STONE

EARTHSINGER CHRONICLES
BOOK ONE

PROLOGUE

In the beginning, there was silence.

The melody of life and breath and heartbeats and change lay locked in a noiseless hush. No green shoots worked their way out of rocky soil. The parched earth was sterile, yearning for change.

The folk had long since shunned the scalding rays of the sun, instead choosing to burrow inside the mountain they called Mother.

And too far away to fathom, another world shattered and died, expelling two refugees who found their way to our shores. The arrival of the Lord and Lady pierced the quiet—their resonant Songs brought to life the hidden power of Earthsong. They were the Firsts.

They sang the grass and seeds and trees into being. They swelled shriveled streams into rivers, and stymied the will of the desert.

Curious, the folk came out of their caves, little by little, to bear witness to the rebirth of the land. Some were suspicious of the newcomers, but others, the young especially, were awestruck by a magic so different from their own.

And it came to pass that the Lady bore the Lord nine children, each as different from one to another as sea is to soil. Each with a Song rivaling the beauty and power of their parents. And they were the Seconds.

These children took wives and husbands from among the folk of the caves, now brought into the light. The fruit of these unions was plentiful, some bearing rich and varied Songs and some harmonizing the echoes of the caves. And they were the Thirds.

The Lord and the Lady ruled their brood with steady hands and hearts overflowing. And all was well.

For a time . . .

—EARTHSINGER CHRONICLES

CHAPTER ONE

A young man beseeched the Mistress of Eagles, How may I best honor my ancestors?

Eagle replied, You could carve your history into the side of a mountain to hold the tale longer, but only those standing before it may read. Or you could write your history on the waves of the ocean so that it may carry your story to all the lands of the world.

—COLLECTED FOLKTALES

Jasminda had wished for invisibility many times, perhaps today she'd finally achieved it. To the best of her knowledge, Earthsong could not be used for such a thing. But when she'd walked into the post station ten minutes ago, the postmistress had promptly disappeared behind the curtain. Now, the clock on the shelf ticked on. Jasminda's fingers drummed in time on the scarred wood of the countertop.

The bell above the door interrupted the duet. Jasminda's back was to the newcomer. A sharp intake of breath greeted her, and she didn't bother to turn around.

Not invisible, then.

The open door let in the sounds of horses and carts rumbling down the tightly packed dirt road, before closing, leaving the shop in silence once again.

With the arrival of the new customer, the proprietress reappeared, smiling warmly, while at the same time shoving an envelope and a large parcel wrapped in brown paper to Jasminda without even looking in her direction.

According to the postmark, the letter had traveled all the way from Elsira's capital city of Rosira on the western coast. The return address was a solicitor's office. Not the piece of mail she was expecting.

"This is it?" Jasminda's voice pitched higher with each word. She held up the envelope. "Everything since last month?"

"It's all that came in," the postmistress said brusquely. Jasminda sighed, her body deflating.

Out of the corner of her eye, she noticed the rigid way the new customer held herself, leaning her entire body away at an awkward angle. The woman was graying and stooped with age, which made the contortion act all the more laughable. She'd pressed herself into the corner of the small shop, carrying on as though she were sharing the space with a rabid animal and not a nineteen-year-old girl.

Unable to help herself, Jasminda closed her eyes and focused on the well of power within her. By itself, her Song was nothing but raw potential, a match waiting for a strike. But when the rush of Earthsong swept over her, the match caught fire, burning bright.

She extended her arms and scrutinized the deep, rich tone of her skin, so different than everyone else in the town, than just about everyone in the entire country of Elsira. The energy rippling through her gave her a deeper connection to her body. She became even more aware of her skin, how it knit together over muscle and bone. Silently, she sang a spell to shift its color to match the muted, less vibrant shade of the astonished women before her.

"Better?" She looked up, wearing a sweet smile as a mask.

The older woman made a sound like a cat struggling with a hairball and stumbled back, grabbing at the doorknob several times before catching hold.

"*Grol* witch," she muttered, then wrenched the door open and fled. The little bell jingled mercilessly.

The postmistress shot her a murderous glare and backed away, once again retreating behind the curtain separating the front area from the back.

Jasminda's brittle smile crumbled. She released her hold on Earthsong, and her skin changed back to its natural hue. She really shouldn't have wasted her power; she was weak enough as it was. There was no telling what she might meet on the journey home, and she couldn't afford to exhaust herself.

Frowning, she ripped open the unexpected letter from the unknown solicitor. She scanned the text, but the words inside were so formal she could barely make sense of them. A telephone exchange and number were printed on the letterhead. Jasminda had never phoned anyone before—hadn't had anyone to call—but the legal language on the page was gibberish, and she needed to have someone decipher it.

The letter and documents included must have something to do with the tax lien against the farm. Could this be the good news she'd been hoping for? Perhaps the tax bureau had turned the case over to the lawyers for her appeal. She didn't know how these things usually happened.

"How do I phone Rosira?" she called out. The post station had installed a public telephone kiosk six months before. Jasminda approached it warily.

The postmistress fought the dividing curtain in her rush to the front. "Who does someone like you have to call in the capital?" Her deep-set eyes narrowed.

"How. Is. It. Done?" Jasminda pressed her lips together, forming a barrier against other, harsher words she longed to say.

The woman paused, hands on her hips, before relenting. "Pick up the handle and click the lever a few times until the operator comes on. She'll tell you how much it'll be."

"Thank you." Jasminda smiled tightly and followed the postmistress's instructions. The operator's staticky voice announced that the call would be five tenthpieces. Jasminda dumped her change in the slot then waited long minutes for the call to be connected.

Once through to the solicitor's office, she had to wait again to be directed to the man named on the letter she'd received, a Mr. Niqolas Keen.

"It's really very simple, miss." His tone was clipped as if he was in a great hurry. "You sign the paperwork in front of a witness, alert us, and forty thousand pieces will be wired into your bank account."

"But why? What's the money for?"

"Your discretion. Your maternal grandfather, Marvus Zinadeel, has recently decided to act on long-held aspirations of running for public office. He's a wealthy merchant with good prospects, you know." Jasminda did not know.

"However, if news of his late daughter's . . . er, unfortunate marriage were to be discovered, that would substantially harm his chances of electoral success."

Jasminda swallowed the rage building inside her. "So you want me to sign these papers which say that my mother was not my mother, and then be *discreet* for how long?"

"Forever. You would not be able to reveal your maternal parentage for the rest of your natural life."

A cold emptiness spread inside her. Forever? Tell no one of her mother's kind eyes and gentle touch? It wasn't as if she had anyone to tell anyway, but the idea chafed. "And the price my grandfather is willing to pay for changing history is forty thousand pieces?"

"That is correct."

Jasminda stared at a spot on the wall, a crack in the paint, just an insignificant blemish. At least for now. Things like this started small, like a cough or a bout of dizziness easily hidden. Then they grew, expanding without warning, narrowing vision, causing periodic vertigo. All of which you assure your loved ones is nothing, a mere inconvenience. Until one day you are caught with such an attack while on the second floor of the barn loft, doing an activity you've done for many years, and fall to your death before anything can be done to save you.

The paint on the wall wasn't ruined yet, but it could be, just as easily as a mother's life.

"Miss, are you still there? Have we been disconnected?"

Jasminda nodded, knowing he couldn't see her. Her voice was small when she spoke. "And if I don't?"

Papers shuffled around on his end. "I understand that you owe a substantial amount in back taxes on the property that is still deeded in your mother's name. Mr. Zinadeel's funds would certainly take care of that expense, would they not?"

The icy sensation seeped through her pores to numb her skin. If her appeal had been rejected, her only option was to petition the board in person—in Rosira. Impossible. This offer could be her last chance. She owed twenty thousand pieces she did not have. "Yes," she said through gritted teeth. "But—"

"Very well then. Once we have word the paperwork is in the

post, the money can be yours the same day. An easy way to solve your problem, true?"

Easy? To sign a paper and suddenly, as if by magic, have no mother. At least not legally. Jasminda didn't know all the implications of such an action, but her heart told her it was wrong. And yet how could she face losing the farm?

She told the solicitor she would consider signing the papers and ended the call. As soon as she stepped out of the booth, the postmistress was there, wiping down the handset and receiver with a cloth smelling of cleaning solution.

Jasminda wanted to smear her handprints on every surface, daring the woman to scrub her presence away. Instead, she scooped up the wrapped package on the counter, cradling it to her chest. The books inside were precious, an escape from the drudgery and loneliness of farm life and the affronts of her rare visits to town. They were her only way to experience the world.

While the postmistress was busy cleaning, Jasminda left coins on the counter to pay for her delivery. The only crime she'd committed thus far was being born, she would not add thievery to the imaginary list the townsfolk had created.

With a silent curse at the jolly bell, she left the shop, exiting onto the main street.

Her steps were heavy as she approached the blacksmith, whose shop was at the end of the short row of buildings in the tiny town. She entered the warm space and rested her parcel on the counter. Old smith Bindeen turned from his forge, wiping his wrinkled brow, and smiled at her. Against her wishes, her heart unclenched. Bindeen had been the closest thing to a friend her papa had made in town and was the only one who didn't make her feel like a five-legged dog.

"Miss Jasminda, it's been a long time."

"As long as I can make it," she said with a crooked grin. She gave him her order, and he gathered the supplies she needed: nails, an axe head, shotgun shells, door hinges.

"Weather's turned a bit cool, hasn't it?" he asked.

"You feel the storm coming?"

He patted his bad hip. "Old bones speak mouthfuls."

She nodded, peering out the shop's front window at the rocky peaks standing guard over the town. "A bad one's brewing. Should hit the mountain tonight. It probably won't make it down here at all, but best be careful."

"How bad d'ya reckon it'll be?" He avoided her eyes as he spoke, but his limbs held as much tension as hers did.

"As bad as two years ago." Her voice was quiet and steady, but her hands clenched into fists involuntarily. She didn't want to get lost in the memory of that last terrible storm. Of searching the mountain paths for Papa and her brothers. Of never finding any trace of them. Mama had been gone for nearly seven years. Papa and the twins for two.

Jasminda cleared her throat to loosen the hold of the past and peered at the old man. He'd lived in this town his whole life, perhaps he knew something she didn't. "Do you remember my mama ever talking about her people?"

Bindeen scratched his chin and squinted. "Not that I can recall, why?"

"No reason." Her voice sagged along with her shoulders.

Mama's family had disowned her for marrying Papa. Now they wanted Jasminda to disown *them*. People she hadn't even met. She hadn't thought she could get more alone than she had been the past couple of years. But she had been wrong.

The old smith pursed his lips and gathered her purchases. "That'll be fifty pieces."

Jasminda frowned. She'd always trusted Bindeen, unlike most in town.

"I'm not tryin' to cheat ya, young miss. The price of everything's gone up. Taxes, too, especially on what comes imported. It's the best price I can give."

She searched the man's face and found him sincere. Using Earthsong would have confirmed his intentions, letting her feel the truth in his heart, but she didn't bother, instead counting out the money and placing it in his hand.

"If ya have any of that magic cream of yours, ya can make some of this back, eh?" He flexed his empty hand, thick with muscle from working the forge for decades, but gnarled with arthritis.

"It's not magic—just goat's milk and herbs." She fished around in her bag and dug out a jar, handing it to him and pocketing the money he gave back to her.

"Works like that magic of yours is all I know."

She held the blacksmith's eye. "You're not afraid of Earthsong like everyone else. Why?"

Bindeen shrugged. "I fought in the Sixth Breach. I've seen the power of those *grol* witches." Jasminda flinched at the epithet, but Bindeen didn't appear to notice. "I've been in sandstorms in the middle of a wheat field, pelted with rocks and hail and fire. It's only by the Sovereign's sweet mercy it can't be used to kill directly. Even so, that Earthsong of yours . . . there's plenty of reason to fear it. But I've also seen your father put a man's bone back in its socket and heal it up good as new without ever touching him."

Jasminda swallowed the lump in her throat. Her papa's Song was so strong. He'd been a good man, bearing the insults and scorn of the locals for decades with his head high.

Bindeen's eyes crinkled. He patted his good hip. "This joint he fixed is the only one on me that doesn't ache." His voice thickened. "Most folks hate easy and love hard. Should be the other way around, I reckon."

"Hmm." Jasminda placed her newest packages into her over-stuffed bag, unwilling to dwell on what couldn't be.

"Get home safe now," the man called.

"Thank you. May She bless your dreams."

"And yours, as well." He bowed his head with the farewell as Jasminda left the shop.

The sun was hours away from setting, and the journey home would last straight through the night. She knew the steep mountain paths well enough to negotiate them in the dark; her main worry now was beating the brewing storm.

Something about the scent of snow in the air gave her an ominous foreboding. Had the bit of her axe not been worn to a nub, she wouldn't have risked a trip to town so close to the storm at all.

She'd reached the edge of the street and was just heading onto the path leading up into the foothills when approaching hoofbeats made her turn.

A huge, black Borderlands pony rode up to her, the county constable astride. "Jasminda, have you been causing trouble again? I just got an earful from that woman what runs the post station about you."

The constable was a jovial, red-faced man whose great belly laugh seemed to echo off the mountaintops. He treated Jasminda like a mischievous child, but at least on most days seemed to realize she was not a criminal.

"No trouble, sir. I just picked up my mail and made a phone call." She willed patience into her bones. She could not handle the opinions of one more Elsiran today.

The constable snorted, then raised his eyebrow. "I believe the magistrate wanted me to remind you about the auction next week. You'll need to be out of that cabin of yours by then. Make way for whoever the new buyer will be."

"I still have seven days to pay the taxes, sir." The wobble in her voice shamed her.

He straightened the bill of his cap, chuckling. "Well, that's right, missy. I suppose you can magic up twenty thousand just like that." He snapped his fingers, and his laugh deepened. "If that witchcraft can spin straw into gold, then we've been fighting on the wrong side of this war all these years." His sizable belly shook, and the pony tossed its head, appearing amused as well.

Jasminda narrowed her eyes. "Thank you for the reminder, sir. I really do need to be heading home now."

"We don't want things to get ugly now, missy. Just clear out like you're supposed to and everything will go real smooth-like."

She wanted to rage. Where exactly was she supposed to go? What was she supposed to do? But pride kept her lips sealed and good sense kept the fury out of her expression.

"Well, on with ya, then," he said, shooing her before turning the pony around. "The sooner you leave town, the sooner these old hens will stop worrying me to death with their nattering."

As horse and rider sauntered away, Jasminda took her first full breath. Once they were out of sight, she turned on her heel and marched up the path leading home.

Still her home, at least for a few more days.

She'd only been walking for a couple of hours when something laying in the path made her stop short. At first she thought a discarded pile of rags had somehow blown up the mountain.

Then she realized it was a man.

CHAPTER TWO

Jackal and Monkey stood at the edge of a wide canyon. Monkey asked, If I leap and make it to the other side, was that my destiny or merely my good luck?

Jackal replied, Our destiny can be taken in hand, molded, and shaped, while chance makes foolishness out of whatever attempts to control it. Does this make destiny the master of luck?

—COLLECTED FOLKTALES

Jack had found himself in a great many hopeless situations in his life, but this one was the grand champion—a twenty-two-year record for dire occurrences. He only hoped this wouldn't be the last occurrence and sent up yet another prayer that he might live to see his twenty-third year.

The temperature had dropped precipitously. His spine was assaulted by the rocky ground on which he lay, but really that was the least of his discomforts.

His vision had begun to swim about an hour ago, and so at first he thought the girl looming above him was a mirage. She peered down at his hiding spot behind a cluster of coarse shrubbery, her head cocked at an angle. Jack went to stand, years of breeding kicking in, his muscle memory offended at the idea of not standing in the presence of a lady, but apparently his muscles had forgotten the bullet currently lodged within them. And the girl was Lagrimari—not strictly a lady, but a woman nonetheless—and a beautiful one, he noticed as he squinted into the dying light. Wild, midnight curls floated carelessly around her head, and piercing dark eyes regarded him. Her dress was drab and tattered, but her smooth skin was a confectioner's delight. His stomach growled. When was the last time he'd eaten?

Her presence meant he was still on the Lagrimari side of the mountain range bordering the two lands and had yet to cross the other, more powerful barrier keeping him from his home of Elsira: the Mantle.

The girl frowned down at him, taking in his bedraggled appearance. From his position lying on the ground, he tried his best to smooth his ripped uniform, the green fatigues of the Lagrimari army. Her confusion was apparent. Jack was obviously Elsiran; aside from his skin tone, the ginger hair and golden honey-colored eyes were a dead giveaway. And yet he wore the uniform of his enemy.

"Please don't be scared," he said in Lagrimari. Her brows rose toward her hairline as she scanned his supine and bloodied body. Well, that *was* rather a ridiculous thing to say. "I only meant that I mean you no harm. I . . ." He struggled with how to explain himself.

There were two possibilities. She could be a nationalist who would turn him in to the squad of soldiers currently combing the mountain for him, perhaps to gain favor with the government, or she could be like so many Lagrimari citizens, beaten down by the war with no real loyalty to their dictator or his thugs. If she was the former, he was already dead, so he took a chance with the truth.

"You see, I was undercover, spying from within the Lagrimari army. But now there are men looking for me, they're not far, but . . ." He paused to take a breath; the effort of speaking was draining. He suspected he had several cracked or broken ribs in addition to the gunshot wound. His vision swirled again, and the girl turned into two. Two beautiful girls. If these were his last moments before traveling to the World After, then at least he had something pleasant to look at.

He blinked rapidly and took another strained breath. His mission was not complete; he could not die yet. "Can you help me? Please. I've got to get back to Elsira."

She stole an anxious glance skyward before kneeling next to him. Her cool hand moved to his forehead. The simple touch was soothing, and a wave of tension rolled off him.

"You must be delirious." Her voice was rich, deeper than he'd expected. It eased the harsh consonants of the Lagrimari language, for the first time making it sound like something he could imagine being pleasant to listen to. She worked at the remaining buttons of his shirt, pulling the fabric apart to reveal his ruined chest. Her expression was appraising as she viewed the damage, then sat back on her haunches, pensive.

"It probably looks worse than it is," he said.

"I doubt that."

Jack's chuckle sounded deranged to his own ears, so it was no surprise that the girl looked at him askance. He winced—laughing was a bad idea at this point—and struggled for breath again. "The soldiers . . . they're after me. I have to get back through the Mantle."

"Shh," she said, peering closely at him. "Hush all that foolishness; you're not in your right mind. Though I'll admit, you speak Lagrimari surprisingly well. I'm not sure what happened to you, but you should save your strength."

She closed her eyes, and suddenly his whole body grew warmer, lighter. The odd sensation of Earthsong pulsated through him. He had only experienced it once before, and it hadn't been quite like this. The touch of her magic stroked him intimately, like a brush of fingers across his skin. The soft vibration cascaded over his entire body, leaving him feeling weightless.

He gasped, pulling in a breath, and it was very nearly an easy thing to accomplish. Tears pricked his eyes. "Sovereign bless you."

Her expression was grave as she dug around in her bag. "It's just a patch. You must have ticked someone off real good. It'd take quite a while to fix you up properly, and the storm's coming. You need to find shelter."

She retrieved a jar filled with a sweet-smelling substance and began spreading it over his wounds. The Earthsong had turned down the volume of his pain, and the cream soothed him even more.

"What is that?"

"Just a balm. Helps with burns, cuts." Her hand paused for a moment. "Never gunshot wounds, but it's worth a try."

He laid his head back on the ground, closing his eyes to savor the ability to breathe deeply again. "A quick rest and I'll be back on my way. Need to keep moving, though. Need to get back."

"Back through the Mantle?" Her tone vibrated with skepticism. "And away from the Lagrimari soldiers chasing you?"

"Yes." Her palm met his forehead again. She thought he was delusional. He wished he was. Wished the last few weeks had been nothing but the imaginings of an impaired mind.

"The Seventh Breach ended almost five years ago." Her voice flowed over him, along with another tingle of Earthsong, cool and comforting. "We've had peace since then. No way to cross the Mantle from either side."

He shook his head, aggravating the hole in his upper chest, inches from his heart where the inconvenient bit of metal was still lodged. "There are ways."

A crunch of boots in the distance set him on alert. He grabbed the girl's wrist to halt her while he listened. The soldiers were near.

He opened his eyes and looked into her startled ones. "Shh, they're coming."

Her head darted from side to side, and he saw the moment she realized someone was indeed coming. Jack couldn't let her be found helping him. Having seen firsthand what these men were capable of, he couldn't let her be found by them at all. The Lagrimari army was filled with men unfit even for Elsira's prisons. This girl had been kind, a trait his people didn't believe the Lagrimari even possessed, but he knew better and felt the need to protect her. He wrestled himself to a sitting position, ignoring the daggers of pain impaling him with every movement, but her strong arms prevented him from standing.

"Hide here, and I'll draw them away," he whispered, and motioned for her to crouch down. "They will find me anyway, but it's best they don't see you." Her gaze darted back toward the sound of approaching footsteps.

As he agonizingly made his way to his hands and knees, the pain flared hot, threatening to blind him. With a tug on her arm, he pulled her behind the shrubbery and half crawled, half dragged himself back onto the narrow, rocky path. Her head stuck up over the grouping of rocks and shrubs, and he motioned for her to get down as he put a little distance between them.

The footfalls grew closer. He turned to face them, not wanting to draw any attention to the girl hiding only a few paces away.

Six Lagrimari men appeared from around the bend in the path. The sergeant spotted him, and a hard smile spread across the man's narrow face. Jack only had time to feel a small amount of satisfaction at the purple bruise around the sergeant's eye before a foot to his midsection stole his breath. A kick to the head stole his consciousness.

CHAPTER THREE

*Monkey said to Jackal, I believe that luck is the master of destiny,
for one cannot be ruled by that which one considers foolish.*

*Then he took a running leap over the edge of the canyon and
disappeared into the setting sun.*

—COLLECTED FOLKTALES

The first snowflakes began to fall as Jasminda crept down the
mountain. She followed the lantern light of the men who'd dragged
away the unconscious Elsiran, staying a few dozen paces behind.
While she'd thought his tale fantastical, there was no doubting the
six Lagrimari soldiers who'd appeared, or their viciousness toward
him. She'd winced as they'd continued to strike him, long after
he'd passed out.

He was an odd one, surely—his manner, his clothing, his perfect Lagrimari speech and accent. She'd never heard of an Elsiran
who could speak the language. Even her mama had never been able
to master it. And with his talk of crossing the Mantle, of course

she'd thought him deranged. The magical border between the two lands followed the mountain range. The Mantle had stood for five hundred years and had only been breached seven times, each resulting in months or years of war.

Her papa had come over during the Sixth Breach. He'd been one of the soldiers stuck in Elsira as prisoners of war when the gap in the Mantle closed. After their release from prison, they'd been unable to obtain citizenship or find jobs, so the Lagrimari had formed settlements, shantytowns really, and eked out a meager living with the help of the Sisterhood. But Papa had met Mama and built a life with her. He never talked much of home or said anything about wanting to go back.

Jasminda had asked him about it, over and over, always afraid that as soon as the chance came, he would disappear into the mysterious country of his birth, just over the mountains. He would reassure her that he wasn't going anywhere—sometimes with a chuckle, sometimes with an exasperated sigh, and occasionally with a haunted look in his eye that made her stop the questions.

The Seventh Breach took place the summer of her fifteenth year. The fighting had ended before her family even heard about it, isolated as their valley home was. Jasminda was glad they didn't find out until the breach had closed. She believed Papa's words that he would never leave her—believed them until two years ago when he'd been proved a liar.

But now her own two eyes bore witness of Lagrimari soldiers on her mountain. The odd Elsiran had been convinced he was still in Lagrimar. That meant he'd crossed the Mantle without even knowing it. Was this the start of another breach war, or something else entirely?

If she'd believed the Elsiran, she would have drained her Song to heal him more. His injuries were beyond her limited abilities, but she'd selfishly only given a little of her power to ease the worst of his pain. She'd wanted to leave a bit in reserve for her long journey. Could she have helped him avoid the men? There was little she could do for him now, not against six armed soldiers, but guilt made her follow them anyway.

It made no sense; he was nobody to her. Just another Elsiran. Except . . . He had not stared at her or been cruel. He had, in fact, shielded her from those men, put himself in their path so they would not find her. Why would he do such a thing?

As the men took wrong turn after wrong turn, she stayed on course, though the direct route she'd planned to take would have had her home and warm in bed by now.

Dawn poked its head over the jagged peaks, and with its arrival came the crowing of a rooster. The soldiers stopped short at a fork in the path. Jasminda knew that crow all too well.

The men conferred for a moment and chose to follow the crowing. The mountain made the sound seem closer than it really was, but the sign of civilization could not be mistaken. Her relief to be headed out of the storm battled with alarm—these strangers were now on a path that led only one place.

Her home.

The Elsiran had regained his senses, and instead of being dragged behind the men like a sack of beets, he stumbled along, his hands tied in front of him. The men climbed down the mountain, leaving the storm behind bit by bit. The snow and ice would grow worse over the next few days, but it would stay at the higher elevations. The valley where her home lay would remain lush and green, protected from the harsh weather by either the mountains surrounding it, or some lingering spell of Papa's, or perhaps a little of both. But there would be no way out. These men would be trapped in an area that was only a two-hour walk from end to end. They would find her cabin; there was no way to avoid it.

She doubled back and took a shortcut she usually avoided, though it had been a favorite of her brothers. It involved a very steep climb, required scaling several large boulders, and brought her far too near one of the caves that peppered the mountain. She ignored the yawning black opening and focused on beating the men to her cabin.

Awake now for over twenty-four hours, she pushed herself far beyond exhaustion. Snow made the rocks slippery, and she lost her footing and slid down an embankment, skinning her hands and forearms. She picked herself up, ignoring the injury, and raced to her cabin, confident she had at least twenty minutes before the soldiers arrived.

She hurried to the barn, where she found the goats already awake, agitated and jittery, no doubt because of the storm. They were like her, craving peace and quiet. Any interruption to their routine or change in the weather troubled the sensitive creatures. She checked their food, then barred the outer barn door to keep them from wandering.

Her next stop was the cabin, where she set down her bag and retrieved her shotgun. She carried a pistol with her on trips to town, but the shotgun was her favorite. It was almost an antique but shot straight and true. She loaded it with the shells she'd purchased from the blacksmith, then sat on the porch steps. Waiting.

Do what you think you can't. That's what her papa had always said. It was a mantra of his. When he'd repeat it, one of her brothers would often make a face, crossing his eyes and mouthing along. But with them all gone now, it had become her own incantation, chanted inside her head at moments like these.

This was her home. The only thing she had in the world. No tax man nor enemy soldier could take it from her. She would do whatever she must to protect it.

It wasn't long before the telltale clomp of boots announced the men. She hadn't gotten a good look at them in the dark, but the cool morning light revealed dirty uniforms and even dirtier faces. All except for their leader, a man of skin and bone, his narrow face overshadowed by both a giant, curling mustache and a blackened eye. He was clean and well groomed, his hair parted and shining with pomade.

She stood as they approached, shotgun dangling almost casually from the crook of her arm. The Elsiran, barely standing, was held upright by a soldier. All her healing work had been undone by their brutality.

The leader spoke first. "Pleasant morning to you, miss. I am Tensyn ol-Trador, Honorable Sergeant of His Majesty the True Father's royal army. My men and I are in need of food and shelter. We must speak with your father or husband." His voice was high and nasal, like a human rat.

"This is *my* home."

His eyebrows shot up, and he glanced back at his men, his mouth twisting into what perhaps was meant to be a smile. "You are alone?"

"I want no trouble here," she responded. The Elsiran's head popped up; he frowned and squinted at her, his bruised face freezing once he recognized her. Astonishment and sorrow settled across his features. His shoulders slumped.

Nerves caused her to struggle to catch hold of Earthsong. The power skittered out of her grasp.

"We have been caught in the mountains by the storm and cannot make it to the capital until it passes. We are tasked with transporting this spy to face the True Father's judgment."

"An Elsiran spy? In your uniform?"

"Yes, he had been spelled to look like one of us. I witnessed it wear off with my own eyes, miss. There are traitorous souls infecting our land, working with our enemies. The Singer responsible for this spell is soon to meet the World After, I think. But that is a matter for the True Father to sort out."

The soldier holding the Elsiran kicked at his legs, causing him to crumple, face-first, to the ground. His upper body heaved as he drew in jagged breaths, but he did not cry out. Jasminda held her breath, keeping her face rigid to hide her horror. The prisoner rolled awkwardly to his knees, then slowly struggled back to his feet. The soldiers beside him snickered as he wobbled before finding his balance. His head shot up defiantly.

Her breath escaped in a rush. The man she'd met the day before on the mountain had been somewhat peculiar, but also gentle. Even with the uniform, he'd struck her as a painter or poet who had fallen upon thieves or been mauled by an animal. She hadn't truly believed him to be a soldier. But now, the sharp lines of his face had turned savage. With his sculpted cheekbones, decisive chin, and that cold power in his eyes, she wondered how these soldiers ever thought they had him cowed. How could she have thought him anything but a warrior?

She forced her gaze back to the sergeant who looked at her expectantly. He'd been speaking, but she hadn't been paying attention. "Excuse me?"

"May we shelter here?" His tobacco-stained smile sent a cold chill rolling through her.

"You and your men may stay in the barn. I will bring you food and water."

A collective grumble arose from the other soldiers. Sergeant Tensyn's grin fell away. "The barn? You must be joking."

"The cabin is quite small, as I'm sure you can see. Plus, I am not in the habit of inviting strange men into my home."

He took a step closer to the porch, bringing his eyes level with her chest. Though his gaze reached her face quickly, she did not miss the route it took. "Miss . . . ?"

"Jasminda ul-Sarifor." She spat out her name as if it tasted vile.

"Miss Jasminda. As the True Father says, it is your duty to aid his representatives to the best of your ability. I'm afraid the barn will not do. For the prisoner, perhaps, but my men have been marching for days with little food or rest." His cajoling tone turned darker. "We have already learned there are traitors among us. Would not a loyal citizen answer the call of our great leader?"

As she had suspected, these men also believed they were in Lagrimar. If they thought her Elsiran they would likely kill her. She closed her eyes briefly and finally connected to Earthsong. With the energy pulsing into her, she could sense emotion and mood. It was not her strongest skill by far, but these men were easy to read.

Danger rolled off them, impatience, barely reined-in malice. And determination. She would not be able to keep them out. Her best chance was to go along with their assumption of her loyalty, be vigilant, and bide her time. Though she knew little of her father's homeland, being a Lagrimari might save her life, so that was what she would be.

She released her connection and adjusted her shotgun in her hands, all while glaring at the sergeant. "You may wait here for the storm to pass, but listen to me clearly. I will kill any man who touches me."

He swallowed. The others shifted where they stood. Finally, Sergeant Tensyn bowed. "I give you my word on the True Father that none of my men will harm you in any way. Food and shelter are all we ask."

Her raw palms burned from gripping the metal of the gun, and her heart stuttered in her chest. The Elsiran looked on, an apology written on his face. She was sorry, as well.

"Well, come in, then."

CHAPTER FOUR

Said a stonecutter to the Mistress of Frogs, How may I complete my work and feed my family, though I am lame?

To which she replied, A stone needs only a trickle of water, unceasing in its focus, to create a groove. If you are the water, take your time to do the work. If you are the stone, best roll out of the way before you are split in two.

—COLLECTED FOLKTALES

It was not in Jack's nature to despair. He'd been through his share of hardships, to be sure—well, less than most but more than some, he suspected. The Seventh Breach in particular came to mind. Ninety-nine days of misery that had felt like a thousand. But even then, he'd been full of righteous rage, which had kept him from sinking into the depression so many of his men had succumbed to.

There was a desolation that sank into the hearts of people who'd lived through war. He saw it in the old-timers who had fought in the tail end of the Fifth Breach, a war that lasted seventy years. But he'd also seen it in the faces of Lagrimari children in the villages the squad had passed through on his spy mission. Before his bloody disguise had worn off.

Now, a kind of melancholy he was not used to threatened to overtake him. He was back where he'd started—captured—and worse, the girl he'd tried to protect had been hauled into this mess. But he couldn't allow himself to sink too far. Giving up was also not in his nature, not while there was breath in his body.

He wasn't sure how many breaths he had left, though. Each one was more difficult than the last. He'd been trained to work through pain, to put it in a box in his mind, then put that box into another box until he had as many boxes as he needed to keep moving, keep fighting. He had lost count of his boxes, and they'd long stopped helping. Pain was all he knew, but even that meant he was alive and still had a chance to escape.

The brute to his left, a lout called Ginko, squeezed a brawny hand over Jack's arm and pulled him forward, toward the girl's quaint cabin, which sat under the shade of several tall trees. A barn stood off to the side with a chicken coop beyond it. Rows and rows of carefully tended plants stretched out on either side of the house, interrupted every so often by thickets of trees.

Most of Lagrimar was desert wasteland, but in the very far west the climate was more pleasant, almost like lush Elsira. He would have imagined that most of the country's population would live in this tiny region, but it was not the case. Aside from the two western Lake Cities, the people were spread evenly across the barren country, with many living in the capital city of Sayya, far to the east.

Jack's travels during his undercover mission had kept him mostly in the west. But he had never been inside a Lagrimari home before and found himself surprised at its warmth and coziness. He had thought they would all look like the tenuously built mud-brick huts of the poor villages, but this was a proper home for a family. Quilts covered overstuffed couches and chairs. Colorful rugs hugged the floor, though they were currently being sullied by the mud tracked in on the soldiers' boots. The mantelpiece featured children's drawings, wood carvings, a cuckoo clock, and a photograph of several people that he couldn't make out from this distance.

The girl, Jasminda, pointed out two bedrooms and a washroom on the main floor for the men to use. Just beyond the living room was the entrance to the kitchen, through which a squat woodstove was visible. A staircase in the living room led up to a closed door that she indicated belonged to her. When he looked back to the mantel, the photo had been turned facedown.

"And what of communications, Miss Jasminda?" Sergeant Tensyn asked. "Our radio equipment is badly damaged, and we've had no contact with our regiment."

"No electricity. No radio or cables here."

Tensyn looked ready to continue his questioning when she broke in. "Sergeant, you hope to bring the spy in alive, yes?" She had not looked at Jack since that moment of recognition outside, and she did not glance at him now, yet he felt her attention on him all the same.

Earthsong moved across his skin like the lips of a lover. When Darvyn had cast the spell to change Jack's appearance before leading him through the crack in the Mantle into Lagrimar, it had felt so different. Less personal, less invasive. But thanks to Jasminda's continued ministrations, finally, the pain could fit in a box. He fought the desire to fall to his knees with relief.

"There is a reward for the return of this man," Tensyn said. "Alive."

Jasminda wrinkled her nose. "He stinks of infection. Why has he not been healed?"

Her words caused a spike of fear. He'd seen many a man die of untreated infection from wounds more minor than his.

"All of my men have already given tribute to the True Father."

"And their Songs have not returned?"

Jack's gaze snapped to her, and Tensyn's expression sharpened. "Tributes are irreversible, as I'm sure you know, Miss Jasminda. Once your Song is gone, it cannot be returned."

All of the men were looking at her now, but her expression did not change. Her eyes flashed for a moment—perhaps with fear or anger—but it was gone so quickly Jack could not be sure.

"I had heard sometimes they did, that is all. This man will die in days if the infection continues." She spun away and stalked into the kitchen.

Was it possible she was more than just a sympathetic Lagrimari? Her ignorance of the True Father's tributes could mean she was a Keeper of the Promise like Darvyn. They often stayed in isolated places like this, free from the dictator's edicts.

"Can you keep him alive?" Tensyn asked.

"Yes." Her voice was clipped.

A cautious hope welled within Jack.

She slammed a basket of fruit on the kitchen table and retrieved more food from the pantry, still clutching her shotgun. The other soldiers, except for Tensyn and Ginko, sat and began eating without ceremony. Jasminda grabbed a bowl, filled it with water, and gathered towels and a knife.

"Back porch. The floors in here are already filthy." Her words cracked like a whip.

"My apologies, miss." Tensyn lowered himself into a bow. "I'll have my men be more careful with the state of your home."

The sergeant motioned to Ginko, who pushed Jack forward. His injuries screamed, but he remained silent. Jasminda's lips pursed and she spun around, leading the way out the back to the porch. She motioned to the top step with her chin. Jack was pushed down until he sprawled across the stairs, gasping for breath.

"Untie him," she said, staring at his lashed wrists. "I need to check his wounds."

Ginko pulled a knife from his boot to cut the rope. The sharp edges of the pain had been bound by whatever spell she'd sung a few moments before, but the weakness in his limbs couldn't be ignored. The lack of food and water, the days of walking and hiding, had all left him teetering on the edge of his endurance. She too had deep circles under her eyes, and he wondered what she'd been doing up on the mountain.

As she settled next to him, his awareness of her pulsed like an extra sense. She smelled of cool mountain air, pine, and something light and feminine that he couldn't place. He closed his eyes and inhaled her nearness, allowing it to soothe and calm him. He imagined himself far away, in the barracks he'd called home since childhood, or maybe even farther away, floating on his back in the Delaveen Ocean, the sun warming his face.

The vision faded when her fingertips grazed his forehead.

"Does that hurt?" Her whispered voice stroked his cheek. He opened his eyes to find her very close. Unable to find his voice, he shook his head.

"Take that off." She pointed to his shirt. He had the absurd desire to chuckle. How many times had he longed to hear a woman ordering him to take off his shirt? What he'd felt of her touch so far had been very soft . . . . She must be soft all over. He'd never imagined a Lagrimari girl could be so lovely. The coils of her hair called to his fingertips and—

"Has your tribute day been scheduled?" Tensyn's oily voice broke through Jack's musings. He and Ginko stood in the doorway, and

Jack hated having anyone at his back. That kind of sloppiness had literally been beaten out of him. He blamed the pain and the fatigue.

His bruised fingers faltered on the tiny buttons as he shrugged awkwardly out of his shirt. Once again, Jasminda assessed his injuries impassively, though he suspected things were quite a bit worse than when she'd seen him yesterday.

"No," she answered Tensyn.

"And your family?"

"Dead." Her unexpressive mask slipped for an instant, and Jack glimpsed a cavernous well of grief in her eyes.

"May they find serenity in the World After," Tensyn said, his voice grave.

Jasminda repeated the blessing. Jack's eyes met hers briefly before she looked away. "Lie back," she told him.

She dipped a cloth in the water and ran it across his chest, cleaning away the blood and grime. He suppressed a groan at the incredible coolness of the water on his skin, relishing it until she stopped suddenly. He craned his neck down to see what had caught her attention. The bullet wound was far worse today, the skin black with infection, blood and pus seeping out.

The screen door slammed. He looked up to find the two of them on the porch alone.

"What is your name?" She pitched her voice low, speaking directly into his ear in perfect Elsiran as she continued cleaning his chest.

He took hold of her wrist, stilling her hand. Even the former POWs spoke only a broken version of Elsiran. How had she been able to learn it when no one in Lagrimar spoke the language? She shook free of his grip and continued cleaning his chest and face. Inside, the soldiers chortled, ensuring they would not be overheard.

"Jack," he whispered, scanning her face desperately. "Are you a Keeper of the Promise?"

Her brow wrinkled in confusion. She darted a look at the door. "No. I don't know what that is."

"How can you—"

"This is not Lagrimar." The door opened again, and Ginko emerged, taking a stance with his arms folded while he chewed on a stick of jerky.

Jasminda switched back to Lagrimari, speaking quietly. "I need to cut away the dead flesh from the wound. Otherwise the infection will kill you."

He nodded faintly, still trying to process her last words. If they weren't in Lagrimar, that meant they had all passed through the Mantle without knowing it. He'd been on home soil the whole time. That must be why she'd acted as if he were deranged.

Escape was so close. The despair threatening to pull him under faded away like mist in the sun.

"My Song is not strong. I can't both stop the bleeding and dull the pain."

He met her worried gaze and smiled, though the action reopened one of the cuts on his lip. Her expression said she thought he was delirious again. Perhaps he was.

"The only way to the other side is through," he said. She blinked, staring at him blankly before the corners of her mouth rose a tiny fraction. He hadn't seen her smile yet, and even this hint of one lightened him. She closed her eyes, and once again the warm buzz of Earthsong poured into him like a fizzy cola. He opened the largest box he could to tuck away the pain and imagined Jasminda's smile.

CHAPTER FIVE

Bobcat and Horse raced to the river to see who was fastest. Bobcat fell behind on a turn in the path, and Horse began to gloat. But when he approached the riverbank, he was shocked to find Bobcat leisurely bathing.

How did you beat me? Horse cried, angry.

Bobcat replied, When the path curved, I stayed straight. A new direction is not enough to throw me off course.

—COLLECTED FOLKTALES

Jasminda lay awake in bed, straining to hear any movement in the house. Dull moonlight filtered in through Mama's frilly curtains. It was several hours to dawn. Exhaustion hollowed her bones. She'd depleted her Song helping Jack. It would have been wise to keep some in reserve to better monitor the soldiers, but the Elsiran's wounds were severe. Though her Song was too weak to effect a complete healing, the infected flesh was gone, and he would live another day.

Her muscles tensed. She held her breath, listening. Tiny frissons of unease burrowed under her skin.

Gripping the shotgun she'd taken to bed in one hand, she reached under her pillow with the other for her father's hunting knife. Another, smaller blade was already strapped to her thigh.

She rose, seized with the desire to check on Jack. The men had left him tied to the porch, saying even the barn was too good for the likes of him. She wrapped herself in a robe, hiding the shotgun in its folds, and slipped down the stairs. Snores rumbled from behind the doors of both bedrooms. Pushing down the anger at having strangers around her parents' and brothers' possessions, she crept through the kitchen to peer out the window.

Jack lay on his back, shivering, hands bound in front of him, feet tied to the porch railing. She doubled back to the main room to grab a quilt, then went out and draped his shuddering body. He didn't appear conscious, but when she began to move away, he grabbed her hand.

"Thank you," he said in Elsiran. She cast a glance into the quiet shadows hugging the porch.

"They didn't feed you, did they? You must be hungry," she whispered, drawing the quilt closer around his neck.

"Mmm." He groaned, leaning his cheek against her hand. His skin was cold and clammy, face drawn and gaunt, and yet she could not pull away. She brushed his forehead and ran her fingers through his short hair. He did not flinch from her touch, but sank into it. His hair was like the soft bristles of a brush, his expression serene as she stroked his head. The fierceness in his face had once again been replaced by a soulful calm.

Such a contradiction, this Elsiran. Neither her skin nor her magic frightened him, yet he had more reason than most to hate

Lagrimari. Of course, she wasn't Lagrimari, but she wasn't truly Elsiran, either. She forced herself to pull away.

"I'll be right back."

"I'll be here," he said, a small smile playing on his lips.

She rooted around the dark pantry to produce a tin of jerky and some dried fruit. She returned to give him a few strips of jerky, then pulled up a loose board in the floor where she could hide the food.

"You can get to this when no one's looking. You'll need to build up your strength."

"We are truly in Elsira?" His accent was lilting and formal, and it put her in mind of her mama's, a good deal more refined than those of the townsfolk.

"We are."

His forehead crinkled in confusion. "But you are Lagrimari?"

"My papa was a settler; Mama was Elsiran. She was in the Sisterhood. That's how they met."

"I've never heard of such a pairing."

Jasminda chuckled, a dry and empty sound. "She fell pregnant, and her family disowned her. Papa found this place and built a home for them." She stroked the board beneath her feet, cut and nailed with her father's two hands, a structure that proclaimed a love that never should have been. That even now, twenty years later, was not accepted. The thought of losing the place Papa had built for his family made her chest constrict.

Jack laid his hand on hers, and her skin tingled at the contact. The intensity in his expression dissolved her creeping sorrow, bringing instead a pang of yearning. She did not touch people. She barely even spoke to people. She was either here alone with no one but the animals as audience, or in town armoring herself against the cutting stares. The tingle in her hand turned into a warm heat that threatened to spread. With great effort, she pulled away from the impossible temptation of his body.

"How far is it to—"

He paused as a floorboard inside the house groaned under the weight of heavy footsteps. Jasminda froze as another board creaked. She grabbed her shotgun, scooted away, and crept down the steps into the yard. The moonlight cast heavy shadows, and she crouched beside a cherry tree, holding her breath.

Two soldiers darkened the doorway before stepping onto the porch. One nudged Jack with his foot, and Jack moaned, pretending to be asleep. The men chuckled to themselves and leaned over him.

"You're sure the sergeant is out?" one of the men asked. Ginko, she thought his name was.

"Thank the Father for thick walls and a soft bed. He sleeps like he's in his mother's arms," the second man said. Based on the outline of his large, misshapen head, Jasminda thought this was the one called Fahl. He'd eaten the last of the boiled eggs earlier, before she'd even had one.

Fahl squatted down and ran his hand across Jack's body. The action took an impossibly long time, and Jasminda's stomach hollowed. When he moved to loosen his own belt, she fought back a gasp. They were going to whip Jack.

"The bitch is upstairs. Are you sure you wouldn't rather . . ." Ginko said.

"I'm thinking the sergeant has her in his sights. Besides, she looks like she's got a mean scratch. No. I'll make sure this one won't make a peep, and who's to care what state he's left in? What Tensyn don't know won't hurt him." He snickered, and Ginko scratched his meaty head, looking back toward the house, appearing uncertain.

Understanding dawned on Jasminda like a blow to the face. She had worried for herself, expected trouble from these men seeking *her* out in the middle of the night, but she'd never considered Jack's vulnerability. Never considered how depraved these men might actually be. She could not sit by and allow him to be violated, though she was not sure what could be done to stop it.

They'd said the sergeant wouldn't approve. Maybe if she woke him, he would stop this. But she couldn't be sure, and going into his room at night could put her in the same predicament. She gripped her shaking hands and prayed to the Queen Who Sleeps for a solution.

The soft bleat of a doe rang out from the barn. The storm on the mountains was still making the goats uneasy. An idea took hold. What she needed was a distraction, and quickly.

Jasminda crouched and felt around for a stone or branch. After finding a good-sized rock, she threw it with all her might. It sailed across the yard to hit the chicken coop. Once the men turned toward the sound, she raced around the front of the house, taking the long way to the barn.

The first distraction bought her a minute, but now she needed something larger to really draw the men away. She slid open the well-oiled barn door. Instead of nestling on the floor sleeping, many of the goats were awake and stumbling around, agitated. She hoped that, for once, the stubborn animals wouldn't need much cajoling. Luckily for her, the buck was eager to be out of doors and the does were of a mind to follow him. Grabbing the shovel, she nudged the herd along, increasing the pressure on their backsides until they bleated in disapproval.

The goats operated almost as a hive mind—when one was upset, they all were—so Jasminda continued poking and prodding at them, pushing them from the barn. Their discontent grew louder.

Whines and cries pierced the night air. She'd often cursed the herd's fickle temperament, but tonight it was a blessing.

She couldn't see the back porch from where she stood, but an oil lamp flickered on inside the house. The goats' racket would awaken the rest of the soldiers, leaving Fahl and Ginko no opportunity to hurt Jack.

Jasminda slipped into the garden shadows as the front door opened and the smallest soldier, Wargi, stumbled out. The sergeant's voice carried over the yowls of the animals as he barked orders. The remaining two soldiers, Pymsyn and Unar, followed Wargi out to investigate what had spooked the goats.

She stifled a laugh at the way the men floundered, chasing after the scattering herd. They wouldn't get much sleep trying to track down each animal. If they asked her in the morning, she'd say she had slept through it. She'd been listening to them her whole life, after all.

When she returned to the backyard, she retrieved her shotgun and found Jack as she'd left him. He opened his eyes, and the moonlight made them sparkle. She knelt and pulled the blanket down from his chin to check him out, not sure what she was even looking for.

"Are you all right?"

"What did you do?"

She shrugged. "A distraction. Have they . . . harmed you?" She grimaced at the foolishness of her question. "Further, I mean."

He shook his head, his face a mask. Warrior Jack was back.

"But they will . . . when they can." Braying cries echoed in the distance.

She gathered up the hem of her robe and nightgown, and reached for the band holding the knife in place around her thigh. Jack's eyes widened. Her face grew hot as she hurried to remove the blade and put her gown back in place. After prying open the same loose floorboard as before, she hid the knife beside the tin of food.

As she laid the board back in place, his hand covered hers. "Thank you."

She flexed her fingers under his palm, ignoring the tingles sparking once again on her skin. "I'm sorry I didn't believe you yesterday."

"You thought I was mad." His mouth quirked. He must have been in a great deal of pain, but it hardly showed. Perhaps he was a warrior jester—fierce one moment, jovial the next.

"I still might."

He snorted a laugh, then winced.

Guilt tightened her chest. "I'm sorry. You shouldn't laugh."

"I'd rather laugh than cry. Wouldn't you?"

She couldn't even remember the last time she'd had something to laugh about.

"Is this a new breach?" she asked.

He sobered. "Not yet, but soon. There are cracks in the Mantle. Places where people can slip through, either knowingly or accidentally. But a breach is coming. The Lagrimari think they've found a way to tear it down permanently."

"Permanently?"

He nodded. "The True Father has never been able to cross during a breach, not while any part of the Mantle is intact. But without it . . ."

"Without it, he could cross. What would that mean?"

His grip on her hand tightened. "The end of Elsira."

The True Father was the most powerful Earthsinger alive. He had ruled Lagrimar for five hundred years, stealing more and more of his peoples' magic through the "tributes" to keep him alive and in power. But the magic had never been enough. Each breach had been an attempt for him to expand his influence.

Though her relationship with the land and its people was tenuous at best, Elsira was her home. She could claim no true allegiance to the Prince Regent or the structures of society, but she wasn't so naive as to believe even her isolated home would be immune to the fall of the country. "Could nothing stop it?"

"There is—" At a sound from inside, his lips snapped shut.

Jasminda whipped her head around. She strained to listen, and felt that same uneasy sensation that had awoken her. Jack was safe for the moment, but something was still not right—something in addition to the six enemy soldiers who'd overtaken her home.

Slowly, she backed away from Jack and crept to the door. It was past time to go back to her room, she couldn't afford to be caught here.

She looked over her shoulder to find Jack's gaze locked on her. The two sides she'd seen before—soulful Jack and warrior Jack—merged before her, giving a complete picture for the first time. She took in a jagged breath as a renewed surge of longing crashed into her. It battered against the solid wall of her fear and aloneness, making her shudder.

Shaking her head, she pulled open the door to the kitchen and slipped inside.

CHAPTER SIX

*Bobcat caught a thorn in his paw and could not remove it. Horse
came by and offered to pull the thorn out.*

Ow! cried Bobcat. I thought you were going to help me.

I removed the thorn, Horse replied.

But you left two more behind!

You are welcome, Horse said, and trotted off.

—COLLECTED FOLKTALES

The blade hidden under the knotty floorboard called to Jack. *Freedom.* He could cut his ropes and head west for home. But it was
doubtful he'd make it more than a few hundred paces in his current
state. His wound was no longer infected—yet it hurt to breathe. A
full day of rest had helped, but it had also brought into focus just
how severe his injuries still were.

He'd awoken to the healing tingle of Earthsong early that
morning. Jasminda was doing all she could, and leaving now would

only increase his chance of recapture. He needed to bide his time until he was at least well enough to walk without aid.

But time was steadily running out. Jack had witnessed the Lagrimari army amassing far too close to the border. Whispers of the True Father's rapidly increasing strength had spread through the countryside like a plague. Word was, tributes were being taken from whole towns at a time. Not just adults but children, infants even, were being drained of their Songs to feed the god-king's unquenchable thirst for power. Darvyn had warned him as much, but Jack hadn't believed the former POW. How could *he* have known, having been trapped inside Elsira since the last breach?

But Darvyn knew a great deal, including the location of a crack in the Mantle. He'd led Jack through that place where the magic had weakened, in order to allow Jack to personally gather the proof his Elsiran government would not accept from a Lagrimari. The two had agreed to meet in a fortnight to return to Elsira, but Darvyn's spell had worn off early, and Jack had been exposed, shot, and forced to go on the run before the appointed date. He rubbed his chest, wondering, not for the first time, what had happened to the young man.

Jasminda appeared through the copse of trees behind the back garden, a full basket on her arm. Her dark eyes flashed as she scanned the area, always alert. The sight of her ignited him as a gentle breeze ruffled her mass of tight curls. Her beauty was raw and pure, and a torrent of desire he had no business feeling rose inside him.

She reached the porch and paused, cocking her head to listen for the men.

Jack kept his voice low. "They do fitness drills first thing in the morning; they're all probably in the front yard going through their paces."

Jasminda tiptoed through the door to the kitchen, but was back in moments with a cup of water in her hands. "You're right. Their calisthenics are . . . interesting." She barely contained a smile.

Jack snorted, recalling the bizarre movements the sergeant insisted they all participate in to stay limber and strong. But when she brought the cool water to his lips, his humor faded as he quenched his thirst.

"Thank you."

She brushed off his gratitude and fidgeted with the sleeve of her dress, a frayed and faded creation that might once have been blue. "So what will you do? About the Mantle?"

He had been pondering just that while on the run from the soldiers, but perhaps the Queen had sent him the solution. Maybe being shot and captured was just what he'd needed. "There is a way to strengthen the Mantle. Prevent the breaches, prevent it from coming down."

She leaned in closer, bringing her scent with her. He breathed in her aroma—delicate and woodsy, both refreshing and fragrant—then cleared his throat.

"An old Lagrimari man in one of the villages recognized me, or rather my disguise. The Keepers of the Promise already had a spy embedded in this unit. Darvyn, the Singer who spelled me, simply switched me in for their agent and gave me his face."

Jasminda's eyes rounded. "I had no idea such power was possible. To change a person into someone else for—how long? Days?"

"Nearly two weeks."

"This Darvyn's Song must be very strong."

Jack nodded, pushing away the foreboding that built when he thought of his friend. One crisis at a time was all he could manage. He only hoped the young man was still alive.

"The elder passed on something for me to give to the Keepers."

He motioned to his left boot and bent his leg to try to reach it, then hissed as pain arrowed through his limb.

Jasminda stopped him with a hand to his thigh.

"Hidden in the lining of my boot."

She nodded and unlaced his ties with nimble fingers, then slid the shoe off. From the lining she pulled a small, irregularly shaped shard of black stone, its surface smooth as glass, then promptly dropped it as if the thing had stung her. It skittered across the wooden boards, landing a pace away.

"W-what is that?" Her lips were parted, eyes round. She shook out her hand. *Odd.* Touching it had not affected Jack in any way, nor had it the old man, though Jack was not a Singer, of course, and the elder had long ago lost his Song.

"He told me it was a map. An ancient one that is supposed to lead to the cornerstone of the Mantle."

Jasminda leaned down until her nose was only a few breaths away from the rock fragment. "The cornerstone?" she asked.

"The old man said the ancient Singers who built the Mantle reinforced it with a single cornerstone, hidden in the mountains. Over time it must have weakened, and now there are cracks in the magic. But it can be shored up, strengthened with Earthsong."

Jasminda's profound reaction puzzled Jack. She seemed horrified by the small stone. Jack grabbed it, feeling nothing but cool, polished hardness. Nothing to match Jasminda's aversion.

He rubbed his thumb across it. "Fortifying the cornerstone will stop the breaches and keep the True Father on his side of the mountain. I was planning for Darvyn to do it, but now . . ."

Jasminda met his eyes with skepticism. "And you believed some random old man with a rock? Where did he get it from, and why has no one heard of it before?"

Jack shook his head. "I don't know. The Keepers have a network of sympathizers hidden across the country. I didn't have long to speak with him before the others returned." He motioned to the house, meaning the soldiers. "But I did verify one thing, the stone *is* magic."

She wiped her hands on her skirt and swallowed. "Of that I'm sure, but I don't know that it's a map."

"What does it make you feel?"

"Bad. Wrong. It's bad magic." She shook her head and rose, backing away from him.

"Jasminda—" he whispered. Footsteps inside the house cut him off. He cursed under his breath, fisted the shard, and closed his eyes to feign sleep.

"Pleasant morning, Miss Jasminda. You certainly rise with the sun, don't you?" The sergeant's obsequious voice made Jack's skin crawl. Jasminda merely grunted. Jack cracked an eyelid to find her trying to get past Tensyn, whose angular form efficiently blocked the doorway.

"If you'll excuse me, I need to get breakfast started." Her shoulders were as taut as her voice.

The man didn't move immediately, and a nasty foreboding caused Jack's fist to tighten until the little shard threatened to slice his skin. Finally the sergeant stepped aside, allowing Jasminda to pass, then followed behind her.

Jack fought to bring his breathing back under control. He did *not* like the way Tensyn looked at Jasminda. He settled his weight protectively over the floorboard where she had stored the knife and food the night before.

He would find the strength he needed to get out of here. And he would have to take Jasminda with him.

CHAPTER SEVEN

*Never give a gift with your eyes closed, said the Master of Sharks
to the rich man. For you may part with more than you intend.*

—COLLECTED FOLKTALES

Six soldiers crowded around the table, devouring the morning meal
Jasminda had set in front of them. Their favorite pastime seemed to
be making fun of the youngest and smallest: bespectacled Wargi.

"This one is more coddled than an Elsiran brat," Pymsyn said
through a mouthful of eggs. "Came into the army straight from his
mother's skirts, he did."

"Thinks he's better than the rest of us because he's not harem-
born," said Fahl. "Just because your mam didn't have to spread her
legs for the True Father doesn't make you top shit."

"And doesn't make your mam any less of a whore than ours,"
Ginko grunted. The table erupted in laughter.

Jasminda always paid close attention to the men's taunting and
verbal sparring. She didn't want to make any more mistakes and

cast suspicion on her Lagrimari identity. But she knew next to nothing of life in that land. Her father had been tight lipped, and it wasn't as if any of her books had information on their culture or practices. Aside from the breaches into Elsira over the years and very limited trade with Yaly, their neighbor to the east, Lagrimar was cut off from the rest of the world. Mountains surrounded the country on all sides, with only a small flat area a few thousand paces wide on the Elsiran border, where all the breaches had occurred.

As the men continued to mock Wargi, the young soldier just smiled and laughed, appearing to take it all in stride. But his eyes remained brittle, and Jasminda almost felt sorry for the boy. His round face hadn't yet lost its baby fat; he couldn't be older than sixteen.

Soon enough, the sergeant called the table to order, issuing instructions for the men to split into pairs to explore the valley and monitor the progress of the storm. All the soldiers except Wargi and Tensyn himself headed out.

"Is there anything my men can help you with, Miss Jasminda?" Tensyn's stained smile verged on lecherous. She swallowed the bile that rose and forced herself to smile back.

"No, sir. Dishes are almost done. Once the spy gets his rations, I'll be back to my chores."

"Wargi, finish the dishes for the lady, then throw some crusts at that vermin outside," he barked.

Wargi stood and gently removed the dishrag from her hand.

"Thank you," she whispered to him. He looked embarrassed and began tackling the pots in the sink.

"Come, rest your feet a moment, dear girl," Tensyn said.

She could think of no way to refuse, and so took the seat offered, cringing as Tensyn slid uncomfortably close to her.

"Beauty such as yours should never have to look upon that filthy Elsiran. Wargi, find a bag to cover the pig's head with."

"Yes, sir."

Jasminda shot a quick glance toward the porch but couldn't see Jack from her position. Tensyn launched into a long and meandering tale of his valor during the Seventh Breach, of the vast number of Elsirans he'd killed and the accolades he'd received from the True Father. Every so often, he would twirl the tips of his mustache and pause to check her reaction. She'd never thought herself a good actress, but she strove to appear impressed.

He finished his story, and she bobbed her head enthusiastically, eyes wide as saucers to portray her awe. He then gave a great yawn and announced he was off for a nap. Jasminda slumped in her chair, exhausted, and noticed Wargi had slipped away at some point. She stood to retrieve the extra food she'd set aside for Jack before heading out to the porch.

He sat propped against the railing, looking like a discarded scarecrow with the sack covering his head. She knelt and uncovered him. He blinked at her, then frowned.

"I was rather enjoying the privacy."

She bounced the bag in her hand. "I can put it back if you like."

He yawned, stretching his shoulders as far as he could with his arms tied. His shirt remained open, and she watched the muscles of his chest bunch and flex. Though he was bruised and scarred, she couldn't draw her eyes away.

Silence stretched between them, and she realized he hadn't missed her stare. Her cheeks grew warm and she ducked her head, pushing the bowl of mashed turnips toward him. He picked it up and awkwardly shoveled the spoon into his mouth with his bound hands, then turned to her with raised eyebrows and a grimace.

"Those are the herbs," she said, voice apologetic. "They're bitter, but good for your healing." Her Song was nearly depleted. She would have to wait until later in the afternoon to be strong enough to help him again.

"I need your help," he said, only speaking once he'd fully swallowed his food, unlike the Lagrimari soldiers. "With the cornerstone."

She shook her head, recalling the vile energy coming from the tiny thing he claimed was a map. "I don't want anything to do with that rock."

"You don't have to read the map, that doesn't require a Song. I can do it. All it takes is a bit of blood."

Jasminda shivered. "Blood?"

"I tried it before. Just a drop, and you'll see the path unfold in your mind. Landmarks, trails, the whole journey runs in your head like a photoplay."

Unease was an army of ants marching across her skin.

"But only an Earthsinger can fortify the cornerstone," he continued. "And you are the only one available." His eyes were all earnestness, gently pleading with her.

But the soldiers, her home, the taxes, the constable. Jack didn't know what he asked of her. In less than a week, she would have to either accept her grandfather's terms or leave her home. Appealing to the Taxation Bureau in person would require traveling across the entire country, and she had neither the money nor the means to do so in time. There wasn't really a choice open to her, much as she hated to admit it. She would have to sign and return the papers before the auction and could not both journey through the mountains with Jack and meet the magistrate in five days.

"There has to be someone else. I can't—I have to . . ." A pulse of energy stole her breath. She shuddered and squeezed her eyes tight.

"What is it?" Jack asked, leaning toward her.

"I don't know. Magic, I think." The faint sensation was not dissimilar to the crawling unease that had overtaken her when she'd touched Jack's map. But this was different. This felt like it was coming from the house. She sucked in a deep breath, rose, and slipped back through the door.

The kitchen was empty, as was the main room beyond. Both bedroom doors were closed, but as she approached, voices rose from her parents' room.

"I don't believe I heard you correctly, mistress. Is that truly what the True Father desires?" Tensyn spoke softly. Jasminda strained to hear. "We have gone through much to recapture the prisoner."

"Do you question your king's commands?" A woman's voice, deadly and elegant, came from behind the door. Jasminda froze and used what was left of her Song to seek out the speaker. But the energy gave no clues. She sensed only one person in the room—Tensyn.

"No, certainly not. I just want to be sure that I understand my orders. I live to obey."

The woman scoffed. "Then follow my instructions. And when this tantrum he calls a storm clears, you and your men return to Sayya. You will be rewarded for your diligence, Sergeant. I will make sure of it."

"Th-thank you, mistress."

Jasminda rushed back to the kitchen, her mind a whirl. The soldiers had claimed their radio equipment was broken. Had that been a lie? But the woman's voice wasn't staticky like it was being sent over the airwaves. It had been as clear and crisp as if she'd been standing in front of Mama's mirror, speaking directly into Tensyn's ear.

The sensation of bad magic had faded now that the conversation was over. Though the Lagrimari had all lost their Songs, it was obvious that some kind of spell was at work here. The sort that left a bitter taste on Jasminda's tongue.

What had the mystery woman's instructions to the sergeant been? The men had wanted to bring Jack back to the capital alive for questioning, but perhaps now that had changed.

Dread danced dangerously down Jasminda's spine. She needed to come up with a plan to save Jack *and* remove these men from her home. Before it was too late.

CHAPTER EIGHT

A boy, having accidentally stepped into a nest of vipers, cried out
to the Mistress of Serpents for aid.

    Serpent turned the vipers to glass and entreated the boy to
leave the nest without breaking the glass. For it is you who have
entered their home without invitation, she said. Why should they
change their nature in their own home?

—COLLECTED FOLKTALES

Night had fallen, and the cool breeze sighed across Jack's heated
skin. Raucous laughter swelled inside the house. Jack winced when
something heavy crashed to the ground. Guilt for his part in leading these men to Jasminda's home had not waned. And now it
sounded as if they were breaking the place apart.

He smelled Jasminda's presence before he heard her footsteps.
She crept up the back steps to kneel beside him. Her palm slid
across his forehead, and he pressed into the touch. Another loud
thunk resounded from within the house, followed by rising voices.

"It sounds like a tavern in there," Jack said.

"It is."

He raised an eyebrow.

"They discovered my father's gin. They're three noses into the still."

There were few things more cruel than a drunken soldier. Jack rolled his cheek back into her hand. "I am sorry for it." The men's intoxication would not bode well for them.

Jasminda's fingers skated across his scalp, soothing the dull ache in his head. The breeze picked up, whistling a warning in the air.

"How much longer will the storm trap us here?" he asked.

A shifting of clouds revealed the moonlight, illuminating her pensive expression. "Another twenty-four hours or so." Her vivid dark gaze drove into him. "Do you think you can walk?"

He rose onto an elbow, searching her inscrutable expression. "I believe so. Are we going somewhere?"

A knife appeared in her hand and with a *snick*, his ropes were cut. "They're all distracted now. I think we should try to get you out of here."

Shock momentarily froze him, but he shook it off and rose to his feet. She wrapped an arm around him, helping to support some of his weight. Jack was grateful for it; much as he hated to admit it, he needed the aid. His wounds and bruises complained noisily, but he ignored them, focusing on finding his footing.

"What's the plan?" he asked as they stumbled down the back steps.

"Stay alive." He wanted to grin at her response, but instead pursed his lips at the shooting pain that stabbed his chest. He boxed it away and concentrated on putting one foot in front of the other.

The two of them sank into the shadows cast by the moonlight, keeping to the tree line, and skirting the side of the house with quiet steps. Inside, discordant voices began a bawdy drinking song.

They had just rounded the corner of the house when the front door slammed open. Jasminda's arm turned to stone around him. Jack held his breath. The moon blessedly chose that moment to sink behind a cloud, leaving the yard in darkness. It was too dim to identify the man who lurched forward, but he walked straight toward them, stopping a handful of paces away before a thick-trunked dogwood. If he looked to his right, he would see them standing stiff as statues, trying to blend into the night.

The soldier unzipped his fly and began to piss. His stream was seemingly endless; how much gin had there been? Jasminda trembled.

Finally, the soldier finished and tucked himself back into his trousers. He turned toward the house, swaying on his feet. Jack exhaled slowly, ready to weep with relief, when the bloody moon broke through the bloody clouds, brilliantly illuminating the yard.

Yet, the soldier—Pymsyn he could see now—had his back to them, staggering toward the cabin. Jack swallowed. Just a few more steps. He counted them down as Pymsyn drew farther away.

On the porch, the soldier's hand met the door handle. From the corner of Jack's eye, he saw Jasminda blinking rapidly, watching the man's every movement. They dared not move, out in the open as they were. Once the Lagrimari was safely inside, they could regain the cover of the shadows.

But instead of opening the door, Pymsyn turned around.

A bone-deep chill took over Jack's body.

Pymsyn's eyes widened. His alcohol-soaked brain took several moments to process before the connection was made. Jack spotted the moment it did, as recognition and outrage crossed the man's face.

In that split second, Jack reacted. He pulled the knife Jasminda had used on his ropes out of the front pocket of her dress, where she'd slipped it. At the same time, he adjusted his hold on her to appear menacing and lifted the knife to her throat.

The maneuver was swift and left him aching. But by the time Pymsyn raised his voice to shout, to all appearances Jasminda was at Jack's mercy. A hostage, not a savior.

"I forced you to do this," he whispered. She struggled against him, though he sensed she was not playing along, but rather rejecting his plan. It did not matter, her tussling would only reinforce Jack's story.

He held her tighter. The sweet fragrance of her hair filled his nose. He inhaled the scent as the soldiers streamed drunkenly out of the cabin.

Jasminda was wrenched away, taking her warmth and aroma with her. Blows from the angry soldiers came down thick and fast. Jack was sorry to have undone all her healing work—he hoped she would not be too angry with him over it.

The severity of the men's punches paled in comparison to what he'd suffered when he'd first been discovered. A few days of rest and relaxation and several fifths of gin had turned the men soft.

"Is that all you've got?" Jack wheezed during a break in the action. Once again a foot to his midsection stole his breath. A kick to the head stole his consciousness.

CHAPTER NINE

Said the Master of Jackals to the soldier, A victorious warrior fights for one of three things: a righteous cause, a broken heart, or a noble death.

—COLLECTED FOLKTALES

"Have you been harmed, my dear?" Tensyn asked, his eyes bleary and bloodshot.

"I'm fine." Jasminda fought to keep her composure. *She* was fine. Jack, on the other hand, had been dragged off back to the porch, insensible. She couldn't tell for sure, but he might have been as bad off again as he was when he arrived.

Tensyn grabbed her chin to peer down at her. He was trying to appear attentive, but she couldn't bear the touch of his skin.

"I assure you, he did not hurt me." She stepped back out of reach.

Tensyn's forefinger was bandaged. It hadn't been so earlier. She was surprised he hadn't asked her to come nurse him whenever he'd injured himself, though it was likely done destroying some valuable keepsake of hers.

She glared at him, holding herself back from railing against Jack's treatment. Tensyn's expression was loose and heavy lidded. He did not seem inclined to kill Jack at this moment—he had ordered his men to stop the beating in an outraged tone—but Jasminda remained unsure as to what she'd overheard earlier in the day.

Something tickled at her memory, but skittered away when she tried to bring it into focus.

"I will post a guard at your door tonight, to ensure your safety. You are under my protection, after all." He bowed. It might have been more gallant if he hadn't stumbled halfway through and messily righted himself.

"That isn't necessary," she said, fear spiking in her veins.

"Oh, I insist." He glanced in the direction the men had taken Jack, his expression sobering for a moment. "*That* is a desperate man."

Jasminda shivered in the cool night. She was growing desperate herself.

She had no intention of falling asleep. Sitting upright on her bed, she kept her shotgun on one side and a long blade in her other hand. But her body ignored her intent, succumbing to exhaustion and its need for rest. Her eyelids drooped, and nothing she could do kept them from closing.

The tinkling of wind chimes—the makeshift alarm she'd hung on her door—was her only warning. A figure loomed above her in the dark. A beefy hand covered her mouth, stifling her scream. Fahl towered over her, reeking of gin. He was strong and had an iron grip on her face, pushing her back into the pillow. The hand holding her knife was stuck underneath her head, and Fahl's other hand felt roughly for her nightgown and grabbed at the hem.

Jasminda kicked out, struggling, fighting with all her might, but Fahl was huge and heavy as he lay on top of her, fully immobilizing her. He eased up enough to continue pushing up her nightgown and then pawed at her thighs as she tried to clench them together.

The shotgun rolled off the bed, hitting the floor. Fahl chuckled when he saw it, launching a blast of alcohol-infused air into her face.

"Keep fighting, sweetheart," he said. "It's been months since I had any, and I don't mind working for it a little."

Jasminda stilled, unwilling to give this man anything he wanted. She hunted for an escape.

He fumbled with his trousers, pulling and tearing at them until his squiggly, limp penis emerged. He made a sound of disgust, then started stroking himself while pinning her down, one hand covering her mouth. Jasminda strained to see what was going on down there—and thanked the Queen he wasn't making much progress.

The terryroot was doing its job. Her herb dictionary listed the odorless, tasteless, plant's use for "wives wanting some peace from their husbands." Her mother had laughed heartily when a young Jasminda asked what that meant, telling the girl that she would find out when she was older. Since the soldiers had arrived, Jasminda had been liberally dosing their food with the herb.

Growling in frustration, Fahl kneeled over her, angrily pulling on himself. Without his weight on top of her, Jasminda could now move her arm but didn't know if she would be quick enough with the knife. The moment of indecision cost her when he stood suddenly, grabbing her by the hair. She winced from the pain as he forced her down the stairs. Her side pressed against his giant chest, immobilizing her arm, but allowing just enough reach for her to slide the knife into her pocket.

"Ginko!" he whispered loudly. "Mate, where are you?"

An answering groan sounded from the living room. The door to one of the bedrooms hung open, revealing another soldier sprawled on the floor inside. Fahl pressed her onto the couch next to a groggy and very drunk Ginko.

"I've brought you a present, mate," Fahl said. His pants sagged, and his flaccid penis hung out shamelessly.

"Eh?" Ginko replied, peeling open his eyes. He perked up when he noticed Jasminda. "What about the sergeant?" he slurred.

"Can't hold his liquor." Fahl grinned evilly, showing off his blackened, stinking teeth. His grip loosened for a moment, and Jasminda tore free with a shout, lunging off the couch toward the kitchen, jumping over furniture in her way. But Fahl and Ginko surprised her with their speed, catching up to her quickly and slamming her down on the kitchen table. She pulled the knife from her pocket and swiped out, slicing through a fleshy arm. A corresponding yowl rang out from whichever of them she'd cut.

She screamed a war cry and lashed out again, but a hand pinned her arm like a vise before the knife met its target. A blow to her face rattled her senses before her legs were pinned as well. She kicked and flailed with all her strength, but it felt like immovable rocks held her in place.

Ginko clutched her legs, nudging her nightgown up. Near her head, Fahl hadn't stopped pulling at himself futilely.

"Perhaps this will go better if I stuff it down your throat." He released her arms to grab her hair and tilt her head back toward him. His grip was tight enough to make her vision blur, but she focused on her newly freed hands. A little closer and she'd be able to reach the two sensitive sacks behind his drooping manhood.

She would rip off whatever she touched and bite off anything that came near her lips.

As Fahl drew closer and Ginko's hands slid toward her panties, the back door crashed open. All movement ceased. Through watery eyes, she saw Jack standing in the doorway, the knife she'd hidden for him in his hand, his restraints dangling from one wrist. He leaped across the room and tackled Fahl, plunging the knife deep into the man's belly. Ginko sprang away.

Jasminda crawled off the table and dropped to the ground. She blinked, clearing her vision, and rose to see Jack duck Ginko's wide punch. The swing threw the Lagrimari soldier off balance. He wobbled until Jack landed a vicious, crunching kick. Ginko crumpled, hitting his head with a loud *crack* on the kitchen counter before falling to the floor. Blood pooled around his head and he stared upward, unseeing.

Fahl, knife still lodged in his belly, had been leaning against the opposite counter, but when Ginko fell, he rushed Jack with a new burst of strength. He grasped Jack in a bear hug and wrapped his hands around Jack's throat, squeezing. Jasminda screamed and ran toward the hulking man, climbing on his back. The fingers of one hand sunk deep into his greasy hair as she pulled back his head, then in one swift motion slit the man's throat with the other, just as she'd do with a goat.

She jumped back and he fell, blood spurting everywhere, covering Jack with its spray.

CHAPTER TEN

The Mistress of Serpents was asked to judge a dispute between two farmers.

This man has diverted the stream so I cannot water my crop, the first farmer said.

For years, this man has kept the stream to himself, the second replied. I am balancing the scales.

Serpent transformed the fields of both men into a magnificent lake. Now there is water for all, she said.

—COLLECTED FOLKTALES

The weight of what she'd done hit her. Jasminda had just killed a man. Nausea squeezed her belly. She released the knife from her shaking hand, startling as it clattered to the floor.

"Are you all right?" Jack asked. She turned to face him and caught sight of Wargi in the doorway. The boy was frozen, eyes on the carnage of his former squad members. And then he was gone.

"Wargi!" she shouted, taking off after him. Jack followed on her heels as she entered her parents' bedroom.

The boy stood over the sergeant's prone body, shaking him awake. Tensyn sat up, bleary-eyed. Long moments passed before he processed what was before him. Both Jasminda and Jack were covered in blood, head to toe.

Jasminda didn't know what to expect, so when the sergeant slowly raised his hands above his head in surrender, she was surprised. She looked back to find Jack training a pistol on him.

"Jasminda, gather the weapons," Jack said. She blinked and jumped into action.

An additional service revolver sat on the dresser. She grabbed it and opened the chamber to find it full of rounds.

She bent to check the ground, when a rucksack in the corner began to vibrate. That same uneasy feeling of bad magic returned, pulsing in time to the movement of the sack.

"What is that?" Her voice hitched.

Jack's brow was furrowed, but Tensyn stared at the bag, eyes wide, before turning away. He swallowed. The noise grew louder, more insistent.

"Answer her." Jack motioned with his gun.

"It's a speaking stone," Tensyn said through clenched teeth.

Jasminda had never heard of such a thing. The queasiness in her stomach grew with each rattle. Jack slipped his hand around her wrist, raising her weapon until it was trained on the two Lagrimari, then he turned to the rucksack and searched its pockets.

A bandana covering his fingers, Jack retrieved a small brownish-red pebble, about the size of his thumbnail. The tiny object shook in his palm, unrelenting. Jasminda winced at the magic coming from it.

"A speaking stone." Wonder laced Jack's voice. "Why is it shaking?"

Tensyn firmed his lips, refusing to answer.

"The shaking must be how it alerts you to a communication." Jasminda could feel the insistence of the magic. She glanced at Tensyn and suddenly the bandage on his finger made sense.

"Blood," she said. Tensyn's eyes narrowed. She turned to Jack who nodded, understanding. He wiped some of the blood covering him onto the stone. It stopped rattling.

"I do not like to be kept waiting, Sergeant. Is it done?" The same imperious female voice Jasminda had heard before came through the stone.

"Who is this?" Jack asked.

A pause. "Who is *this*?" The voice was smiling. It was as though the woman already knew who she was talking to. "I suppose introductions can come later. Time and the True Father wait for no man. Ta-ta."

With a cry, Jack dropped the stone and shook out his hand.

"What happened?" Jasminda asked, but the speaking stone ignited like a match as it hit the ground. The flame instantly caught hold of the bedroom rug and raced across its length, impossibly fast.

As if possessed with some kind of intelligence, the fire leapt up the legs of the dresser. Before Jasminda could move, one of the oil lamps exploded, showering the room in sparks and flame. She screamed and ducked. Jack was on her in an instant, leading her out of the room, away from the blaze.

Wargi and Tensyn, coughing and sputtering, raced out behind them and disappeared through the kitchen. Jack pulled the bedroom door shut and stuffed the quilt from the couch in the crack at the bottom of the doorframe.

"Do you have a fire suppressor?"

His words scrambled in her head. "A what?"

"No, I suppose you wouldn't, all the way out here. We don't have much time. Save what you can." He dashed into the kitchen, leaving her staring at the door, still not believing what lay on the other side.

A coughing fit caused by the acrid smoke filling her lungs shook her from her stupor. Tears like acid stung her cheeks. Her house was burning. Her home.

She raced upstairs and replaced her blood-soaked robe with a dress and boots. Tossed items blindly into a sack. Some part of her was still in her parents' bedroom, watching the flames consume the walls. She stared at the bag in her hands, not remembering how it got there, not knowing what was inside, only that the tightness in her chest was not just smoke, it was the mouth of an endless river, a wash of despair sweeping her away.

She found herself in the living room again, standing in front of the cabinets. Had she run down the stairs? Was that why she was struggling to breathe?

No . . .

Everything here was precious. Sooty fingers skimmed each shelf, committing the feel of each object to memory. Her chest contracted. Was that her heart shrinking away to nothing?

Jack appeared next to her, carrying a basket stuffed with what remained of the pantry. "Give that to me." He plucked the sack from her grasp. She stared at her empty hands for a moment, then at Jack, and felt grounded by the firmness of his expression. His uniform was tattered and stained. She pulled out a set of her brothers' clothes from the cabinet and tossed them at him.

"These should fit—the boys were tall for their age."

Flames reached out from under her parents' door, the quilt

having been eaten away. In mere minutes there would be nothing left of her life.

"Jasminda."

Time spun without her knowledge. She turned to find Jack changed and ready. He'd even pulled on Papa's old coat, the one the three children had saved up over the course of a year to replace. Papa had been wearing the new one the last time she saw him.

Tears formed, and her throat began to close up. Jack said her name again. "We have to go."

She nodded, throat too thick to speak, and allowed him to take her hand and pull her from the house.

In the front yard, Wargi dragged Pymsyn's body, laying him next to the charred, motionless form of Unar. Tensyn sat on the ground, enthralled by the vivid flames. Their reflection danced in his dark irises.

Jasminda's knees hit the ground as a crash sounded behind her. Heat crawled over her skin. Pungent smoke punched her nose. She could not bring herself to look. Jack wrapped his arms around her and pressed her into his chest. He whispered something she couldn't hear above the rush of blood in her ears.

Gasping, she worked to pull herself together, clutching at the coat Jack wore that had long since lost her father's smell. Finally, she could breathe steadily. His arms were a cage of safety around her, but she still felt like her chest had cracked open and everything inside was leaking out.

"This is all I have. I have nothing else."

He held her tighter and rocked her gently, but she found no solace in his arms.

CHAPTER ELEVEN

Now Spider was more crafty than any of his brother or sisters.
And he was the only one who wept not a single tear when his
parents met the World After.

—COLLECTED FOLKTALES

The cock of a hammer made Jasminda freeze. Slowly, she pulled away from Jack and turned around. Wargi held a pistol trained on them. He shook with fear and made little hiccupping sounds.

Jack raised his palms; Jasminda did the same.

"W-Wargi?" she said, voice shaking. "Please." The boy looked broken, so unsure.

His grip tightened on the gun, and with his unsteady hand, she was afraid he might shoot them without even meaning to.

"There, there, my boy," Tensyn said, rising. "Give that to me, then."

With relief, Wargi gave the revolver to his sergeant. Jack's shoulder brushed against hers as they stood side by side. Jasminda closed her eyes on a long blink, then opened them to face her fate.

Tensyn glared at them. Soot covered half the man's face, and his normally coiffed hair stuck out all over his head. Part of his mustache had burned off. He looked from Jack to Jasminda, taking in their close proximity, and snorted.

"You think this Elsiran will think twice about you when he no longer has use for you?" He sneered and lowered the gun, pushing forward the hammer and placing it in his waistband. "But by all means, run off with this scum and see for yourself."

His yellow smile gave Jasminda a chill. "Y-you're letting us go?"

The sergeant turned so his face was in profile. He affected a magnanimous expression and shooed them away with a flick of his wrist.

"I don't understand. Why would you do this?" Jack asked.

Tensyn *tsked*. "I've lost the bulk of my squad." He motioned to the dead men, the dwindling fire. "I doubt very much that Wargi and I could get you back to Sayya with our necks intact. Let us call it a tactical relinquishment. Now go, before I change my mind."

Suspicion had both Jasminda and Jack backing away. She fully expected the sergeant to shoot them in the back as they fled, but he paid them no attention. They walked backward to the tree line, then rushed behind a large trunk.

"What was that?" she asked.

Jack's face was drawn, worried. "I have no idea. I don't trust it."

"He wants us to leave. But why?"

Jack lifted his shoulders. "I think we have little choice but to go."

Jasminda forced herself to view the wreckage. The barn did not appear in danger from the rapidly dying flames. Some idiot had left the door unbarred, but perhaps that was for the best. The goats would be able to leave and forage for food. They were tough animals and too stubborn to die.

She led Jack through the grove of crab apples, deeper into the valley. Once they were a good distance from the ruined cabin, she stopped. Tears stung the backs of her eyes as the reality of the night's events sank down on her.

"What do you think Tensyn and Wargi will do?" Jack's voice cut through her self-pity.

"Go back. The speaking stone—that woman, I heard him talking to her before. She ordered him back to Sayya. I'd thought he would kill you first, but . . ." Her head was clouded from grief, and she couldn't connect all the dots clearly.

Jack bent over and breathed deeply. His face was ghostly pale, and the energy that had been fueling him seemed to ebb.

"I need your aid," he said.

She rushed over to help him sit. "I'm surprised you're even standing."

"That is not what I meant. The cornerstone." His gaze held hers, and she couldn't look away.

"Jack, I want to help you, but in five days I will have no home." At his incredulous look, she went on. "This valley is so far out, so isolated, the Prince Regent didn't even know we were here for many years. But when the crown found us—found me—they determined I owed a small fortune in back property taxes." She took a deep breath. "I researched the statutes. By law, since we didn't get any notices for all that time, we can apply for something called safe harbor and not have to pay."

She blinked back her tears and sniffed. "I sent an appeal detailing everything, but it doesn't seem to have helped. According to the magistrate, on Seconday of next week they will auction the land if I don't come up with the money."

Jack reached for her hand, threading his fingers through hers. The sensation calmed her, gave her something to hold onto.

"What will you do?" he asked.

She shrugged. "Renounce my mother and save my home. And then rebuild."

"Renounce your mother?"

She told him of her call with the solicitor and her grandfather's offer. The paperwork he wanted her to sign. "I don't want to, but I don't know what else to do."

Jack was quiet for a moment. He reached into the bag he'd slung across his back. The bit of silver he pulled out took Jasminda's breath away.

"I found it in the back of the pantry when I was gathering food. It was your mother's?"

The pendant hung on a slightly charred chain. Snaking lines of metal had been designed to curl in on themselves in a beautiful tangle. Jasminda smiled at the familiar necklace.

"The sigil of the Queen," she said, running her finger along the warm metal, tracing the endless curving line. "I haven't seen this in many years. All in the Sisterhood wear them. I always thought it looked much like a spider."

Jack smiled and tilted his head. "I can see that. Here . . ." He grasped the chain with nimble fingers. "Let me fasten it for you." She swept her hair from her nape and presented it to him. His fingers brushed her neck, leaving goose bumps in their wake. She swallowed as the weight of the pendant settled just below her collarbone.

Rubbing the silver charm between her thumb and forefinger was soothing. It was an action Mama had done several times a day. Jasminda used to wonder if the motion aided in prayer. The Queen Who Sleeps visited the dreams of some—a very rare few—though Papa was included in the number.

He'd never spoken of the words of wisdom he received during these dreams, so Jasminda could only guess. Her own dreams had always remained silent, though she prayed for a visit just as most Elsirans did.

Mama had described joining the Sisterhood and devoting her life to service of the Queen as the best decision she'd ever made. Even when she'd left the order to start her family. That hadn't stopped her generosity. She'd made up baskets for the sick, those who would have benefitted from Papa's healing but refused it out of fear. She was kind to those who shunned her, and even coolly polite to those who only accepted her and the twins— who all three appeared Elsiran and had no magic—not Papa and Jasminda.

Her mama had been too good for this world and was needed in the World After to spread her love there. At least that's what Papa had said. It was just a platitude to soothe grieving children, but as Jasminda grew older, she believed it more and more.

She released the pendant and spun around, the realization hitting her like a blow to the chest. "I can't sign those papers, Jack."

His eyes rounded with concern. "They burned, did they?"

She paused, thinking. "No, I never took them out of my bag. But I wish they had, because I won't sign. Mama never distanced herself from me. She walked away from everything she knew and everyone just for us. I can't—I won't disrespect her memory by giving in to my grandfather's shame." She stood and paced, her boots rasping across the fallen leaves.

A nagging doubt had chafed against the back of her mind since her call with the solicitor. She couldn't put her finger on it, but her gut told her there was more to her grandfather's offer than what had been stated.

"You do have another option, you know," Jack said.

She stopped her pacing.

"The in-person appeal. Go to Rosira. Your grounds are sound.

There's no reason why the Taxation Bureau won't listen." He reached for her hand, and she gripped him. "I will help."

"You'll help me get to Rosira? I don't have any money, and"— she motioned to herself—"traveling across the country would be difficult for me." She could only imagine that the rest of Elsira would be far worse in their regard for her than those in the tiny Borderlands town.

Jack pursed his lips. "Yes. Of course I'll help you. I could even . . ." He bit back whatever he'd been about to say. "I will do whatever it takes to help you save your land so you can rebuild."

Her free hand found the pendant again, worrying the smooth silver. "All right. And I will help you with the cornerstone . . . as much as I can."

CHAPTER TWELVE

The Mistress of Eagles lived atop the tallest hill in all the land. From there she said she could hear the voice of the wind more clearly, and who better to listen to than the greatest traveler in the world?

—COLLECTED FOLKTALES

"Are you sure you don't want to rest some more?" Jasminda asked. "The storm seems to have lessened a bit, but it will still be a treacherous climb." A trickle of Earthsong zipped through Jack. He did his best to straighten and pretend he did not hurt everywhere.

"No, we don't have any time to waste. And you had better save your magic for the Mantle."

Her lips thinned, but the tingle of power ceased. She marched over to a wide tree and retrieved a thick branch from beneath it, then presented it to him. He accepted the walking stick gratefully. His shoulder and abdomen were both ablaze with pain; each breath was a struggle.

He fished the little map stone from his pocket and rubbed his thumb across the sleek surface. Then he pulled the knife from his belt—the same one he'd used to kill the soldier. It was clean now, but still he hesitated before pricking his finger and touching it to the stone the old man had given him.

The valley disappeared, the smell of smoke left his nose, and every sound was silenced. All of his senses were overtaken by the magical vision stored in the map. He was transported onto the mountain, walking high in its peaks behind a darkly hooded figure. The summer sun shone overhead, and sweat trickled down Jack's brow. His body was whole and healthy. Gravel crunched under his feet and birds trilled nearby.

The most recognizable landmark was up ahead. A peak that was flat on top, making it look like a table sitting high above the earth. The hooded figure's path took him straight toward the flattened pinnacle. He approached, but then veered north-northwest, toward a ridge that in summer was coated with a dense layer of green shrubs. It was across this rise they had to travel.

Jack wondered if the person in the hood was the one who had created the Mantle. Such things were lost to history without so much as the whisper of myth to give any clues. The Mantle had always been, at least for the past five centuries. And whoever had created this map had been to the cornerstone before. For now, that was all Jack needed to know.

He struggled to leave the vision—though it had been much harder the first time he'd tried it, the night the old man had given him the map.

Jack peeled his lids open and found himself staring into the eyes of a scowling Jasminda. She looked from him to the ground where he'd dropped the map after being torn back into the present. "That's an ugly bit of magic," she said, nudging the rock with her toe.

Ugly or not, it was the only way to find the cornerstone, and he needed it. When he bent to retrieve the map, she stopped him and picked it up after wrapping her hand in her scarf. Grimacing, she dropped it into his palm like a hot coal.

Jack described the flat peak and the green ridge to her. "I know that place," she said. "We can take the path on the north side of the valley."

They set out through the garden rows and trees, Jasminda holding the sack containing the items saved from the house. He protested, but she would not let him carry anything, giving a pointed look at his limping legs when he tried to insist.

"I'm not an invalid."

Her arched eyebrow contradicted him. "Focus on staying upright. I'll do the rest."

He noticed the wince she tried to hide from some injury she wouldn't acknowledge, but overall, she was in far better shape than he. Common sense told him she was right to insist, but his pride stung.

The moon peeked out from the overhead clouds, brightening the way out of the valley and up the trail leading into the mountains. Though the valley was calm, the storm raging ahead worried him. Their path rose, and the temperature fell drastically. Beneath their feet the ground changed from grassy, to dirt covered, to snow covered. Each torturous step brought not only a deepening of the snow but increased pain.

Jasminda led the way, the light from her lantern reflecting off the icy whiteness, now knee deep. But the surrounding darkness swallowed up the illumination. He trusted that she could find the landmarks at night. The walking stick was a godsend as each step became more difficult than the last. Pausing to catch his breath, he was struck by a coughing fit, leaving red splatters on the pristine white.

When he straightened, he found Jasminda staring at the blood on the ground. Almost immediately, the warm hum of Earthsong rippled through him.

"Save it," he rasped. "I'm all right."

She scowled. "You are not all right. You are worse than when you arrived. Stop being such a fool." The buzz of Earthsong continued for a few moments before she turned and stomped away.

They battled the storm for hours, their progress arduous. Strong gusts of wind blew against them, sometimes knocking them on their backs and forcing them to stop until the intensity eased. Icy blasts whipped through Jack's coat, freezing his fingers until he could no longer grip the walking stick and had to leave it behind.

"Let's stop here for a moment," Jasminda shouted, pointing to a notch in the rock wall just big enough for two people. Underneath the overhang, the snow stood only ankle high, and the sidewalls protected them from the worst of the wind. They crouched down together, shaking from the cold. She took his hands in hers and rubbed, bringing some feeling back into them. In the flickering lantern light, worry etched a frown on her face.

"Does this storm seem strange to you?"

"Strange how?"

She swiveled her head from side to side. "I don't know. It's almost like it's . . . alive."

Jack's teeth were chattering so hard that he wasn't sure what sort of expression crossed his face, but Jasminda blinked and looked down. "Never mind."

"Is that possible? Can Earthsong do such a thing?" Jack flinched at the thought. A living storm? Could this be the first wave of attack? The True Father had long used environmental means to wage war, but such a storm was unprecedented.

Jasminda brushed away the snow that had accumulated on her

lashes. "It would take a great deal of his power, I'd think. An unbelievable amount, but it might be possible." She shivered in a way that didn't seem like it was purely from cold.

"How much farther is it?" Jack asked.

She motioned with her head, and he craned his neck around. The tabletop crest of the next mountain was just ahead of them, glowing in the filtered moonlight reflecting off the snow.

Excitement coursed through his blood, and Jack rallied, drawing whatever inner strength he could into his depleted limbs. He cracked his knuckles and tried to fashion his frozen face into a grin. "We're nearly there."

Jasminda nodded, and they stood. Some previously untapped fount from within propelled him forward. Though snow covered everything, he recognized the change in elevation as the green ridge from his vision.

"Where to now?" she shouted over the vicious wind.

"Just across there."

They had to hold each other up to continue, but pushed forward. Jack had no feeling in his feet or hands, and not much in his face, either. He could almost believe that the storm did have some evil intent.

The wind battered them as they crossed the narrow ridge single file. Jasminda held the lantern, leading the way across the icy path. Snow crumbled, tumbling down steep inclines, and was swallowed by the darkness.

Jack's foot slipped. He tipped forward, crashing to his hands and knees. Jasminda wrenched him up, and they shuffled forward, bitterly slowly, but his legs would not move any faster. The path disappeared over a slight incline in front of them.

"It's j-just . . ." He raised a hand to point. Jasminda looked over her shoulder, her expression more grim than he'd ever seen it. They crested the rise, and Jack blinked snow out of his eyes, wonder growing at the sight before them.

He slipped again and thundered to the ground, sliding down the hill on his back. Jasminda cursed behind him, falling on the ice as well.

When he caught his breath, he lay looking up at a giant pillar of stone rising from the ground. It had to be five stories high. Another stood ten paces away. Jack turned his head to find an entire circle of such irregularly shaped pillars, but the more astonishing sight was that none were touched by snow or ice. Inside the perimeter of rough columns, green grass covered the earth.

Jack crawled forward, seeking the warmth. Once he crossed the perimeter, the thrall of the storm no longer touched him. The stone circle must have held magic that protected it from the elements. Feeling returned to his senseless limbs. Wondering if he was hallucinating, he made his way to his feet. But beside him, Jasminda's slack-jawed face reflected his awe.

"Is this what you saw?" she asked.

"Yes." The first time he'd used the map, he'd seen the hooded figure enter this circle of stones. In the vision, it had been summer. Now, it seemed, no other season existed here.

"What now?" Jasminda's voice held an edge of wariness.

Jack tore his attention from the stark delineation of winter and summer to look to the center of the circle. The space was twenty paces across. But unlike in his vision, the inside of the circle was empty. "It was there. Just there in the middle." He turned to Jasminda.

"A red obelisk rose higher than the outer stone columns. In the vision, I knew it was the cornerstone." He stared at the empty space again. Well, not entirely empty. Where the obelisk had once stood now lay a smooth patch of what looked to be dark glass. Somewhat irregularly shaped, the sleek surface held ripples, as if a stone had been tossed in a puddle and then the whole thing had frozen.

Jack moved toward it, studying the area.

"Could it have been moved?" Jasminda asked.

"I don't . . . I don't know." He dropped to his knees, exhaustion catching up with him. Was it his imagination, or did the glass move? Jasminda kneeled beside him, her attention caught as well. Had she seen it?

Like they had practiced the movement, both reached a hand forward at the same time. Only the tips of their fingers brushed the surface, but the glass shattered as if hit with a hammer.

Shards exploded outward, lacerating their hands. Jack dove for Jasminda, using his body to protect her from the spray of sharp fragments. She landed with an *oomph* beneath him, and Jack struggled to catch his breath. Blood seeped from the many shallow wounds on his hands. It was not so much that it should have made him feel light-headed. He'd had worse wounds only the day before. But still, before he could move off Jasminda, his head dove toward the ground and all went black.

CHAPTER THIRTEEN

Failure is like Frog who wished that she, like a tree, would lose her green in autumn.

—COLLECTED FOLKTALES

Jasminda's eyelids felt at least three times their normal weight. The last thing she remembered was the breath leaving her lungs as Jack's weight crushed her. Now, the pressure on her chest was gone. She opened her eyes and found Jack two paces away, still out cold. And the world around her had changed.

When they had entered the stone circle, the storm still raged outside its boundaries. But now, she had been transported into a different season altogether. Beyond the pillars, the sun was up, the weather serene. The outside now matched the inside of the circle.

She sat up and looked again at Jack, sprawled beside her. In his open palm lay the map stone. That was odd. She was sure he hadn't been holding it when they entered the circle.

She looked around again and gasped, scrambling backward at

the sight of a hooded figure standing across the shattered glass from them. Only now, the glass was whole again, like it hadn't burst apart and sliced her. Her fingers no longer stung from the cuts, and there was no blood slicking her palms.

"Who are you?" she called out.

The figure, covered head to toe in a dark cloak, walked around toward Jasminda. She stood her ground, not wanting to move farther from Jack's vulnerable form.

The cloaked person's arms rose to remove the hood, and Jasminda's chest contracted. Standing before her was a woman, a Lagrimari woman. Her dark hair was pulled back into a thick braid, and her eyes, slightly downturned at the corners, gave her a sad look.

She peered in Jasminda's general direction, but the woman was looking through her. Jasminda turned—there was no one else there besides her and Jack.

The sad woman opened her mouth and spoke, shocking Jasminda even more. "You are here for the cornerstone." Her voice had a slight echo to it, a distant quality, though the woman stood only a few paces away. "My father built the Mantle. When he died, protecting it fell to me. Father told me that one day there would be seekers. Either to destroy the barrier or to strengthen it. You must prove which you are before the cornerstone may be revealed."

The woman clasped her hands in front of her. "The test is simple. Return the map to the center of the circle."

Confusion furrowed Jasminda's brow. "Return?" She took another look at the odd patch of glass. It was, perhaps, four paces across. But once again, it had changed. Now in the very middle, a chunk was missing. The irregular shape of what was left behind matched that of the map exactly, it was a perfect fit.

"That's all I have to do?" She looked back over her shoulder, but the woman had disappeared.

The test was simple indeed, though a flutter of apprehension sped her heartbeat. Jack still hadn't awoken; concern for him pummeled her, but she knew what his priority was. With a deep breath, she removed the map stone from his palm, gripping it as gingerly as she would a dead rodent.

To get to the center of the glass, she would have to walk across it—the place where the map fit was too far to reach from outside. But the last time they'd touched it, the glass had shattered.

Jasminda kneeled, feeling on the ground for a pebble or stone. Finding one, she tossed it onto the dark brown glossy surface. It fell with a *thunk*, but the glass held.

She rose and tentatively placed a toe at the very edge of the glass and pressed her weight. It still held, giving no indication of being brittle or delicate at all.

Her heart beating double time, she stepped fully onto the surface. It bore her weight without a groan of complaint and felt just as solid as the ground. When she looked up, her breath caught in her chest.

A different woman stood just in front of her, one she hadn't seen in nearly seven long years. Jasminda's throat thickened. Tears bit her eyes. "Mama?"

Eminette Zinadeel smiled sweetly, but looked off at an angle, staring into the distance. Her auburn hair held streaks of gold. A dusting of freckles lay scattered across her nose. Their pattern was as familiar to Jasminda as her own face.

"Mama!" She reached out to embrace her, but her mother flinched back. Eminette turned to regard her daughter with empty eyes.

"You could have saved me."

"What?" The accusation in her mother's gaze was an arrow through Jasminda's flesh.

"How did you not know? The sickness inside me. How did you not sense it?"

Jasminda blinked through freely flowing tears. "I-I'm sorry, Mama. I didn't know. My Song isn't—"

"Your Song is weak. If you were stronger, you could have saved me."

A sob yanked itself from Jasminda's chest. In the back of her mind, a thought whispered that Papa hadn't sensed Mama's illness, either, and his Song had been much stronger than hers. But most of her acknowledged that her mother was right. If Jasminda had only been stronger, had only worked harder at learning Earthsong, she would have known.

Mama shook her head bitterly and faded away.

"No!" Jasminda fell to her knees; her bones shook from the impact with the glass. She could not catch her breath. Her lungs spasmed, fighting for air.

The map stung her fist. She choked down her grief. The center of the circle was so close, just another two steps. Though this simple test might be the end of her.

She closed her eyes and steadied her breath.

"Jasminda?"

She looked up. Her papa stood just in front of her, the twins on either side. She fell back, taking them all in.

"Papa? Roshon? Varten?" Neither the boys nor her father had changed. The twins were identical except for their expressions. Roshon scowled down at her, and Varten shook his head. Her father's heavy eyes echoed the boys' disappointment.

"If you had come with us that day, you could have saved us," Papa said.

Roshon crossed his arms. "You never wanted to go to town, always begging off, afraid of the townsfolk."

Varten pursed his lips and didn't speak.

Jasminda's stomach lurched, threatening to empty itself. "B-but how could I have saved you?"

"I never thought I'd raised a coward, Jasminda." Papa's voice cut through to her core.

She tried to tell herself this was the magic, the test, none of it was real. But there they stood, and they *looked* so real. Not a hair on their head had changed. They blurred from her tears.

Jasminda tucked her chin to her chest and crawled forward, pushing through the place where they stood. Their legs faded away into mist, and although part of her was relieved, a larger part would have endured anything—would have gladly accepted their blame, if only they had been real.

She stretched out her hand for the center of the circle. It was only an arm's length away. It should have been easy to reach, but her whole body had turned leaden.

A heavy foot nearly stomped on her wrist. She looked up yet again to find the county constable towering over her. The smell of smoke filled her nostrils.

"That fine young couple has big plans for that cabin. They don't mind rebuilding. Even if the thing hadn't burned, they would have torn it down and started over. Said it was too rustic for them." The red-faced man gave a deep belly laugh before piercing her with his gaze.

"A shame you couldn't hold onto your family's legacy. Now, not only is it up in smoke, not a chicken or goat will remain once these new homesteaders get their way." He shook his head and adjusted his cap. "Ah, well, that's progress, innit?"

Jasminda's head dropped, and all the fight went out of her. The farm lost? The cabin torn down instead of being rebuilt? She shook in agony as the words of her family and the constable rained down on her like an avalanche. Her limbs were too heavy to move. She was locked in place as if she had turned to stone. Perhaps she would become one of the pillars that guarded this place.

Try as she might to take one more step, she couldn't do it.

Her fingers were pried open, and the map was removed from her hand.

She opened her eyes to find Jack, red eyed and red faced, but determined, lurch forward on his hands and knees and drop the small stone into place.

As soon as it settled into the spot of its origin, the ground began to vibrate. An invisible force pushed her back onto the grass as the entire interior of the stone circle shimmered and shifted. A giant red obelisk popped into existence where the map stone had lain.

Jack crouched next to her. His eyes slowly rose to meet hers. He scrubbed away the tears tracking his cheeks.

What had he seen? Whatever it was, it seemed no less harrowing than her own test, only Jack had passed.

The cornerstone rose before them, radiating power.

Jack's golden gaze dimmed. His breathing stuttered, and his eyes rolled up into his head. Blood gushed from one of his nostrils.

"Jack?" Jasminda reached for him, but he fell to the side, unconscious. Fear drummed a cadence inside her chest. She could not heal Jack and have any hope of fixing the cornerstone.

Though it tore at her heart, she swallowed and focused her attention on the obelisk. Her breathing had still not returned to normal, so it took several tries before she could successfully connect to Earthsong. The raging river of power felt wild, rough, and choppy.

She filled her Song to its limited capacity and felt for the magic of the cornerstone. A power ancient and unfamiliar met her. The spell was a tangled webbing of complex pieces, far beyond her skill level.

She could see cracks in the intricate latticework of energy, but trying to fill them would be like mortaring a brick wall with twig and a bit of mud. She was just too weak. She had the absurd desire to laugh.

The voices of her family echoed in her head. She swatted them away, but they persisted.

"It's not just me," she muttered aloud as if their apparitions were still before her. "No Singer alive could repair this spell." The magic was hundreds of years old. Papa had told her the ancient Singers must have had godlike powers to create the Mantle. And yet slivers of doubt pierced her.

She poured her Song into the attempt, feeling her way around the spell, trying to patch even one crack. She drained herself to no effect. The old man who'd given Jack the map must have been delusional. Or was she simply the wrong Singer for the job?

She shivered, suddenly cold. No longer able to hold on to Earthsong, she opened her eyes to find swirling eddies of snow had invaded the protection of the pillars. The remaining grass shriveled before her eyes as the storm breached the circle.

What had happened? How had the magic failed? She drew her coat tighter and bent to Jack. He was still breathing, but his injuries had been severe, and the climb up the mountain had only worsened them.

She leaned her head to his chest to find his heartbeat slow, his body temperature scarily low. She lay across his body to try to warm him, but it looked more and more like he would die on this mountain. Likely, they both would.

Tears froze on her face. She squeezed her lids shut against the pain of defeat in so many areas.

Pins and needles skittered across her skin, alternating between tiny jabs of pain and numbness. The evil presence lurking in the storm felt even nearer. She stared up at the obelisk as hope fled.

The ground shook—aftershocks of the cornerstone's appearance? But the gentle vibrations increased in intensity. The rattling grew until the snow bounced and the earth groaned in complaint. Violent, shattering shakes rattled the ridge where the circle stood. The stone columns trembled and crumbled as the shaking grew stronger. Large chunks fell away, barely missing where Jasminda lay protecting Jack with her body. Beneath them, cracks appeared in the earth.

She gripped Jack tight, whispering the Promise of the Queen through stammering lips. "While She sleeps this promise keep; That She dream of us while for Her we weep; May She comfort, counsel, guard, and guide; Those whose love will never die; And when Her betrayer pays for his lies; And finally the World After occupies; May love's true Song with Her remain; And awaken Her that She may rule again."

What was left of the disintegrating columns swayed and tilted. Two of them crashed into the obelisk. They tore through the gleaming red stone. The other pillars followed suit, and rocks tumbled down from somewhere above. They all fell, pounding the ancient artifact into powder until no trace remained.

The ground opened up where the columns had once stood.

Jasminda had repeated the prayer twice through, her words a mere whisper at the end, when the earth beneath her fell away, leaving her clutching Jack's limp form as they tumbled down the mountain.

CHAPTER FOURTEEN

When bonds of friendship would hold him down, Bobcat cuts his ties to run free.

—COLLECTED FOLKTALES

Jasminda lost Jack in the free fall. In the pummeling of rocks and snow and debris, her curled fists could not hold on, and he fell away.

Then the rapid descent stopped. The buzz of Earthsong surrounded her, lifting her until she was weightless. A soft, glowing light approached, floating upward as if on wings. Rising along with her lantern was an unconscious Jack. She grabbed his hand and pulled him into her arms as they floated straight up. Having him back calmed her enough that she could take a breath and enjoy the healing warmth surrounding them.

Her nicks and cuts disappeared; even her frayed emotions were soothed—an accomplishment achievable only by a very powerful Singer. She wished she hadn't exhausted her Song. She longed to reach out and sense the intentions of the Earthsinger who'd

found them. Though his or her actions so far had been benevolent.

The spell—strong enough to carry two adults in the air—
brought them down the mountain and set them gently on a patch
of snowy ground. They were protected from the snow and cold by
a bubble of insulated air.

Jack stirred. Jasminda brushed a hand across his brow and exhaled when he blinked his eyes.

"Welcome back," she whispered.

"Delighted to be here." He looked around, confused. Flexed his
arms and legs.

She crawled closer. "What's wrong? Are you hurt?"

A brilliant smile spread across his face. He shook his head.
"Not at all."

She wanted to check for herself to be sure, but the relief in his
expression told the story. He was well. Thank the Sovereign.

"What happened?"

She shook her head. "Someone saved us. An Earthsinger."

Jack's eyes widened. "And the Mantle?"

Jasminda swallowed her regret. "It didn't work. I couldn't do it.
I wasn't strong enough."

The light in his eyes dimmed, and a new fissure formed on her
heart. There was nothing she could do to make it better—their
chance to stop the war was gone because she had failed.

She longed to ask him what he'd seen in his vision, but the
darkness around them moved. Shadows broke away from the rock
wall, stepping into the weak circle of light. Two men and two
women, all Lagrimari and armed with rifles, came forward. Jasminda scrambled back, her hand diving into her coat pocket where
she'd stored her pistol. Jack, too, produced a revolver, holding it at
his side.

Perhaps the Singer who'd saved them hadn't been as benevolent as she'd hoped.

The Lagrimari held their weapons at the ready, pointed down. Instead of uniforms they wore clothes made from tough, gritty-looking material similar to burlap. The men and women themselves seemed tough and gritty as well. Jasminda held her breath as the group regarded them with hard gazes.

Footsteps crunched in the snow behind the Lagrimari. A small head appeared and pushed its way to the center.

"I told you to go back to the cave," one of the women spat as a little boy pulled away from her grasp. The woman's face was badly scarred on one side with jagged lines. The boy was around six or seven, with a shock of black hair and round cheeks. He smiled brightly, revealing two missing front teeth.

Jasminda pointed her pistol at the ground, peering at the boy.

"Well, hello there," Jack said in Lagrimari. "Are you the welcome wagon?"

The boy beamed at Jack, who smiled back uncertainly. Jasminda watched the exchange, confused.

"He's an incorrigible child," the scarred woman said.

"He is only trying to counteract your pigheadedness, Rozyl," another voice said from the darkness. An old woman stepped into the light, her face leathered and wrinkled. She was gray-haired and stooped, and wore a ragged coat of matted fur. "It's too cold out here for all this bother. *Pssht.* Put those away." She waved her hand, and the armed men and women strapped their rifles to their backs and retreated into the shadows. Rozyl was the last to do so— she scowled at Jasminda before she went.

"Come, children. Come inside where it's warm." The old woman placed a hand on the boy's shoulder. "Thank you, Osar. We wouldn't want our guests to feel unwelcome."

"Who . . . who are you?" Jasminda asked.

"I am Gerda ul-Tahlyro. This little one is Osar, always trying to do good deeds." She smiled down at the child, who seemed a bit abashed.

Jasminda could only stare at the boy. "That was *his* spell?"

"Oh yes. He's the strongest of us all."

"They don't need to know that," Rozyl growled from somewhere in the darkness.

"Osar has already said these two are safe. What reason have we not to trust them?"

"I don't trust anyone." Footsteps crunched away. The cave entrance must be there, hidden in the darkness. When the last footsteps disappeared, Jasminda stood, taking Jack's offered hand.

He was peering at Gerda, his brows drawn. Jasminda expected him to say something, but when he didn't, she offered her hands to Gerda, palms out in greeting. "I'm Jasminda ul-Sarifor, and this is Jack . . ." She waited for him to provide his surname, but he remained silent.

Gerda squinted at her outstretched hands. Jasminda blinked rapidly, unsure of her mistake. Though she'd never actually had anyone greet her properly in Elsira, she hadn't thought this Lagrimari woman would shrink from her touch.

"In Lagrimar, they greet one another by bringing a hand to the forehead," Jack said, reaching for Gerda's right hand and bringing it up to touch his head. Jasminda swallowed and dropped her hands, heat rising in her neck and cheeks.

"Sarifor, you say?" Gerda cocked her head to the side. "Any relation to Dansig ol-Sarifor?"

The world fell away for an instant as an image of Papa's disapproving face crossed her vision. She blinked past it and forced herself to breathe. "You knew my father?"

Gerda nodded. "Long ago." She turned and disappeared into the shadows. "Come along now. There's a warm fire inside."

Utterly shaken, Jasminda moved to grab the bag and lantern, but Jack's quick fingers plucked them away first. He chuckled at her exasperation, but his eyes lacked their usual sparkle.

"What do you think?" Her voice was hushed and cautious. Warily, she watched the storm bluster just on the edge of their little invisible wall of protection.

"I'll go first," he said, then grabbed hold of her hand and charged ahead.

She was glad for his hand in hers. The mountain caves and tunnels frightened her. They had been strictly off-limits growing up, and even her intrepid brothers had listened to Papa's words and stayed away. Half a dozen cave openings lined the mountain path her family used on their way to and from town. But they had never ventured in. Something about the gaping openings sent off danger signals. On a primal level, they felt like places to be avoided.

Like the wretched map and Tensyn's speaking stone, a similar crawling unease pervaded the caves. All set her teeth on edge in their own way.

But the others did not shudder the way she did upon entering the cavern. Jack gave no evidence that his skin was crawling with the oppressive atmosphere. With each step, the temperature grew steadily warmer, but cold goose bumps irritated her skin.

A short tunnel opened to a huge chamber many stories high. The interior was wholly unexpected; instead of the rough surface of rock, the walls and floor were glassy and smooth, like the patch of ground surrounding the cornerstone. The entire interior of the mountain looked as if it had been blown in the forge of a glassmaker. She struggled to calm her rioting belly. Her breath pulsed in short gasps.

Jack's expression mirrored her concern.

"Do you feel the *wrongness* of this place?" she asked. "It's like . . ." The lifeless eyes of the soldier she'd killed swam into her vision. The cave stank of pungent earth and stale air, but underneath it all, she smelled blood. She was glad her Song was depleted for the next half day or so. The idea of trying to sing here caused a ripple of nausea to overwhelm her. That same instinct screaming the danger of the caves told her that this was not a place for magic. For the first time ever, the thought of using Earthsong filled her with dread.

Jack pulled her closer, wrapping an arm around her. "We can just wait here for the storm to end." His warm breath on her ear pulled her back from the edge of panic. She focused on him, the strength in his body now that he was no longer in pain. He was a solid thing to hold onto.

"And then what?" she asked.

"I think these Lagrimari must be Keepers of the Promise. Rebels against the True Father. Perhaps their young Singer could help to bolster the cornerstone—if we're able to find it again."

A sob escaped Jasminda's pressed lips.

"What is it?" Jack's eyes were frantic.

She sucked in a breath and met his gaze. "It's gone." He grew stricken as she told him of the shaking earth. Of how the cornerstone had been destroyed.

"I don't understand." He pulled away from her and dropped his head in his hands. "What happened? How could it just be crushed like that?"

Jasminda drew away. She wanted to offer some comfort, but what words could she say? If she had been stronger, could she have prevented the rock slide? The avalanche?

Off to the right, an opening in the cavern wall was lit by a flickering fire. Voices buzzed from within. Jack trudged forward, toward heat and light, his face a desolate landscape. Jasminda followed, her arms wrapped around herself, poor protection from the fears and regrets that pummeled her.

They stood outside the cave in silence. Jasminda watched Jack for a clue of how to proceed, but he was lost in his own mind.

"Come," Gerda called, her voice cracked. "No use skulking about in the corridors."

Jasminda peeked inside to find a well-tended fire roaring in the center, sleeping packs spiraling out from it. A handful of careworn women, each huddled with a small child or two, looked up at her. Osar sat with a slightly older girl near the fire. Rozyl and the others from outside stood grouped together in the corner, hovering over Gerda who sat on the ground with two other elders.

With a hand on Jack's shoulder, Jasminda nudged them forward. Two dozen Lagrimari watched their entrance. She had never seen so many people who looked like her in the same place. But each face she peered into held a sort of quiet desperation, a somberness that hinted at a life of struggle. Except for Rozyl. She merely glared.

Oddly enough, the obvious antagonism was comforting for Jasminda. At least she was in familiar territory. She set her jaw and scowled back, refusing to be cowed by this woman who didn't even know her. Rozyl's gaze dropped to her hand on Jack, and Jasminda froze. He was the only Elsiran there.

He shook himself, his eyes sharpening and scanning the room, then shifted into a protective stance, placing his body in front of hers.

"Have a seat," Gerda said.

Jasminda was still wary of the smooth cave interior. However, with no other options, she settled on the ground in front of the elders. Jack positioned himself by her side, but turned slightly, keeping an eye on the entire space. Rozyl and her crew moved a few paces away.

"This is Turwig ol-Matigor and Lyngar ol-Grimor." Gerda pointed to the old men.

"You are Keepers of the Promise?" Jack asked with a sidelong glance.

"We are," Gerda said, motioning to the other elders, Rozyl, and the three guards with her. Rozyl groaned. The other women and children were out of earshot.

"Did you know my father as well?" Jasminda asked the old men. A look passed between them that she couldn't decipher.

"It was many years ago, child. I can hardly recall," said Turwig, whose kind face held a grandfatherly quality.

The one called Lyngar had deep lines etched into his face, his perpetual scowl making her wonder if he was related to Rozyl. "I can. He was a scoundrel. He abandoned his regiment. Unforgivable!"

Jasminda tensed and focused on the unpleasant man. "He was captured in the Sixth Breach. A prisoner of war." She forced the words out through clenched teeth.

"Is that what he told you?" Lyngar snorted. Gerda shot him a murderous glare, and he looked away, not exactly chastened, more like he'd grown bored with the conversation.

"He journeyed to the World After two years ago along with my brothers . . . to join my mother, who was Elsiran." She said the last as a challenge, to see how he would react. Lyngar's head whipped toward her before his gaze shot to Jack.

"So that is why you cavort with them."

Jasminda moved to stand, wishing she could throttle the old man or, at the very least, get away from him. Jack's hand on her arm stilled her, and she sat stewing in rage. Either the fire was far too hot or her blood was ablaze.

"Why have you brought these people across the Mantle?" Jack motioned to the women and children in the center of the room.

"It will fall soon," Gerda said simply. "Better to be on this side than the other when that happens."

Turwig spoke up. "How do you know about the Keepers, boy?"

Beside her, Jack swallowed and cleared his throat. "I met one years ago. After the Seventh Breach, I was stationed at the Eastern Base—"

"You're a soldier?" Rozyl asked through gritted teeth.

Jack nodded tersely. "When we transferred the POWs to the settlement, as per the terms of the treaty, I met a young man called Darvyn." More than one person in the cave sucked in a breath. "You know him?"

Gerda silenced everyone with a glance. "Go on."

Wariness crept into Jack's expression. "We used to talk. We became friendly. He let me practice my Lagrimari with him. One day, a few months later, I went to the settlement, and he was gone. Disappeared. I called for a search, thinking something must have happened to him, but we found nothing."

Jasminda listened, impressed that he had even tried to find a missing settler. It was more than most Elsirans would have done.

"Then, just over three weeks ago, he returned and called for me at the base. He wouldn't tell me where he'd been, just that the Mantle was going to be destroyed and Elsira needed to be warned. I contacted the Council and the Prince Regent, but they wouldn't take the word of a Lagrimari settler. But I believed him."

Jack scrubbed a hand down his face, his eyes growing faraway. His voice dropped as he told of the spell Darvyn had cast to make him appear Lagrimari, of hiding within Tensyn's squad and discovering the terrible truth. "Not just cracks, not just a breach—the entire Mantle will fall. Soon. And the True Father will be unleashed on us all. But then, you already knew."

A chill rippled over Jasminda's skin. The faces of the Lagrimari were pensive.

"And Darvyn's spell just . . . failed?" Turwig asked. The old man had leaned forward, intent on every word of Jack's story.

Jack nodded, his shoulders sagging with weariness.

"He must be dead," Lyngar said matter-of-factly.

"Or so badly injured he could not maintain the spell." Gerda placed a comforting hand on Turwig as the man shuddered.

Jasminda wondered who Darvyn was to them. "You know this Darvyn?" she asked.

"Since he was a small child." Turwig's voice faded almost to nothing.

Lyngar's face was perpetually twisted, as if everything smelled bad to him. "You've got your proof now, boy. What will you do with it?"

Jack made a fist so tight his knuckles cracked. "Now that the . . ." He blinked, looking stricken, and cleared his throat. ". . . the Mantle is beyond saving, we must prepare for war. I will go back and make them all listen to reason. Organize our troops. Then ready ourselves for a fight to end all others."

Gerda and the old men shared another meaning-laden glance. Rozyl stalked up, towering over the seated group. Her face was taut as she stared at Gerda, pleading silently. Whatever was going on, it was obvious Rozyl did not want Jasminda or Jack to know about it.

Gerda held up a hand to wave Rozyl off. "What if there were another way?"

Jack looked up, his jaw set. "What other way?"

"You Elsirans worship the Queen, do you not?"

"Yes, of course." He looked from face to face. "Do you? I thought religion was not allowed in Lagrimar."

"Oh no," the old woman said. "The only religion allowed is reverence of the True Father. There are the Avinids, of course, but they believe in nothing. However, the Queen Who Sleeps graces the dreams of some, and there are many who believe in secret."

Turwig hummed in agreement. "If She were awoken, it is said Her power is great enough to stop the True Father."

Jasminda gaped. "Do you believe that?"

"Do you doubt it?" Turwig's dark eyes lit from within with wisdom.

She swallowed, turning to Jack. "She has never graced my dreams," he said slowly. "I've prayed to Her many times without response."

"Just because She didn't speak to you directly, doesn't mean She didn't hear you, child," Gerda said. "I believe She hears us all."

"But She has slept for hundreds of years; there's little chance She will awaken now." Jasminda wondered if the others were all crazy for contemplating such a thing.

"Hmm," was Gerda's only response.

Jack's flame-colored eyes danced in the firelight, the desolate look in them banished with this talk of the Queen. Though Jasminda could not even begin to hope for such a miracle as the Sovereign's awakening, she was grateful for anything that erased the blight of defeat from his brow.

For with the cornerstone's destruction, the miracle of the Queen's awakening might be the only thing that could save them.

CHAPTER FIFTEEN

On the same day every year, the Mistress of Horses received the gift of a pot of honey. However, she never knew the giver and so never tasted its sweetness.

—COLLECTED FOLKTALES

Jack's arms were wrapped around something warm and soft. He opened his eyes; any hint of drowsiness fled as a spark tickled behind his ribs. Jasminda lay curled on her side, her back pressed against his chest. Her head was tucked just under his chin, and his heart sped as he watched the rise and fall of her gentle breaths.

After their discussion of the Queen the night before, the elders had insisted it was time to sleep. Jack had no idea how long it had been since they'd left Jasminda's farm, but even healed, his weary body was ready to shut down.

Jasminda hadn't wanted to stay with the others, and Rozyl's hostility had led Jack to agree. So they'd bunked in a smaller cavern a few hundred paces away.

Without a fire, this chamber was quite a bit cooler. They'd curled up on the ground next to each other, using her lumpy sack as a pillow.

Jack didn't want to wake Jasminda by moving too quickly. He brushed her hair back, letting his fingers get caught in its tangled softness. Her scent was enticing, soothing, and he lay for a moment breathing it in. Once again, thoughts inappropriate to their current situation stole into his mind. The curve of her buttocks grazed his groin, and he inched backward so as not to scandalize her with his growing erection.

He owed her his life, there could be no doubt of that. So perhaps these feelings that had sprung up inside him could be traced there. All he knew was that he'd slept better on this hard, cold ground with her in his arms than on the most luxurious mattress in Rosira.

Light footsteps echoed outside the cave entrance. Jack removed an arm from around Jasminda and palmed the pistol he'd left within easy reach, keeping it down by his side. Though he had trusted Darvyn, he could not be completely certain that *these* enemies of his enemy were, in fact, his friends. They could prove to be great allies in the fight against the True Father, but they held secrets. There must be more to their reason for braving this journey than they'd shared.

Lantern light brightened the entrance as a curly head appeared—a head much lower than he'd expected. Osar stood gripping the lantern shakily. Jack released his weapon. The boy's huge eyes glittered, and he beckoned Jack forward with one hand.

"Jasminda." He shook her gently. "We have a visitor." He nodded in the child's direction. Jasminda sat up, yawning.

Osar motioned again for them to follow before disappearing down the hall. They gathered what was left of their things and joined the others in the larger cave. The fire had been put out, lanterns had been lit, and most were packed and ready to go. The armed Keepers and elders stood in the center; Gerda's quiet tones carried over Rozyl's hard voice and wild gesticulations. But all grew quiet once he and Jasminda arrived.

"Sit, sit," Turwig enjoined. "Have something to eat." He rooted around the pouch at his side and passed them a sparing amount of jerky and dried berries.

"Thank you," Jack said, realizing his own hunger. How long had it been since he'd eaten? He must have lost the basket with their food in the avalanche. He would even have settled for Jasminda's bitter herb mash, but though the Lagrimari food was not tasty, it was far more filling than he'd expected.

Jack inhaled the simple breakfast. He looked up to find that Turwig carried another, smaller pouch, this one cradled in his palm like it was precious.

Jasminda, who'd been wrestling with a tough bit of jerky, froze. Her gaze narrowed on the old man's hand. Gerda appeared next to them, leaning in intently. She made Jack a bit uneasy; her gaze seemed to peer directly into the soul.

"Feel that, do you?" Gerda asked Jasminda. "I suspected you might."

"I don't trust her," Rozyl announced from the corner. "Who knows where her loyalties lie? I think this is a mistake."

"Hush," Gerda replied, still staring at Jasminda. Jack looked to her as well; she was obviously uncomfortable, though she'd been somewhat squirmy since they entered the caves. But now she visibly shook and leaned back as Turwig held the pouch out to her. With obvious reverence for the little bundle, he reached for Jasminda's hand and placed it in her grasp.

She gave a soft cry and jumped. "What is this?"

Jack was on alert, hovering over her, wanting to render aid. Gerda halted him with a hand on his arm.

"Open it," Turwig said.

Jasminda shook her head. Her hand trembled. "I can barely stand to hold it. What's in it?"

"Jasminda, get rid of it," Jack said, not liking her reaction. He went to grab it from her, but she shifted out of reach. Gerda's hand tightened on his arm, displaying impressive strength. He didn't want to hurt the old woman, but if that thing was dangerous, he needed to protect Jasminda. That was, if she would accept his aid. She seemed conflicted.

"Open it," Gerda repeated gently.

A hush fell upon the cave. Jack held his breath as Jasminda slowly pulled the tie on the pouch, revealing its contents.

Nestled in the folds of fabric was a deep red stone—the same color as the cornerstone, but small enough to fit in the palm of her hand. It was multifaceted, but smooth, like an oddly shaped gemstone.

Jasminda held it up to her face, inspecting it. Jack was entranced by the stone as well. A surge of longing shot through him. He wanted to touch it, feel its smoothness beneath his skin. But he could not move.

Lyngar brought one of the lamps closer to illuminate the stone better. Embedded within were dark, swirling lines. Was this the fossil of an insect like the ones he'd been intrigued by as a boy? But the curves of the shape trapped inside were no skeleton. Jack recognized the familiar symbol embedded beneath the surface.

"The sigil of the Queen," he whispered.

Jasminda raised her free hand until it hovered over the bloodred stone. She met Jack's eyes—hers sparked with anticipation and fear.

He wanted to tell her not to touch it, but the longing was so strong within himself that he couldn't speak the words. His breath caught in his chest when he tried to voice the warning.

Jasminda's finger traced the surface of the stone. Her eyes closed and long, dark lashes brushed her cheeks. Then, as if she'd instantly fallen asleep, her face slackened, and her whole body pitched backward to tumble to the ground.

CHAPTER SIXTEEN

We run through the woods laughing. Yllis's fingers are intertwined with mine, and when he looks over, the love in his eyes makes my breath catch. My heart is so full.

Eero is behind us, thundering through the underbrush. I do not have to turn to sense my brother tripping over a root that Yllis and I had jumped over. It would be funny to let him fall, but it is not his fault he has no Song and cannot feel the forest around him the way we do. In the blink of an eye, I sing a spell to lift him back upright and set him on his feet. He stumbles a bit but rights himself, his emotions confused for a moment, before refocusing on the competition.

We clear the tree line, and Eero races ahead, beating us to the water's edge. He dives underneath and swims out a little ways, shouting, berating us for our slowness. Yllis and I splash into the waves, soaking each other, and I think this is the happiest I have ever been. The two people I care most for in this world are here, and it is the most beautiful day I could have dreamed.

Yllis said he would not let it rain on Eero's and my birthday, and he did not. I shall bring the clouds back myself tomorrow to keep things in balance, but for today, watching the smiles on his and Eero's faces as the sun shines down on us is the best present ever.

Later, the fire crackles before us, and I lean back into the strong hold of Yllis's arms around me. Eero sits just across from us, roasting tubers on a stick. His melancholy calls to me and I yearn to soothe it, but long ago he made me promise not to sing away his moods. I endeavor to respect his wishes, though it is difficult to see my twin so sad.

"What ails, Eero?" I say to him.

He continues to stare into the fire, his eyes faraway. I disengage from Yllis and move around to sit beside him. "We celebrate our birth today. Why are you downhearted?"

I nudge his shoulder. His mouth quirks slightly in the beginnings of a smile.

"I do not aim to diminish any happiness of yours. I only wish . . ."

I remain patient as he forms his thoughts. Words are not always easy for him, but they eventually flow. I do not push.

"I wish I could sing, as you do. As Father did."

I reach out to him, placing my hand on his. "And I wish I shared Mother's talent at drawing the way you do. The pictures you create are unequaled. Everyone's talents lie in different directions."

"Yes, but to control the earth and the sky? It is magnificent." Wonder fills his voice. I feel ashamed for taking for granted the Song that swells within me, the feeling of oneness that I have with the life energy of the world.

"We are different," I say. He looks pointedly at my hand, still on his arm, an example of the difference clearly displayed by the contrasting hues of our skin. Mine like our father and the other Songbearers with our dark hair and dark eyes, his the shade of Mother's and the other Silents, with eyes of vivid golden copper. "The blue of the day's sky and the black of the night's are different, but one is not better than the other. We need both. If I could give you part of my Song, I would, so you could feel what *it is like. And perhaps you could give me some of your talent so that I could paint the murals that bring such delight to all who see them, and it will equal out."*

He pulls away from my touch and stands, offering me his roasted tuber before turning to look at the water. "We will never be equals, Oola." My name on his lips has never sounded so hopeless.

My twin walks toward the water, and I move back to Yllis's arms.

"He offered for the daughter of the Head Cantor," Yllis says as I watch Eero's retreating form. "She turned him down for one of the Healers." A fissure forms in my heart.

"I did not know. He tells me little of his love life. Once upon a time, we were close as heartbeats." I shift to face Yllis. "Do you think there is a way?"

He leans his forehead to mine, his Song dancing at the edge of my perception, offering solace and comfort. I do not reach for it, but I am glad it is there.

"A way for what?" he says.

"To share my Song with him?"

A thoughtful look crosses his face. His studies with the Cantors are progressing; he is learning much about new spells, new ways to funnel and control the massive energy of Earthsong. "If there is a way, we will find it. I promise."

His lips slide to mine. The kiss is not all-consuming, it is simply a reminder that he is here for me and that any problem I face, he faces as well. My worries flee. I would do anything for my twin, and if it is a Song he desires, I will do all I can to give it to him.

CHAPTER SEVENTEEN

The Master of Sharks carries duty like a parcel he would deliver
to someone else.

—COLLECTED FOLKTALES

Jasminda winced at the burning sensation in her palm. Her empty palm. When her vision focused, an anxious face filled her view. Firelit eyes regarded her, and a familiar scent filled her nostrils. Jack. His face relaxed as she stared up at him, hypnotized by the color of his eyes.

"What happened?" she asked, dazed.

He frowned. "I should ask you that. You collapsed."

Clarity came back quickly. The cave, the storm, the elders, the stone . . . which had disappeared from her hand. She looked over to find Turwig wrapping it up again. Jack helped her to a seated position as the chatter of several voices quieted.

"You saw something, didn't you?" Gerda asked.

Unlike the vision in the circle of stones, when she'd touched this stone she'd been drawn in to someone else's life. She'd actually *been* someone else. Someone deliriously in love. The girl, Oola, was an Earthsinger with skin the color of Jasminda's own, and she had been born a twin to Eero, a Silent—as Oola called him—who resembled an Elsiran, like Jasminda's brothers. This was a world where Singers and Silent wed and apparently lived in peace with their children, normal and accepted. There had been no feeling of isolation in Oola's thoughts, no sense of being always mistrusted or feared for her magic. On the contrary, her brother was jealous of her power.

The vision had been all-encompassing, and it took a moment to adjust to being torn away and inhabiting her own body again. Jasminda related the brief vision and watched the elders' reactions, everything from puzzled to stupefied.

She flexed her arms and legs, bringing feeling back into them. "What is that stone, and why does it cause visions?"

Turwig and Gerda shared one of their meaningful looks. The old man still held the wrapped stone. Jasminda's fingers itched to snatch it from him. She couldn't explain the strange possessive instinct that had arisen within her toward the thing, but she wanted it back.

After a few moments of silence, Rozyl spoke up. "She passed the test, you might as well tell her."

"Test?" Jasminda was not interested in any more tests. Anger fired within her. Jack grew rigid as well.

"Throughout the war," Turwig began, "the Keepers have fought against the True Father's tyranny, searching for a way to overcome his great power in order to awaken *Her.* We have always believed that killing the True Father was the only way to awaken the Queen. But the masked fiend is hard to kill."

"Almost impossible," Gerda said. "And there are those who

believe he walks among us in secret, taking on the appearance of our trusted friends and confidants."

Rozyl crossed her arms and sniffed. Could the woman's paranoia be justified? "It's true that no one has ever seen his face?" Jasminda asked.

"No one has seen any part of him," Turwig replied. "He is always covered from head to toe and wears a jeweled mask to hide his face. The women of his harems are kept blindfolded when they are with him. And aside from the Cantor, only the Songless are allowed in his inner circle."

"The Cantor?" Jasminda frowned. "Who is that?"

"Every few generations, a powerful Earthsinger is spared the tribute and serves as the True Father's Cantor, someone who studies Earthsong, finds new ways to create the breaches. They develop new spells and increase the True Father's power."

Jasminda had never known how the breaches were created. She doubted anyone on this side of the Mantle knew. "And what about those who give tribute? They must be able to get close to him."

Turwig's expression grew grim. "Tribute is given while unconscious. Only the Cantor and the True Father know how it is done. But we have chipped away, little by little, doing what we could, saving who we could. We've grown a network to hide as many as we can, so they may retain their Songs." He looked to Osar and the other children who were busy on the other side of the cave, far out of earshot.

"Do you all still have your Songs?" Jasminda asked.

"We lost ours long ago," Gerda said, motioning to herself and the elders. "Aside from some of the young ones, only Rozyl and Sevora have their Songs."

Sevora was the other female Keeper. Jasminda hadn't heard the woman utter a word, but her dark eyes were engraved with sorrow. Jasminda shuddered to imagine life without her Song; it was a part of her, weak though it was. Rozyl caught her stare and turned her closely shorn head away from the scrutiny. But for once, there was no spite from the Keeper.

Jasminda faced the elders again. "You all helped the young man who disguised Jack?"

"Yes . . . Darvyn. The poor boy spent his entire life hiding from tribute-camp thugs, being shuffled from place to place. His power . . ." Turwig shook his head at some memory clouding his mind. "His power is blinding. Darvyn was the one who discovered this." He motioned to the stone. "Years ago, when he was a small boy, we were secreting him away one night—there had been some betrayal at his previous residence, as was often the case. The boy was hidden in a wagon of straw pallets, but when we arrived at the checkpoint, he had disappeared.

"We doubled back, searching for him, but it was the middle of the night and the roads in Lagrimar are not somewhere you want to be caught after dark. I tracked him to the ruins of Tanagol, one of the first border villages destroyed early in the war."

Turwig's eyes softened as he became lost in the memory. "Imagine a child of four or five digging through centuries-old rubble, only to come out covered in dirt and muck with this treasure. He had felt the pull of the ancient spell within calling to him. Later, Darvyn began having the Dream of the Queen. She gave him certain instructions that we have been endeavoring to bring to pass for many years."

"She told him to disguise me and send me over the border," Jack said.

Understanding dawned on Jasminda. "She told Darvyn that you all should bring the stone here?" Turwig and Gerda nodded. "And did She say what it was? What it does?" She held her hand out for the stone, and to her surprise, Turwig gave it to her.

"No, She does not have control over the length or frequency of the dreams," he said, "so sometimes information is disjointed. We believe this is a caldera, an object that serves as a container for spells."

"Like the map and the speaking stone," Jack said, leaning forward. "Are these objects common in Lagrimar?"

"Not at all," Turwig answered. "About a hundred years ago, a Keeper managed to get his hands on the journal of the Cantor. Everything we know about calderas comes from that book, and it's not much. Only the most powerful Earthsingers can create such objects. They can serve various purposes and even hold parts of their Songs. It requires . . ."

Jasminda looked up from her inspection of the bundle in her hand. Part of her longed to touch it again, but another part was afraid. "It requires what?"

"A blood sacrifice. And with the strongest ones, a death."

Jasminda froze. "Blood magic?" It didn't exist anymore, at least not according to Papa. But merely saying the words brought to mind the wrongness of these caves, the skin-crawling feeling she'd gotten from both Jack's map and the speaking stone. This caldera was different than the other ones, potent certainly, but it didn't feel tainted. And it hadn't required any blood before sharing its vision with her.

"It's magic we've never seen before," Turwig said. "Stronger than any known today, saving the Cantor and the True Father."

"Did you all have the same vision I had, then?" Jasminda asked.

"Oh, no, child," Gerda said. "Nothing at all happens when any of us touch the caldera."

Jasminda shuddered. *"No one* else has seen a vision when they touch it? Not even Darvyn?" The Keepers all shook their heads. "You've tried using your blood?"

"We've tried everything," Turwig said.

"So what made you think to test me with it?"

Gerda tilted her head to the side, regarding her. "Intuition."

Jasminda looked at her skeptically.

"And you wear the Queen's sigil around your neck," Lyngar said. "Maybe it was a sign." He didn't sound as though he was happy about that.

"But why does it work for me?" Jasminda's hand flew to her mother's pendant. It wasn't unique, all Sisters wore them.

Turwig shrugged. "Perhaps because you're half Elsiran. Perhaps some other reason. But since it opened itself to you, I believe you must be the one to unlock the mysteries of this stone. None of us are able."

Her failure with the cornerstone—to even pass the test to reveal the cornerstone—gnawed at her. The words of her family echoed in her head. Too weak. Too afraid. Jasminda shook her head in disbelief. "What were the Queen's instructions? What did She say specifically?"

"She is rarely specific," Gerda said. "Her guidance has led us this far, though it has taken twenty years to find a way to get the caldera safely into Elsira. We had to trust that once we made it here, a way would be shown." She leaned forward, her intensity piercing. "You are that way." She placed her hand on top of Jasminda's closed fist, and the caldera pulsed in response.

The trust these people were placing in her was staggering. And very much undeserved. "Who else knows about it?" Her voice was small.

The elders shared a glance, looks of resignation appearing on their faces. Rozyl sighed. "The Cantor knows, so we must assume she's told the True Father—"

"The Cantor is a woman?" Somehow Jasminda had assumed the powerful Earthsinger must be a man.

"Yes," Rozyl spat. "Her name is Ydaris, and she is menace personified."

Jasminda shared a look with Jack. His eyes lit. Could he be thinking what she was? Could this Ydaris be the mystery woman giving orders to Tensyn?

"Anyway, we believe the king is searching for the caldera. All along we had planned to use decoys to sneak it out." Rozyl waved her hand toward the women and children at the far end of the cave. "Word spread more quickly than we'd planned, and many have heeded the call to leave Lagrimar."

"There are more refugees?" Jack asked.

"Yes, being led by groups of Keepers through known cracks in the Mantle. And more will follow them."

Jasminda's heart drummed, ready to beat out of her chest. "Can you stop them? Send word somehow?"

"Why?" Gerda asked. "Why should they not seek better lives for themselves?"

"Better lives like those in the settlements?" Jasminda scoffed. "There are no better lives for those who look like us here. Those who can sing. There will be no welcoming party for you. In fact, I would be surprised if they don't send you right back the way you came."

"They would not do that." Jack's voice was grim. "It is the Prince Regent's duty to protect all within the borders of Elsira. He is honor bound."

Jack had not suffered the stares and cutting remarks. The bad trades and cheating merchants. The insult "*grol* witch" uttered over and over.

Jasminda reached out for Gerda's gnarled hand. "I do not think it will be a good place for the children. I do not think they will be safe there." From the corner of her eye, she saw Jack's jaw tighten, but he stayed quiet.

"You have never been to Lagrimar, have you, girl?" Gerda said.

Jasminda shook her head.

"Of course not, for you seem to believe they were safe back there." Her voice was kind but stern. Admonishing her ignorance. Jasminda looked again at the gaunt and hollow expressions of the mothers, the wordless appeals in the eyes of the children. They clung to each other like lifelines in a raging storm.

Rozyl's voice broke the silence. "Do you know what awaits these children? Slavery. For most it's either the mines, the labor camps, the harems, or the army." She ticked the list off with her fingers. "In the mines, at least you get to keep your Song. Though you exhaust it every day chipping away at bits of rock, pulling precious jewels from the mountain, and filling your lungs with dust. And after fifty years of service, you are released to die in poverty. The camps are for the boys to have their Songs sucked away, then be sentenced to hard labor for the rest of their lives. Girls go to the harems to 'bless' the Father with sons for his army."

"The suffering is immense," Gerda added.

Jasminda brought her hands to cover her face, not wanting these people to see her cry, especially not after what they had all been through. She'd had no idea how terrible Lagrimar actually was. Life in Elsira would not be easy, with little opportunity and even less dignity, but it was not slavery.

"More are coming," Rozyl said, "and the caldera is the last hope for all of us. If it falls into the True Father's hands, then all is lost. If he breaks out of Lagrimar, not only will Elsira fall but other lands will follow. The world could be his to control. We've got to end this."

Jack turned to face Jasminda. "She's right. This caldera is the best option for winning the war. You must have been chosen for a reason, Jasminda. Maybe everything that's happened was supposed to."

Jasminda snorted. If Jack's suffering, the soldiers invading her cabin, the fire—if all of those things were the Queen's plan, and if Jasminda was truly chosen, then the Queen had quite the sense of humor.

The weight of the expectant eyes peering at her sealed her mouth shut, silencing the doubts she longed to raise. She'd started this journey with one impossible goal, to help Jack so that he would help her save her land. Now an even more unattainable task was being set before her.

"So what do I do?"

Uncertainty crossed more than one face. "We'd planned to bring the caldera to Rosira, to be near the Queen's resting place in the palace," Turwig said. "After that, simply rely on Her guidance." The old Keeper smiled at Jasminda. "For now, follow the visions. Learn what the caldera wants to show you. It must lead to a way to awaken Her."

Anxiety lay heavy on her shoulders. Perhaps the Queen would lead them to another, someone truly able to solve the mystery of awakening Her. For now, Jasminda had little choice but to accept the duty and pray the person they really needed would reveal themselves.

Jack squeezed her arm, lending her strength. She would need all of it to face disappointing those who'd placed their faith in her.

CHAPTER EIGHTEEN

The Mistress of Horses never met a field she could not coax to grow just a little brighter. Her voice can still be heard in the whisper of the leaves that shoot from the ground.

—COLLECTED FOLKTALES

"Are you going to try again?" Jack's voice hummed in Jasminda's ear.

The others completed their preparations to leave, but Jack's gaze never left her. She felt it like a physical touch. "I should, shouldn't I?"

"But you don't want to? What's stopping you?"

She opened her mouth to admit to him her failures—if she could not save those closest to her, how could she do something so big? Thankfully, Rozyl's raised voice kept her from answering.

"We have little choice. It makes no sense to travel down a tunnel we can't feel or see the ending of."

Jack rose and moved to where Rozyl and the elders stood. Jasminda followed. "What's the problem?" he asked.

To Jasminda's surprise, Rozyl answered. "We can't connect to Earthsong in the caves. Somehow, the mountain is blocking us. Without singing, we'll never find our way through this maze of tunnels."

"Has the storm not stopped?" Jack asked.

Rozyl was grim. "It's getting worse."

"Worse?" Jasminda cried out. "No storm has ever lasted this long."

"Not a normal storm, is it?" Lyngar raised an eyebrow.

Dread snaked its way across Jasminda's skin "So what do we do?"

"I bloody well don't know," Rozyl said, exasperated. "What *can* we do? Wait until we can cross above the mountain."

"That storm won't die a natural death, I promise you that," Lyngar said ominously.

"What happens when you try to sing?" Jasminda asked. For the first time, she realized that her Song, which should have been fully restored by now, was not at full capacity. It had been hours since she'd used the last of her power on the cornerstone. Had the caldera sapped her?

Turwig spoke up. "The children say their Song calls out but nothing's there to answer it. Like the world has disappeared. Try it yourself if you like, child."

Jasminda drew in a shaky breath, then closed her eyes. Part of her was afraid to try—the foreboding she'd felt when first entering the cave had not dimmed. That sense that her magic had no place here was as strong as ever, but curiosity won out over the fear. She opened herself to Earthsong. The normally strong pull of the power was nearly overwhelming; the tide tried to pull her under, harder than ever before. "I feel untethered. I can barely hold on."

"But you can draw upon Earthsong?" Rozyl asked.

Jasminda nodded, eyes still closed. Her attention was on her awareness of the cave, the tunnels beyond, and the mountain surrounding them. Ghosts of the ancient inhabitants brushed the edge of her senses. She thought briefly of the legends of the Cavefolk, the race of people who had lived within these mountains generations ago and then disappeared. There was a kind of primeval power here, locked in the fabric of the rock, but it thrummed with a different pattern than Earthsong.

Still, a thread of life wove through this place. Insects and creatures too small to see, and mosslike vegetation that needed no light. She pulled the energy inside her; it formed a path, though faint, that led through to the other side of the mountain.

She let the power slide away. "I can sense the route, but it's long. I'm not sure I'll be able to stay connected and sing for the whole journey. The caldera sapped my Song."

"Why in pip's name must it always be her?" Rozyl grumbled. "She's not even full Lagrimari."

Jack's breathing turned heavy as he glared. His reaction lit a spark of satisfaction within Jasminda.

"Perhaps she can link with someone," Turwig suggested.

Rozyl gave him a look that could have sheared the shell off a beetle. "Why can she sing and no one else? Why does the caldera respond to her only? Her magic must be different. I'm not linking with her." Jasminda flinched internally at the bite in the woman's voice, though she had no desire to link with Rozyl, either.

"What is linking?" Jack asked, looking from Rozyl to Jasminda.

Gerda patiently began to explain. "It's when two Earthsingers share their connection. They—"

"It's when one Singer gives control of their entire Song to another to do with as they please," Rozyl interjected. "And *that* is not going to happen."

"It's a sharing of power," Gerda continued, "but only one Singer can be in control. It must be done voluntarily, of the giver's free will. If we still had our Songs, we would do it."

"Speak for yourself," Lyngar hissed. Jasminda had linked with Papa when she was young and still learning. He'd shown her how to control her power through the link, but she could not imagine linking with a stranger. To do so was to become extremely vulnerable to another. It was like letting someone into her soul.

The elders and Rozyl bickered over what to do. Neither Rozyl nor Sevora would link with Jasminda.

A small hand slipped into her own. Osar's round face beamed up at her. She squeezed his hand, and he leaned in, resting his head against her leg.

"You would link with me, wouldn't you?" she asked, smoothing down his hair. "You're not afraid?" He shook his head, then offered her his other hand, which was closed in a fist.

"What do you have there?"

He unfurled tiny fingers to reveal a shoot of green with delicate white petals sparking out of it.

"Where did you get this?" she asked, incredulous, picking up the tiny flower. It could not have grown in the cave, and with the snow outside it was doubtful he'd brought it in with him. Yet here it was. Something beautiful and impossible amid the bleakness. "Thank you."

Silence descended. Jasminda looked up to find the others staring at her and the blossom in her hand. She straightened her shoulders, looking at Rozyl and Lyngar as she spoke. "Osar will link with me."

Rozyl narrowed her eyes. Lyngar merely turned toward the exit, speaking over his shoulder. "Fine. Let's get going. We've wasted far too much time as it is."

CHAPTER NINETEEN

What of peace? asked a soldier to the Mistress of Serpents.
A warrior who fights for peace is like a man leaving the shore
to climb a hill so he may better view the ocean.

—COLLECTED FOLKTALES

Jack kept to the rear of the party as they made their way through the tunnels. He did not like to be so far from Jasminda, who led the group with Osar at her side, but he also did not want Rozyl or the other armed Keepers at his back. They seemed to feel the same about him, which left him walking side by side with Sevora, the tall Lagrimari woman who never said a word to him.

On the whole, the refugees were not a talkative bunch. The only sounds were footsteps that echoed against the oddly smooth cave walls and the soft babbling of the youngest children. The group did not dawdle, either, deftly navigating the twisting path, which edged steeply downward, leveled off, then dipped low again.

They took no breaks, and not even the smaller children walking on their own complained. Nor did the elders, who were remarkably spry for their ages. Hours passed like this, the silence companionable but complete.

Slowly, the air began to change. A thick humidity replaced the cool, earthy scent of the mountain. They extinguished their lanterns when light glowed softly up ahead. Over the thump of their footsteps, water trickled, insects whirred, birds called.

Home.

The tunnel ended abruptly, leaving them at the edge of a huge cavern, much like the one they'd entered on the other side with some key differences. This cave was filled with trees and vines and greenery. Rain poured down through openings in the rock far overhead. A narrow and somewhat hidden path led down to the forest floor. Just beyond it, a stream of water flowed gently down, vanishing below. The view stole his breath.

The group formed a queue, as the path was only wide enough for one. Jasminda disappeared from sight first. Not being able to see her made Jack's palms itch. He was returning to civilization and, with it, all his duties and responsibilities. Not the least of which was Jasminda.

She had stolen into his life—his very complicated life—and he was in no hurry for her to leave. But the war on the horizon would make everything immeasurably harder. Anti-Lagrimari sentiments would kick into effect once again, and Jasminda's Elsiran blood would not protect her from the ire of the people who saw only her skin. He could tell from the way she spoke, the haunted look in her eye when the refugees discussed Elsira, that it never had.

The path ended in a wide cave mouth overlooking the Elsiran Borderlands. A steady rain fell from the overcast sky. Jack had little sense of the time of day but was very glad to be once again on Elsiran soil.

Still in the shadow of the mountain, the group wound their way through a thick copse of trees; Jack struggled to get his bearings. How far had their trip through the mountain taken them? How close was his army base?

A gathering of flimsy structures became visible a few thousand paces ahead. This was a place he recognized: the community was called Baalingrove, one of the settlements of former Lagrimari prisoners of war. It was here he had first met Darvyn years ago.

As always, Jack was struck by the living conditions of the settlers: makeshift wooden shacks with leaky tin roofs, tiny patches of garden, no running water, no electricity—though the last wasn't uncommon in the Borderlands. The men gardened and hunted in the foothills, but survived in large part due to the kindness of the Sisterhood, devoted followers of the Queen who provided food and supplies. Neither the Prince Regent nor the Council saw fit to do any more, and the Elsirans preferred to pretend the settlers didn't exist.

The refugees walked through what amounted to the main road of the settlement, an unpaved path that was slowly becoming a river of mud in the insistent precipitation.

Unease prickled his spine. No one emerged from any of the shacks to peer at the group of newcomers. So far they hadn't seen a single soul in a place that housed nearly one hundred men.

Jack approached Gerda and pulled her to the side. "Why don't you and the civilians stay here? I think something may be wrong."

"We go together." Gerda's response was maddening.

"There might be danger." Jack's plea fell on deaf ears.

Turwig patted his arm. "There is danger everywhere, son. Who's to say it won't find us here as well?"

Jack muttered under his breath and moved to the front, but stopped when angry voices rent the air, shouting in Elsiran. He couldn't make out the words through the clatter of rain on metal but recognized the heavy Borderlander accent. Gunshots rang out.

"For Sovereign's sake, get the children back!" he shouted.

He shared a frenzied glance with Rozyl, who pursed her lips and made a hand signal to her crew. One of the men peeled off and helped direct the mothers and children to squat behind the nearest shacks.

Jack and the four armed Keepers remained on the main path, along with Jasminda and the elders.

"Go with them," he told Jasminda. She merely rolled her eyes and cocked her pistol.

The voices came from the edge of the settlement. As they approached, gunfire continued to pop, and the shouting grew louder. Movement flickered in the corner of Jack's eye; a Lagrimari woman sat huddled with two children behind another shack under the limited protection of the roof's overhang. She had not been part of his group. Her eyes widened when she saw him, confusion crossing her features as she took in his companions.

Rozyl rushed over to speak with her. "What happened here?"

"There was some trouble in the town, I think. A girl went missing. Seems her father got it in his head that one of the settlers took her, and a mob of farmers came here to search." The woman's eyes kept darting to Jack. He took a few steps back, aware that, to her, he must look like one of the men in the mob.

"Are you injured?" Rozyl's voice was softer and kinder than he'd heard it before.

"No, but my boy's up there. He wanted to fight with the men. I can't leave him." She pointed toward where the noise of battle was audible.

"Not even for the safety of these little ones?" Jasminda said. The solemn, dripping faces of two boys, each under five, stared up at them.

"We made it out together. I won't lose one of them now."

Jack's heart stung for the woman. "Are you a refugee?" he asked. She shrank back at his voice, her face twisted in fear. Her gaze, full of questions, shot to Rozyl.

"He's"—Rozyl looked back at Jack and shrugged—"with us."

The mother's expression was still rigid with suspicion. "We crossed with ten others two days ago, but I don't know what became of them once the fighting started."

Jack broke away to investigate, only dimly aware of the others trailing behind him. A turn in the road revealed a makeshift barricade made from an overturned wagon. It offered only meager protection but blocked the mouth of the narrow dirt road.

A half-dozen Lagrimari crouched in the sodden muck behind the barrier. Around twenty more were gathered nearby, seeking cover behind the dilapidated structures on the edge of the settlement. Several were armed with hunting rifles, the others with pitchforks, machetes, and one man even held a sword. A boy of about twelve was among their number. He must have been the woman's son.

In the road and scattered among the living were the bodies of more settlers. Some had been shot where they stood, but many had wounds in their backs. They'd been cut down while trying to flee the violence.

The insistent rain created a river of blood that streamed down the road. The carnage here was senseless. Jack vibrated with anger.

On the other side of the overturned wagon, a small band of Elsiran farmers, only a dozen strong, clustered together at the base of a tree. They were all armed, but most clutched their rifles like bats, striking at the icicles and dirt clods being flung at them. Every so often, one would get a shot off in the direction of the settlers.

The way the boy knelt among the older men, looking slightly off to the side, his body alert but unmoving, made Jack believe it was he who was singing the spell to attack the farmers.

The Elsirans were penned in a tight group. Whenever one of them tried to break out of it toward the settlers, a chunk of mud or an icicle would hit him in the face or body, knocking him back. Two of them did manage to peel off and run away, back down the road toward the town.

The settlers cheered, and one man finally noticed Rozyl and her group advancing on the barricade with their rifles drawn. The Keepers took up positions and began firing on the farmers. The ice-and-mud attack stopped as the boy looked up, startled. This gave the farmers a chance to dive for cover among the nearby trees and shrubbery. Then the Elsirans returned fire.

The armed settlers must have been out of ammunition, for they didn't shoot, but Rozyl and her team were methodical, efficiently finding their targets and hitting them as man after man fell.

Jack felt no sympathy for the farmers, though they were his countrymen. There had been incidents such as these over the years, when tensions between citizens and settlers had bubbled over, but this would go down as the worst yet.

Jasminda crouched at his side. "I convinced the woman and her children to wait with the others."

The woman's son was staring up in awe as the Keepers made short work of the remaining farmers. Those who hadn't been shot were now beating a quick retreat.

"I knew many of the men who lived here." Jack's voice sounded hollow in his own ears. He was soaked to the skin, but the numbness in his limbs had nothing to do with the weather.

A dead settler lay only a dozen paces away, eyes open and sightless. Jack stayed low as he moved to the man's side to close his eyes. "May you find serenity in the World After."

The gunshots stopped, and now the sound of engines took their place. Through the gaps in the trees lining the road ahead, thick wheels churned through the mud.

Jack's tension flared, then quickly fled. An open-topped four-wheeler drove up bearing four Elsiran soldiers. On its heels were two transports, a dozen men to each if they were following protocol. Sure enough, twenty-four men hopped out of the trucks and dispersed strategically, forming a perimeter around the settlement. The soldiers in the four-wheeler exited, guns drawn, and advanced on the barrier.

Jack stood ready to greet his men. Before he'd taken more than two steps, the soldiers opened fire. They gave no warning, no orders or instructions, just began shooting. Those at the barrier dove for cover, and Jack stood, dumbfounded, until Jasminda pulled him down again.

What in Sovereign's name?

"Can you do the thing with the ice and mud?" The idea of firing upon his own men was something he could not fathom at the moment, and he didn't want the other Lagrimari to do so, either. He needed a distraction.

"I think so." Jasminda drew in a breath and closed her eyes.

The firing stopped as the ooze on the ground rose into a wall of mud to block the view of the soldiers. Jack ran to the barricade, passing the shocked Lagrimari gathered there, and hurdled across.

"All right, Jasminda," he called, pulling out his weapon. When the mud once again fell to the earth, Jack stood face-to-face, pistol drawn, with the lead officer, a captain he recognized but had never personally spoken to before. From the corner of his eye, he saw the soldiers nearby train their weapons on him.

"Hold your fire!" the captain shouted, a dazed look coming over him.

"Do you know who I am?" Jack asked through clenched teeth.

"Y-yes, sir."

"Who am I, then?" he pressed.

"High Commander Alliaseen."

Soldiers nearby gasped in shock.

"I-I have to ask for your identification code, sir."

"Ylisum two five three zero nine." Jack squeezed his hand around the butt of the pistol still pointed at the captain's head, anger vibrating through his every fiber. "Verified?"

"Verified." A moment was all it took for the demeanor of the other soldiers to change radically. Guns were put away swiftly, and the men all stood at attention. Jack lowered his weapon as well and tried to control his breathing.

"Commander, I am Captain Daveen Pillos. We had heard you'd been lost."

"I was found, Captain." Jack took in another steadying breath and unclamped his jaw by sheer will. "On whose order were you firing upon these settlers?"

Pillos's gaze darted to the barricade and back. "No one's order, sir. We were engaging combatants."

"When you engaged these combatants, were they firing upon you?"

A tic jumped in the captain's jaw. "No, sir. But reports said they had attacked some civilians."

"Under the rules of engagement, under what conditions is it permissible to fire upon residents of your own country when you are not under immediate threat of harm?"

Pillos blinked rapidly as if trying to recall.

Jack exhaled in exasperation. "Has martial law been declared, Captain?"

"No, sir."

"Then am I correct in stating there are no conditions under which it is permissible to fire upon residents of your own country when you are not under immediate threat of harm?"

"Y-yes, sir. But, sir . . . they are settlers."

Jack took a step back and raised his voice so that all present could hear. "Yes, Captain. These are settlers. And as of the Treaty of the Seventh Breach, they have non-enemy status in Elsira. Unless they directly provoke you and are not, as in this case, merely defending themselves against attack, it is our sworn duty as defenders of Elsira to protect them. Is it not?"

"Yes, sir."

Jack took a deep breath, exhausted from the display of leadership. Pillos was doubtless no different than most of his men, than most of Elsira, if he could stand to believe such a thing.

"See if anyone needs medical attention and gather their weapons. But for Sovereign's sake, don't shoot anyone."

Pillos gave the commands, his eyes darting back to Jack every few seconds. "What are we to do with them all, sir?"

Jack scrubbed a hand down his face. "Call in transportation and take them to the Eastern Base for now. And contact the Sisterhood. More refugees will be arriving."

Jack recalled Jasminda's words in the cave. The Lagrimari were coming here searching for a better life, but if this was what they'd find when they arrived, maybe they were better off in Lagrimar.

CHAPTER TWENTY

Beware the Master of Monkeys. He would sell you the night as a cloak for the sun.

—COLLECTED FOLKTALES

Jasminda's gaze followed Jack as he dealt with the soldiers. After the initial incident, the men's sudden change in attitude and obvious deference toward him piqued her curiosity. He only had to say a few words and they would take off like startled horses.

Several soldiers came over to ask, somewhat hesitantly, for the weapons of the Lagrimari. The settlers understood the commands and translated for the others. Rozyl scowled but added her rifle to the pile.

Once the guns had all been put away, the other refugees were brought out from their hiding places, including nearly two dozen people she hadn't seen before who'd hidden in the trees just beyond the settlement. They all gathered, seated behind the remains of the makeshift barrier, still wanting some distance between themselves and the Elsirans.

Gerda sat next to Jasminda as she watched Jack giving commands and instructing his men.

"You follow him very closely," Gerda said. "Do you think he will disappear?"

Jasminda pulled her gaze away. "I'd almost forgotten he was one of them." Her heart tied itself in a knot. He'd been so different, so kind, but now, standing in a huddle of other Elsirans, it was difficult to pick him out from the group. The idea of finding warmth and comfort from his presence seemed foreign.

What had she expected? She knew he was on a mission. He'd risked his life to gain information to save his country. With the cornerstone gone, her only use to him was in unlocking the mystery of the caldera. Just because she'd grown to think of him as a possibility, perhaps even as a friend, did not mean he felt the same. She was an ally; she must do her part and he do his.

With a sigh, she pulled out the pouch that held the caldera.

"Watch over me while I try this again?" she asked Gerda. Jasminda had been insensible to the world during the last vision.

Gerda patted her shoulder. "Of course."

Jasminda inhaled deeply, unwrapped the caldera, and lowered her palm.

In the distance, the clouds have not yet begun to form, but I feel them coming. A raw wind races across the mountain ridge, but I do nothing to block its bite. The sensation of the air whipping against my skin grounds me.

Above my head, Eero turns circles in the air, riding on the wind. I briefly wonder who taught him the trick, but no one needed to. He has been a quick study. He swoops before me, hovering just out of reach.

I grab for him anyway, knowing it will make him smile, and he races away.

"You will burn yourself out," I call up to him, making sure my voice carries as his form becomes smaller and smaller. Within minutes, I sense him weakening. He has just enough Song left to land gracefully by my side, laughing, his face full of joy.

"A little more, please," he says, holding out his hand.

"More? So you can waste it flying through the air like a deranged bird? There is a reason you do not see any other Songbearers tearing through the skies disturbing the clouds."

He snorts. "Because you are stodgy curmudgeons with no sense of adventure."

I roll my eyes. "No, because we respect the energy and do not squander it on frivolity. If you needed to fly to escape danger or forestall some terrible event, that would be one thing."

His resonant chuckle echoes off the mountain peaks behind us. "If you give me a little more, I will endeavor to seek out some poor soul in peril and give aid straightaway."

I turn away from him and cross my arms.

"My dearest, most beautiful and talented sister." He leans into me and makes his most pitiful face to engage my sympathy.

"Your only sister."

"Yes, and a more wonderful sister there could never be. I promise not to squander it. I shall give the Song the respect it deserves. Please?"

I want to hold my ground against him. But in the weeks since Yllis discovered the spell that allows gifting a portion of a Song from one to another, Eero has been happier than I have seen him since the loss of our parents. Perhaps happier than I have ever seen him.

We thought it best not to make the spell widely known, and so are all sworn to secrecy. At first, Eero and I would go up into the mountains above town to let him practice so as not to be spotted. But this week we are on assignment in the east, checking in on the colony that has sprung up here in the shadow of the eastern mountains.

It is a quiet place, so far from home. A bleak and dry environment where nothing grows, but the colonists are working to transform it into lush farmland, as our parents and grandparents did long ago in the west. We could not have found a better place for Eero to practice away from prying eyes.

I relent and take his hand for the spell. The power is always there, humming inside me, a leashed beast waiting for release. I set a trickle free and sing it into my twin, deep into the core of him where it would last him quite a while if he did not waste it.

I give just a little, but he has been using it up faster and faster, asking for more and more. Some part of me advises caution—having been born Silent, there is no telling how the power will affect him—but it brings him such joy.

"No more until tomorrow," I admonish. His eyes shine as he nods his understanding.

With a flick of his wrist, he pulls the moisture from the air until it forms a tiny dense cloud hovering above his palm.

"What are you going to do with that?" I hold back a laugh.

His grin is mischievous. He winks at me. "My tongue is a bit parched. The terraforming is moving at a snail's pace, and the water rations here barely slake my thirst." He opens his mouth, and the little cloud becomes a stream of water that arcs, landing on his tongue.

I shake my head and turn back toward the imposing mountain range. "The storm will be here in a few hours," I say. "We had better head back so I can help the Songbearers with today's work. That way they will not fall too far behind because of the weather."

The Songbearers work together to sing the barren ground to fertility. One day, farms will grow where this desert stands. That is the true power of Earthsong.

My brother squints into the distance, unable to see what I see. "Would it not be better to halt the tempest and leave more time for the work?"

I shrug. "If we stopped every storm, nothing would ever grow." A greater unease pushes at me, but I brush it away. One storm at a time is all I can deal with.

Jasminda stared ahead blindly, replaying the last vision in her mind. Changing desert into farmland—she was awestruck by the power of these ancient Singers.

To the west of the settlement of Baalingrove were green fields and rolling hills. Clusters of trees sprang up here and there, and according to the settlers, the nearest farming village was about two kilometers away. But the settlement stood in the shade of the bordering mountains. Jasminda recognized the profile from her vision. Baalingrove was very close to where this colony of Earthsingers had been. All of this beauty and greenery had been transformed from desert wasteland long ago.

She stood, wincing at the way her sodden clothes stuck to her, and turned to the distinctive peaks. In her mind, she tried to triangulate the location of the colony. How long ago had it been since the Singers had done their work here? Was this vision a clue of some kind? Could the colony's location offer some insight into how to awaken the Queen?

"They wish the refugees to sleep at the Eastern Base tonight," one of the settlers told the others. The men sat together, appearing impervious to the rain that poured down. "The Sisterhood is setting up a camp for them near Rosira. The plan is to travel there tomorrow."

This elicited a chorus of grumbles from the other men. "I reckon we should go with them," another grizzled man said.

"And leave our homes? Who are they to us?" Voices murmured in agreement.

The first man stiffened. "Those who need protecting." Protests rose, but he leaned forward. "Most of us were born in the harems and grew up in the army. No family and no choices. We've been cast off here going on twenty years, but these women and children coming across need our help. They don't know the language, nor do they know what to expect from these flame-haired bastards—though after today, I'm sure they can guess."

The others quieted, and he continued. "I can't make none of you go. All I know is a man protects those weaker than himself. And no matter what they think, we're still men."

Jasminda blinked back tears. Had Papa not met Mama, he would be one of these men. The settlers remained silent, but she saw renewed purpose in the set of their jaws. They would go to protect the others.

And she would go as well—it was where she'd intended to end up all along. Appeal to the Tax Bureau, save her land. And discover a way to awaken the sleeping Queen. No, not difficult at all.

But first, she needed to visit the site of the colony. If the way to awaken the Queen was truly tied to these visions, then she couldn't ignore any possibilities.

She looked for Jack, but didn't want to ask any of the Elsirans. Finally, she spotted him near one of the vehicles talking with some of the soldiers. She called to him, waving to get his attention. Their eyes met, and a chill raced through her. She told herself it was just the unyielding rain. Jack broke away from the group; the other Elsirans looked her way, confusion evident on their faces.

He approached wearily. He looked so tired and burdened. Perhaps that was her imagination, however, his demeanor *had* changed.

Gone were even the hints of the man she'd once confused for an artist. He was all warrior now.

His presence beside her dried her throat. Whatever she had been planning to say flew out of her head.

"You are in charge of these men?" The question had been weighing on her since the soldiers had lowered the weapons pointed at him and showed him such deference. She didn't know much about military ranks, but High Commander sounded awfully important.

"Yes," he said simply.

Her heart grew heavy. Though he stood next to her, suddenly he seemed very far away. "You are very young."

"I started early. Practically at birth. And my family is very . . . well connected." There was no pride in his voice.

"The men respect you. It isn't false regard in their eyes. You must be quite good."

He shrugged and looked away, as though uncomfortable with this topic of conversation. She changed the subject.

"You're taking us all to the base?"

"Yes, all the refugees and any of the settlers who want to come. Tomorrow, we'll head for Rosira."

And what would happen after that? Would she ever see him again? She pushed the question back. It would probably be for the best. Before she got any more attached.

She cleared her throat. "I saw something with the stone."

Jack's brows raised; he stepped closer. "What?"

She briefly relayed the last vision. "The twins were near here. I recognize the formations." She pointed to the mountain. "Perhaps a few kilometers north. I thought maybe we could go there and look around. There could be something we're meant to find."

"Do you think the caldera is like the map?" he asked, following her line of thought.

"We know so little. There might be nothing there, but since we're so close, I thought we should check."

He looked off into the distance. "The only thing I can think of up there are the ruins of the Citadel. Do you think that's where this colony was?"

"Could be."

Jack nodded, his decision etched on his face. "Then we'll go. It's very near the base, so we can stop at the ruins on our way." He moved to walk away, then stopped and turned back to grab her hands. "Thank you."

The contact zinged all the way up her arms. "Don't thank me yet. I still don't know how any of this will help awaken the Queen."

He grinned at her. "Still. Oh, and I don't think we should mention the caldera or the plan to wake the Queen to anyone else. Getting anyone in the government involved could be . . . complicated."

"All right," Jasminda agreed. "I don't have anyone to tell, anyway."

He squeezed her hands, then marched away, barking out orders. Jasminda clenched her fists, willing the tingling to stop before it reached her heart.

CHAPTER TWENTY-ONE

The Mistress of Frogs was called to the bedside of an old woman who wanted to be assured of peace in the World After.

She said, Peace can be found only in memory. To seek it in the future is folly.

—COLLECTED FOLKTALES

Jack watched the transports carrying the refugees and settlers rumble away. Only he, Jasminda, and Benn, his assistant, remained. Jack had been grateful when Benn drove up an hour before. He'd embraced his old friend like a brother.

Jasminda's expression was unreadable as the other Lagrimari were driven off. Jack didn't have to explain himself to his men, but he'd noticed their questioning looks as Jasminda was held aside while the Lagrimari were gathered together.

Now Benn, the only person Jack trusted, was in the driver's seat of a four-wheeler. He wouldn't ask any difficult questions, and he would be discreet. Benn had known of Jack's undercover mission—only the broad strokes—and had kept his every confidence.

"Where to?" Benn asked. He'd greeted Jasminda politely, palms out, without any questions, and for that Jack was grateful. The fact that *she* appeared surprised at the action gnawed at him.

"The Citadel. We need to take a look at the ruins."

The Citadel had been built after the First Breach, just a few decades after the Mantle's erection. The invading Lagrimari had taken over much of the eastern farmland. They'd built a wall to keep the Elsirans out and used their considerable power in the form of earthquakes, fires, storms, and floods to do battle.

Elsiran engineers responded by constructing a mighty battle ram that eventually tore down the wall. Their superior numbers pushed the Lagrimari back, and the tear in the Mantle closed again, without the Elsirans quite knowing how.

That's when the Citadel was built—a walled city that could withstand a year-long siege. The Elsirans bolstered their army, making the city its headquarters. That long-ago Prince Regent knew it was just a matter of time before the True Father attacked again.

Their four-wheeler came to a stop at the edge of the ruins. A vast sea of tumbled rock and stone stretched out before them. Tough grasses and shrubbery pushed their way through gaps in the stones. Here and there an archway remained mostly intact. The foundations and first stories of many of the buildings had also lasted, though the formerly cobbled streets were just greenery now.

"Why was it never rebuilt, I wonder?" Benn asked.

"I don't think we had the heart. A city of stone is no match for men who can cause it to crumble with a thought." The Elsirans had underestimated the Earthsingers, and they had suffered for it. Jack exited the vehicle, wading through the somber atmosphere that had settled over them.

"But this city stood for hundreds of years," Jasminda said, coming to his side.

"Because the True Father wanted to use it." Jack snorted. "After all the work it took to build, the Lagrimari tunneled in during the Second Breach and took over. It changed hands throughout the years more than once."

The rain had subsided for the moment, though the gray sky promised more. Jasminda turned in a circle, taking it all in. She shivered, wrapping her arms around her middle.

"Are you cold?"

Jack still wore her brother's pants, but had changed his wet shirt for a dry one and donned a brown army jacket back at Baalingrove. The refugees had been issued blankets while waiting for transport, but Jasminda must have left hers behind.

He took off his jacket and handed it to her. She smiled, almost shyly, before accepting it.

"Thank you," she whispered. It engulfed her, and she had to roll up the sleeves. Jack looked away. The jacket wasn't even really his, but it sparked something possessive in him that was wholly inappropriate.

The Citadel sat slightly to the southwest of the only gap in the mountain range. This stretch of land was a few thousand paces wide and was the sole location from which you could see the country of Lagrimar.

"That's it, isn't it?" Jasminda asked. "Breach Valley? I've never . . ." She looked visibly shaken.

The Mantle was invisible to the eye, but try to cross the gap and you would hit an impenetrable force. Well, mostly impenetrable.

Every breach had occurred right here. Every breach save for the current one.

"What does he want?" Jasminda asked. "Why invade this place again and again?"

"Farmland, food for his people. I suspect everyone is easier to control when they're well fed." Elsirans certainly were. The most unrest always happened in times of strife.

"But he has magic."

Jack turned away from the valley, back to the ruins. "They say he hates to use it. Darvyn told me that the True Father's power is tainted, so he himself cannot transform the land from desert to fertile. Apparently, he tried at the beginning and it only made the land worse. But he had already stolen the power from the strongest Earthsingers, so there were few left to terraform. So he set his sights on this side of the mountain."

After the Citadel's destruction, the Eastern Base became the hub of army operations. It was to the north of Breach Valley, just out of sight of the constant reminder of failure the destroyed city held.

Benn walked a bit farther out of earshot. "Do you recognize anything?" Jack asked Jasminda.

"This does seem to be the location of the colony I saw. But I don't know." She headed down an overgrown path that was once, no doubt, a vibrant city street. Every so often she would stop and squint. He wondered if she was using her Song to search for clues but didn't pierce the quiet to ask.

The low hum of voices rose nearby. Jack grabbed his sidearm and moved in front of Jasminda, scanning the area.

His skin tightened with apprehension until a bugle trilled out. They turned a corner and found three dozen old men gathered before the remains of the clock tower. Though not much of the structure was left, it was still the tallest thing standing in the city.

Some of the old-timers were in military dress uniforms, some in suits and ties with sashes of honor covering their chests. They all stood at attention while a lone bugler played a plaintive melody. Two at the front of the group folded the Elsiran flag, its blue and gold symbols of the country's crest disappearing into the folds.

Jack came to attention and saluted. When the bugle died, the men's voices rose, singing the Elsiran national anthem.

"From sandy shores near oceans deep,
To mountains near and far,
Her memory, alive we keep
Elsira's in our hearts
Shining brightly, coast to hill
Her beauty waning never,
Elsira lives on by our will
Elsira is forever."

Quiet replaced the voices, and then the ceremony was done. The skies picked that point to open, dousing them in a cold drizzle.

Some of the men looked up, noticing Jasminda and Jack for the first time. Jack wore only the plain brown shirt, and none of his stripes were visible to indicate his rank, yet one of the men recognized him. The old-timer snapped to attention and saluted.

"High Commander Alliaseen. It's a pleasure, sir." The other men followed his lead.

Jack reciprocated, conscious of his intrusion upon them. "As you were," he ordered.

By the age of the men present, he gathered they must be Fifth Breach veterans. Some tough old bastards. What he'd heard about those fights made his stomach sour.

"Jasminda?" one of the men called out, stepping forward. She grew rigid beside Jack before her expression morphed into a smile.

"Bindeen?" A graying figure approached and bowed slightly as she beamed. "What in Sovereign's name are you doing here?"

"I might ask you the same. Those what are left from our regiment get together this time every year to pay our respects. It's the anniversary of our last stand here."

"This is Master Bindeen, the blacksmith in town," Jasminda said by way of introduction. Jack liked that she smiled fondly at the old man. He sensed there were not many who could claim her friendship.

Bindeen nodded at him. "Sir."

Jack looked more closely at the uniforms of the men. "You say you shared a regiment?" Bindeen wore the patch of the 23rd Infantry, the Black Skulls, while the two who'd folded the flag were both from the 18th, the Stormwalkers. And over there was a fellow from the 49th.

Bindeen eyed the others with a sidelong glance, then grinned. "We share a regiment that no patch was ever made for, sir." The old man peered at him meaningfully.

"The Phantoms?" Jack was incredulous.

"Aye."

Jack viewed the man with renewed admiration. He bowed slightly. "It is an honor."

Bindeen scoffed, his face reddening. "It was Qerwall over there who brought me in and watched our backs every day of that mission." He motioned to a wiry man with a full head of gray hair still tinged with the red of his youth.

Jasminda looked back and forth between them. "What are the Phantoms?"

Bindeen's mouth clamped shut, a guilty look crossing his face, but Jack grinned. "I think fifty years of being classified is long enough. What do you think, Sergeant?"

The man smiled. "Why don't you step into our office? I'll tell you all about it."

CHAPTER TWENTY-TWO

The Master of Monkeys came across a hunter caught in his own trap in the forest.

Will you free me? the hunter cried.

Nay, answered Monkey. However, in leaving you ensnared, I free your prey from your pursuit.

—COLLECTED FOLKTALES

Jack followed the others into a large tent erected just outside the ruins. Tankards of ale poured from fat barrels were shared liberally. The rain pattering against the tent's fabric lent a steady soundtrack to the tale the old men spun.

Benn, Bindeen, and Qerwall sat together with Jack and Jasminda on folding camp chairs. The other soldiers sat in small groups nearby sharing memories and catching up.

"We're honored to have you here, Commander," Qerwall said. His steely eyes were so light they almost seemed leached of all color. Different from the amber shade of most Elsirans.

"I'm honored to be here. Will you tell us about the Phantoms?"

Qerwall eyed Jasminda with more curiosity than suspicion and launched into his story. "I had the dream of the Queen once when I was a lad, no more than three or four years old. I didn't rightly know what I'd seen, but when I told my mama, she nearly fainted dead away. Got a lot of attention from that, I did, in our village. A group of Sisters came and questioned me for the Dream Record. But it wasn't until years later, when we deployed during the Fifth, that I had another one."

He rested his elbows on his knees and spread his gnarled fingers apart. "The Breach had been open going on sixty years, and at that point we were in a long standoff. They'd send a storm and then we'd bomb the living daylights out of them, and on and on. But when I got to the front line, things had just started turning ugly.

"The day before had been the first time we'd been hit with those bloody apple bombs they conjured." He snorted at Jasminda's questioning expression. "They didn't whistle or hiss like normal shells. But if you smelled apples, you were in for it. Those blasted things eventually destroyed the Citadel."

"Haven't been able to eat an apple since," Bindeen added.

Qerwall grunted in agreement. "But that first night I had the dream. I was transported to this dark place where I couldn't see anything, not even myself. I heard *Her* voice. It flowed through me like lava in my veins. Never heard a sound like it before or since.

"She told me that there were others I had to find. Men I could trust, plus a few names She gave. Also, there were Lagrimari working against the True Father and we had to meet up with them. Said they'd found a weakness in the True Father's plan and we had to be ready."

"See there's this fella called a Cantor," Bindeen broke in. "The True Father's second in command. I suppose they don't last long, that madman kills people close to him after a while, but this one's name was Morryn. He's the one what made the apples. This Morryn had a son in secret. The True Father didn't know about him, and Morryn wanted to keep it that way."

"That was the weakness, see," Qerwall continued smoothly. "These Lagrimari rebels had found it out and taken the son captive. They brought him to us, and we hid him in Elsira. Then got word to Morryn that we had his boy and if he didn't stop shelling us with them apples, we couldn't guarantee his son's safety."

"That's when the tide turned in our favor," Bindeen said. "We couldn't do much against those bloody bombs, but once Morryn stopped creating them, we were able to mount an offensive."

"That's how we won the Fifth Breach." Qerwall nodded and sat back, taking a long drink of his ale.

Jack took in Jasminda's stunned expression. He had studied military history, and while there were no public records of the classified mission, when he'd taken over as Army High Commander, he'd been briefed on the broad strokes. But he had never actually met any of the men involved.

"What happened to Morryn and his son?" Jasminda asked.

Bindeen sobered. "The father wanted to defect. We had a plan to get him and the boy out of the country and on a ship headed for Raun. But . . ." He shook his head.

"The True Father found out. Killed the son. Drained the father's Song." Qerwall stared into his mug.

"But left Morryn alive?" she asked.

"For a time." Qerwall nodded. "We got word from one of our contacts that the man escaped after his tribute. Don't know what happened to him. Can't imagine the True Father didn't hunt him down and have him killed. After the breach closed, we were cut off from the rebels and heard nothing else about him."

"It wouldn't have been easy for him to hide with that hair of his," Bindeen mused. "When we had him, we shaved his head so he wouldn't stand out so much, but you could still see that mark he had."

Jack looked up sharply from his ale. "What mark?"

"Birthmark. Shape of an *S* running from the front of his head to the back. A streak of white in his dark hair. All the way down to his scalp."

A vise gripped Jack's chest, making his breath short. "Describe him to me. How tall was he? How old then?"

Bindeen scratched his chin. "Average height for a Lagrimari. Thick build. Would have been in his fifties back then, I reckon. Why?"

Jack looked at Jasminda. "The old man I met, the one who gave me the map. He had a white streak in his hair just like that. The rest had turned a dark gray, but that streak was pure white."

Jasminda stared at him, her eyes reflecting the foreboding he felt.

"But he would have to be going on one hundred years old now," Bindeen said.

"You think it could have been this Morryn who gave you the map?" Jasminda's voice was hushed. The conversation in the tent stayed at a low hum, but to Jack's ears it was deafening.

He sat back in his seat, hands shaking. He pushed away the vision he'd seen during the quest to find the cornerstone. That had broken his heart, but this suspicion rising within him threatened to break his spirit.

"What if Morryn is still working for the True Father?" Jack asked. "What if giving me the map was a trick, a plot to find a way to destroy the cornerstone and keep their plans in motion?"

A growing dread unfolded as his thoughts continued. "You said the storm was magical, and after we revealed the cornerstone, the storm demolished it." He met Jasminda's gaze. "The current Cantor. She must have ordered Tensyn to let us go. Because she *knew* what I was going to do."

Jasminda shook her head. "But you can't know. We don't . . ." She frowned, staring at the ground. "The fire at the cabin? The stone caused it. They were . . . manipulating us. Forcing us to leave."

It was harder and harder to deny. The bottom dropped out of Jack's stomach. "This is my fault. I believed Morryn. I didn't ask enough questions, and I walked right into a trap."

He recalled the first time he'd touched his blood to the stone and been taken into the map's vision, seeing the cornerstone and knowing that he had a chance to avoid the war. It had consumed him, made him foolish.

"They knew who I was, and they used me to further weaken the Mantle." He massaged his head as the truth struck him. "By pursuing the cornerstone, I brought about its destruction."

"If this is true, the True Father destroyed the cornerstone, Jack. Not you." Jasminda placed a hand on his forearm and squeezed gently.

"But remember the hooded woman in the vision? No one the True Father sent would have passed the test and found the cornerstone. He needed someone to lead him to it." A pained expression crossed her face. "You said you felt like the storm was watching you. What if it was? I should have listened to you. It *was* bad magic."

A crackle of static interrupted whatever she'd been about to say.

Benn sat up and grabbed the portable radio at his waist. He stepped outside to hear the caller, but ran back in almost immediately.

"Urgent call for you from the capital, sir."

Jack stood, his whole body heavy as he walked out of the tent to take the call.

"Jack? Is that you?" a familiar voice warbled down the line.

"Usher? What's wrong?"

"Oh, Jack." The man exhaled in relief. "Thank the Queen you're alive!"

"What's happened?"

"It's Alariq." The old man's voice cracked, weighed down with misery. "Your brother is dead."

CHAPTER TWENTY-THREE

And what of evil? said the town's mayor to the Master of Bobcats.
Evil is a powerful man's greatest friend. It will either fill
his heart or line his pockets.

—COLLECTED FOLKTALES

Jasminda pulled Jack's coat around her tighter. The thick, wet fabric did relatively little to keep out the driving chill of the rain. He hadn't worn it long enough for his scent to permeate—and the dampness would have washed it away in any case—yet since she could not hold him, she settled for the jacket.

Dusk had fallen, and the murky haze was penetrated only slightly by the vehicle's headlamps. Benn navigated the four-wheeler with ease despite the sodden roads.

Jack's pensive mood was so present, it could have taken up an entire seat. He was eating himself up with blame for the corner-stone's destruction. Jasminda wished she could soothe him. If he hadn't taken Morryn's map and tried to use it, the True Father would have just found another. And that person might not have been so lucky as to have been saved by someone like Osar.

But guilt was guilt, and Jack continued to stew in his. The unvoiced question was this: had the cornerstone's ruin hastened the fall of the Mantle?

Nothing catastrophic had happened in the days since the avalanche, but maybe the worst was yet to come. A headache formed at the base of Jasminda's skull. They could only move forward, not back. What was done was past.

The four-wheeler approached a grouping of low, gray structures hugging the earth. The Eastern Army Base was all bland concrete, straight lines, and harsh corners, made drearier by the persistent rain.

Benn pulled to a stop beside a row of other vehicles, and Jack faced Jasminda, his expression grim. "I need to check on some things. Benn will have sleeping quarters located for you."

"I won't be with the others?"

Jack shook his head emphatically. "You are an Elsiran citizen, not a refugee. That must be made clear."

He leaned in to speak a few words to Benn and then was off, disappearing into one of the nondescript buildings.

"Miss Jasminda, if you'll follow me."

Benn led her into the largest building on the base. Concrete floors and cinder block walls did not make the hallway inviting. Harsh overhead light gave everything a pallid sheen. They passed a number of doors with square glass embedded within. Beyond was a large space, a gymnasium perhaps, holding rows and rows of cots. Lagrimari huddled together as Elsiran soldiers finished setting up the pallets.

Jasminda shivered, glad she would not have to spend the night among so many strangers.

Benn led her down another hallway and motioned her to a small row of metal chairs. "Would you like something hot to drink? Coffee or tea?"

She sank into a seat. "Coffee would be nice." He nodded and disappeared into one of the many rooms. Though she sat alone, the building buzzed with energy. She reached for Earthsong to sense the people around her, hidden behind walls and doors. Wariness and anxiety pervaded.

The Elsiran soldiers were now tasked with housing those whom they'd only ever seen as the enemy. The atmosphere was taut with tension.

Two soldiers tramped down the hall. Their conversation halted when they caught sight of her. Jasminda averted her eyes, but couldn't avoid the hostility rolling off them.

The men continued on, but their voices reached her. "Looks like the commander has himself a new pet."

A snort. "A *grol* bitch to fetch the paper and eat the table scraps." Laughter.

Jasminda hunched over, ducking her head. But her shame was quickly replaced by anger, which raced like a streak of lightning sizzling through her veins. The sensation of pins and needles pricked her skin. The hair on her arms stood up.

"Wonder what he's thinking, keeping them all here. Could be the lot of them are spies seeking intel."

One man chuckled derisively. "Fat lot of intel available in the mess hall."

"That's not the point. We should gut every *grol* we come across. That's less of them to fight when the next breach comes."

A third voice spoke up. "I don't know. There's a couple of fit birds out there I wouldn't mind tussling with." More laughter.

Jasminda clenched her fists until her knuckles hurt. Though

the area around her was empty, she was aware of another presence nearby. At first she thought her Song sensed someone in an adjoining room, but this was closer than that. As close as frost coating her skin. An unseen entity stoking her anger like bellows to a fire.

Untethered emotions swirled inside her. Her Song pulsed, drawing in more Earthsong until she was pregnant with power.

"The one the commander picked out is the fittest, though. Maybe once he's done with her, he'll give us a turn."

She couldn't hold on anymore. Her rage exploded, funneling itself through her Song.

Her chair vibrated. The floor shook in gentle waves, then more forcefully. A violent wind basted down the hallway. Doors slammed wildly. Furniture rattled.

Frantic soldiers rushed into the hall. Jasminda kept her head down, trying to control herself. In moments, the flare-up was over. Her Song was simply too weak to sustain that much energy. She was burned out and, moreover, horrified at what had just happened.

The foreign presence had disappeared, and the building was in chaos. Men with guns drawn raced past her and around the corner.

What in Sovereign's name had she done? She stood on wobbly legs and followed them into the mess hall. The refugees were crushed together in the center with weapons trained on them by wild-eyed soldiers.

Jasminda covered her mouth, stifling a gasp. She caught Gerda's terrified gaze and wanted to melt into a puddle of shame. Jack appeared, calling for calm. Despite his words, the tension in the room was oppressive.

"What happened?" he asked, looking around. "Who was responsible for that?" He repeated it in Lagrimari.

Jasminda swallowed her fear and took a deep breath, preparing to step forward.

"The children are frightened, sir. They acted without thought." Gerda's voice was calm and even. She stood beside Osar, an arm around him.

Jasminda's breath staggered. She couldn't let the old woman shift the blame to the poor children. When she moved forward, Gerda held out a hand surreptitiously to stop her. "We will make sure it doesn't happen again," the gray-haired woman said.

Jack expelled a breath and rubbed his face. His shoulders sagged. He stepped closer to Gerda. "Tensions are high, as I'm sure you know. If my men feel threatened they will react, and I may not be here to stop them. Many of these soldiers were in the Seventh Breach. Any display of Earthsong will inflame them."

"I understand." Gerda's gaze seemed to cut through Jack straight to Jasminda, who stood several dozen paces behind him, hovering near the wall. "We will stay watchful and calm."

"I would appreciate it." Jack turned and spoke to his men, but his words blended together in Jasminda's ears. As the soldiers left to go back to wherever they'd come from, Gerda approached.

"You must beware, child. We are not the only ones slipping through the Mantle's cracks."

"What do you mean?" Jasminda's voice shook.

"You felt something, did you not, in the wind and rain and snow?"

Jasminda's eyes widened. "How did you know? I sensed . . . someone. Something. And just now it happened again. Only this time it set upon me, made me lose control of my Song."

Gerda nodded. "The storm, it is tainted. The True Father is breaking free of his chains. And you are a target now because of the caldera."

"He knows I have it?"

"Not exactly." Gerda tilted her head to the side. "While the

Mantle stands, he is limited. But his spell is drawn to the stone like a tracking dog. This storm will seek you out looking for weakness to exploit. Feeding on your anger. You must be stronger than it. Protect your mind." She tapped a wrinkled finger against the side of her head.

Jasminda tightened her arms around her waist. "Why didn't you warn me before?"

Gerda shrugged. "We weren't sure it would affect you. I was hoping you would be immune."

"Well, I'm not." Jasminda stepped back. At least her Song was depleted until tomorrow. She could do no further damage.

Benn appeared, bearing a perplexed expression and a mug of coffee.

"I have to go," Jasminda said, sullen. Gerda smiled and shuffled away.

Jasminda accepted the coffee gratefully, allowing the liquid to scald her tongue. The discomfort grounded her. The invasive vileness of the True Father's magic was nothing she would soon forget. She only hoped she could somehow steel herself against it.

CHAPTER TWENTY-FOUR

Eagle and Shark were once as close as petals closed for evening.
Not even a strong wind could tear them apart.

—COLLECTED FOLKTALES

Jack left his office well after midnight and trudged out into the soggy night. The rain had tapered to a light mist, matching his downcast mood. He wound his way through the narrow lanes of the base until he reached the supply building where Jasminda was staying.

There was no place in the barracks secure enough for a single woman, and Jack wanted to make sure Jasminda was protected. Sleeping space was at a premium, so a cot had been set up for her in this small warehouse.

He opened the door; a tall stack of boxes cluttered the entryway, blocking his view.

"Jasminda. It's me," he called out, rounding the mountain of crates to find her crouched on her cot, a knife in hand. Her skirt had rucked up, revealing the garter that had housed the blade.

Warmth shot through him. With a shy look, she set her skirt to rights. He swallowed and forced his gaze up to her face. She was looking anywhere but at him, so he pulled up a box and sat beside her. "How do you like the accommodations?"

"It's no cave floor, but it will serve." Her eyes finally rose to meet his, and he relaxed a notch. For some reason he'd needed to see her after this endless, excruciating day.

He reached for her hand and threaded his fingers through hers, drawing comfort with every breath they shared so close together.

"Are you all right?" she whispered.

"I've been worse." He tried to inject lightness into his voice but failed. Guilt had nearly paralyzed him, and now grief threatened to finish the job.

"And you've been better?" She dipped her chin to meet his lowered gaze.

"Haven't we all?" He stood on a tightrope with doom on one side and failure on the other, but in only a handful of days Jasminda had become the bar he gripped to balance him. Under his fingertips, her velvet skin soothed him. "How is your skin so soft?"

"It's the balm." She shrugged off his question, but he could not recall even the hands of the gently bred young ladies often trotted out before him being so smooth. How was it that a girl who worked a farm could have skin like this?

Her eyes narrowed, as if seeing inside him. "Something happened. Before we left the Citadel." Her soft voice clung to him in places unused to such tenderness.

"You mean besides discovering that I've nearly singlehandedly brought down the Mantle myself?"

She squeezed his hand. "Unless you've developed a Song in the past day, you did not."

"I led him to it. It's the same thing."

"It's not. And that's not why we left the tent so quickly."

He swallowed, closing his eyes. "My brother . . . is dead." Saying the words aloud made them all the more real. Alariq was gone, and with him, Jack's chance at a normal life.

"I-I'm sorry. I'm so sorry, Jack."

Her emotions showed on her face, but his were buried. He was not supposed to tell anyone yet, but he found himself opening up to Jasminda. "He was piloting his airship and ran into a thunderstorm. The craft crashed. He was thrown through the window."

Imagining his elder brother broken in such a way was simply too much. He pushed the vivid images out of his mind. Jasminda stared, sorrow and pity in her eyes. He took a deep breath. "I haven't told you all you need to know about me."

His mouth opened, but no more words would come. Pain clawed at his heart.

"Will you tell me?" she asked.

He would have to. It would soon become unavoidable, but this day had already gone on for too long. "I want to, but let us wait until tomorrow, if that is all right. It is not something I want to think about now. Worries on top of worries."

"Of course." She smiled, but it didn't reach her eyes. He had no wish to make her unhappy, however, his heart was too heavy for much more. "Was he your only family?"

The sole relative he still spoke to, if only occasionally. He shook his head. "My mother lives in Fremia now." He didn't mention her abandonment. He supposed Jasminda would find that out soon enough.

"Has she been told?"

"She's in seclusion. But we are half brothers. Were . . . His mother is long passed. He and I were never close. We didn't see eye to eye, but . . ."

"But he was kin."

Jack nodded. "Kin. And now it falls to me." He stroked each of her knuckles and massaged the delicate skin between her fingers.

"What falls to you?"

"I . . ." He dropped his head. Shook it. "It is late. You should rest."

"Tomorrow, then." Her hand slipped out of his. He wanted to grab it again, but he wasn't being completely honest and perhaps didn't deserve her touch.

He should leave, and yet sat firmly rooted in place. Was it only last night she had slept in his arms? Could he admit to her that he wanted to do so again?

Her voice shook when she spoke up. "Jack, what do you see when you look at me?"

He was tongue-tied. Beauty. Bravery. An intensity that took him by surprise, even when it shouldn't. He wasn't sure what to say.

"Your men . . . they see me as the enemy. How is it you don't?"

His back straightened. A haze of anger colored his vision. "You're not the enemy. Did someone say something to you?" She grabbed his arm when he went to stand. He didn't know what he was going to do, but it involved finding whomever had caused her pain and inflicting some of his own.

"No, no. Just . . . they think it."

He froze. "Does Earthsong tell you that?"

She shook her head. "I can just tell."

"You're safe here, I promise." He was responsible for this base and these men. He'd reiterated to them that if something happened to one of the refugees, it better be because one of the Lagrimari had caused some bodily harm, else a court-martial was in store. But he would protect Jasminda himself.

She smiled weakly and lay down on her cot looking over at him. Without consciously thinking about it, he slid onto the ground, stretching out beside her.

Jasminda shot up like a catapult. "You're not going to sleep here, are you?"

"I made you a promise, and I plan to keep it." He settled back, propping his head on his hands behind him. This was better. His muscles had balked at the idea of leaving her, but lying beside her on the unforgiving concrete floor was almost soothing.

"You don't need to do that. You can't sleep on the ground!"

"I've been doing it for the past few weeks. Another night won't hurt anything."

"But you have a whole set of rooms here. With comfortable beds, I'm sure."

He held her gaze, willing her to feel his truth. "I won't let anything happen to you. Besides, this is better than sleeping standing up, which I've done a time or two. I wouldn't recommend it." He grinned, but the worry in her eyes didn't fade.

She lay back down, then shifted to her side, watching him. Though he could stare at her all night, he forced his eyes to close. There she was behind his eyelids; at least she wouldn't feel uncomfortable with him gaping at her openly.

Her steady breaths lulled him to the edge of sleep. Then she spoke. "You could probably fit on the cot."

His eyes flew open. He waited half a moment to be sure she wasn't joking. When she made no move to rescind the offer, he shot up so quickly she gasped in surprise. In a heartbeat, he was squeezed in behind her on the narrow cot. It was not much more pliant than the concrete had been, and yet the tension of the day flowed away completely as they lay on their sides, his body spooning hers. She shifted her hair out of the way, baring her neck to his gaze.

Her back sank into his chest. He squeezed her waist and exhaled, feeling content for the first time in many hours.

Suddenly, she stiffened. "What's wrong?" he whispered.

"Nothing. Nothing's wrong." She pulled his arm tighter against her abdomen. His shoulders dropped; he splayed his hand out, feeling the rise and fall of her breath.

Her neck was so inviting, smooth, and fragrant, with her unique scent filling his nostrils. He couldn't resist, his lips met her skin almost of their own accord. Jasminda shivered and pressed even closer to him, so he did it again, whispering his lips across her aromatic skin.

"Jack." Her voice held a plea that zipped through him, heightening his attraction.

He kissed her again at the spot where her neck met her shoulder.

"I haven't ever . . . I mean, I want . . ." She was breathless and trembling.

"What do you want, Jasminda?" he asked, speaking against her neck. He had wanted to do this for so long, and she was soft and pliant in his arms.

He took a chance and nudged the fabric of her dress aside to press a kiss to her shoulder. "Tell me. I'll give you anything I can."

When his lips touched her, she gave a little moan, which made him never want to stop. But then she turned in his arms to face him. Her tears threatened to overflow, halting him.

"Some things are not for me." She raised her gaze to meet his, sorrow evident, but no regret, to his relief. Her fingers hovered above his lips. He held his breath until they descended in a feather-light touch, tracing his mouth. "*You* aren't for me."

"So why is it that I can't stop thinking about you?"

She leaned even closer, until she was only a breath away, and then she kissed him.

Jack was drenched in sunshine and light, the gray day and dreary night burning away as he sank into her kiss. He threaded his fingers through her hair, holding her to him. When he prodded her in gently with his tongue, she opened, giving him entry.

He lost himself inside her mouth, her lips, the occasional, sensual clash of teeth. When they broke apart, both breathing heavily, he captured her hand in his and pressed a kiss to her palm. He wanted to kiss her everywhere.

Their foreheads met. He stroked her cheek and slid an arm beneath her before rolling them so he was on his back with her on top of him. His hands rested on her lower back, just above the rise of her bottom. He went no lower, though, merely captured her lips in another scorching kiss.

She wiggled on top of him, brushing against his erection. A pulse shot through him, and he turned his head to the side to exhale the deep longing. "Please don't move," he begged.

Slowly, she rubbed her thigh against his hardness again. Any more of that and he could not guarantee his sanity would stay intact much longer. He flipped them over to hover atop her on shaky arms.

There was no shyness in her expression. She leaned up and kissed him, stroked from his jaw down his neck, to his chest. Her hand came to a stop at his belt. Jack swallowed.

When her hand moved lower, he grabbed it and placed it next to her head. Before she could tempt him with her other hand, he grabbed that as well. She was well and truly trapped now. He claimed another kiss before rising from the cot. He adjusted himself, though there would be no relief in that quarter tonight, and settled on the ground again.

Jasminda peered down at him, pouting. "You can come back. I'll be good. I promise."

"I don't want to make you an oath breaker. And I will make no such promises." He took deep, calming breaths, trying his best to ignore the pull of desire that would have him once again on top of her and far more. "Tonight, we should sleep. I do not want to do something that you will regret."

"Would *you* regret it?"

He wanted to laugh but instead reached for her hand and drew it to his lips. "No. But it is not my virtue we are speaking of." He kept her hand in his as he stretched out on the ground.

Jasminda was an innocent, of that he was certain. And though he wanted her beyond reason, it would not be right. Not here, not now. With so much about to change, the last thing he wanted to do was hurt her. Not in any way.

He gripped her hand and enjoyed the play of her soft skin against his rougher hands. Sleeping on the ground was no hardship when he was near her.

CHAPTER TWENTY-FIVE

One day, Eagle discovered a jewel nestled in the branches of a tree. She caught it and brought it to Shark.

Is this for me? Shark asked, beaming at so generous a gift.

Nay, it is mine, I only wanted to show you, Eagle replied, peeved at the assumption.

And so the first fissure was cast.

—COLLECTED FOLKTALES

Yllis careens around the corner, nearly crashing into a servant. His dark eyes are stormy.

"Did you find him?" I ask, breathless.

He shakes his head. "What exactly did he say to you, Oola?"

I twist my fingers in frustration, recalling my brother's words. "He wanted more, begged me for a little more power. When I refused, he got upset. Yllis, I've never seen him like this before. He was . . ."

Eero's eyes had bugged out of his head. The veins in his forehead and neck had been so prominent, I thought he might burst.

His frustration and jealousy and anger ripped at me. Clawed me open. I knew then that his gift had been a terrible worst mistake. I could never give him any more of my Song.

My voice is a quiet hush. "He said that he would find a way to get more. That I could not stop him."

Yllis wraps strong arms around me. I sob into his chest, feeling the weight of my failure drag me down. He calms me with tender, wordless sounds and his solid presence, but I feel selfish for relying upon him.

"You have not told anyone, have you?" I say into his chest.

"No, of course not. And none of the other Cantors know the spell nor have an interest in it."

That, at least, is something. "But still, someone could discover it. Or craft a similar spell. Eero has a way of getting what he wants." Or maybe that was just with me.

"I think we have created a monster," Yllis says. He pulls back to look into my eyes. I can only agree.

Whatever happens next will be my fault. I crumple inside to consider it.

The vision was interrupted by the bleating of a horn as the base residents were called to the mess hall for breakfast. Jasminda tucked away the caldera and followed the blaring noise to the morning meal.

She hoped to see Jack again—he'd woken her with a kiss before disappearing back to his work—but as soon as the plates were cleared away, a line of soldiers led the refugees to a caravan of buses for the trip to Rosira.

Benn appeared and directed her to a special vehicle, a boxy, close-topped four-wheeler. He explained that for security purposes, Jack rode in an armored vehicle, which couldn't legally transport civilians. Jasminda had wanted to share the long journey with him from the eastern border of Elsira to the capital city on the western coast, but it wasn't to be. Instead she had to put up with a lonely trip, complete with a driver whose eyes would flick to the rearview mirror, shooting cold, suspicious glances at her. She didn't waver, meeting his gaze each time until he looked away. He was no doubt wondering why he was chauffeuring around a Lagrimari-looking Elsiran girl.

The rain stopped as they drove west, and a tension she hadn't realized she was holding released. She admired the rolling hills and dense forests of Elsira's picture-perfect countryside. Night fell, and dusty, unpaved roads eventually gave way to wider, paved highways, illuminated by electric lights and full of vehicles of all shapes and sizes.

Jasminda sucked in a breath when she got her first glimpse of Rosira from the crest of a hill. The city swept up and away from the ocean like a gentle wave. Lights sparkled from thousands of houses, which from this distance gave the impression of being stacked on top of one another, but as they drew closer, were really etched in layers going up the steep hillside.

There were no skyscrapers or especially tall buildings like in the pictures she'd seen of the megacities of Yaly. The main industry here was commerce, and docks stretched the entire length of the coastline with an assortment of vessels anchored there like great beasts asleep in their pens.

She tested her connection to Earthsong, then dropped it, immediately overwhelmed by the dense press of so many energies. How could anyone use magic in a place so heavily populated? Did Lagrimar have cities, and if so, how were the residents able to cope?

Her vehicle traveled a serpentine path through the city. Jack had assured her he would find lodging for her, though he hadn't mentioned where. She suspected the Sisterhood had a dormitory of some kind where she could stay. Surely women whose mission was to feed and care for the settlers would not view her as terribly as the soldiers had. She could only hope.

The steep road through the densely packed buildings turned back on itself several times, dizzying her. After half a dozen twists and turns, the truck approached a gilded gate guarded by soldiers wearing black uniforms with gold trim and fringed epaulets. The gates swung open, revealing a brightly lit, curving drive that ascended even higher.

The Royal Palace of Elsira loomed in front of them, white stones gleaming under the illumination of a shocking quantity of electric lights. The pictures in her textbooks did not do it justice. Columned porches ran along the first floor with a seemingly endless number of arched windows just beyond. Carved into the stone above each window were images of the Founders, the magical Lord and Lady in various poses showing how they'd transformed Elsira.

Somewhere within this building lay the sleeping body of their descendant, the Queen Herself, protected by the Prince Regent who ruled in Her stead until She awoke and returned to power. Seeing it in person, Jasminda was transfixed. Though there was no longer any magic in Elsira, the palace seemed to give off its own energy and spoke to her in an unfamiliar way.

The driver exited the vehicle, and Jasminda remained, hoping that whatever business Jack had here would be quick. The trip had been exhausting, and she wanted nothing more than to fall into whatever bed she was assigned. The door she leaned against jerked open and there stood Jack, holding out his hand.

She stared at it uncomprehendingly. "Can I not wait here for you?"

"You would prefer to sleep in the truck?" The corner of his mouth quirked, shattering his grim expression.

She looked from him to the palace and back again. A knowing smile crept up Jack's face.

"When you said you'd find lodging for me, I didn't think . . . Jack, I can't sleep in the *palace*."

"Why ever not?" He crossed his arms and leaned against the truck.

"Because I'm a goat farmer. Palaces are for royalty. The Prince Regent cannot possibly allow someone like me here."

"Trust me, it's all right. Many officials and dignitaries live in the palace. A whole wing is devoted to ranking officers and their families. Honestly, it's more like an inn than a proper palace these days."

"But—"

"I'm well acquainted with whom the Prince Regent allows under his roof." A flicker of pain crossed his face, and he took a deep breath. "Jasminda—"

"Commander!" an insistent voice bellowed from across the driveway.

"One moment, General," Jack responded while his eyes pleaded with her. She accepted his offered palm, gripping it as she stepped from the vehicle and approached the palace.

A battalion of servants greeted them inside the entry. Jack announced her as an honored guest and conferred with a matronly woman who must have been in charge of things. Two maids whisked her away before she could even thank Jack or say good night, let alone find out what he had wanted to tell her. Hopefully it was whatever he'd said she needed to know about him. Her heart burned to know his secrets, even as part of her was glad she didn't.

She barely registered the dazzling hallways of the palace, the opulent room she was led to, the plush carpeting, detailed tapestries, or hand-carved furniture. She saw only the bed, canopied and enormous, and then the backs of her eyelids as she sank into the extravagant mattress.

CHAPTER TWENTY-SIX

The Master of Jackals walked into the desert bearing only one skin
of water.

Are you not afraid? a boy cried, as Jackal disappeared into the
sands.

I will return or I will not, he said. My fear has no bearing
on the outcome.

—COLLECTED FOLKTALES

A knock at the door brought Jasminda fully awake. She garbled a
greeting and a tiny maid, not yet out of her teens, appeared with
yards of fabric in her arms.

"Have a nice rest, miss?" the girl said in a crisp city accent. Jasminda tried to prop herself on her elbows but gave up after a few
moments and collapsed back down.

"I've never slept better," she said, mostly to the pillow.

The girl chuckled, then flitted around the room, opening the
curtains. Late-afternoon sunshine filtered in.

"It's time to bathe and change, miss. The Prince Regent has requested you for dinner."

She startled into wakefulness. Was she to be the main course? Neither the servants last night nor this girl had reacted to her appearance, but Jasminda remained on her guard. Why could the prince want to dine with her? Jack must have set it up, though after enduring the suspicious glares and harsh words of the soldiers, she could not imagine the prince would be more welcoming to her than they had been. However, it stood to reason that Jack would be in attendance as well; he was the reason she was staying there, after all. Her excitement to be near him again grew as she followed the maid into the gold-trimmed bathroom.

Marble floors and walls greeted her. She gaped at the ivory-handled sinks with hot water flowing from the taps and marveled at the modern efficiency of a water closet with a seat that warmed her bottom. Papa had devised a plan for plumbing in the cabin, using some spell she suspected, but water had still needed to be heated on the stove.

The bathtub proved to be a stumbling block. The little maid was adamant about bathing her. Jasminda protested that she could very well bathe herself—she wasn't a child—but finally gave in to the girl's steely determination.

At least a bucketful of dirt disappeared down the drain. Her hair was washed and doused with a sweet-smelling concoction. Nadal—for if another woman was to see her naked, Jasminda insisted she should at least know her name—carefully combed Jasminda's thick, tightly coiled locks free of snags in front of the fire, drying it as much as possible. Then she helped Jasminda into a complicated dress she wasn't sure she'd be able to get out of again. At a gentle tap on the shoulder, Jasminda turned to face the full-length mirror in the dressing room.

She gasped at the vision in front of her. Shiny golden fabric flowed around her body, hugging her curves and making her appear, for the first time, like she was worthy of staying in the palace. Her hair was even tamed into a cascade of thick waves.

"You are a miracle worker," she praised Nadal, who blushed.

Nadal searched the pocket of her apron and pulled out a tiny oval mirror on a gold chain. "Where would you like it, miss?"

Jasminda gaped. "Who is it for?" Mourning mirrors like the one Nadal held were worn after the death of a loved one. It was said those in the World After could peer through the mirrors and say their final good-byes to the living. After Jasminda's mother died, she'd worn one around her neck for a year. When her father and brothers died, she hadn't had the heart.

"You haven't heard?" Nadal's hushed voice filled with wonder. "I'd thought since you arrived with . . . Miss, the Prince Regent has gone to the World After."

Jasminda took the mirror from the girl, gripping it lightly, and shook her head. "When did this happen? And how could he have invited me for dinner?"

"They made the announcement this morning, but he could have been dead for days. They never proclaim the death of a royal until his heir has been sworn in. Fear of attack during the changeover or some such. I heard from a girl who works in the prince's wing that she'd seen His Grace last week, Thirday. But she's just a duster, and she didn't see him that often." The torrent of words seemed to take something out of the girl, and she dropped her chin, staring at the floor as if embarrassed to have spoken at all.

"So the new prince invited me?" Her skin went clammy. The air in the room suddenly grew thin, as if Jasminda stood at the peak of a mountain. Jack had wanted to tell her something that night at the base, and again before they'd entered the palace. . . .

She shook her head, unwilling to believe such a thing. He was a warrior, and perhaps a poet. He was almost certainly not a . . . She couldn't even attach the word to him. An image of his face slightly twisted in one of his grim smiles filled her vision. He would have told her something so monumental.

"Is this dinner special in some way? Is it in honor of the prince?"

Nadal shook her head. "It is just dinner. The changeover is seamless. Outside, the people will mourn and most here will wear the mirrors for a week or so, but the business of the palace never stops, not even for death."

Jasminda sucked in a breath and fastened the gold chain around her neck. It fit snugly at the base of her throat. Not quite tight enough to choke her.

"It's time, miss," Nadal said.

Jasminda steeled her nerves and ignored the questions battling for dominance in her mind. They exited the rooms, and Nadal led her to the top of a grand staircase where a black-clad butler ushered her down and through a maze of hallways to a grand dining room. The grandeur of the palace was a blur, the empty feeling in her bones stealing most of her attention.

"Jasminda ul-Sarifor." A hush descended over the vast room as her name was announced by a silver-haired attendant. Every head swiveled in her direction, and she froze under the weight of expectation in the air. The sense of foreboding remained, but she tilted her chin a few notches higher and stepped farther into the hall. Yet another butler appeared at her elbow, a kind-faced man who, despite his Elsiran appearance, reminded her of Papa.

"Miss Jasminda, this way, please," he said, and led her deeper into the dining room. She followed his straight back, walking carefully in her delicate gold slippers. A four-piece string ensemble sat in the corner playing muted orchestral music. Three enormous U-shaped tables took up the majority of the room, with seating around the sides and a wide space for the servants to come and go in the middle. The end of the center table faced a slightly raised dais on which stood a smaller table. She surmised that must be where the Prince Regent sat. The space was magnificent—more carvings of the Lord and Lady adorned the tops of each window, and the ceiling was a grid of carved stone. Around each table sat several dozen people, all watching her. Conversations restarted, but the stares drilled into her as the butler led her to a setting only a half-dozen paces away from the dais.

She was seated next to a posh woman in an elaborate, feathered hat, her snakelike figure poured into a silken black sheath dress. Directly across from Jasminda, an old man with a hearing cone pressed to one ear and thick spectacles leaned toward the man to his right, complaining loudly of the noise. Each wore a mourning mirror. The most ostentatious display was from an older gentleman farther down the table whose mirror was affixed to his eye patch.

Jasminda fought the urge to squirm as the gazes of so many in the room raked over her, not bothering to hide their inquisitiveness. Her glass was filled by a passing waiter, and she grabbed at it, gulping greedily to soothe the sudden ache in her throat. The hall quieted again, and Jasminda turned to see what had captured everyone's attention this time.

A hidden door built into the wall behind the dais had opened. A group of guards in fancy black uniforms emerged, then flanked the door. Chairs groaned across the floor as everyone at the tables stood, almost as one. Jasminda raced to catch up.

The same man who had announced her stepped forward and cleared his throat. "Jaqros Edvard Alliaseen, High Commander of the Royal Army, First Duke of Cavill, and Prince Regent of Elsira."

The servant slid away, and Jasminda's heart dissolved into a pool of liquid at her feet. Directly in front of her, in full regalia, stood Jack.

CHAPTER TWENTY-SEVEN

The Master of Monkeys built a maze to dissuade those who would visit his home.

He received no visitors.

—COLLECTED FOLKTALES

Jasminda had thought him beautiful in dirty fatigues and covered in bruises and blood, but in his royal uniform and freshly trimmed hair, he was nothing short of divine. The spark of hope she'd held inside, the one she'd foolishly allowed to grow into a tiny flame, flickered then snuffed itself out completely.

Jack—*Prince* Jack—sat stiffly at the raised table mere steps away from her. His face was a rigid mask. He looked straight ahead, acknowledging no one.

The head butler was speaking again, making announcements about the dinner, the soup, the ingredients, but Jasminda's attention was wholly focused on the man in front of her.

Gone was the ragged creature she'd discovered on the mountain and thought mad, the bruised and bloodied soldier who had sacrificed himself to protect a woman he didn't know. A woman who could have been his enemy. When did he become this statue sitting before her, neither warrior nor poet, but prince?

The coronation must have happened as soon as he'd arrived in the palace, but even more than the shock at his new position, she couldn't believe how his whole nature seemed to have transformed. The light in his eyes that had withstood capture, gunshots, and beatings was now dimmed.

The kindly butler approached and cleared his throat politely, placing his hands on her chair. She pulled her attention away from Jack to find that she was the only one still standing. As every eye in the room, except Jack's, bored into her, she took her seat as gracefully as possible, smoothing her dress and thanking the butler in a trembling voice as he slid her chair in.

Her hands shook. She flattened them on the table, imprinting the grooves of the wood onto her palms. Anger flared hot for a moment, then melted just as suddenly into despair. Neither emotion would help her. She was lost in an unforgiving sea. There was no way to escape the glares from around the room, and the one person who had given her comfort during these past days of upheaval was now a stranger to her.

Tears stabbed the backs of her eyes. She used every trick she could to hold them back, resorting to digging her nails into the inside of her elbow until she could focus on the external pain a little more than the internal.

The first course began, and chatter resumed around the room. The soup set before her was completely foreign. The stunning silverware of her place setting offered four spoons. Jasminda took a deep breath and clasped her hands together, darting glances around the table. The woman next to her had already chosen a spoon, and Jasminda couldn't see from her position which one it had been.

She didn't want to make a misstep. Jack had invited her here, whatever his reasons were, whoever he was now, and she was determined to get through this meal with as much dignity as she could muster. She buried her shock and dismay, replacing it with determination. If she was the only *grol* these snooty city folk ever encountered, she wasn't going to give them any more fuel for their fire of scorn.

Jack filled her peripheral vision, but she refused to look at him again. He cleared his throat, then did so again a few moments later. A waiter hurried to tend to his water glass, but he brushed the man aside. The third time he cleared his throat she snapped her head toward him, narrowing her eyes and clenching her jaw against the swarm of emotion rising inside her.

He slowly drew his hand down and selected the second spoon from the left, all the time staring down at his bowl. At her place setting, she chose the same spoon. The woman next to her tilted her bowl toward her body, then shoveled the spoon in the opposite direction before bringing it to her mouth.

Jasminda glanced back at Jack as he slowly, slowly ate his soup in the same way. She copied his movements, happy to get something in her stomach. She had slept all day and hadn't eaten anything since the day before. Dinner went on like this, course after course. She would be presented with some new obstacle—bread, salad, three entrées—and Jack would model the behavior for her.

The Prince Regent—she vowed to stop being so familiar with him, even in her head—did not speak to anyone during dinner, and this appeared to be taken as normal by those present. It made her feel better that she would not have to talk to him. Just hearing his voice would make it that much harder to mend the gaping hole inside her.

Blessedly, after what felt like hours, dinner finally ended. The last dessert dishes were cleared away by the staff, and the various characters at the table patted their bellies obnoxiously. Jasminda had never eaten so much food at one time in her life. Guiltily, she thought of the refugees. What rations had they been provided? Her meal sank like lead in her stomach.

The company rose from the table and, just when she thought there would be a reprieve from the unrelenting pressure of the evening, the butlers ushered everyone into a huge adjoining sitting room. Small groups split off and clustered around settees or card tables, chatting amiably. Jack was nowhere to be seen. Jasminda stood alone next to the massive fireplace, enduring the uncomfortable heat.

Glances sent her way ranged from mere curiosity to outright contempt. Her back remained straight, head high, but inside, she was wilting.

A girl about her age approached the other end of the fireplace, setting a glass on the mantel. She stood for a moment peering at the flames before approaching Jasminda. Slender and beautiful, she wore a peach-and-gold dress that made her skin appear to glow. Amber eyes the color of her hair appraised Jasminda, not unkindly.

"These things are positively awful."

Jasminda stared at her, unsure of the girl's intentions.

"I'm Lizvette." She held out her hands.

"Jasminda." She placed her palms to Lizvette's and pressed gently.

"Welcome. I'm told you're responsible for saving the life of our new prince." Lizvette's friendly smile seemed genuine, but Jasminda did not dare attempt a connection to Earthsong to determine her true intentions. She scanned the room to find they had attracted a great deal of attention.

"I did save him once, or perhaps twice. But I cannot take credit for the last time."

"Our Jack, always getting into trouble." Lizvette smiled, but her eyes were lakes of sadness.

"You are . . . friends with the Prince Regent?"

Her smile changed, though Jasminda could not determine precisely what was different about it. It was bleaker, perhaps. "I was betrothed to his brother."

"May he find serenity in the World After," Jasminda responded, bowing her head. Lizvette repeated the blessing. Jasminda considered the young woman's dress more closely. What she'd initially thought was shiny gold beading were actually dozens of mirrors embroidered into the material. A conspicuous show of grief that seemed at odds with Lizvette's unassuming manner.

There were not enough mirrors in the world to adequately represent everything Jasminda mourned. So many lives gone, so many failures. She'd thought for a moment as she lay beside Jack that perhaps . . . But now that was gone, too. Perhaps it was for the best. She did not want to imagine the look in his eyes when she failed him, too.

An exceptionally tall man stalked toward them, his face contorted in indignation. She could read his intention quite clearly without Earthsong and took a step backward. Lizvette followed Jasminda's gaze and turned to face him. He took hold of Lizvette's elbow and leaned down to whisper loudly in her ear.

"What do you think you're doing?"

"I'm greeting our visitor, Zavros. She is the Prince Regent's guest. Jasminda, this is my cousin—"

"It's time to go, Lizvette. You're keeping your father waiting."

Lizvette smiled apologetically at Jasminda. "It was lovely meeting you. I'm sure we'll be seeing each other again soon. May She bless your dreams."

Jasminda repeated the farewell and stood rigidly as Lizvette was towed away to a card table in the back. The blazing fire had grown unbearable, and the perimeter around her was a quarantine zone. What a surprise not to be the belle of the ball. With a final glance about the room, in which she refused to admit she was searching for Jack, she slipped out the door.

Thick silence draped the empty hallway; each direction stretched on identically. She had absolutely no idea how to get back to her rooms. With no orientation or memory of the route she'd taken to get to the dining room, she took a few tentative steps to the left before a voice halted her progress.

"Leaving?"

She turned to find Jack standing behind her, regal and gorgeous. He was so close, but now untouchable. She hardened her features, not looking directly at him, not wanting to give away the storm of emotions fighting for dominance within her. Her fists clenched and opened as her body stiffened with tension. Traitorous tears welled; she blinked them back.

"I'm not sure if I should bow or curtsy or what," she said, gripping her hands in front of her to stop their movement.

"I am sorry I didn't tell you," he said, voice pitched low. "I wanted to. I should have. It's inexcusable, I just . . ."

She longed to hear an excuse that would satisfy her and return things to the way they were. No words came. He shook his head and rubbed at his chest, just below his collarbone where his bullet wound had been.

"Jasminda." He stepped closer, and she took a step back.

"That wound was healed. Does it still bother you?"

He dropped his hand to his side and drew even closer, backing her against the wall. She stared at the carpet, but he tilted her face up with a finger on her chin. Wanting to numb herself to the feeling of his skin on hers, she refused to meet his eyes and focused instead on his chest, covered in rich-looking fabric with brightly colored insignias on his uniform. He released her chin, but she stubbornly continued avoiding his face.

"Jasminda," he repeated. Her name on his lips was more than she could bear. "If I could change who I am, I'd do it in a heartbeat. You deserved the truth. I owed you that much."

"You can have no debt to me. I helped a captive soldier, not a prince." As much as she tried to avoid it, she was drawn to him. Perhaps this was the last time she'd be this close to him. The tears escaped; she could not stop them. "Now if you'll excuse me, Your Grace, I have urgent business in my room that needs attending to. Pleasant evening."

She slid out of the cage of his body and gave a wobbly curtsy before picking up her beautiful skirt and running. When one hallway ended, she picked another at random. She had no idea where she was going, but she'd rather be lost in the palace for a thousand years than see Prince Jack again.

Blinded by her tears, she finally stopped in a blue hallway full of mirrors. She leaned against a little table but refused to look at her face, ashamed of her reaction to him. He could no longer be Jack. He could no longer be her hope. He could be nothing to her at all.

CHAPTER TWENTY-EIGHT

*The Mistress of Frogs held a banquet for her closest friends.
Friendship is like a mirage in the desert, she said. It gives you
great hope and encouragement when you need it the most.*

—COLLECTED FOLKTALES

"One of the maids escorted her to her chambers," Usher said, entering the dimly lit space. Jack paused midstep from where he'd been pacing the floor of his sitting room, only half listening to the evening news.

"Thank you, Usher. Make sure she has a servant assigned to her at all times so she doesn't become lost again."

The old man nodded.

"But don't let her know that I ordered it. I don't think she would like that."

To his credit, Usher didn't even raise an eyebrow. The valet had been with Jack's family since before he was born. The old man's kindly face was a warmer, more familiar sight than his own father's had been. Jack switched off the radiophonic, silencing the newsreader midsentence, then fell into an armchair in front of the fireplace. He could not begrudge Jasminda her anger and pain. It had been unacceptable for him to keep the truth from her.

But each chance he'd had to tell her—that night at the base, or the morning before they'd left for Rosira when he could have found a quiet place to explain—he'd avoided it. Reality was coming faster than he had wanted, and he'd been certain he could outpace it.

His return had been chaotic, with the secret coronation last night and then a flurry of briefings. He'd ordered the bulk of the armed forces to the eastern border in preparation for the breach, and logistics had taken up much of his time.

Aside from the pending disaster with Lagrimar, he'd had calls with the leaders of their allies Fremia and Yaly, letters to read and sign, introductions to staff and security personnel to make. He'd hardly looked up when he was being called for dinner, and then it was too late.

He'd been a fool—and worse, a cowardly one. His desire to put off any change to the way she saw him had won out over his good sense, and Jasminda had suffered. The weight of the crown threatened to press him down into the earth.

But her expression as she'd stood in the dining hall, the devastation marring her lovely face, made him feel like a villain. It gutted him. The guilt and shame were heavier than the crown.

Somehow, he could not keep the women in his life from hating him.

"Has word been sent to my mother?"

"Yes, sir. But it may be some time before she receives the message."

The last he'd heard, his mother was cloistered in a jungle sanctuary, hours from the nearest Fremian city. "She finally has her wish—her son is the Prince Regent. Too late to do her any good."

The little he'd heard of the news report had confirmed his fears that his coronation was being met with more than a few misgivings. His mother's defection to Fremia, Elsira's southern neighbor, twelve years earlier had cast a long shadow, especially on her only son.

"I only hope she's found peace," Usher said.

Jack hoped so as well. He stared at the crackling fire until the flames burned themselves into his vision. His fingers picked at the fringe on his jacket, unraveling one of the threads, and he tapped an impatient rhythm on his knee.

"Say what you must," he said, after the silence had grown more oppressive than companionable.

Usher's bushy gray eyebrows rose. "What makes you think I have something to say?"

"Twenty-two years of knowing you, old man. And I suspect I won't like whatever it is, so spit it out."

"I believe I said everything I had to say before you left on your foolhardy mission."

Jack raked a hand through his hair. "Protecting Elsira is my only mission, and I would do anything, even sacrifice myself, to see that happen. The opportunity was once in a lifetime, too great to miss."

"The opportunity for the army's High Commander to go undercover in enemy territory? It is unheard of."

"I was the only one for it. The only Elsiran to speak their bloody language well enough to blend in with them. If I hadn't gone and verified what they were planning, the Council would never release funds for the preparation we need. We would have been blindsided by the breach." Although if he'd acted with more circumspection, the cornerstone might still be intact, but he could not say those words out loud.

"You paid a heavy cost for that information, young sir."

Jack absently rubbed the place on his chest where the bullet had pierced his flesh. The pain had been gone for days, but now there was a phantom ache. He must have been imagining it. "I don't regret accepting the mission."

"And being captured?" Usher's voice was soft, without a hint of censure, but a pinprick of guilt stabbed at Jack.

The fire crackled and jumped, flames leaping upward. The vibrancy of the fire reminded him of her, on the porch with her shotgun, of the blade she kept strapped to her leg. Fearsome beauty. The pain in his chest shifted and grew. It lay mere inches from his heart.

"Being captured nearly killed me. But it also brought me a wonderful gift."

He slumped down in his chair. When had he come to care so much for her? She had been a bright light at the end of a tunnel of pain and desperation, but what Jack felt was not merely due to the debt he owed her for saving him, not just for her kindness toward him. She was strong, with a sharp mind, passionate, and brave. So unlike the giggling, gossiping society girls who had vied for his affection for so many years. Jasminda slit a man's throat and kept her wits about her, for Sovereign's sake; she had a warrior's heart.

Usher steepled his fingers below his chin. "This gift you speak of, is it the kind worth keeping?"

Jack looked up sharply.

"Is it the kind that you would regret allowing to slip through your fingers?" the old man asked.

"She is angry and hurt. I was, if not dishonest, at least not forth-coming. She has every right—"

"You do not balk at walking across enemy lines and pretending to be one of them, at great peril, I might add, yet you quiver with fear at one young woman."

"I'm not quivering with fear," Jack scoffed.

"I believe I see a quiver, young sir. Just there." Usher extended his finger, waggling it about, pointing at most of Jack's body.

A smile edged its way across Jack's face. "The Queen Who Sleeps must have a sense of humor to send you to look after me."

"That She must," Usher said.

Jack regarded the fire for another moment before jumping from his seat, what he must do now suddenly clear. "And I thank Her every day for that," he said, kissing Usher on the forehead.

He raced out of the room and down the corridor, flying up the stairs to the great alarm of several passing servants. Jasminda's rooms in the guest wing were on the other side of the palace. He wished she were closer, though visiting her rooms, wherever they were and especially at this hour, was unseemly and could put her reputation in jeopardy. Based on the chilly reception she'd received from the gathered aristocracy at dinner, however, her current reputation was no great asset.

Jack had been caught in the dining hall after dinner by Minister Stevenot, who had profusely dispatched his condolences. Over his shoulder, through the cracked door to the adjoining parlor, he'd watched, heartsick, as Jasminda stood alone, an island in an unfriendly sea. He'd been on his way to her when Lizvette approached Jasminda, and her kindness filled him with gratitude.

As if conjured by his thoughts, Lizvette now appeared on the staircase above him in the grand hall.

"Your Grace," she said, curtseying, an amused smile playing upon her lips.

He climbed up to the landing to stand beside her. "You know, you must try to keep a straight face when you say that."

She nodded, her eyes alight. "I shall keep that in mind." Her expression sobered, and she laid a hand on his arm. "I haven't gotten a chance to tell you how sorry I am for the loss of your brother."

"No, I'm sorry I haven't been to see you. And for your loss. Not only a husband gone, but you were to be the princess."

Her lips pressed to a thin line. "Yes, well, Mother and Father are inconsolable." Her voice was light, but shadows danced in her eyes.

He and Lizvette had raced around the palace as children, under the disapproving eyes of their parents. Her father had been a close friend and advisor to his, and still retained a place on the Council. She and his brother had been engaged for two years and were to be married in just a few weeks.

"And you?" Jack asked, craning his neck down to look her in the eye.

"It happened so fast." She dipped her head and ran her fingers across the mirrors embedded in her gown, avoiding his gaze. "Alariq did love his gadgets, though. He would probably have lived in that airship if he could have." She managed a weak smile. "I can't imagine what was going through his mind, piloting through that kind of storm."

"Nor I. He was always so reasonable. I just hope I'm up to the task of filling his shoes."

"You are. Of course you are. You will be a wonderful prince." She finally met his eyes, beaming up at him, though her smile overflowed with sadness. She took hold of his hand and squeezed. He hoped she was holding up well, despite appearing so tired. Dark circles under her eyes were starting to show through her makeup.

"I don't want to keep you," he said, pulling away. She held on a moment longer before releasing him.

"Whatever are you doing on this end of the palace?"

He shifted on his feet, his gaze involuntarily drawn toward the hall leading to Jasminda's room.

Lizvette looked, then frowned slightly. She sighed. "Are you . . . *with* her?"

"I owe her an apology. One that is overdue."

Lizvette took a step back. "The whole palace is talking. They're watching her. Wondering."

"I don't have time for Rosiran busybodies." Indignation shaded his voice.

"Jack, she will be trouble for you."

His protective instincts kicked in. Jasminda was not anyone else's concern. She belonged here, had more right than most who called the palace home.

The worry in Lizvette's face cut through his rising ire. His anger was not for her. "May She bless your dreams, Vette."

"And yours as well, Your Grace."

He walked away, his skin prickling with the sensation of being watched until he turned the corner.

CHAPTER TWENTY-NINE

The Mistress of Horses oft traversed the countryside at night singing the moon's song. Sometimes the moon would sing back.

—COLLECTED FOLKTALES

Jack stood outside Jasminda's door, gathering his courage before knocking rapidly. His breathing grew shallow as the seconds ticked by. When the door finally opened, he schooled his features, attempting to hide his wonder. She was radiant in the outfit she'd worn at dinner. The gorgeous golden dress highlighted the color of her skin and made him want to feel its softness. Her hair was tamed somewhat, but still wild, gorgeous, and free, like her. But her eyes were red-rimmed from crying.

That phantom ache above his heart flared again. He rubbed at it unconsciously. She studied his movement, worry creasing her forehead. He swallowed the lump in his throat and bowed low, causing her to take a step back.

"Excuse me, my lady, but you inquired as to the completeness of my healing. I . . . I fear I may have reinjured myself and wondered if you would be so kind as to inspect it for me."

She tilted her head up at him, her brow furrowed. He was afraid she would shut the door in his face at so flimsy an excuse. Instead, she took another step back, allowing him entry. She turned on her heel and headed to the fireplace where a chair had been dragged over quite close to the flames.

"Are the palace physicians not up to the task, Your Grace?" She motioned to the chair; he sank into it.

"They are the best in the land."

"I'm having trouble singing here. There are too many people. But I can take a look." The bag she'd brought from home lay on the floor, and she crouched, retrieving her jar of balm. She approached him, her focus solely on the spot beneath his clothes where the wound had been. When her eyes finally met his, something passed between them, but she firmed her mouth into a frown. "That will have to come off," she said, motioning to his covered chest.

He unbuttoned his coat and laid it aside, then undid his dress shirt and slid out of it. Her focus never left his chest the entire time. When he'd disrobed enough, she knelt in front of him, one hand resting on his thigh, the other gently prodding the newly healed skin.

"What makes you think you've reinjured yourself?" she said, voice full of accusation. "Your Grace," she added, yanking her fingers away.

"Because it hurts. Just here." He pulled her hand back, holding it in place against his heart. "And don't call me that. I'm still Jack."

Her lips trembled, the pools of her eyes swam with tears. "No, you're not just Jack anymore. You never were."

She again tried to draw her hand away, but he held on tight, grasping the other, as well, and bringing them up to meet. He stroked her silken skin and lifted her joined hands to his lips, kissing each softly then placing a palm on each side of his face.

"I'm sorry, Jasminda." He squeezed his eyes shut, unable to take the pain evident on her face.

"What are you sorry for?"

"For not telling you. For being unable to be just Jack for you. Trust me, I never wanted any of this."

"Why not?"

"My elder brother was groomed to rule. I was never as smart or accomplished as he. Never as good at all of this." He waved at the lavish room. "Most of my childhood was spent in barracks, training for the army. I don't believe I'll ever feel like a prince, not on the inside. I should have told you . . . I just couldn't bear to."

Her thumbs skimmed his cheeks, and she slid out of his grasp to brush his forehead, his chin. A finger grazed his lips, causing him to shudder.

She kept hold of his face but rose from the ground and sat on his knee, leaning her forehead to meet his. He wrapped his arms around her waist and held her tight, never wanting to let go.

"I don't know what to do with you," she whispered, stroking his face, her lips a breath from his own. "I cannot keep you, but I cannot turn you away."

Jack nudged her head up and drank her in. When her gaze dropped to his lips, he leaned forward, capturing her mouth. They kissed tentatively at first. He allowed her to explore, touching her lips softly to his, then with more pressure. Eventually, she tilted her head and opened for him. He caressed her tongue, his control nearly slipping when she groaned into his mouth.

She gripped the back of his head tighter, her mouth hungrily attacking his. Her taste was so sweet, the scent of her slowly driving him crazy. He pulled away, but she leaned in, not letting him go.

"Last night I . . . Perhaps we should slow down," he said, shifting her in his lap, moving her away from his rapidly growing erection. His desire for her was intense, but she would likely need time to trust him. He couldn't push. It was enough that she was in his arms again.

Her chest heaved, thrusting her breasts up seductively as she sat atop him, eyes still closed, kiss-swollen lips slightly apart. "Slow down?"

"Yes, darling. I may be a prince, but I'm only human." That night at the base he'd lain awake, convinced every nerve ending in his body was connected to the place where their hands had touched. Now, she was so much closer and he was having an even harder time holding himself back. "I don't want you to feel pressured."

She dragged her hands through his hair, igniting sparks of pleasure that rolled down his spine.

"I want you to be certain . . . ." He sucked in a breath as she ran her fingers down his chest, then up again. She ducked her head and kissed his collarbone. He did not trust himself for much longer.

"Jasminda." He groaned.

She shifted her knee ever so slightly, rubbing against his straining crotch. "Yes?" She smiled wickedly, her mouth edging closer to his nipple.

"You're killing me."

"Then let it be a warm death," she said, hiking up her skirt so she could fully straddle him.

CHAPTER THIRTY

When the Master of Sharks met his beloved, he longed to gather all the roses of the world for her.

His sister, Eagle, warned that tenderness can be a torturous touch.

—COLLECTED FOLKTALES

Sitting on his lap, she delighted in his unmistakable desire for her as it settled between her legs. A blast of pleasure assaulted her as she brushed against his hardness. She should have been appalled at her forwardness. The rich city girls he was used to were probably far more demure. Even prettied up in a fine gown after a fancy bath, Jasminda would never be like them. But he had come to her. He wanted her. It was not possible, and yet here he was.

Jack's skin burned beneath her hands. The contrast of hard and soft made her fingers long to stroke him everywhere.

He stilled her hands. "Jasminda, are you certain?" The heat in his eyes was tempered with concern.

She nodded. "I would like to have this with you." Unspoken was the reality that this could well be her only chance. He could be her lover. Perhaps not for more than this one night, but if that was all she had, then she would take it and hold it close in her memory forever.

"You have done this before, I would imagine." She laughed at his sheepish expression. "Handsome soldiers are not the lonely sort." She pressed a kiss to his forehead, nose, and lips, then brought his hand to her breast and trapped it under hers. "You can show me."

"But I've . . . I don't want you to think . . ." He shook his head. "It was different before."

She sat back, dropping his hand, her skin rapidly cooling. "Am I so different?"

"You are. In every way."

Her mind raced as doubts swarmed. She drew away and moved to stand, but he wrapped his arms around her.

"Jasminda, don't mistake me. You are like nothing I ever thought possible. Like no one else I have ever met. And I am glad of it. You are remarkable."

She did not want to feel the joy his words inspired, the resurgence of hope within her. Nothing had changed. He was still a prince and she a farm girl with the wrong skin color and too much magic. Tonight was just a night. But as his arms tightened, pressing her against him, her heart threatened to revolt.

He kissed the shell of her ear, her jaw, her chin. "I will show you, if you will show me."

"Show you what?" she whispered as his tongue tickled her neck.

"Your secrets."

"I haven't any secrets."

He focused on her other ear, tugging on her lobe with his teeth. She shivered, the tiny motion sending a spark all the way to her toes.

"Your body begs to differ." He stood, lifting her easily. After she settled on her feet, he leaned in for another endless kiss. Molten longing pooled between her legs.

"There is sylfimweed in the kitchens, I trust?" she asked.

"I should think so, with the number of soldiers I reprimand for being found sneaking out of storerooms with maids." He placed a hand on her belly. The thought of having his child was not something she could entertain at the moment. Yet another fanciful idea to quell. She would go to the kitchens in the morning to obtain the herb.

Jack frowned as he pressed against her stomach. Thinking of half-breed bastards, no doubt. Before she could reassure him that she had no such designs, he kneeled and placed a kiss over her navel through her dress. She froze. He reached down to the hem of her dress, then slid his hands underneath to caress her ankles and legs. Her breath hitched. She needed the damnable dress off. Now.

Fumbling with the strap wrapped around her bosom, she found the end and gave it a strong tug, causing most of it to unravel. Jack watched with rapt attention as the dress loosened and eventually gave way, leaving her top half bare and only a thin silk slip covering her bottom half.

Hot with undiluted desire, his eyes traveled up her body to meet hers. Never breaking their locked stare, she walked backward to the four-poster bed overtaking the room and sat facing Jack. He still kneeled by the fireplace, staring at her.

She crawled back until she hit the pillows, then lay down, her legs barely spread apart. Jack prowled in her direction like a cat ready to pounce. He grasped one leg, tugging it to the side, mirrored the movement with the other leg, and then crawled between them.

A shiver rippled through her as he caressed her legs, hands sliding under her slip, running up her thighs, pulling the material up to her waist.

"No knife?" He sounded disappointed.

"It didn't match the dress."

The silky scrap of underwear Nadal had provided for her was all the protection she had from his thumbs as they ran up and down her. He kissed her once there, through the fabric, before moving his tongue up her stomach to circle her navel. The anticipation of feeling him inside her swelled.

He worshipped her body with his tongue, pressing kisses every place he could reach. Hands on the curves of her bottom, he spread her legs wider, settling his weight between them. Jasminda arched up, wanting more but at the same time longing to touch him, too. She freed her arms from her sides and slid her hands down his back, digging her nails into his flesh when he did something particularly delightful with his tongue or fingers.

The panties had to come off. Jack's head popped up, focused on the material sliding down her legs before she kicked them away. She reached for the front of his trousers but stopped, perplexed at how to undo them.

He grinned and showed her the buckles and buttons, easing them off along with his drawers. She sat up, enthralled with the sight of him. She reached out for him, stroking his length. His eyes closed on a hissed breath. Jasminda loved learning him, changing the pressure and monitoring his reaction as she squeezed and caressed.

With a low rumble in his throat, he pulled away and came to

rest on top of her, bringing his face close to hers. He was settled at her entrance but made no move to go farther. Just cupped her face and kissed her silly once again. She wrapped her legs around him, urging him to keep going, to go all the way.

He eased a hand between their bodies and stroked her. She tried to widen her legs even more. Finally, one finger worked its way inside her. She bucked and wriggled beneath him, wanting more, and he chuckled softly before inserting another finger and working them in and out of her, sliding deliciously.

She moaned when his thumb circled her most sensitive area. He kissed and caressed her, creating an amazing buildup of longing and desire. She teetered on the precipice, overwhelmed by what was coming, when he pulled out his hand.

Gasping at the loss, she looked up at him, wide-eyed. He positioned himself once again at her entrance, his expression seeking approval.

"Jack," she cried. "Please."

With permission granted, he eased himself into her. A sharp, stinging sensation accompanied the feeling of being stretched wide. She strained as he pushed farther inside her and focused on his face inches from her own. The discomfort was expected, and tempered in large part by her excitement.

Their pelvises met, and she curled her legs tight around his waist.

"Are you all right?" he whispered.

She kissed him in response. "What happens now?"

"Now I start moving, but I want to be sure not to hurt you."

She wriggled against him, delighted by the fullness of his invasion of her body. Jack grimaced, the tension of not moving evident in the veins bulging in his forehead and neck.

"You're not hurting me," she said, and kissed him again. He slid out of her a bit then plunged back in, then did it again with a gentle movement, a rocking in and out of her, creating a sweet friction between them.

Jack voiced unintelligible, impassioned sounds, his arms straining as he kept the majority of his weight off her. Their dual rhythms harmonized as they moved together.

She ran her hands down his back and even lower, wanting to push him even deeper inside her, wanting to hold all of him with her body. When he sped up his pace, she matched him, and the wave built up again. It rose, rose, rose, until she didn't think anything could ever be better.

Then it broke, a dam shattering, and she came completely apart, nothing but pleasure rushing through her unbridled. She screamed but wasn't aware of it until the rawness in her throat brought her back to reality and the crest that felt like it had lasted a lifetime slowly faded away.

Her breath came in short bursts, and Jack, on top of her, was doing little better. His face was flushed, and sweat dripped from his hair down to his chin. He gave her a look of pure tenderness and peppered her face with more kisses. He remained inside of her, still pleasant, even as his swell reduced. When he moved to get off her, she clutched him to her more firmly.

"No, not yet."

He rolled them onto their sides, still intertwined, still one. Jasminda wiped the sweat from his brow and kissed him everywhere she could reach.

"Jack."

"Yes, my darling?" he said, breathless.

"Just . . . Jack," she said, and smiled. He brought her even closer, kissing her until they both had to stop to catch their breaths again.

She locked her legs tighter around him, determined to imprint this moment not just in her memory but into her skin, her bones, her soul, and her Song. When she left, it would be all she had to remember him by.

CHAPTER THIRTY-ONE

Shark wished for Eagle's prophetic knowledge, and Eagle envied Shark's generosity.
  And the petals of their closeness wilted.

—COLLECTED FOLKTALES

Jasminda reveled in the feel of Jack's fingers winding through her hair as they lay in the enormous bed. "I have something for you," he said.

"What is it?" She grinned and he beamed down at her, appearing lost for a moment. Then he shook his head as if coming out of a fog and stood, crossing the room to his discarded jacket.

Jasminda appreciated the view of his strong back and the muscles working there and lower. He turned to find her staring and flushed, his face and chest growing red.

"Am I not supposed to look?" she asked saucily.

He shook his head and returned to the bed, a thin, rectangular box in his hand. Gathering her again into his chest, he held the box out. She brushed her fingertips across dark blue velvet emblazoned with Elsira's crest and looked up at him questioningly.

"Open it."

Gingerly, she plucked the box from his palm and lifted the lid. A shiny gold medal winked up at her in the dim light. A five-pointed star with the profile of a man wearing a crown at its center hung from a wide blue-and-gold ribbon. Around the man's head circled the words IN FEAST AND IN FAMINE WE SUSTAIN.

"It's the Order of the Grainbearer. Elsira's highest honor for service to the crown." Jack's voice was full of pride.

Jasminda's heart stopped beating. "For me?"

He squeezed her shoulder. "You saved my life. This is just a token, but you deserve it."

"But . . . but . . ."

"There's generally a nomination process and months of paper-work and a fancy ceremony, but I didn't want to wait for all that. I may do away with it entirely from now on. I just went into the storage room where they keep these and got one for you."

Her mouth gaped open.

"Don't worry. It's official. I signed you into the registry myself."

She snapped her jaw closed, but a minute passed before she could form words. "Thank you."

"I suppose I should call you Dame Jasminda now." He smiled and bowed. She laid her head on his chest again, admiring the finery of the medal. On record as having been of service to her nation. A lump grew in her throat.

Somewhere, a clock struck midnight.

"You know, it may be easier if . . ." Jack trailed off. Jasminda lifted her head, not liking the tone of his voice.

"If what?"

He stroked a hand across her jaw. "I don't want them to make

your life here miserable. There will be questions, speculation ...
gossip. About us." Worried eyes searched her face.

The tiny light that had flickered to life in the center of her chest
faltered. But she'd known. When he'd showed up at her door, she'd
known. When she'd let him in, and when she'd chosen to go down
this path, she knew where it would lead and where it would not.

"So what would be easier?" The question fell from her lips on a
whisper. She must not have done enough to mask her feelings, for
he pulled her closer, tightening his grip around her.

"If we remain discreet." His voice wavered. That tiny wobble
stole the strength from her growing hurt. It was not exactly a rejec-
tion, but the reality was clear. He could never truly be hers. He
belonged to the people now, and the people were fickle masters.

"You are right," she said to his chest, then pressed a kiss there to
show she bore no ill will about the state of affairs. She did not. If
her heart broke the tiniest bit, it was only because she had allowed
it to grow weak and sentimental. That would never do.

She sat up, pulling herself out of the fortress of safety his arms
provided. "This is no one's business but ours. We don't ever have to
speak of it again, if you'd prefer."

"No, that's not what I ..." He reached for her, but she pulled
away, turning to sit on the edge of the bed with her back to him.

"You should probably go. You will be missed if you leave it until
morning." She wished she had something to cover herself with.
There were robes in the great wardrobe hulking in the corner of the
room. She'd peeked in it earlier. All she had to do was walk over
there and retrieve one, but she did not trust her shaky legs.

Tears formed in the corners of her eyes, and she pushed them
back. She tried to force that same will into her legs to push her to
stand, but just when she thought she'd found the strength, nimble
hands enfolded her waist, sliding her across the bed. Jack turned

her over until she was on her back with him straddling her, his face inches from her own.

He kissed her. She closed her eyes involuntarily and lost herself in it. Even if by some miracle she found someone to kiss again, it would never be like this.

"If you want me to tell the world, I will," he said. "I will call for a press conference on the steps of the palace and shout your name from every roof and balcony." He placed kisses down her jaw, pausing to nuzzle the crook of her neck and inhale deeply.

She threaded her fingers through his hair, so short now there was barely anything to hold on to, and pulled his head up so she could peer into his eyes. "Don't be ridiculous."

"I don't want you to think that I . . . that I care what anyone else thinks. I just don't want it to be harder for you than it has to be."

"All right." A quiet acceptance of an unavoidable fact. "What have you said about my presence here?"

He settled onto his elbows, still on top of her, and her center warmed at the press of him against her.

"You are my honored guest. You saved my life at great risk to yourself, and are welcome to stay as long as you like." He grasped a lock of her hair between his finger and thumb. "I will erase the debt. Your taxes. I would have done it anyway."

She shook her head and looked around the room; even in the dark its finery was visible. "I don't want to owe you any more than I do already."

"You owe me nothing—"

She hushed him with a finger across his lips.

"I will not allow you to lose your home," he said around her fingers.

"I don't intend to. I'm going to lodge my appeal in person tomorrow at the Bureau of Taxation. It's my last day to do so, and my case is solid."

"I know it is. I'll have Usher, my valet, assign you a driver. You can go and get it cleared up."

"Thank you." She smiled, battling the sadness that kept creeping in from the corners. The clock struck the quarter hour.

"You really should go and get some sleep," she said, smoothing a finger across his brow. "Can you discreetly get back to your rooms?"

He sighed, rising to a knee. "I can use the back passageways. There are secret corridors throughout the palace too narrow for the servants to bother with. I used to hide in them as a child." He reached for her. "How I wish I could stay beside you the whole night."

She did not give voice to all the things she wished that would never be.

He stood, finally, retrieving his scattered clothing and dressing. Jasminda admired each of his body parts as they were hidden from her view. When he looked at her one last time, she glimpsed a well of pain inside him she had never seen before, one that tugged at her in a new way. And it made it all the more difficult when he kissed her good-bye and walked out the door.

CHAPTER THIRTY-TWO

"Lady Oola, are you ready to begin?" My cousin Vaaryn stands in the center of the amphitheater that is the Assembly Room. Rows of benches spiral around him, filled with the other children of the Founders. He is aged and stooping, the eldest of the Thirds. Next to him, spine as rigid and unyielding as his face, sits my beloved Eero.

When I shudder, Yllis squeezes my hand. I stand, all the heavier for the weight pressing against my heart, and force myself to look upon my twin.

"Eero, son of Peedar, second-born to the ninth child of the Founders, what say you to the crimes of which you are accused?" My voice sounds strong, but inside I quiver from nerves. The closest relative of the accused must stand up for him in Assembly, but I do not want to be here, not as observer, judge, or Advocate.

"My only crime, sister"—the word is a sneer falling from his mouth—"was being born Silent in a world of Songbearers." He is not chained or bound in any way and crosses his arms in front of him defiantly.

I clear my throat and take a breath, still amazed at the cruel way he speaks to me now. "Your crime is the kidnapping of Sayya, Fourth descendant of the Founders. Do you deny this?"

He looks straight ahead, his gaze boring into the wall. "As a Third descendant, I see no reason to dignify this proceeding with a response."

I swallow. "As you well know, only Songbearers are counted in the line of descendants. The Silent are not—"

"Did you not gift me part of your Song, sister? Does that not make me a Songbearer?" The accusation in his voice cuts me. There are so many feelings swirling inside—anger, pain, despair, even hatred. The person before me cannot be my beloved brother. He simply cannot be.

I step closer, and Yllis rises beside me, lending his support, as always. "You are not a Songbearer, and it was my mistake to use that spell. I take responsibility for that. Because I love you and would do anything for you."

"Anything?" The venom in that one word burns.

"Anything but give you more of the power you abused. You forced me to cut you off by your actions."

"I was innovating, the way the Cantors do."

"You set things out of balance. Earthsong is not to be used for better prices in the marketplace or to cheat at cards. You cannot ruin a crop because a farmer insulted you." Tears well even as the anger rears its head. "And you cannot steal a girl away from her bed at night and attempt to force her to gift you her Song!" I do not ask the question I want, whether he has actually found a way to take power from someone. The fact that he tried with Sayya must mean that he has discovered some new way—a way that does not require Earthsong.

A shiver rolls through me. I force myself to fulfill my role as Advocate. "You have heard the accusation and evidence presented against you. And as you have not denied it, now is the time. Unburden your conscience."

He shakes his head, and a smirk crosses his face. "You all think you can continue to subjugate us. That the Silent will continue living as second-

class citizens for the rest of time. Sayya made me believe that she cared for me, but when I offered for her she could not bear to wed a Silent. And now my own sister forsakes me. This Assembly is a sham. If you want to judge me of a crime, then have my peers judge me. Why are there no Silent in the Assembly? Why must we make do with the scraps of life while Songbearers reap all the benefits?"

"What are you talking about, Eero?" I crouch down, near enough to look into his eyes, yet far enough so that he cannot reach out and strike me. The fact that I even think this is a possibility is sad proof of how much has changed over the past two seasons. Last summer he was the other half of my heart, but by the time the leaves fell from the trees, he had become my enemy.

"There are no Silent in the Assembly because only a Songbearer can read a man's heart, can know the truth buried within. How can a Silent judge? What scraps has life given you? We ate at the same table, all our lives. What inequities have you suffered, brother, that makes you hate us so?" My voice cracks on this last sentiment.

His eyes harden, but still he does not look at me. His jaw is set, and his body may as well be made of stone. As his Advocate, I cannot use Earthsong to determine his state of mind, but as his twin I would never need to.

Yllis pulls on my shoulder gently, and I allow him to lead me back to my seat. Vaaryn struggles to his feet and calls upon Cadda, Sayya's mother and Advocate, to have the final word.

"It is so rare for us to hold one of our own in judgment; crime in our land is so infrequent. The guidance of the Founders steers us toward mercy." Her voice is soothing and calm. "Though my daughter was troubled greatly by Eero's actions, she was not harmed. We ask for his captivity so that a Healer may give him the aid and comfort he so obviously needs."

Eero snorts and rolls his eyes.

Vaaryn stands before Eero, and suddenly my brother's expression freezes. He rises into the air, his arms locked to his sides, his legs still bent in the sitting position. For criminal proceedings, a random sampling of nine Assembly members serve as judges, communicating using Earthsong to make their decision. Eero floats for a few moments until Vaaryn speaks again.

"The Assembly agrees with the recommendation of Cadda. It is decided that Eero, son of Peedar, will be delivered to the Healers, who will tend to his mental instability until a time wherein he is determined to again be in his right mind."

"Be it so," the Assembly says in unison.

I do not want it to be so, but I cannot change reality. I watch my brother float away and wonder when I will see him again.

CHAPTER THIRTY-THREE

And what of justice? the lawman asked the Mistress of Serpents.
Justice is a beautiful woman, who when courted by numerous
suitors, chooses whom to wed by having the men draw straws.

—COLLECTED FOLKTALES

The memory of Jasminda's touch still shivered across Jack's skin. He could have sworn her scent suffused the air. He breathed deeply, fortifying himself as the Council Room filled with grumbling men.

"What is the meaning of this?" the Minister of Finance asked as he stalked in sulkily. "How dare you summon us so early?"

Jack bristled at the man's tone but held his tongue. Years of commanding the army had accustomed him to a certain amount of respect. Who would have thought that being the Prince Regent would afford him less? But in the eyes of these men he was a less than suitable alternative to his brother, Alariq.

A Council meeting had been on the schedule for the afternoon, yet as soon as Jack had entered his office, still riding on the bubble of elation after leaving Jasminda's room, he had been brought swiftly back down to earth. He'd asked his secretary to move the meeting to first thing in the morning. "We will begin once everyone arrives," he said curtly. No trace was evident of the good humor he'd had only an hour before.

When the last minister appeared, Jack took a deep breath. He opened the folder before him and pulled out a curling sheet of paper.

"I received this early this morning. It appeared in my offices. And when I say *appeared*, I mean it popped into existence in midair right over my desk."

Gasps came from around the table. Jack cringed recalling how he'd plucked the page from the air, feeling the residual vibrations of Earthsong on the single sheet.

"It pertains to the True Father's terms for peace."

Another round of gasps and murmurs resonated.

Jack ran his fingers across the letter. He had read it over and over again and could almost recite it by heart. He peered at every shocked face around the table, then repeated each word.

"It has come to the attention of the beloved leadership of the Republic of Lagrimar that preparations for war are being made by the Principality of Elsira. While We assert Our right to pursue the protection of Our people against the ambition and reckless dominance of all outsiders, We acknowledge that a peaceful and permanent solution to the many years of strife between our lands would be advantageous.

"Our offer is peace in exchange for the immediate return of every Lagrimari within the borders of the Elsiran principality. Our people are Our greatest resource, and it is within Our right to negotiate for their safe return to home soil.

"The entire power of Our crown is united behind this generous offer of peace. If Our people are returned within three days, a guarantee will be made to honor all current borders in perpetuity for the length of Our

reign and to immediately cease and desist any actions that may be deemed by the Principality of Elsira as acts of war.

"In witness whereof We have hereto set Our hand the eighth day of the tenth month this five hundred and twelfth year of Our reign."

Silence descended. Jack released the paper and let it fall back onto the table.

"The refugees," Minister Nirall, Lizvette's father, said under his breath.

"Yes," Jack replied. "He's promising to abandon whatever scheme he has for destroying the Mantle if we return them."

Zavros Calladeen, Minister of Foreign Affairs, leaned forward, not meeting Jack's eyes. "But why all of a sudden? Of what military value are they?"

Nirall shook his head. "Women, children, old men. Some of the children may have powerful witchcraft, but would that prompt the offer of permanent peace?"

"Perhaps this is a blessing from the Sovereign. After all, these *refugees*"—Pugeros, the Minister of Finance, spat the word out like he would a rotten bite of food—"are already straining the Principality's coffers. With this year's abominable harvest *and* the increase on import tariffs out of Yaly, we are already facing difficult financial waters. The latest debacle with the King of Raun means an even more dire situation for our economy. We simply cannot afford to provide food and care for the refugees for too long. At most we could support them for a few weeks."

Jack was incredulous. "Then we take out a loan." Guffaws sounded from around the room. He raised his voice. "And we work to educate the people on why ejecting political refugees is not only a callous move but is fundamentally un-Elsiran. We would send these women, children, and elders back into the grip of a madman?"

"Your Grace is surely not suggesting that we destroy what's left of our economy and plunge ourselves further into debt for a handful of savages?" Pugeros asked.

Jack slammed his hand on the table. "What of our honor?"

Calladeen's voice was low and measured. "Honor is not about doing what is right in a vacuum of consequences. Honor is doing the hard thing and letting history determine your legacy." He quoted words Alariq had said many times. Jack wanted to punch him in the face.

"There is international precedent," Stevenot said. "We are under no obligation to burden ourselves with their care."

"This is not a financial question, gentlemen, but a moral one," said Nirall. A former professor and the Minister of Education and Innovation, he was most often the voice of compassion and reason. "They are fleeing a brutal dictator. We must treat them the same way we'd treat our own women and children. There must be a way to find enough resources to care for them all."

"Minister Nirall." The timbre of Calladeen's voice resonated as he addressed his uncle formally. Calladeen, the youngest on the Council save Jack, owed his position as Minister of Foreign Affairs not to his uncle's influence but to his own keen intelligence, politicking, and ruthless ambition. "I visited this camp the Sisterhood has erected, and much as I would like to feel sorry for these refugees, I am moved by something less like pity and more like suspicion to see them crossing our borders in such increasing numbers."

"Surely, you do not suppose that those miserable creatures could be spies? I'm told they practically kiss Elsiran soil when they arrive," Nirall replied.

"Never forget their witchcraft," said Calladeen. "This Earthsong they possess is dangerous. What is to stop them from bringing down a violent storm or a rockslide or a fire?"

Jack simmered just below a full boil. He'd never understood what Alariq saw in Calladeen. "Earthsong saved my life. On more than one occasion. Like anything else, its bearer determines whether it's a weapon or a blessing. Now is there a chance there are spies among them? Certainly. But does that mean we turn our backs on all those seeking aid?" Jack shook his head. "A Lagrimari man is the only reason the coming war is not a surprise, unlike every other breach. Instead of treating them as enemy agents, we should be trying to learn from them, gaining additional intelligence, and working together to find a way to stop the True Father."

"That is a naive way of looking at things, Your Grace," Calladeen said haughtily. "The Lagrimari are not tacticians. Additional intelligence has never defeated them. Superior force, training, and discipline have done that for nearly five hundred years."

Jack bit his tongue, recalling the Fifth Breach veterans' story. Intelligence and tactics had indeed won the day fifty years ago. Not even the Council knew the truth of what really ended that war. Nor were they likely to believe him if he told them. "Things are changing, Minister Calladeen. My time embedded with the enemy showed me that. We cannot be so arrogant."

Calladeen seethed. If he thought he could intimidate Jack with a stare down, he was wrong. While these men might have been superior politicians, Jack was no stranger to conflict. And he would not back down from a battle.

He ground his teeth together. "And what makes you think the True Father would keep this promise of peace? What confidence do we have in his word?"

"We have negotiated peace treaties before," Pugeros said.

"And they have all been broken. Whether in five years, fifty, or one hundred, there is always another breach!" Jack stood suddenly, his heavy chair sliding against the floor with a groan. "He wants out of that Sovereign-forsaken desert he's been stuck in. That hasn't changed. What happens when we return the refugees and the Mantle falls anyway? He will be that much more powerful before he comes to invade us. We have no leverage here."

"It is a risk," Stevenot said thoughtfully.

"A great one," said Nirall, adjusting his spectacles. "We will need time to consider the ramifications. We have three days to decide. Let us table this for the moment to give it the proper reflection." He looked to Jack for confirmation. But Jack shook his head.

"There is nothing to consider. We are honorable Elsirans. Let's start behaving as such. I want the latest budget audit on my desk this afternoon." Pugeros visibly paled. "We will find the funds to care for those seeking refuge in our land. No excuses."

Jack's pronouncement was met with withering gazes from almost every seat at the table. He didn't care what they thought, he just wanted it done.

He moved toward the door, needing to get out of the airless room and all of the closed-minded intolerance. Perhaps Alariq would have dealt with the situation more diplomatically, but Jack was a soldier. He gave orders, and they were followed. Couldn't these men see that if they gave in to the True Father's demands, they would not be so unlike him? Jack couldn't—he *wouldn't* allow Elsira to sink into unfeeling barbarism. He'd thought the war was against a foreign enemy, when really he just might have to save his land from itself.

CHAPTER THIRTY-FOUR

The Master of Bobcats faced down an enemy with far greater numbers proclaiming, Woe unto he who trusts the odds. For he is defeated before he is begun.

—COLLECTED FOLKTALES

Jasminda saw Rosira in the daylight for the first time as the town car she rode in rolled through the streets. She reached the city center more quickly than she would have liked. The government offices were housed in a sprawling building of white marble that straddled three city blocks. Its architecture was similar to the palace's, with arched windows and carved columns, only a great dome sat at the center of the government building, and its copper roof had corroded to green long ago.

The auto pulled to a stop in front of a set of grand steps leading to one of the building's many doors. The driver—a friendly man with sparkling eyes—had assured her this was the correct entrance to the Tax Bureau. Now Jasminda swallowed nervously, smoothed out her skirt, and began to climb.

Earlier that morning, Nadal had arrived with a stunning array of clothing for her to choose from, with hemlines ranging from a respectable midcalf to an eyebrow-raising above-the-knee. Beading, sequins, and tassels adorned the collection. But Jasminda had chosen the simplest frock, navy blue and stylishly loose-fitting, with a waistline that grazed her hips. Now she wished she'd selected something fancier, something that screamed, *I'm staying in the palace and am the very close acquaintance of the Prince Regent.*

Inside, she crossed the lobby to the information desk. The woman seated there peered curiously above the rim of her spectacles but directed Jasminda to the property tax office without further comment. After traveling hallways only slightly less convoluted than the palace's, she located the proper door. The office's tiny antechamber was a waiting room. Though the hour was early, already three people sat in the wooden chairs lining the walls.

Jasminda scanned the small space and spotted a clipboard sitting on the open half door leading to the inner office. She added her name and took the seat farthest from everyone else. The two men and one woman couldn't seem to take their eyes off her. She sat up straight, determined to ignore their scrutiny.

A portly security guard ambled by and did an almost comical double take. "Oy," he called. "What are you doing here?"

"I'm here to see the Eastern Manager about my property taxes," Jasminda replied coolly, maintaining eye contact. The guard tilted his head, gaping at her like she'd grown horns.

A harried-looking woman appeared in the half-door and called a name from the clipboard. One of the waiting men stood and was admitted into the office.

The security guard stared a bit longer at Jasminda, who looked straight ahead, sitting up tall. Eventually, he muttered something unintelligible and sauntered away. What could he do? She wasn't breaking any laws, and despite all appearances, she *was* a citizen.

It was an hour before her name was called.

"Jasminda ool-Sareefour?" The clerk pronounced the words as if speaking around marbles in her cheeks.

Jasminda stood and marched to the door. Everyone else had been let in without comment; however, the clerk made no move to grant her entry.

"What are you here for?" the woman asked, eyeing her up and down. Dark auburn strands escaped from her messy bun.

Jasminda bit back an exasperated sigh. "My case number is Y seven oh three three. I've appealed my tax judgment in writing and was told that the only option was to come here and appeal in person. You see, we never received—"

"Wait here," the woman said brusquely, then turned to rummage around in the large file cabinet behind her. She retrieved a folder and riffled through it for a few moments before her gaze shot back to Jasminda.

"I'm sorry, I can't help you. Only the Director can hear in-person appeals, and he's not here today."

Jasminda chanced a connection to Earthsong to test the woman's statement. The press of the city made her stumble in place almost drunkenly as the energies pressed into her from all sides. Thousands upon thousands of people so close by. She barely managed to keep hold of the connection and sense the woman before her.

Lying. Or rather, hedging. Confident that she was doing right but still scared. It was confusing. But Jasminda gathered her file had been marked somehow.

"When is the Director expected to return?" she asked through clenched teeth.

"Oh, I don't know. It may be some time." Another lie.

"Just enough time for my window to appeal to close? Today is my last day."

The woman blinked and slammed the file closed. "I can't help you."

Almost the truth. She wouldn't help, that was clear. Jasminda released Earthsong and fought the urge to sag with relief. She turned away, then back again, an idea forming in her mind. The clerk was pale, her eyes wide and frightened.

"I don't suppose the Director knows a man named Marvus Zinadeel, does he?"

The woman swallowed nervously. "Y-yes. They have lunch together once a month." She narrowed her eyes. "Why?"

Jasminda snorted and turned on her heel. She strode through the government building, her steps echoing on the marble floors. At the town car, she was ready to wrench open the door in anger, but the driver beat her to it.

"Do you know a merchant named Zinadeel?" she asked him.

He seemed surprised, but nodded. "Yes, miss. He owns several department stores in midtown."

"Which is the biggest?"

Fifteen minutes later, she stepped in front of Olivesse's, a three-story monstrosity in the middle of the bustling merchant district. Mannequins wearing the latest fashions filled the windows. An irrational burst of pride zinged through her to see that the very dress she wore was currently displayed, only in sea-foam green.

It reminded her that she did have allies. At least one, and he was a fairly important one. But she could do this on her own. She was not a leech and would not earn any of the gossip sure to follow in her wake. Before she could second-guess herself, she went inside.

In all her life, she'd never seen so many clothes in one place.

She'd thought the wardrobe Nadal had procured for her was fine, but this was unimaginable.

She fought to hide her amazement as she walked down the center aisle, passing racks upon racks of clothing. Her fingers itched to reach out and explore the fabrics. Silk and chiffon, lace and linen. This was the true wealth of her family. This was what Mama had walked away from to live in their little valley, which suddenly seemed like it was on the other side of the world, not just the country.

A sprightly saleswoman approached, her forehead lined with uncertainty. "Is there something I can help you with?"

"Where is the owner's office?" Jasminda asked.

With a bewildered look, the woman pointed her to the back of the store. In moments, Jasminda stood in front of Marvus Zinadeel's secretary, who appeared just as flummoxed to see her as everyone else she'd encountered this morning.

"He doesn't know I'm coming, so I'm certain he hasn't given you any excuses as to why he can't see me," Jasminda said. "I'll be going in now."

"But, but you can't—" The secretary stood, however, Jasminda towered over the diminutive woman, glaring at her fiercely. She flinched, allowing Jasminda to smoothly step around her and open the great mahogany door to her grandfather's office.

The interior was all dark wood, somber, heavy furniture, thick hand-woven rugs, and bulky brocades. The intercom crackled to life as the secretary's warbled voice announced the arrival of an unwelcome visitor.

Jasminda stopped short just inside the door, her confident forward motion arrested by the sight of the man before her.

He stood, cutting an imposing figure in his tailored suit. His hair had gone white at the temples but retained its reddish-blond color on top. He was handsome in a distinguished, distant way. Tall and lean and more intimidating than she'd imagined.

"Grandfather?" she said, her bravado falling away under the intense scrutiny of his golden eyes.

"Jasminda." His face was inscrutable. He leaned against the side of his highly polished desk and crossed his arms, looking her up and down. Finding her lacking.

She took a few more steps but stopped, not wanting to stand too close to him. She didn't bother to greet him properly, and he made no move to do so with her. With effort, she steeled her spine. "I went to the Taxation Bureau to lodge my appeal in person this morning, but it seems I won't be allowed to."

His expression didn't change, but something in his eyes flashed.

"I believe you and the Director are quite chummy. Perhaps you have some insight as to why he will not be able to hear my appeal."

Zinadeel's eyes burned into her. "Can't say that I do. Best take it up with them if you have some complaint."

This would be a test of wills, then. "And what of this document you want me to sign?" She produced the folded and crumpled paper from her pocket. It had gotten soaked in the rain and then dried out and was overall a bit worse for the wear.

Zinadeel tracked the paper with his gaze. "What is there to discuss? It is a generous offer. You should be speaking with my solicitors at any rate. They handle these types of affairs."

"But I wanted to talk to you in person, Grandfather. I have questions." Gathering her strength, she strode forward and sat in front of him, perching gently on the very edge of one of the two chairs facing his desk. A deep furrow appeared in his forehead, but he walked behind his desk and sat.

"Well?" His voice was suspicious. Unyielding.

"I know that Papa contacted you after Mama's death." She

wasn't sure if she imagined the wince he gave. This was the man who had cut Mama off two decades earlier without a word—was it possible he felt some regret?

"And I myself wrote to you on numerous occasions over the past two years. Yet you did not see fit to respond until now. The first time I hear from you is mere months after the first time I heard from the Taxation Bureau. Twenty years without a tax bill, can you imagine?"

She forced herself to smile. "And then, out of the blue, your *generous* offer arrives, which would provide enough to pay this sudden debt. I am very curious why that is. Can you enlighten me?" She sat primly, hands clasped on her knee.

His frown deepened. "Is it not obvious why? I am a respected man. I am running for city Alderman in the spring. My daughter Eminette's poor decisions reflect back on me, on all of us. I am doing my duty as head of this family by trying to mitigate the unsuitability of her choices."

Jasminda held her face very still. "So you want me to accept hush money to never reveal your daughter's transgressions?" She shook her head. "You cannot erase my mother from this world. She loved my father, and I am the result of that. It happened, and your money cannot destroy it."

Zinadeel snorted. "Money is a great motivator. It makes people forget. Or remember, depending on which is convenient." He peered down at her, sizing her up. "What do you really want?"

"I want to know the true reason you offered me this deal."

"I've told you." He waved his hand impatiently.

She shook her head, watching his brow descend.

"And where do you expect to live once your little farm is sold at auction *tomorrow*, hmm? What will you do? How will you eat?" He gave her a self-satisfied smirk. "If forty thousand isn't enough, how about fifty? Is your sense of nostalgia worth fifty thousand pieces? Eminette is dead, she can have no opinion on the matter."

Red stole across her vision. She gripped the arms of the seat to keep her limbs still. "My parentage isn't for sale."

"Everything is for sale. It's just a matter of negotiating the proper price. Your home and your life for mine. It is a fair exchange, I should think." His shrewd gaze seemed to cut right through her. "Or have you some other option?"

She thought of Jack. He had offered to pay off her debts, and then what? Would that make her the whore the soldiers whispered of? She shivered at the thought. That was nearly as bad as renouncing her mother and taking *this* man's money. But she was well and truly stuck.

She stood. "I will not make this easy for you," she said through gritted teeth.

Her grandfather chuckled maddeningly as she stalked out of the office, past the wide-eyed secretary. The timbre of his amusement echoed in her ears as she left the store without another look at the fine clothing or beautiful things.

Back at the town car, the driver rushed to open the door for her.

"Back to the palace, please."

She didn't look back as they pulled away.

CHAPTER THIRTY-FIVE

A wise man asked the Mistress of Eagles, How can I hear the voice of the Divine?

All voices are the Divine, she answered.

But what of those speaking evil?

Eagle replied, Evil is heard with the heart and not with the ears.

—COLLECTED FOLKTALES

Jasminda jumped at the knock on the door. She scrubbed away the stubborn tears that had escaped, despite her best efforts, and approached.

"Who's there?"

"Miss Jasminda, it's Usher."

She relaxed and opened the door, glad to see him. His gray head and kind face were welcome sights. That morning he had led her through the palace to the vehicle depot to meet her driver. Usher held Jack's trust, and hers by proxy.

"The prince requests your presence."

Surprised at the summons, she followed. Usher led her through the bowels of the palace and down many steep staircases, each older than the last. Here, the original stone walls and floors had not been plastered over or carpeted. Kerosene lamps instead of electric shone dimly, lending an acrid tinge to the cool air, though to Jasminda's mind, torches would not have been out of place.

"This is the oldest part of the palace, Miss Jasminda. It is used exclusively by the Prince Regent."

Something odd brushed against her senses. The energy of this place was overwhelming. The hallway in which they stood ended with a door. Usher pushed it open with some difficulty and motioned her through. Giving him a quizzical look, she stepped cautiously, then gave a yelp when her feet slid down.

The floor was like a bowl, the inside of the room a white sphere with the door hanging in the middle. Candles glowed eerily from little alcoves notched into curved walls made of no material she could fathom. Everything was smooth and white, but the shadows from the candles flickered gloomily.

Jack knelt on one knee at the bottom of the bowl, underneath a long white capsule floating in midair. The smooth, seamless surface of the capsule was made of the same strange material as the walls. The object resembled an elongated egg, about six feet in length. It hovered courtesy of an ancient, intensely powerful spell that tingled against the edges of her senses like static electricity.

Jack rose, facing her as she found her footing and gingerly stepped down the concave floor. Exhaustion wearied his features, but his expression brightened at the sight of her. She slid into his arms, and he held her so tightly she could scarcely breathe. But she did not complain.

"Are we where I think we are?"

Jack lifted his head, looking up at the floating capsule. "The resting place of the Queen Who Sleeps."

She stared in awe. "But this chamber is sacred. Can I be here?"

"Not even the Sisterhood may come down here—only the Prince Regent and those closest to him." He took her hand and pulled her directly underneath the Queen's encased form, then led her to kneel with him. "We come to seek Her counsel and wisdom, to pray for the knowledge and strength to lead in Her stead."

She wrenched her gaze from the smooth surface of the Queen's tomb. Not a tomb, for She slept only, and it was promised that She would awaken.

"Being here, does it spark any insights into the visions?" Jack asked.

She stood and walked the length of the Queen's encasement, staring up at it. A crushing sense of defeat teetered at the edge of her awareness. She shook her head. "This place is full of power, but I don't know. It's not like anything I've seen."

Shame for her weakness and the little progress she was making with the caldera filled her. She relayed what she'd seen to Jack—Eero's trial, his being taken away for treatment. "I wish I could go faster. I'm sorry." She sank down to the ground, and Jack came to sit next to her.

"I know you're doing your best. I'm not trying to pressure you, just help." He grasped her hand, but the worried look never left his face.

She ran her fingers through his somewhat disheveled hair. "Something's wrong. Something new."

His shoulders sagged. He told her of the letter from the True Father and the terrible demands.

Tears once again stung her eyes at the thought of all it had taken for the refugees to make it to Elsira in the first place. Only to be sent back . . . It was unthinkable, but she knew too well how little value a Lagrimari life held here.

"What will happen?"

"I have three days to ensure the Council doesn't make a grave mistake."

Jasminda shuddered. If only she could make more progress. She would try again now if her Song weren't still depleted from this morning's vision and her trip downtown.

Nothing was going right. The auction was tomorrow, and she was no closer to saving her farm or awakening the Queen. Jack was lost in his duties. She was glad he hadn't asked about her visit to the Taxation Bureau. She didn't want him to offer his aid again.

Relying on him and his princely connections would be lovely. But where would she turn when this dream dissolved back into reality? Even now he was not really hers, and if she grew to depend on his care, on his help, then she risked so much more when it was over. More than she could bear.

Lost in thought, Jack's expression was dark.

"They will come around," she said, leaning against him. "They have to."

Jack snorted. "Those old men are so stubborn and callous, and they have little respect for me." He sighed. "What if I can't save the refugees?"

Jasminda didn't know what to say. Odd that they both felt so powerless, she the only one for whom a magical object worked and he the prince of the land. But they battled forces much more powerful than themselves. She could only hope those forces wouldn't win.

CHAPTER THIRTY-SIX

What can I do to gain favor? asked the tax collector to the Master of Jackals.

Marry well.

—COLLECTED FOLKTALES

The newspaper cartoon displayed a baby with a shotgun in one hand and a scepter in the other, a crown of bullets sitting askew on his head. On one side, grotesque caricatures of Lagrimari refugees gobbled food from huge bowls, while on the other, waifish Elsiran farmers split a single loaf of bread.

An editorial on the same page detailed Prince Jaqros's plan to starve his own people in favor of the refugees. It dredged up the swirling chaos surrounding his mother's emigration after his father's death—she had renounced her citizenship before fleeing the country. Those had been dark days.

Of course the reporters did not mention his father's mistreatment—that was a secret no one knew. The damage the former Prince

Regent had caused with words and occasionally with fists. How Jack hadn't been able to protect either of them. How the light had fled his mother's eyes until she'd had to leave. Jack's fingers dug into his palms at the memory.

Today's newspaper article reported "no confidence that the offspring of a woman who many consider a traitor to her country could effectively rule." His recent reckless undercover mission and subsequent disappearance were laid out. He was young and headstrong and prone to rash behavior.

Jack slammed the paper shut and tossed it to the ground. Usher stooped to pick it up, smoothing the folds and placing it neatly on the bureau.

"What happens if I abdicate?" he asked, seriously considering the idea.

Usher sat next to Jack in the armchair in front of the fireplace, a finger to his lips in thought. "Your second cousin Frederiq is a lovely boy, but a twelve-year-old Prince Regent would fare little better in the press, I'm afraid."

Jack groaned. "The Council would run that child ragged and rule unchecked. Sovereign only knows what manner of damage they'd cause if left entirely to their own devices." He rose and leaned against the mantelpiece. "I don't know what to—"

His secretary knocked on the door then stuck her head in when he replied.

"Minister Nirall for you, Your Grace."

Jack sighed. "Show him in, Netta. Thank you."

Nirall entered, his normally jovial face grim. Jack forced a warm greeting and bid him to sit.

"You've seen today's paper, Your Grace?"

"Unfortunately."

"What passes for journalism these days is offensive," Nirall said with a sniff. He shook his graying head. "However, this refugee business has the people on edge."

"And they blame me? For failing to turn away these threadbare women and children? Is that what the people are saying?"

"Your Grace, the people simply want to know that their Prince Regent and their Council hear their voices and have their best interests at heart. They're afraid helping the refugees is taking away vital resources from our own people."

"And the rest of the Council has concern for their interests? Giving in to the True Father's demands is madness." Jack shook his head. "If we could only get more of them to see reason . . ."

Jack closed his eyes, weary of the task in front of him. Whenever he dropped his lids he saw Jasminda's face smiling back at him, and the thought soothed him. The cares of the world disappeared in her arms; how he longed for nightfall and the comfort of her touch.

"What do you think Alariq would have done?" he asked.

Nirall exhaled slowly. "He would have examined all sides of the issue very carefully. Measured them twice to cut once."

A hint of a smile cracked Jack's bleak face. "My brother would have measured them no less than four times. That's why he was a good prince."

Nirall leaned in, resting his elbows on his knees. Round spectacles and a gray-streaked goatee in need of trimming gave him a professorial air. "Alariq was also very good at deflecting."

"How do you mean?"

"Sometimes, when people are up in arms about something, they need their attention to be redirected elsewhere."

Jack frowned. "What could redirect them?"

Licks of fire reflected in the man's spectacles, setting his eyes aglow. "The people have been displeased over the shortages for

some time, but the royal wedding was going to be the perfect distraction. The right mix of glamour and austerity, of course, but an
event to capture the public's imagination all the same."

With a sigh, Jack slumped farther in his chair. "I'm sure that
would have done the trick. It's too bad they could not have wed. I
hope Lizvette's spirits are not too low."

"She's quite well. And she would still make a very fine princess."
Nirall's gaze held Jack in its grip.

He was dumbstruck. Several moments passed before he could
respond. "You can't be suggesting . . ."

Nirall reached for Jack's arm. "Our two families are still a good
match. A strong princess will go a long way to improve your public
perception. A wedding, an heir, it would be—"

"That is ludicrous!" Jack stood. "Lizvette loved my brother. How
could I . . . It would be extraordinarily inappropriate, not to mention in very poor taste. I'm not sure how you could even think such
a thing."

Nirall stood and bowed his head. "I did not mean to offend you,
Your Grace. I was simply trying to offer a potential solution."

Jack backed away. "The title Minister of Innovation fits you too
well. But this is outlandish. I could never do such a thing to the
memory of my brother, nor to Lizvette."

"You could honor him by maintaining his legacy. He chose my
daughter for a reason, and you and she have always been friends. I
do not believe the idea would be as unappealing to her as you
think."

Jack held up a hand. "Please stop. I do not want to hear any
more of this. I cannot."

"Forgive me, Your Grace. I won't speak of it again." Nirall
bowed formally and took his leave.

Usher shut the door and came to stand by Jack's side.

"Has everyone gone mad, Usher?" When the valet did not respond, Jack looked over. "What? You can't think that lunacy makes sense?"

"Alariq was popular with the people. He had the luxury of waiting to marry. An unpopular man is aided by a well-loved wife."

"Don't spit platitudes at me, old man. How could she be well loved, jumping from one brother to the next?"

"Your grandmother did the very same thing to much regard when her first husband died. The people like continuity."

"The people are idiots."

Usher set a hand on Jack's shoulder. "I'm sure the feeling is mutual."

Jack scowled and shrugged off the contact. "I do not love her."

"Many things will be required of you in your new position, young sir. Unfortunately, falling in love is not one of them."

Jack's gaze fell upon the newspaper. He stormed over to the bureau, snatched up the offending sheets, and threw them into the fire. He rubbed his chest while he watched the pages burn; the spot just under his shoulder where he'd been wounded had suddenly begun to ache. Or maybe that was just his heart.

CHAPTER THIRTY-SEVEN

*The Mistress of Frogs intervened in a feud between two brothers.
Family is a two-bladed sword, she said. It must be maneuvered
expertly to avoid injury.*

—COLLECTED FOLKTALES

"What's your name?" Jasminda asked her driver—the same one as
the day before—as the town car curved through the streets. In the
rearview mirror his eyes were a sparkling shade of green. She'd
never seen eyes that color.

"I'm called Nash, miss."

"Have you lived in Rosira all your life?"

He chuckled. "Oh no, miss. I'm Fremian. I've been here . . .
going on thirteen years now. I reached master level in the Hospitality Guild, and when I passed my Level Ones—that's the exam—
I had my pick of positions. Most go to Yaly, but I've always liked
living by the sea. I started in the resorts up north, and let me tell
you . . ."

Nash certainly wasn't short on conversation. During the short trip, he told her how he came to Rosira following a young lady who had eventually relented and agreed to marry him. Nothing in his manner indicated any suspicion or distaste for Jasminda.

"Nash, I'm sorry to interrupt, but are there many Fremians in Elsira?"

"Not so many, miss. A few servants in the palace and at the premiere vacation spots, some professors at the university, too, but the immigration laws are strict. Down in Portside, you'll see folk from every corner of the globe working the ships, but they're prohibited from entering other parts of the city."

Nash's native Fremia was a land that valued knowledge and excellence above all else. They had the best schools and universities and offered elite training in everything from art, to science, to warfare and hospitality. Around the world, no one was better at what they did—no matter what it was—than a Fremian.

"And do your people have any . . . opinions on the Lagrimari?"

He gave her a knowing smile. "Fremia has always been neutral, miss. We stay out of the conflicts of other lands."

Just outside the city limits, Nash turned onto a rough path cut into the dirt, and drove another half kilometer or so before stopping. A miniature city lay stretched out ahead, made up of orderly rows of white tents with oil lanterns strung up on poles to form the perimeter.

Nash turned in his seat to face her. "It isn't like here. So many people from all over the world come to study back home, we're used to differences of all kinds. It must be hard living in a land with so much sameness that any deviation at all stands out."

She nodded but couldn't find her voice to respond. Nash sobered, then straightened his hat and exited to help her out of the vehicle.

"I shouldn't be too long," she said.

He tipped his hat to her. "Take as long as you like, miss."

The warm feeling she had from her conversation with Nash faded slowly as she approached the refugee camp entrance. Soldiers milled around, at odds with the nearly half a dozen women of the Sisterhood busily unloading supplies from several trucks.

Jasminda had come to find Gerda and tell her and the others what she'd learned so far from the caldera. Perhaps the elders could provide some guidance, but at the very least, she wanted to update them. She twisted her hands, dreading disappointing the Keepers with her lack of progress, when her attention was captured by two people on the other side of the vehicles.

An Elsiran man and woman stood arguing. The woman was clad in the blue robes of the Sisterhood. The man was slim and rather short, wearing a black suit and cap similar to Usher's. He looked like a driver.

Jasminda could not hear the words of the dispute, but the man's motions were emphatic. However, the voice rising with emotion was high pitched. When both turned, Jasminda's breath caught. The fellow was really a woman, dressed in male clothing. But what really caught her eye was the face of the Sister.

With her golden auburn hair tied in a topknot the way all Sisters wore it, her topaz-colored eyes, and straight nose peppered with freckles, she was the spitting image of Mama. The only thing that kept Jasminda from crying out and running into the woman's arms were the burn scars across her left cheek and jaw extending down her neck.

Jasminda drew closer until she could hear better.

"Clove, *please*." The Sister's voice was lighter and breathier than Mama's. Jasminda almost didn't trust her memories. There was no way two people could look so similar.

The shorter woman gave an exasperated sigh. "You promised you would be there, Vanesse. I needed you."

Vanesse. Jasminda knew that name. Her mother had spoken it often enough. Jasminda had even tried addressing her letters to Vanesse Zinadeel when those to her grandparents kept being returned unopened. But her mother's sister had not responded, either.

Aunt Vanesse.

Her only proof was a first name and a face nearly identical to her mother's.

"I wanted to be there," Vanesse was saying, "but Father needed me at his presentation. He insisted."

"You are a grown woman," Clove said. "You can tell him no." Vanesse's hand went to the burn on her face self-consciously.

Clove sighed, her shoulders lowering. She reached up and caressed Vanesse's cheek, right over the scar, in a very intimate way. Vanesse leaned into the touch before pulling back sharply, her eyes scanning the area. She caught sight of Jasminda and froze.

Clove looked over her shoulder, her gaze glancing off Jasminda. Her expression was dejected.

"Can we talk about this later?" Vanesse asked. Clove shrugged and shuffled off to a town car parked at the end of the row of military vehicles.

Vanesse sniffed, watching Clove walk away. Then she turned and slowly headed toward where the other Sisters were working. Her eyes were downcast as she passed Jasminda.

"Your father is a beast," Jasminda said, unable to hold her tongue.

Vanesse jumped and stared at her as if she was crazy for her outburst. "You speak Elsiran." She looked at Jasminda more closely. "How do you know my father?"

Jasminda held the older woman's gaze. "He is my grandfather."

She stood tall, daring her aunt to deny her. For a moment, Vanesse just stared mutely as if not comprehending what she was seeing.

"Jasminda?" She let out a gasp, almost a sob, and rushed forward, wrapping her arms around her niece. Jasminda was frozen in place as Vanesse crushed her. "I can't believe it. You look so much like Eminette," her aunt whispered into her hair.

"No, I don't. But you do." She found the strength to wrap her arms around the other woman and hold on as Vanesse continued to squeeze.

When Vanesse pulled back, tears streamed down her face. She cupped Jasminda's cheeks. "No, I see her in you. Your chin, your forehead." She stroked each part as she mentioned it, and the tears continued. They welled in Jasminda's eyes also.

Vanesse released Jasminda and wiped at her eyes, sniffling. "Come, let's sit." She motioned to a log lying in the grass a few paces away. They settled in next to one another, and Jasminda studied the burn scars marring her aunt's cheek and jaw. Her left ear was mangled as well.

Vanesse touched her face and dipped her head. "Your grandmother did that."

Jasminda's jaw slackened as she struggled to comprehend a mother burning her own child. "Was it an accident?"

Vanesse snorted. "No. I was sixteen and she caught me with"—she looked over toward where Clove had disappeared—"someone she thought unsuitable." Jasminda could imagine her grandparents would find another woman unsuitable.

"Emi had been gone for four years, sending us letter after letter. Mother and Father would burn them, so I started going for walks to meet the post carrier so I could read them." Her voice hitched. "Mother had told everyone Emi died of a fever out in the Borderlands, but Emi had written letters to her friends telling what really happened. Our parents were incensed. So when it looked like I was going to end up an embarrassment as well . . ." Vanesse's gaze lengthened. She stared across the makeshift car park toward the expanse of tents, lost in the memory.

"When she came after me with the oil, I thought she wanted to kill me. She doused my bed and then lit the match before I even knew what was happening. Said she wanted to make sure no one at all would steal me away from her. No one would want me. I would never shame her the same way my sister did." Vanesse's hand fluttered near her face, never quite touching her scars.

Jasminda's breathing was shallow. A tear escaped as she took in her aunt's misery. "And your father? What did he say?"

She sniffed. "'All actions have consequences.'" Her voice was deep in an imitation of Zinadeel.

"But the Sisterhood. How could your parents support you joining a group that aids the settlers?"

Vanesse straightened and wiped her eyes again. "The Sisterhood is respectable. The Queen has shown us Her blessing many times. Providing for the less fortunate is something that brings honor to the family. The irony that Emi met your father while in the Sisterhood is perhaps lost on them. Or maybe they just believe that I'm too ugly to be a temptation."

Vanesse dropped her head. "I'm sorry I haven't been there for you. My parents are very . . ." She searched for a word, her eyes clouding.

"You're afraid of them," Jasminda said, growing cold as a guilty look of assent crossed her aunt's face. She could not fault the woman. How would she feel if she'd been burned by her own mother for falling out of line? Her grandmother must have a tenuous hold on her sanity to do such a thing. And she knew firsthand how intimidating her grandfather was.

"How did you come to be here? Where are you living?" Vanesse asked, appearing truly interested.

Jasminda allowed herself to revise her opinion of her aunt and told her of the events leading her to Rosira—leaving out the caldera and her exact relationship with Jack—and of visiting her grandfather. Vanesse listened to the story, her horrified expression growing with each twist and turn.

"You must be careful of Father. I believe he's capable of anything," she whispered, shivering a little. Any lingering anger Jasminda had held toward the woman dissolved into pity. The family Jasminda had known was kind and loving. She'd never once feared either of her parents and couldn't imagine doing so.

Vanesse grabbed Jasminda's hand and squeezed. "I hope that we can get to know one another. I would very much like that."

"Me, too." Jasminda's heart lightened at the thought of having a family again.

"There's a place we can meet where no one will see. Though you may have to invest in a good-sized cloak, or perhaps some face paint so you're not recognized."

Whatever else Vanesse said was lost to the rushing in Jasminda's ears. Her aunt could only get to know her in secret. Hidden corridors, cloaks, and face paint. Late-night rendezvous and secret trysts. Was there no one who would bring their acquaintance with her out into the light of day?

She pulled her hand out of Vanesse's grasp and stood on shaky legs. "I'm supposed to meet with some of the refugees now. I have to go."

Someone else's secret. Someone else's shame.

She left behind the question on Vanesse's face and the call of her name on the woman's lips.

CHAPTER THIRTY-EIGHT

How may I gain power? asked a servant to the Master of Bobcats.
Bobcat replied, A man who seeks power believes he can control
his kite in a furious gale. A man who has power, releases his string.
—COLLECTED FOLKTALES

Jasminda wasn't certain of how to find the elders. Each tent she passed was identical to the last. Fortunately, the camp was rather small.

Within a few minutes she stumbled upon Rozyl, Sevora, and the other two Keepers from the mountain. Jasminda dreaded asking the woman for anything, but she had little choice.

As she approached, a ripple of unease charged the air. The Keepers had their faces to the sky, as if they were listening to something.

"What's wrong?" Jasminda asked. No one answered.

She reached for Rozyl, brushing the woman's arm to get her attention. Her fingers merely glanced across Rozyl's skin where she'd pushed up her sleeve. But a violent press of Earthsong rose and slammed against Jasminda like a physical shove. She couldn't separate herself and was plunged directly into the flow of Rozyl's connection to Earthsong.

Jasminda cried out, suffocated by the maelstrom of energies of so many people around her. Pain, white and hot, lanced through her body, blinding her. Somehow she had linked to Rozyl's power, and it felt like being crushed into paste. Suddenly, a filter emerged between her and Rozyl's Song, like a window shade pulled down to hide the glare of the sun. It muted the volume of the energy, and the vise around her chest loosened.

She was still uncomfortable but could now pick out details in the Earthsong surrounding them. The nearby soldiers—tension rippling through them, fear and distrust pulsing along with the blood in their veins. The despair of the refugees, the hope and the hopelessness. Their heavy hearts and minds.

Finally, she was able to tear her hand from Rozyl's arm. She coughed and gasped, relieved to break the connection. Rozyl regarded her with disbelief.

"Don't you know better than to touch someone when they're linking?" Rozyl asked, looking at her like her hair was made of spiders.

Jasminda realized that Sevora had been holding Rozyl's hand. "I-I didn't realize—"

"And why did you not shield yourself?"

"Shield?" So that must be how Earthsingers coexisted in large numbers. Jasminda shook her head. "My father was the only other Earthsinger I knew. He did not teach me." She wondered what other lessons she had missed.

"Your Song is so weak," Rozyl spat.

Jasminda cringed and wrapped her arms around herself. "My brothers could not sing at all."

"I don't know why it must be you," Rozyl said with disgust, and took off down one of the wider paths through the tents, the others on her heels, their disapproval evident.

"I don't know what just happened, but I didn't ask for it, either. I didn't ask to be the only one the caldera will work for," Jasminda called out, racing after Rozyl's quick steps. The woman continued to snub her, and soon they emerged at the camp's entrance where a crowd had grown. The Keepers disappeared into the throng of people.

Still shaking from the unexpected force of the link, Jasminda strained for a better view of what had captured everyone's attention. "What's happening?" she whispered to a woman cradling a sleeping baby.

"I think they're holding back the rations."

Jasminda moved to the front of the group to verify. Vanesse and two other Sisters stood near a line of soldiers arguing with the captain. At their feet were crates of rice, potatoes, and vegetables.

"You cannot keep rations from these people. I won't allow it," a gray-haired Sister said.

Jasminda approached. A few other refugees broke away from the crowd and drew nearer to the soldiers as well.

"Is there a problem delivering the rations, Captain?" Jasminda asked.

The man looked at her sharply, evidently surprised at her command of Elsiran. He glanced at her dress, obviously expensive and so different from the threadbare fabric covering the refugees. She'd not seen this man before, and he probably had no idea of her identity, but he could plainly see she was different than the rest.

"This witchcraft will not be tolerated," the captain said.

Jasminda crossed her arms and stood her ground. "Exactly what witchcraft are you referring to?"

The man glowered at her. "That." He pointed an accusing finger at the first row of tents.

The field on which the refugee camp had been built was covered in brittle, end-of-the-season grass shedding its green for the impending autumn. But each tent in the row had a bed of blooming flowers before it—grouped into different colors.

White desert lilies graced one. Red bristlebrushes another. A golden flower she didn't recognize blossomed in front of a third tent. Before their eyes, green stalks shot through the dry earth of another canvas structure and opened, revealing brilliant purple petals.

"Flowers?" Jasminda asked, unable to keep the derision from her voice. "You're afraid of flowers? Something to brighten the landscape and bring a little joy? What is wrong with you?"

The man's face hardened. "It's evil. The whole lot of you *grols* are evil." He spat, aiming at Jasminda's feet. The Sisters raised their voices in protest.

A boy of about twelve came to stand next to her. She did a double take, recognizing him as the child who'd aided the settlers in Baalingrove. On her other side, two settlers regarded the confrontation warily.

Outrage overcame the pain of the words she'd heard so many times before. "You have no right to withhold the rations, Captain. Not for something so innocent. Do you not have orders to feed these people? Where is your honor?"

The captain's face contorted. "You'll not speak to me of honor, witch."

"Just leave the food here. We'll carry it in ourselves." She moved toward the nearest crate. The boy at her side approached as well.

"Stay back. Don't come any closer." The captain's hand hovered near the pistol strapped to his waist.

Jasminda stilled, but the boy kept moving, not understanding the captain's command. In the space of a heartbeat, the captain pulled his sidearm and pointed it at the boy. The entire line of soldiers drew their rifles on the gathered refugees. The Sisters, startled, took several steps back.

"No!" Jasminda screamed. In Lagrimari, she shouted, "Stop!"

The boy looked over at her, brows drawn. His eyes glittered, warm and golden brown, lighter than most Lagrimari's. His face still held the roundness of youth, but those enchanting eyes were hard.

The child took another defiant step toward the food. Somewhere close by, a woman screamed, "Timmyn!" He tensed, hearing his name, then took another step.

Time slowed as Jasminda shook her head and opened herself to Earthsong, struggling to work out the shield technique she'd witnessed Rozyl using during their unexpected link. It worked just enough so that the other energies weren't screaming in her head, drowning out her thoughts and severing her connection, but she was far from proficient. The soldiers' emotions were a whirlwind of fear and aggression. Too far gone to be soothed by Earthsong, even if she'd been strong enough to do so.

She reached out to Timmyn and found the well of pain to be deep. He was in a place beyond hearing. *You don't have to prove anything,* she wanted to tell him. *We will not let you starve here. The prince would never allow it.* Her helplessness crushed her as she felt his hurt.

When the shot rang out, Jasminda lost her connection to Earthsong. She grabbed at the air in front of her, too far away to catch him as Timmyn fell backward onto the ground. A deep crimson stain ballooned across the fabric of his shirt. Jasminda looked up at the captain in horror. His face was an emotionless mask.

She fell to her knees. Her breath came in short, shallow bursts. Tears blurred her vision. She vaguely registered a group of refugees taking the boy away to be healed. Through the fog she heard Vanesse speaking. Her words were just a jumble of sounds that didn't penetrate. Time ceased to exist. All she could hear was the crack of the gun and the thud of Timmyn's body hitting the earth, over and over again.

A hand on her shoulder brought back her awareness. Nash stood over her, grim. She took his offered hand and struggled to her feet. Her legs were stiff from kneeling for who knows how long.

The soldiers parted for them as Nash led her back to the town car. Jasminda looked over her shoulder. The rest of the crowd had long ago disappeared into their tents; all that remained was a ghost town.

CHAPTER THIRTY-NINE

The Assembly Room grows quiet as all eyes focus on me. Their expectant gazes draw me back to the present. My mind had been aloft, far from this room and out in the early summer sunshine, feeling the waves gently lapping at my feet. That is how I wanted to spend my birthday, at the sea, as I always have before.

I straighten my shoulders and regard the room. Every face holds a tension it never has held before. And it is all my fault.

"All here are agreed?" My voice is low. I speak out loud, as has been the custom during Assembly for the past half a millennia. I will not give in to the paranoia of so many of my cousins gathered here, afraid of eavesdroppers.

We are agreed, murmur many Songs against my consciousness.

"Today is the first day of my twenty-first summer. I am the youngest Third. Vaaryn, you are two hundred years my elder. Your leadership has been unblemished. I am untested. Is this really wise?"

When Father, the last Second and the youngest son of the Founders, passed into the World After, Vaaryn assumed his responsibilities in the Assembly. The idea of leadership passing to me was unfathomable.

"Yes, dear cousin," Vaaryn says. "I am not much longer for this world. It is best that the youngest should lead us."

Most Thirds lived only a few years past their two-hundredth birthday. Fourths less than that, and Fifths barely made one hundred. The Silent were old at seventy.

"But it is because of me that we face war with the Silent. It is because of me—" I choke on the words as a sob rises to my throat. Yllis is there with an arm around me, steady and stable, my rock in the storm.

Yllis's mother, Deela, rises. "So it must be you to lead us through. We have lived in peace for hundreds of years with the guidance left by the Founders, but perhaps it has been too easy for us. We have never been challenged in this way before."

"Eero and those who follow him have poked at a sore that has been dormant for a long time," Yllis says. "The Silent have no voice in the Assembly. Their parentage is not claimed. If it was not Eero now, it would have been someone else in the future. It is not all because of us."

He wants to take more of the burden of Eero's fate away from me, absolve me of some guilt, but it is mine to hold. Yllis developed the complex spell that allowed me to share my Song with my twin, but I was the one who used it. Who kept using it and ignored the truth for too long—giving Song to the Silent would cause them to go mad. The Silent were so for a reason.

"Very well," I say. "I accept. So be it. See to it."

It is as if the Assembly takes a collective breath. "Be it so."

And with three little words, I have been made Queen.

CHAPTER FORTY

The Master of Monkeys told his betrothed, I will steal for you the juiciest fruit from my neighbor's tree.

When he returned, he found the neighbor's cape stuck in the window, and his love nowhere to be found.

—COLLECTED FOLKTALES

BEDLAM STRIKES REFUGEE CAMP

An attack by Lagrimari refugees on Elsiran military personnel resulted in the shooting of a young refugee. Witnesses say the refugees had been threatening violence with their magic, causing the soldiers to respond with force.

Tensions have been high in the camp, which was established by the Sisterhood to answer the refugee crisis impacting Elsira. The influx of foreigners through reported cracks in the Mantle has been a hotly contested issue. Many are unhappy that the Prince Regent seems to be allowing unfettered immigration by these unknown persons.

Jack crumpled the thin newsprint in his fist. He knew very well there had been no attack by the refugees. The evening papers had gone from printing gossip and long-ago scandals to outright lies.

News of the incident had enraged Jack the moment he'd heard. The captain had been arrested immediately, and while the boy had made a full recovery due to the camp's Earthsingers, Jack was resolved to court-martial the offending officer. A decision that would no doubt be met with opposition.

The door to his office opened, and Usher stepped in. Faint music filtered in from the hallway.

"You will have to at least make an appearance, young sir." Usher stood looking reprovingly at him.

"I don't know why they didn't cancel the bloody thing. Now is no time for a ball."

"Third Breach Day falls on the same day every year. They cannot cancel an entire ball because the Prince Regent is in a foul temper."

Jack stood, rolling down his shirtsleeves and buttoning them. "Don't I have the right to be in a temper when unarmed children are being shot? When this entire country seems to have fallen victim to lunacy? At what point, I ask you, am I permitted to be upset?"

Usher picked up Jack's discarded formal dinner jacket and held it out for him. He slipped his arms through and focused on working up some joviality for the ball he was being forced to attend. It wouldn't do for him to scowl his way through, giving more fodder for the papers. Only one thing would truly make him smile, though.

"Is she coming?" he asked, unable to keep the hope from his voice.

"Would it be wise for her to?"

Jack's shoulders slumped.

"She would prefer not to be at the center of any undue attention. Isn't that what you agreed to?"

"I know, I know. It's just . . ." He sighed and checked his appearance in the mirror. He looked tired, older than he had even a week ago. For a moment, he had an inkling of how this position could have turned his father into a brute. Jack could feel his edges hardening. The bit of himself that he'd always held back when he'd been in the army, that person he would have been if he'd been born to a baker or a farmer, had always remained inside him, catching the odd glimpse of sunlight in stolen moments when he hadn't had to flex his muscles as the High Commander. But that hidden self was now being choked. The only times he could seem to breathe anymore were when he was with Jasminda, and even then they had to remain hidden, secret. He couldn't acknowledge anything true about himself, and he was afraid it was changing him.

He stalked down the hallways toward the cacophony of the ball. The ballroom had been decorated, somewhat garishly, in orange, the color of Third Breach Day. Each of the seven breaches had a holiday attached to it, initially as a memorial for all who had been lost in the wars, but more recently it was just an excuse for a celebration. None were as lavish as the yearly Festival of the Founders when all work ceased for three days, but each Breach Day was commemorated by excessive decorations in the color of the holiday and a palace ball for the aristocracy.

Jack entered the corridor outside the rear of the ballroom where a dozen butlers were organizing trays of appetizers. The lead butler did a double take and rushed over, admonishing him, in the most respectful way, for being in the servants' hall. Jack brushed off the man's request to stop the band and make a formal announcement of the Prince Regent's arrival.

"I just want to watch for a bit," Jack said. "I promise you can announce me once this dance is finished. I'd hate to interrupt." The butler's obsequious expression barely hid his displeasure at this interruption to the normal order of things, but he backed off, allowing Jack to peek through the curtains separating the hall from the ballroom.

This was the vantage from which he'd watched these events when he was too young to attend and still longed to. The elegance, the glamour—long ago he'd found them fascinating. Now all he wanted to do was escape.

The band played one of the up-tempo, syncopated melodies that had become popular of late. Couples on the dance floor marched back and forth to the beat of the music. He wasn't the best at these modern dances but enjoyed them more than the tamer, boring classic steps.

A delicate fragrance reached his nostrils, and for a moment, his heart rose in his chest. But the light feminine scent wasn't Jasminda's. He turned to find Lizvette standing next to him.

"How did I know I'd find you hiding back here?" she asked, a smile on her lips. There was still tension around her eyes, but Jack knew that would take time to fade.

"What can I say? I'm terribly predictable."

She stepped to him, linking an arm through his and peering out at the crowded dance floor. "Perhaps *consistent* is a better word."

"Yes, I far prefer that. And I'm not hiding. I'm biding my time."

She chuckled and pulled him toward the doorway. "Come, Your Grace. There is no time like the present. And yes, I would love to dance."

He barely masked his grimace but followed her out past the bewildered lead butler just as the band finished the current song. The man scampered up to the microphone on the bandstand and rushed through the recitation of Jack's titles at top speed as all present bowed.

Jack suppressed a groan as the band started in on a tame, traditional melody. He danced the long-practiced steps with Lizvette, holding her stiffly. Just beyond the dance floor, glass doors opened to the terrace and gardens beyond. A cool breeze filtered in, reminding him of his time in the mountains.

He could almost imagine he was holding Jasminda. They had never danced, though. Perhaps he would have a phonograph delivered to her rooms so he could hold her against him and feel her heartbeat as they moved in time to the music. The thought loosened the tension that was binding him. He would dance a few more songs, then steal away to be with her.

"My father came to see you, did he not?"

Jack tuned back in to the room, almost having forgotten it was Lizvette he held. "Ah, yes. He told you about that. I'm sorry he had to bother you with that business. Don't worry. The thought never crossed my mind."

She grew rigid beneath his fingertips. "Would it be so bad?" Sad eyes blinked up at him, and he missed a step, nearly bumping into a burly man dancing inelegantly beside him.

"What are you saying?" He was barely able to get the words out through his shock.

"I know the press has been harsh . . . with everything about your mother and this dreadful business with the Lagrimari. I just . . . Well, perhaps Father is right. Perhaps I can help."

Her face was open and hopeful. He couldn't sense any guile there, but her words were madness.

"What of Alariq? His memory?"

She lowered her head. "I will always hold Alariq's memory dear. He was truly one of a kind. But wouldn't he want you to be at your best advantage? I think he would want this."

Jack snorted. "My brother would not so much as let me borrow a pair of his shoes, much less his future wife."

"Alariq is dead." Her voice was clipped. "And I am not a pair of shoes." The eyes staring up at him were full of hurt.

"Of course not, Lizvette. I didn't mean to say . . . I only meant that . . . Wouldn't Alariq have wanted for you to find love again? Happiness? Not just sacrifice yourself to aid my popularity."

Her expression melted as she looked up at him. "Love?" She said the word like it was a curiosity, some foreign species of fruit that had appeared on her table. Her hand on his arm squeezed gently, then turned into almost a caress. Discomfort swirled within him. "Do you not think something could grow? Here?" She placed a hand on his heart.

The music stopped, and the other couples on the dance floor clapped. Jack drew away from Lizvette, from the unwelcome pressure of her hand on his chest, and turned to politely applaud, as well. He used the moment to gather his thoughts. She was in mourning, perhaps confused. He and Alariq were not much alike, but perhaps she was only grasping for the last threads of him left. He'd known her his whole life . . . at least he thought he knew her.

He bowed to her. "Thank you for the dance." Ignoring the question in her eyes, he rushed off the dance floor to stand near the doors leading to the terrace. The collar of his shirt constricted like a noose. He longed for fresh air to breathe.

"Your Grace," a voice called out behind him. He turned to find a cluster of men from the Merchants' Board regarding him expectantly.

He could see now how the conversation would go: a few minutes of pleasantries, how beautifully the ballroom was decorated, how fine the musicians. Then possibly a round of complaints when he inquired after their families—a son too enthralled by the weekly radio dramas for their liking or a daughter being courted by an unsuitable beau. Then, far too quickly, they would get around to what they really wanted to talk to him about. Some favor or request, with just a nudge so that he recalled how useful their support was and thinly veiled threats of the damage that would take place if that support were withdrawn. Nothing overt, but enough pressure exerted on any joint could eventually cause a break.

The men wrangled from him a promise to consider a proposal to reduce worker wages. He didn't tell them that as soon as the plan escaped their lips he did consider it . . . and found it untenable. No, he smiled and nodded, shook hands and wished them back to wherever they'd come from as quickly as possible. Just when he thought the Queen had finally smiled upon him and the conversation had reached its death throes, a rotund character called Dursall spoke up.

"Quite a shame what happened to that little *grol* boy."

Jack's jaw clenched at the epithet.

"Well, with so many of them there, something like that was bound to happen," a wine importer named Pindeet said.

"I don't know," said Dursall. "I don't suppose a *grol* is any more likely to commit violence than, say, an Udlander. If they were brought up in a proper environment, I'd think you could almost entirely erase their more barbaric tendencies." The gathered men nodded in agreement. "Speaking of which, what's this I hear of a Lagrimari woman staying in the palace?"

Jack chose his words very carefully. "She is Elsiran. Born of a settler and a woman of the Sisterhood."

"Quite unusual," Dursall said. "But it proves my point. Perhaps it is in large part due to the gift of half her parentage, but from all accounts she is well spoken and well groomed. I daresay almost fit for polite society. How do you find her, Your Grace?"

Eight pairs of eyes were trained on him. He tasted each word on his tongue before allowing it to leave his mouth. "In truth, I don't know her that well. In the handful of times in which I've made her acquaintance, I've found her to be quite . . . acceptable." He swallowed.

The conversation continued for a few minutes but was impossible for him to follow. He regretted the words as soon as they'd left his mouth, but what was he to say? To mention that he was in a constant state of longing for her touch, that a day without seeing her was incomplete, that she was the most fearless and impressive woman he had ever encountered would have been more than these old hogs needed to know.

He was about to slip out to the terrace when an elderly woman dripping in diamonds, the wife of a former Council member, stopped him to attempt to wrangle an invitation for her *very eligible* granddaughter to the next state dinner. Jack looked longingly at the doors to freedom before plastering on a smile.

CHAPTER FORTY-ONE

Eagle warned Horse, Tread with caution and tranquility; the ground ahead is full of brambles.

Horse shook off the warning saying, Watching your feet is a sure way to bump your head.

—COLLECTED FOLKTALES

The pounding of rain against the window left Jasminda anxious and on edge. The storm had caught up with her. Each drop of water held untapped menace and eroded whatever sense of calm she'd held since that night at the Eastern Base.

Her emotions were raw, not just from the arrival of the True Father's storm, but from her sleepless night.

The evening before, she'd watched the ball from the shadows of the terrace. She'd merely wanted to glimpse the festivities and to see Jack in his finery once again. Hiding amidst the billowing folds of the curtains, she'd felt like a ghost, as though her existence was mere myth.

Her heart had leapt when Jack had come so near, almost close enough to touch. But she'd also been close enough to overhear what he said to those aristocrats, how he'd called her "acceptable." The words echoed in her head, seizing her heart in an icy grip. She knew she wasn't being fair, she understood his evasion, but nothing about this situation was fair, nothing about her life had ever been.

He hadn't come to her that night, either. Usher had brought her a note with Jack's apologies. Urgent matters of state kept him away.

Now she sat in the palace's Blue Library, books spread around her, trying to concentrate. She forced herself to focus on the book in her lap—Elsiran history. Wanting to start at the beginning, she'd pulled down dozens from the shelves, growing more and more uneasy with each one she read. The history before the war was treated like a fairy tale or a parable. Tales of the Founders were little more than children's stories written for adults. There were no dates, no names or locations—just stories of wonder and generosity from the esteemed Founders and whimsical folktales about their offspring.

Even the fates of the Lord and Lady were never mentioned, only that leadership eventually passed to one of their descendants, the Queen Who Sleeps, who continued their wonderful work. Then, inevitably, each book would contain a short and very vague passage on her betrayal by the True Father and the spell he cast that placed her into an endless sleep. A sleep that could only be broken if he were sent to the World After. His true identity or where he came from were never touched upon. Nor were his motives.

It was as if history and myth had intertwined somehow, and vital facts had been lost or obscured. And now she was beginning to understand the truth through her visions. Nothing in the recorded histories could disprove what the caldera showed. And the emotions she felt when she was Oola, the Queen, were all too real. Every sorrow, every bit of angst and guilt and fear became hers, and lasted long after she came back to herself.

The time between the visions was shortening as well. This morning she'd seen a brief vision of Yllis asking Oola to marry him. It was not the first time he'd asked, and she again denied him. Her emotions had been unstable—finding her brother and restoring peace to their land had been all she could think about—but her Song sensed Yllis's frustration and pain. The vision ended abruptly, almost in the middle of a thought, and Jasminda hoped she would be strong enough to try the caldera again later that night.

She looked up from her spot on the floor and stifled a gasp to find Lizvette standing before her, willowy and elegant in a cream-colored gown.

"I didn't mean to shock you. Please forgive me," Lizvette said.

"No, I'm sorry. You haven't been standing there long, have you?"

"No." The generous way she smiled made Jasminda think that wasn't precisely the case.

Jasminda rose and tiptoed her way out of the prison of books she'd created, motioning to a set of chairs at one of the study tables. Lizvette perched in her seat, back straight, hands folded neatly in her lap. Jasminda copied her pose, but her body didn't take to it naturally.

Lizvette looked around. "I never come in here. It's so odd that I've lived in the palace all my life and rarely take advantage of its resources."

Jasminda shrugged. "It's easy to take things for granted. Hard to believe that what seems permanent could ever be taken away." She sank in her seat like a deflating balloon.

"You have had a great many losses?" Lizvette's body was rigid, but her voice was kind.

"I've lost everything. Everything I've ever had." Jasminda snapped her back straight again and refused to give in to the melancholy. "But I'm sure you don't want to hear about my sorrows."

"I cannot imagine what it must be like."

"You've had your share."

Lizvette's only response was a thinning of her lips. Jasminda opened herself to a trickle of Earthsong, becoming better at shielding each time she tried. Lizvette's emotions swirled in a storm of grief and longing. Surprised at their strength and depth, Jasminda lost her hold, and the connection slammed shut. The other woman's placid, controlled face hid a maelstrom of pain.

Jasminda's heart went out to her. "Would it . . . help to talk about him?"

Lizvette's eyes widened, and her hands clenched in her lap.

"Prince Alariq?" Jasminda prompted. "It's said talking about our departed ones keeps them alive in our hearts."

Lizvette released her hands to the arms of the chair and took a deep breath. "Oh, Alariq. Yes. I mean, no, thank you. I . . ." She smoothed out the fabric of her pristine dress and smiled. "I came to see you to give you a warning. I'm afraid it might not be safe for you here in the palace. Things are becoming quite strained with public opinion regarding the refugees. Jack is doing his best, but he faces heavy opposition."

Jasminda's slippered foot tapped the floor as tension seeped into her limbs. "You think someone will harm me?"

Lizvette's long neck stretched impossibly longer. She stood and crossed to the shelves, holding the most recent newspaper. "Have you seen today's paper?"

When Jasminda shook her head, Lizvette brought it over, smoothing the pages on the table.

MYSTERIOUS LAGRIMARI WOMAN
HAS PRINCE IN A TWIST

His Grace, the Prince Regent has tongues around the palace wagging with his reported admiration for a young half-breed Lagrimari woman. Miss Jasminda ul-Sarifor, age and birthplace unknown, is a guest in the palace and has received the royal treatment. Records show that she was awarded the distinguished Order of the Grainbearer in a secret ceremony. Miss ul-Sarifor apparently saved the prince's life shortly before his coronation, though the details of the rescue have not been forthcoming.

Prince Jaqros has turned down the social invitations of several lovely young women in the Elsiran inner circle, purportedly to further his relationship with the exotic and interbred ul-Sarifor.

Her stay in the palace is said to be ongoing, and while officials are tight-lipped as to the true nature of her relationship with our new, young prince, our eyes and ears remain open.

"The *Rosira Daily Witness* is not much more than an extended gossip column," Lizvette was saying, though the oceanic roar of blood rushing through Jasminda's ears made it difficult to hear. A bubble of despair burst in her chest as she read the headlines and scanned the other articles. She pushed the paper away, not wanting to see any more.

Lizvette's eyes were glassy, her face sorrowful. "The press has always bothered him. They've never cut him any slack. Ever since his mother's emigration. And now it's worse than it was then." She clucked her tongue. "She was too young and possibly too delicate for the demands of palace life. It broke her."

Eyes the color of dying embers singed Jasminda. "He needs to be seen as strong. He needs to fill Alariq's shoes and be loved by his people and not hated. Do you understand?"

Jasminda nodded, fighting the approaching tears.

"Father says if he marries well, he can put these troubles behind him."

Cold fingers gripped Jasminda's heart. Lizvette's head lowered as she stared at the carpeting. A chilling knowledge bit Jasminda. She reached out for Earthsong again, this time prepared for the woman's hidden emotions. The longing pervading her was not a futile thing, as it would be for a departed lover. It was vibrant, vigorous, and full of life.

"Are you in love with him?" Jasminda asked, her whole chest numb.

Lizvette blinked, momentarily taken aback by the question. A crack of vulnerability broke through her poised demeanor. In an instant, it was gone. She rose. "I only offer you advice. Please be careful. It would break him if anything happened to you."

She left the room in a cloud of soft perfume, completely extinguishing the cooling cinders of hope still clinging to life inside Jasminda.

CHAPTER FORTY-TWO

Horse trotted into a briar patch. She struggled savagely to free herself, but the thorns dug in deeper.
Eagle passed by saying, Avoidance will always trump escape.

—COLLECTED FOLKTALES

Jasminda was unable to focus on the thick and dusty books any longer. A build-up of pressure sat on her heart, searching for an escape valve.

She pushed the restlessness down, determined not to allow the foul power threading through the rain to affect her again. Though she had not set foot outside since the storm had struck the city early in the morning, its repulsive energy penetrated the palace walls.

Her stomach grumbled; it was long past lunchtime. Thinking it best to avoid as many people as possible, she decided to locate the kitchen herself. No need to bother Nadal when she was perfectly capable of the task.

However, her confidence in her ability to manage the often

crisscrossing, often dead-end passageways of the palace had been optimistic at best. Swiveling her head back and forth at the T-shaped intersection in which she stood, she fought against the rising tide of hopelessness. The events of the past days rooted her where she stood. She feared she would never find her way again.

"May I be of assistance?" a deep voice purred behind her.

Jasminda turned to find the unpleasant man who'd practically dragged Lizvette away from her at that first dinner watching her from a doorway. Tall and broad-shouldered, he had unusually dark hair and a precise goatee. But he stared at her as if she were an item in the display case of the butcher's shop.

A surge of anger flared inside her at his self-important expression, tempting her to grab hold of her Song. She took a deep breath to release the tension and shook off the tingling in her limbs. The storm was playing its tricks again. "I don't believe we've been properly introduced. I am Jasminda ul-Sarifor." She held out her hands, challenging him to greet her properly.

"Zavros Calladeen, Minister of Foreign Affairs." He ignored her outstretched palms but bowed deeply. The bow was more formal than the pressing of hands and indicated a higher level of respect, but she got the sense he found it distasteful to touch her.

"I was searching for the kitchens," she said.

"Are your servants inadequate?"

"Not at all. But I'm the independent sort." She tilted her chin higher, with each breath battling the desire to give life to her rage and wipe that haughty sneer off his face. She could rattle the ground beneath his feet or pull the moisture from the air and soak him where he stood. But she held herself very still—on the edge of a knife blade of control.

"Allow me to escort you." He offered his elbow, though his expression made her think he meant to jab her with it.

"Oh, that's not necessary." Spending another moment in his company might just tip her over the edge.

"I must insist," he said. "You never know when there may be unsavory characters around." He spread his arms to indicate the potential villains lurking about, but the only unsavory person here was him. "I'm sure our Prince Regent would never forgive me if harm were to befall you."

"I appreciate your concern for my welfare, but I am in no need of escort from you."

He quirked an eyebrow. "You have had a stimulating few days here, I'm told."

She remained silent, practically vibrating with tension.

"The incident at the refugee camp? I hear you were quite near the action."

She gripped the fabric of her dress in tight fists to stop the shaking of her hands. The images flooded her, only serving to heighten her building fury. "If by stimulating, you mean horrifying, then you are correct. That soldier had no honor, shooting a child."

Calladeen drew uncomfortably close. Her Song slipped free of her grasp, reaching for the well of Earthsong, filling her with vibrant energy. Her shield came up effortlessly.

"You feel the Prince Regent is acting honorably in subjecting the captain to a court-martial that could result in his execution?" he asked.

A spell escaped her, lowering the temperature in the hallway. Her voice was layered with ice when she responded, "That captain would have killed the boy for no reason if there had been no Earthsingers present. The prince is doing the only honorable thing."

Calladeen shivered visibly in the rapidly cooling corridor. "Such a shame that honor is not the most important quality in a leader. Leadership is about making hard choices and not indulging one's every whim. For example, bringing home a stray pet is not in line with effective governance."

Jasminda narrowed her eyes as the space between them chilled so drastically she could see her breath in the air. "Say what you think you need to say to me."

He pulled his collar closer to his neck as he pinned her with an accusatory glare. He must have known it was her doing this. Satisfaction unfurled within her, warming her blood. She smiled cruelly as he took a step back, a tinge of fear leaching some of the contempt from his expression.

"Your presence is a problem," he said. "You make him weaker. Unfortunately, Jaqros is the only prince we have. He is not strong enough to survive the scandal of an attachment with you. He needs a princess the people can rally around, not some mongrel whore installed in the palace."

The crack of her hand against his cheek echoed across the marble floors. She had never slapped someone so hard before. She had never slapped anyone ever. But the bubbling madness inside of her applauded. Her Song surged, seeking other ways to retaliate.

Calladeen smirked, crystals of frost gathering in his goatee. Jasminda took a deep breath, vibrating with energy seeking an outlet.

"Zavros." Jack stepped into view from behind Calladeen. The prince was all warrior now, face cut from stone. His voice was low and deadly, forcing the taller man backward a step. "If you ever so much as look in her direction again, I will personally ensure your eligibility for the Order of Eunuchs. If you have a problem with me, you bring it to me. You do not speak to her. You do not look at her. As far as you are concerned, she does not exist."

Calladeen's eyes widened.

"Now get out of my sight."

The man lowered into a hasty bow before fleeing down the hallway.

The ferocious rage that had built inside Jasminda deflated with a pop. She released her Song, and the hallway warmed instantly.

Jack reached for her. She longed to fall into his arms but instead took a step back. His forehead crinkled in confusion. "Are you all right?"

Shaking her head, she took another step away from him. She didn't trust herself, and as glad as she was to see Jack—glad that he'd intervened before the storm pushed her even further—the pain building within her came rushing to fill the space the anger had occupied.

"I caught the tail end of what he said." Jack looked angrily toward the direction Calladeen had departed in. "You know I would not let anyone harm you. You're too important to me."

"Me? Important? I thought I was merely acceptable." The words flew from her mouth, a final, bitter assault from her stung pride.

Understanding dawned on his face. "You heard that last night? You know I didn't mean—"

"Shh. Someone may overhear. Voices carry up here, don't they?" She motioned along the long, resonating hallway.

Jack took another step toward her, but she motioned him to stop, shaking her head. "Please don't."

With a final look in his pleading eyes, she turned and fled. His expression was burned into her memory, but she had to escape. She didn't want to be near Jack with the storm's venom running through her veins.

Eventually, a passing servant stopped and, at her request, directed her to the vehicle depot. Lunch could wait. She had to find Nash.

CHAPTER FORTY-THREE

The Mistress of Serpents came upon a man sleeping by the riverside. In slumber, all are powerful, she thought. But awake, we are trapped by our memories of liberty.

—COLLECTED FOLKTALES

Somber men in dark suits with even darker expressions lined the streets. A few women were scattered among the group, as well, many waving hand-painted picket signs with slogans like WAGES NOT WITCHCRAFT! and FEED THE PEOPLE NOT THE REFUGEES!

Jack's motorcade wound its way back to the palace. He had spent the afternoon fulfilling a guest appearance Alariq had scheduled at the Export Council. Smiling and touching palms and glad-handing bigwigs and fat cats was not how he'd wanted to spend his day. And now, it seemed, the poor were having their say as well.

He did not begrudge the people their anger, if only they would focus it in the right direction. They needed someone to blame for the misfortunes of late, and the Lagrimari refugees were simply convenient. But the asylum seekers had not caused the poor harvest or the shipping embargo. And their absence could not fix them, either.

A smaller group of refugee supporters standing closer to the palace lifted his spirits somewhat. Not everyone in his land was so callous. Then a woman with a sign reading WHY NOW? rapped on the window as the limo slowed for a sharp turn. Yes, why now?

Back in his office, he'd barely gotten his coat off when his secretary ran up out of breath. "The Council called an emergency meeting an hour ago, Your Grace. They're voting."

"Voting on what?"

"I'm not sure, Your Grace. They wouldn't say."

"Thank you, Netta." Jack straightened his suit coat and rushed to the Council Room. He opened the door and six faces regarded him. Some looked shocked, some guilty, and several entirely too smug.

"What is the meaning of this?" he asked, dropping heavily into his seat. The Council could meet as long as a quorum had been reached, but to do so without the Prince Regent present was unheard of.

"Your Grace." Stevenot's eyes were wide and round. "The people are demanding action. We could not afford to wait."

"Action?" Jack's brows raised.

"Yes, we've received a petition with well over two thousand names."

"And what do all these people want?"

Calladeen leaned forward, hands clasped in front of him. "To eject the refugees from Elsira."

"We have already voted," Pugeros added.

Jack held himself very still, reining in his ire. "I see you've been most efficient, doing so without the added burden of my presence."

"It was urgent." Calladeen's voice was a rumble.

"The terms the True Father demanded," Nirall said, looking a bit green. "We've agreed to them."

"You bloody well haven't!" Jack roared.

"We had to. Public safety is at risk. There was a riot down in Portside this morning." Nirall's expression was apologetic.

"You are falling right into his hands! This is what he wants. I will not let you do this. I will veto."

"And what happens when news of the True Father's letter gets out and the people learn that we had a chance for peace and did nothing?" Pugeros asked.

"How would word of the letter be made public unless someone in this room does so?" Jack peered at faces gone suddenly blank. "You threaten to reveal classified national secrets to get your way?"

Calladeen spoke. "The Council vote was unanimous, Your Grace. The only way to veto would be to invoke Prince's Right and dissolve this body."

A hush fell across the room.

Jack fisted his hands on the armrests. *Unanimous?* Not even Nirall had seen reason. Jack's veto would have stood if even one Council member had dissented, but Calladeen was correct. In the history of Elsira, only one other prince had invoked Prince's Right. That ancestor of his had been branded a tyrant and beheaded in a coup. With the enflamed emotions of the populace being what they were, Jack could not expect his fate to be any different.

The meeting continued around him, wrapping up. The ministers gave him a wide berth. Jack was certain his anger could be felt, radiating off him like waves of heat. He hoped it singed everyone it touched. He had been outmaneuvered, and deftly so. These men wouldn't have dared do this to his brother, box him into a corner in this way.

The wood grain of the table was smooth against his flattened palms. The voices of the men faded as he studied it.

Here he sat in the chair his brother had occupied. And his father. And his grandfather and great-uncle. A member of the Al-liaseen family had been the Prince Regent since the loss of the Queen. The blood in his veins was noble, royal. That was supposed to mean he possessed the best qualities of an Elsiran.

And yet he had lost.

The refugees would be sent back to a life that was not a life. Back to die. He could not save them, any of them.

His mother, gone without a word. His brother, determined to pilot that wretched airship, no matter how foolish. Jasminda, harassed by a member of his own Council, the press nipping at her heels.

He was unworthy of the crown, the responsibility, the power. Even unworthy of the woman he loved.

She had walked away from him in the hallway earlier, as she should have. She'd been in pain—pain he had caused. His heart splintered.

What would his legacy be? Would the pages of the history books be kind? Or would they only remember him for dooming hundreds of innocents? For the loss of an entire nation?

This illusion of peace would be short-lived.

The True Father would destroy the Mantle—perhaps tomorrow or next month or next year. And what then? Being right would not save his people.

The knots in the wood of the table kept their silence, though they stared back at him in accusation. He did not blame them.

CHAPTER FORTY-FOUR

War.

    Silent versus Songbearer.

    Blood in the streets.

    Silent outnumber Songbearers more than ten to one, and while Eero has not turned them all against us, he has managed to bring many more than I ever imagined over to his side.

    I always thought he was able to wrap me around his finger because of my weakness for him, my love. But it is a talent of his. He is charming. When he talks, people listen. They believe and trust him. They follow him, taking up arms against their neighbors, rending our land in two.

    Our Songs make us fearsome foes, though Earthsong cannot be used to kill. But none who have felt the energy of a million lives strumming in his or her veins can rejoice in sending any living creature to the World After.

    Early on, we healed any Silent harmed in an attack. The Assembly believed this would bring them to our side. But it did not. I cannot understand if the Silent are jealous of our Songs or fearful of them. The truth likely lies in a combination of the two.

Swords clash. The Silent fight through the rain and ice, the mudslides and fire. They are pelted with rocks, tumbled by earthquakes, but they persist.

It is within the power of the Songbearers to entirely unmake the land from the fabric of its being, in the same way that we do the reverse, creating a beautiful landscape where once a desert stood. But we think of the future—a future of peace.

Eero knows my weaknesses. He knows me too well. I should never have been made Queen to lead the fight against him. I am the last person who should have been chosen.

Yllis studies with the Cantors day and night. His guilt is an anchor around his neck. It pulls him away from me. I have not allowed him to answer for his part in the scheme to help Eero sing. And I have not agreed to marry him. How could I with things the way they are? I thought I was protecting him by accepting all the blame, but that and my repeated refusals of his marriage offers have changed things between us.

The hurt in his eyes when he looks upon me cuts deep. So deep I do not believe I have a heart any longer. My heart was never my own. It belonged more to the ones I loved than to me.

War.

It drags us under.

It tears us apart.

CHAPTER FORTY-FIVE

A traveler stood at a crossroads, uncertain of which way to go.

The Mistress of Frogs whispered in his ear, Just as lightning transforms the tree into cinder, so does doubt change progress to stagnation.

—COLLECTED FOLKTALES

Jack padded into Jasminda's chamber well after midnight, unsure of what his reception would be. His heart was weighed down by heavy chains, and the only thing that could lift his spirits was her—even though she would be well justified in refusing to see him.

She was still awake, sitting by the fire, staring pensively into the dancing flames. He approached with halting steps. She looked up, eyes shining with unshed tears, and Jack dropped to his knees.

"The servants are gossiping something fierce. Is it true? The refugees are being sent back to Lagrimar?"

A great hollow space opened in Jack's chest. He nodded.

"Oh, Jack." She collapsed against him. He exhaled the breath he'd been holding since he'd seen her last.

"I have prayed to the Queen, but She has given no counsel. I do not think I hold Her favor."

"Jack," she whispered, wrapping her arms around him and drawing him closer. His body relaxed, at home with her in his arms. "You are a good prince. You are selfless and fearless."

His head dropped. "I am constantly afraid."

She grabbed his chin and tilted his face up. "But you rise above it."

He smiled grimly. "Even you are too good for me."

"Nonsense," she said, and pressed her lips to his. He kissed her back greedily, holding her head firmly in his grip.

"I'm so sorry about earlier," she said. "I wasn't myself."

"No, I'm sorry."

She brushed her fingers across his lips. "I have no right to change the rules we both agreed upon."

He shook his head. "I don't want there to be any rules for us. I just wish . . ." He squeezed her tightly to his chest again, not sure even of what to wish for. A different world, a kinder one.

He rose and lifted her so he could sit in the chair with her on his lap. He rubbed circles into her back, noting the tension in her muscles.

"What will happen to me?" Her voice was empty as an echo.

He shifted so he could peer into her eyes. Misery suffused the beauty of her face. "Jasminda—"

"Half-breed. Mongrel. That's what the papers say, right? I do you no favors by staying here. And didn't the True Father's letter say every Lagrimari must be sent back?"

Jack's lungs compressed as if he were at the peak of a mountain sucking in air too thin to quench his need. "You are not Lagrimari."

"Am I not?" Her eyes were almost wild. "I may have been born in your land, share half your blood, but I'm not one of you. I'm not one of them, either. I don't belong anywhere, Jack."

"No," he said, voice steely. "No, you belong with me." He held her tighter, his chest vibrating with the racing of her heart.

"For how long? How long until you must find an acceptable princess? One that you need in order to regain the people's trust? We were only ever going to be temporary."

He crushed her to him and stroked her soft, springy hair. "Are you saying you want to leave?"

"No."

"Then—"

"But I cannot stay."

He shook his head rapidly, desperate to jostle a solution into his brain. "If being prince is good for anything, then I should get to be with the woman I love." He pulled away and clutched her hands to his chest. "Do you hear me? I love you."

Saying it out loud took the edge off the panic building at the thought of her leaving. "You are strong and intelligent and fearless and beautiful. I had never even hoped a woman like you existed. I love you, Jasminda."

Tears traced her face. "I love you, too. You must know that. You are my whole heart, Jaqros Alliaseen. My whole heart. I never thought I would . . ."

She looked away, and he wiped her streaming cheeks.

"Do you want to know what I saw, in that awful test to find the cornerstone?" Jack's voice sounded hollow to his own ears.

Jasminda looked up, eyes wide. They hadn't spoken of their visions. He had no wish for Jasminda to relive whatever horrors she'd seen, but now he felt the need to tell her.

"I saw my land in flames. My people dying in the streets because of my failure. And I saw you." His voice cracked. "I saw you being carried away from me. Ripped out of my arms, screaming."

She cupped his cheeks, tears filling her eyes. She kissed him softly, first on his lips, then his cheeks, eyelids, nose, forehead, before returning to his mouth.

She was so gentle it made him anxious. He did not deserve such tenderness. He deepened the kiss, grabbing hold of her waist and stroking her side. The tightness she'd held melted away as her arms came around his neck.

Jack lifted her and carried her to the bed. She kneeled on the mattress as he stood devouring her mouth with needy kisses. She slid her palms down his chest and began working on the buttons of his shirt. Her expertise at removing men's clothing had grown, and she had the shirt hanging open and the trousers pushed to his knees in record time.

As he was undoing the ties of her dress and sliding it over her head, a blade of awareness sliced into him. Jasminda was soft and pliable, her body receptive to his touch, but something was different. There was a distance present between them that had never been there before, even as she discarded her slip with a seductive smile and lay back, inviting him between her thighs.

Vowing to make this night more memorable than any other, he set upon her with a fervor, licking and stroking his way up her legs. He reached her core and lapped at her, stroking her entrance teasingly. She panted and cried out his name, begging for more, but he held off giving her what she wanted. He brought her to the brink of climax, then eased her back down, ignoring her protests.

Satisfied when her limbs shook with need, he kissed his way up her belly. One hand glided to her breast, and with the other he plunged two fingers into her center, causing her to buck, her back arching as moans of pleasure escaped her. She was more than ready.

All it took was a thumb flicked across the right spot and she went over, cresting the wave.

When her cries gentled, they kissed and she guided him into her. The indefinable sensation of sinking deep inside her was so much more than lust. The gentle rhythm of their lovemaking sped up to a pounding beat as he fought to chase away the nagging worry, guilt, and fear. She loved him. She would stand by him in this dark time.

He drove into her, spurred on by her nails digging into his back and her mewls of pleasure. Losing himself in her skin, her scent, her cries, he could almost outrun the gloom of what was to come.

Afterward, she lay in his arms stroking his skin, not seeming to mind the sweat and stickiness after so much exertion. He held her tightly against him, as tight as he dared without crushing her. For even though she had been right with him the entire evening, a voice in the back of his head told him she was slipping away.

CHAPTER FORTY-SIX

The Master of Sharks visited a merchant dealing in rare and precious gems. How much of your profit do you give to the poor? he asked.

Why should I share the fruit of my labor? the merchant responded.

Shark replied, The gem that is most valuable, is the one shining upon the most people.

—COLLECTED FOLKTALES

Jasminda awoke alone. It was just as well. She would rather remember Jack as he was last night, holding her close, whispering how much he loved her. The vision he'd spoken of chilled her. She hated that she was going to make a small part of it a reality, but she had no other choice. Her love for him would do him little good in the long run.

She located her dress, the one she was wearing when she arrived. It had been washed and pressed and was the only thing she truly owned here. She also strapped a serrated knife, nicked from her dinner tray, to her thigh using a garter.

Though her heart was fracturing, it was time for her to go back home. She would continue to unlock the secrets of the caldera for as long as it took to gain answers. Once she knew more, she would contact the palace, but in the meantime she needed to find a way back east.

The palace hallways were quiet. Jasminda managed to locate the office nearest the vehicle depot and asked for Nash. Within a few minutes he appeared, a newspaper tucked under his arm. With a nervous glance at the paper, she wondered what today's story was.

"Is it done?" she asked.

"Yes, miss." His keen green gaze never strayed from her. "An account has been set up at the Royal Elsiran Bank. I have the deposit slip—"

She waved her hands to stop him. "I don't want to know how much. It was enough for the taxes and to buy back the land?"

He nodded. "And then some. The dealer's eyes nearly bugged out of his head when he caught sight of your Order of the Grainbearer medal. Very rare they are. It brought in a tidy sum."

"Well, you keep the rest. I—I don't want it." Her fingers twitched, remembering the feel of the soft velvet case and cool metal. Jack's cautious smile as he'd given it to her. It was done. On her terms at least. Her grandfather could take his shame-laden contract and swallow it whole for all she cared.

Rebuilding the cabin on her own would be slow, but she would manage it. What did she have if not time? A wave of dizziness swept over her at the thought. "I need to get out of here."

Nash's face softened. "Of course." He led her to the door, picking up a large, black umbrella from a stand full of them, and protected her from the driving rain as they stepped outside. Though there was a steady torrent, Jasminda was calm. The storm's power over her had always required a catalyst—her anger. When she was collected and even, she could stay in control. So leaving now was doubly necessary, before something else sparked her rage.

Just as she and Nash reached the row of town cars, rapidly approaching footsteps caused her to turn. Four Royal Guardsmen marched up, splashing across the pavement, stiff and imposing.

"Miss," one of the Guardsmen called as she backed toward the auto, "I need you to come with us."

She had never before been summoned by the Royal Guard. Usher had brought messages from Jack, but he'd never sent anyone else. She cast a glance at Nash, whose brow was furrowed, before turning and following the Guardsmen back into the palace.

Despite the large umbrella, her dress was soaked from her few minutes outside. She shivered, following the men through the halls to a wide doorway. They descended a staircase, wet steps squishing on the stones, then followed a hall leading to another staircase. At the end of a sparse hallway, a fifth Royal Guardsman stood before an elaborate brass gate that he unlocked as they approached, before ushering them through. Jasminda froze when the iron bars of the dungeon cells came into view.

"What is this about?" she asked, whirling around.

The door to a cell hung open, and the Guardsmen all stopped walking, blocking every direction except into the cell.

"I'm being arrested?" Her gaze darted around the small space, sparse but clean. "By whose order?"

The young, bland Guardsman did not look at her as he spoke: "Miss, by order of Prince Jaqros you are remanded here for your own protection."

"My protection? From what?"

"Please, miss," he said, pointing to the cell.

"Why am I here? Why won't you tell me?"

"Miss Jasminda," a familiar voice said. Usher stepped out from behind the row of Guardsmen. "There has been a threat made against you. He doesn't know who to trust. He's trying to protect you."

Fear stole the strength out of her budding anger. Lizvette had hinted as much the day before, but an actual threat turned her blood cold. "Then perhaps I would be safer elsewhere. He should just let me go."

With no other options, she stepped inside the cell and shuddered as the door clanked shut behind her.

"He is not strong enough to do that." Usher stepped to the bars and slipped a thick, warm blanket through a gap. Jasminda accepted it, lay down on the thin cot, and cried.

CHAPTER FORTY-SEVEN

That is impossible, *Vaaryn says through his Song.*

Then how would you explain it? *Deela, Yllis's mother, replies. She, Vaaryn, and I sit in the Great Hall. There are still loyal Silent working as servants here, but there are no doubt also spies for the other side, as well. No important conversation is held out loud any longer.*

No Songbearer would gift Eero their Song. There are only two who even know the spell. *Deela looks at me, and I shrink a bit more inside.*

So you believe he has actually learned to steal a Song from a bearer? *Vaaryn's forehead wrinkles in disbelief.* That would be . . .

A disaster, *I finish. But it must be true. Eero is singing again. Through the window, the battle for the skies is clear. Only hours ago, the placid, clear day was interrupted by sudden, unnatural clouds. Songbearers on the front lines have had to fend off tornadoes, hurricanes, snow, and ice all afternoon.*

Who has he stolen from? *Deela says.*

I shake my head. We are still accounting for all of the Songbearers in the city.

Will all the Silent want Songs now? *Vaaryn wonders.*

I frown, considering. I do not think he will want to share. My brother was never generous.

How do they still follow him? Do they not find him a hypocrite? Especially when his demands are for a separate land for the Silent. *Deela's face is so like Yllis's, even more so when working out a difficult problem.* He has split us apart and wants to make it official, by creating a land just for them, yet he steals the Song of a Songbearer.

His gift is winning the hearts and minds of others, *I say.* Logic is not always required for that. And as for his demands, perhaps we should give him what he wants.

Vaaryn's rheumy eyes go wide.

Hear me out. If we take the abandoned land east of the mountains, we could reform it and rebuild, just as we did this land, *I say.* We could leave the west to the Silent and rebuild to the east.

I let them mull over my suggestion for a while. The thought of leaving my home sickens me, but this war must end.

We must bring this to the Assembly, *Deela says.*

I nod, certain I can convince them.

At least once he is separated from the Songbearers, he will not be able to steal what the Silent do not possess. *Deela seems reassured by this.*

Eero has already stolen so much from the Silent—their peace, their stability, their future—but I keep these thoughts to myself as we take our leave.

Yllis finds me before sunset as I pace the floors of the Great Hall, awaiting updates from those on the front lines. He is rumpled and creased, his hair is lopsided, but he is as beautiful to me as ever.

"You must come with me," he says. I startle at hearing his voice aloud,

but I am so grateful he has spoken. He leads me to his office in the labora-tory of the Cantors.

"I think I have found a way."

"Do you think it wise to speak?" Though I love to hear his voice, I, too, have been seized by the paranoia affecting the other Songbearers.

"You, too, Oola?" He pins me with a withering glare, one I must grow used to seeing from him. What once was soft and cherished between us is now all hard edges. "No Silent are allowed within the walls of the Cantors."

"Very well. You think you have found a way to do what?"

He points down to his leather-bound notebook. Tight handwriting fills every page, obscuring the color of the original paper.

"I have studied everything we have on the ancient ways of the Cavefolk. They are Silent but manage to harness a vast power different than Earthsong—from a different source. Just as powerful but not as lim-ited. Cantors have long used the Cavefolk techniques, but only with Earth-song. They have never attempted any of the more robust spells because they all require one key ingredient." His finger stops below one word, written boldly, traced over and over.

Blood.

I meet Yllis's eyes, which gleam in the lamplight.

"With blood magic, we can create a spell to silence any Song," he says.

"Blood magic?" I shake my head and step away. "We cannot."

He steps toward me, his eyes on fire. "We must."

"No, there is another way." I tell him of the plan I shared with the others. "What he wants is his own land. The war will end once we give him this."

Yllis stares at me for a long while, and shivers run up my spine. "You were always blind when it came to him."

"What do you mean?"

For a moment, the hard shell he's constructed around himself cracks, and I see a glimpse of the man I fell in love with. Yllis moves closer to me, placing his hands on my shoulders. "He wants what he has always wanted: power."

I shiver. Both from the truth of his words and his close proximity.

"So this spell . . . how does it work?"

"It is a binding spell to prevent connection with Earthsong."

"And we will need someone's blood?"

His eyes darken, and he nods. "Let me worry about that. Link with me, and I will teach you the spell."

His hand is the same as I remember. Warm and big, it swallows mine. I hardly get to relish the feeling of his skin when I'm thrown into his link. The feel of the spell sours my tongue, but I commit it to memory.

CHAPTER FORTY-EIGHT

The Master of Jackals waded into the sea and found a fish floundering in a forgotten net.

When he went to free it, the fish responded, Leave me be.

Said the Jackal, Don't you want to be free?

The fish replied, I do not trust you not to eat me. I will take my chances with the will of the ocean.

—COLLECTED FOLKTALES

The young maid standing in Jack's office sniffled and wrung her hands. "No, Your Grace. I would never let anyone else in Miss Jasminda's rooms. Never." Red-rimmed eyes overflowed with tears. "I always saw to her myself, just as Usher asked."

Jack sighed and paused his pacing. "And you have no idea how anyone would have gotten hold of this?" He pointed to the low table where the beautiful, delicate, golden gown Jasminda had worn her first night in the palace lay. It had been found, slashed and partially burned, outside the doors to the Prince Regent's office suite.

"No, Your Grace." The girl shook her head violently, took another look at the gown, and burst into a fresh round of sobs.

"All right, all right, Nadal," Jack said, motioning for Usher to comfort her. "I believe you. But you haven't heard anything from the other servants?"

She leaned into Usher and quieted. "Some of them have been cool toward me since I wouldn't gossip about Miss Jasminda with them. I haven't heard anything."

Jack dropped roughly onto the couch, nervous energy rattling through him. He answered the question in Usher's gaze with a nod, and the man led Nadal away, returning alone a few minutes later.

"She's going to hate me," Jack said as he rubbed his burning eyes, wishing he could rub away the weariness and the heartache. "She has every right to. But she's in the safest place in the palace. Almost anyone could have sneaked into her rooms. Any person in this palace could mean her harm."

Usher clucked his tongue; Jack looked up. "What?"

"You should go to her, young sir."

"Was she really leaving?" Jack sank down, every bone in his body feeling twice its weight.

"It appears so," Usher replied, apologetic.

Jack groaned, closing the lid on the emotions that threatened to spill out at the thought of Jasminda's absence. A horrifying idea struck him. "Mother often talked of wanting to leave. I would hear them arguing. . . . Father would never let her." He scrubbed a hand over his face. "I'm just like him, aren't I? I will never be able to escape the shadow of his cruelty."

He stood and walked to the terrace doors, looking out at the city stretching before him and beyond, to the endless waves of the ocean, turned dark and ominous, churning from the force of the storm.

Usher came to stand by him. "You are nothing like him."

Jack rested his forehead against the cool glass. The weather outside matched the agitated whirlwind inside him. "Then why do I feel like the villain here?"

The buses with the refugees were now on their way toward the border. By this time tomorrow, they would all be back across the mountain. Only the Queen knew what their fates would be, but Jack could guess. He chuckled mirthlessly.

"What have I done, Usher? Sending the woman I love to the dungeons. Allowing the refugees to be sent back. What does this make me?"

"It makes you a prince."

"And what is that worth when I can't save anyone?"

The darkness in his heart was in danger of overtaking him. He rubbed his chest as if he could massage the broken organ from the outside. "I must go to her. Either she'll forgive me or she won't. Besides, I don't want her staying in the palace any longer than necessary. You've gotten in touch with Benn's wife?"

"Yes, she's happy to let Jasminda stay with her down in Portside. The family will keep watch for trouble." Usher's reassuring voice was a balm to Jack's soul.

"All right. She should be safe there while I ferret out whoever's responsible." He cast another glance at the ruined dress; anger beat a rhythm inside his chest. "I can't fail her, too," he rasped, nearly choking on the words.

Usher clapped him on the shoulder and squeezed. Some days the only thing keeping Jack upright was the man's presence.

He gave Usher a sidelong glance. "How do you stand me, old man?"

"I don't really have a choice, now, do I?" Usher said with a droll smile.

Jack shook his head and left for the dungeon, feeling even more guilty for keeping Jasminda locked away a moment longer than necessary. He had wanted her safe while he questioned the servants, but the task had taken longer than anticipated. As he entered the outer chamber leading to the cells, the guards snapped to attention.

"Captain," Jack said. "It's time to let her out."

The captain's eyes widened. "L-let her out, Your Grace?"

"Yes, open the cell. I'll take her with me."

The captain's gaze darted to his fellow guard, rigid beside him, then back to Jack. "B-begging your pardon, Your Grace, but she's already been let out."

Jack stilled, every muscle in his body tensing in alarm. "I gave explicit orders that the young woman was to be held here until I ordered her released."

"Yes, Your Grace."

"Then by whose authority was she released?" Jack roared.

"Yours, Your Grace." The captain held out a folded letter, stamped with the official seal of the Prince Regent. Jack snatched it from his hands and read the contents, instructions to release Jasminda to the custody of the letter's bearer.

He motioned for the guard to open the door to the cells and strode through, needing to see for himself that Jasminda was really gone. A blanket lay neatly folded on the cot inside an empty cell.

He spun back to face the captain. "Who brought this note?"

"A servant, Your Grace. A maid. I didn't know her."

"And you thought I'd send a maid to retrieve someone from custody?"

"The letter bears your seal, Your Grace."

Jack turned away, trying to tamp down the rage boiling in his bloodstream. At its edge was a cold fear. Whoever had stolen Jasminda's dress and destroyed it had wanted to send a message to Jack. They must have taken her as well. Would they really harm her? All to punish him?

One person had clashed swords directly with Jasminda recently. Someone who could gain access to the royal seal. Jack's breathing came in short spurts as he exploded from the dungeon, racing up the stairs three at a time.

"Where is Minister Calladeen?" he growled to the young man at the main Royal Guard station.

"He's in his offices, Your Grace."

A red haze swallowed Jack. His whole body quivered as he stalked down the hall and slammed his way into the offices of the Minister of Foreign Affairs. A startled young secretary yipped in alarm when Jack stormed into the inner office.

Calladeen stood, eyes wide.

"What did you do?" Jack demanded.

"I don't know what you're talking about."

Jack marched across the room until he was nearly nose to nose with the man. "Where is she?" he yelled. Calladeen shrank back, leaning almost comically away.

"Where is who, Your Grace?"

"Don't play games with me, man. Where is Jasminda?"

Calladeen placed two hands up in a motion of surrender and stepped away from the wall of anger radiating from Jack's body. Jack clenched and unclenched his fists, waiting for the moment when he could release his frustration in a flurry of violence.

"Your Grace, I swear by our Sovereign, I do not know."

Jack's glare was ruthless, and the man seemed genuinely afraid.

Jack held up the letter. "You did not forge this message from me ordering her release?"

Calladeen plucked the letter from Jack's hand and read it over, a frown pulling down his mouth. "No, I did not. But I do recognize the handwriting."

Jack had paid little attention to the curling script of the letter. "Whose is it?"

Calladeen's sharp face grew pensive. "Lizvette's."

CHAPTER FORTY-NINE

The Master of Monkeys was lost in his own maze for several eve-
nings. He would follow the moon thinking the light would show
him the way but found the moon to be an inconstant navigator.

—COLLECTED FOLKTALES

The caravan of buses rolled across the country as the wet day darkened into a tempestuous, thundery night. Rain pelted the metal of
the bus's roof so hard it sounded like hail. Jasminda sat near the
front, handcuffed to a bar running under the window.

On the bench across from her sat Osar, squeezed together
with a woman and two smaller children. All the mothers held
their children close, blanketed in fear and sadness. The refugees
had taken a risk in trusting their Elsiran neighbors, and they
had lost.

Jasminda felt her own loss acutely, the loss of Jack and now her
freedom. The cold metal bit into her skin when she jangled the
chain connecting the cuffs. The soldier sitting in front of her craned

his neck, glaring at her. She narrowed her eyes at him, hardening her stare until he turned around.

She'd thought being locked in the dungeon would be the worst this day would hold. She'd been wrong.

While imprisoned, she had mulled over the latest vision from the caldera while waiting for Jack to appear and explain himself. Then the clank of keys approaching had made her sit upright.

A young maid appeared outside her cell with two Guardsmen in tow. The door opened, and the girl motioned Jasminda forward. She stood, shocked the Guardsmen allowed the maid to lead her away.

"Did Jack send you?" Jasminda asked as she was passed a hooded cloak, large enough to cover her face. "Where are we going?"

"There's a car waiting for you, miss."

"To take me where?"

"We must hurry," the girl said, leading her through the servants' passages at a rapid pace.

The last vision had left Jasminda's Song depleted, so she could not test the maid's emotions. Jack would not have allowed her to be released to just anyone, though it was odd that he'd sent a servant she didn't know instead of Nadal or Usher. They soon arrived at an outer door. Just under the overhang, protected from the driving rain, Lizvette waited with an unfamiliar driver and vehicle.

Jasminda froze. "Jack didn't send you, did he?"

"It isn't safe here for you," Lizvette said, scanning the area as if a ruffian would spring from the bushes at any moment.

"Who wants to hurt me?"

"Please believe me. This is for the best." Lizvette wouldn't meet her eyes but nodded at the driver before turning away. "Do not harm her."

The burly man narrowed his icy gaze and approached. Fear

spurred Jasminda into action. She spun away and ran, but the driver reached out a long arm and grabbed her. She kicked and flailed, but her shout was muffled by his large hand covering her mouth. A pair of handcuffs clinked as the metal slid across her skin.

He manhandled her into the backseat where another man, who she hadn't noticed before, waited. In the brief moment when the driver removed his hand from her mouth, she gasped for air to scream, but a gag was stuffed between her lips and tied around the back of her head. She continued thrashing, but the second man held her in a crushing grip. The driver took his seat and slammed the door. Jasminda struggled to look out the window, seeing only Lizvette's retreating form disappearing into the palace.

Jasminda writhed and twisted, but the fellow holding her had arms of iron. Deciding to save her strength, she relaxed her body. Stealthily, she inched her skirt up to reach for the serrated knife strapped to her leg. She removed the blade and twisted again, preparing to slam it into her captor's thigh. The driver's gaze flicked to her in the rearview mirror, and he wrenched the steering wheel, swerving the car on the rain-slicked streets and knocking the knife from her grip.

Her captor growled and smashed her head against the window, momentarily blacking out her vision. She stilled as her wits returned and rested her head against the glass to cool the pounding.

Lizvette's betrayal shouldn't have been as shocking as it was. The woman's coy warnings the day before had been for what? To simply mask her own desire to do Jasminda harm?

As the car wound through the city, the storm pounded away. Once again Jasminda was relieved her Song was exhausted. She would cause no destruction now. Her head swam as the auto made a turn onto a muddy road that led to only one place.

The camp was in chaos when they arrived, stopping just past a line of waiting buses. The man holding her, whose face she still hadn't seen, pulled her from the auto. Cold rain sliced through her dress, numbing her. Rage roared inside with no outlet.

Dozens of Sisters stood before her, arms locked together, dresses plastered to their skin, topknots unraveling, attempting to form a human barrier between the soldiers and the refugees. The Sisters repeated a prayer over and over, asking the Queen Who Sleeps for protection.

Starting at the end of the line, the soldiers pried the Sisters' hands and arms apart as the women's prayer grew louder. Mud lapped at their ankles, and more than one man and woman slipped and splashed in the muck.

Behind the Sisters, refugees lined up solemnly in rows, waiting to board the buses, resigned to their fate. However, some would not go quietly. A handful screamed and wailed, planting themselves on the ground and refusing to move.

As the soldiers broke through the resistance of the Sisters, they also handcuffed protesting refugees and held them under armed guard before forcibly placing them on the buses. The man holding Jasminda transferred her to a young soldier who dragged her over to the group of restrained refugees and pushed her to the ground. Water and dirt oozed into her boots and coated her dress. Four men trained their rifles on the group.

Jasminda shivered. She angled her head down until she could pull the gag from her mouth, then sucked in deep breaths, surveying the turmoil around her.

A white-haired general barked orders, instructing his men to ensure every Lagrimari made it across the border. No exceptions.

"What if they won't go?" a lieutenant asked.

"Shoot them."

Jasminda's shivers turned into uncontrollable shaking. Those weren't Jack's orders, but it didn't seem to matter. Screams and cries filled the air.

Among the protesting Sisters was Aunt Vanesse, who spotted Jasminda and broke away from the others to rush to her side. She was distraught, wet hair caught in thick tangles down her back, her blue robes covered in mud.

"Oy!" Vanesse hailed one of the officers and pointed to Jasminda. "She is not a Lagrimari. She is an Elsiran citizen."

The lieutenant looked at Jasminda askance and raised his eyebrows. "Do you have proof of that, Sister?"

"You have my word as an Elsiran. This girl's mother was my sister," Vanesse pleaded.

The lieutenant shrugged. "Even if that were true, we're under orders." He looked Jasminda up and down again. "How Elsiran can she be if she looks that much like a *grol*?" He shrugged and stomped away.

Vanesse screamed, and Jasminda reached for her hand, clasping it in her bound ones. They were both icy cold. Vanesse fell to her knees, sobbing, but a strange calm had fallen over Jasminda. Her anger had changed, transforming into a bitter sort of pity that coated her tongue.

"We both know I don't really belong here."

"No. You're all I have left of Emi. I will find someone who will listen. You don't belong over there, either." Vanesse shuddered. "We can find a place for you. I promise." She squeezed Jasminda's chilled hands.

"Do *you* even have a place here? A way to be who you really are? With the person you love?" Jasminda's voice had an edge to it that she hadn't meant to put there.

Vanesse reared back as if slapped. Her mouth hung open. "What do you know of that?"

"I know that I love someone I can never be with. Not openly. And I thought stolen moments would be enough, but they're not. I don't want to be a secret, hidden away, never allowed to see the light of day. I don't want to be a liability. I want to be a treasure."

Recognition lit within Vanesse. "You *are* a treasure. I'm sorry that you haven't felt that way." She placed her palm on Jasminda's cheek, then leaned forward to kiss her forehead.

"I wanted to tell you—I discovered why Father needed you to sign those papers. It wasn't just because of his run for Alderman." Vanesse sniffed, regaining her composure to brush a sodden chunk of hair from her eyes. "Emi had a trust fund worth hundreds of thousands. Seven years after her death, if unclaimed by her legal heirs, it would go back to our parents. Father had a large investment go badly, and this shipping embargo has hit his business hard. He had his eye on Emi's money and wanted to be sure it was uncontested. If you had signed . . ."

"I would have given up my right to an inheritance I never even knew of," Jasminda said. Her mind spun.

Vanesse nodded. "I didn't know all the terms of the trust before I started looking into it. But I—I claimed the bequest in your name. The money is yours if you want it."

Something split inside Jasminda's chest. The warmth and love from her aunt gave her the push to drive out the lingering bitterness. Emotion clogged her throat as she felt freedom from the rain. It was a moment before her voice returned. "Thank you, Aunt."

"There is no need. It's what Eminette would have wanted." Vanesse dropped her head. "I envied her courage in grabbing what she desired out of life. I envy it now." Another Sister called her name, and Vanesse stood jerkily. She pointed to the ground. "This injustice will not stand."

"Aunt, if you can get a message to the prince . . ." Jasminda said.

There was little chance that Vanesse could get through to Jack in time. An unknown woman, even one of the Sisterhood, was unlikely to receive an audience with the Prince Regent.

Vanesse's brow furrowed, but she nodded. "I will pray for us to meet again." And then she was gone.

After another half hour in cold, wet misery, Jasminda was herded toward a bus with the others. A soldier pushed her roughly into a seat and locked her handcuffs around the bar, securing her in place.

Rozyl tripped up the steps, a soldier at her back. The two locked eyes. "I guess you're one of us now," the Keeper said, her lip curling. The soldier shoved her toward the back of the bus.

Jasminda pressed her head against the fogged window and slumped in her seat. Vanesse's revelation beat against the impossibility and danger of her situation. If she could get out of this, she could start over, rebuild.

But the caldera was heavy in her pocket. Besides the obvious lack of appeal of being forced to live in a land she knew nothing about, she could not allow the stone to fall into the hands of the Lagrimari. She needed a plan, but didn't know where to begin.

Through the windshield, the headlamps illuminated only a few feet ahead of them. The rest was inky blackness, rain tapping a staccato beat on the roof. The driver took to the radio, inquiring whether they would be stopping due to the hazardous conditions. The only response was static.

The True Father's storm flooded the countryside, turning the lush, fertile farmland to swampy lakes of woe. It had tracked her this far, and now here she was, bringing the caldera directly to the enemy.

She had to protect the stone—with her life, if necessary.

CHAPTER FIFTY

The Mistress of Horses quarreled with an astronomer over the shape of stars in the sky.

What you see as a fine lady dancing, Horse said, I view as a stampeding herd.

—COLLECTED FOLKTALES

Lizvette's only movement came from the rise and fall of her chest as she breathed. She didn't move so much as an eyelid to blink. She sat rigid in the chair, hands clasped neatly in her lap.

Jack, on the other hand, was all motion, pacing the floor of the sitting room in the Niralls' residence suite. "Where is she?" Gravel coated his throat.

"On a bus with the other refugees."

He dropped his head into his hand. "Why?"

"It was the best place for her."

Jack spun to look at her. "And that was your decision?" His supposedly healed wound throbbed angrily, as though the grief and pain were trying to claw their way out through his chest. He wrenched open the door and ordered the Guardsman outside to radio the refugee caravan and pull Jasminda off the bus.

"And was it you who destroyed her dress?" He resumed his pacing.

Her head shot up, eyes wide. "Her dress?"

"Her gown, ripped and burned and left in front of my office today."

Lizvette blinked slowly and took a deep breath. "That wasn't me."

"Do you know who it was?"

She notched her chin up higher and stared straight ahead.

Jack made an exasperated sound and crouched before her, careful to maintain his distance. "Tell me."

A single tear trailed down her cheek. Her jaw quivered. "I think it was Father," she whispered.

"Nirall?" Jack reared back on his heels, almost falling. He braced himself with a hand on the floor and shook his head. "I don't understand."

Her hands were squeezed together so hard, the tips of her fingernails had lost all color. She shook her head and another tear escaped her eye. Those were more tears than Jack had ever seen her shed in her entire life. She had always been a stoic child, never screaming or crying, not even when injured. Everything kept bottled up inside, even now.

Her whole body vibrated as if the strength it took her to remain composed had run out and pure chaos reigned underneath her placid exterior. She was at war with herself. Jack could see it plainly. Her distress stole a measure of rancor from his anger.

"Vette, we have known each other all our lives. You must tell me."

Her jaw quivered, but she nodded, darting a glance at the closed door. "He wanted me to be the princess. I suppose it would make up somewhat for me being born a girl. Alariq was kind, but he never held my heart."

She looked at him pointedly, and his stomach sank in understanding. He opened his mouth, unsure of what to say, but she continued. "When Alariq died, Father didn't miss a beat. He was determined to be the grandfather of the next Prince Regent, no matter what it took. Jasminda was an obstacle, but one that worked in his favor. If you would not choose me of your own free will, then he would give you a push."

"What kind of push?"

"Feeding information to the press. Giving them fodder for the fire. Presenting me as the solution."

"And you went along with this, Vette? Why?"

She swallowed and brushed away the wetness from her cheeks. "I never wanted to hurt you, and I certainly never wanted to see her harmed. But Jack, you are the Prince Regent of Elsira. You must marry well. Your wife is not just for you; she will be the princess of the land. Did you really think there was a future with her? It's for the best that she leave now with the others."

Jack shot to his feet as the ache in his chest seemed to spread to his whole body. His hands pulled at the short ends of his hair, searching for a release from his frustration. "Lizvette, there is no future for me without her."

"So she should have stayed here, hidden away for the rest of time so you could sneak into her chambers? And then what? What about when you need an heir? She's to be content being your mistress while you sire the next prince with someone else?"

"You had no right! Not to decide her fate. Did she get on that bus willingly?"

Lizvette turned her face to the fire. "I gave explicit instructions that she was not to be harmed."

Jack leaned against his desk, imagining Jasminda fighting tooth and nail against whatever hired thugs Lizvette had acquired.

"Did you think of what it must have been like for her?" Lizvette looked down to her folded hands. "If, one day, someone ever loves me, I would hope they would scream it from the rooftops." Her smile was brittle.

Jack fell onto the couch and slumped down. Lizvette was right. In a perfect world, he would have shouted his love for Jasminda from every window in the palace . . . but the world was far from perfect.

A knock sounded at the door, and a Guardsman entered.

"Your Grace, radio communication with the refugee caravan is down due to the thunderstorm. We're unable to contact them."

"Then send a telegram to the Eastern Base and keep trying the caravan. I want to make sure she doesn't step one foot inside Lagrimar."

"Yes, sir." The Guardsman spun on his heel, readying to leave.

"Wait." Weariness lay over Jack like a blanket. He looked at Lizvette and sighed. "Take her to the Guard's offices for questioning. The charge is kidnapping. And arrest Minister Nirall, as well."

Lizvette stood and brushed her dress off, her sad eyes relaying an apology. Jack's head fell to his hands as the weight of the crown grew even heavier.

CHAPTER FIFTY-ONE

Said the astronomer to the Mistress of Horses, And what of when the stars fail to shine?

Horse replied, The day the stars forsake the sky is a day not worth contemplating. For it will be our last.

—COLLECTED FOLKTALES

"There is too much interference, sir." The communications officer flipped a switch, testing yet another connection.

"What kind of interference?" Jack asked, peering over the man's shoulder.

"It's very unusual, but we're not able to contact any unit east of the Old Wall." Static could be heard through the man's headset.

"So the entire northeastern sector of the country is radio silent?"

"Yes, sir. No telephone, two-way, or cable communication is operational. They're all down."

Jack rubbed the back of his neck. "It's almost as if this were intentional."

The officer looked up, startled.

Jack did the math in his head. The caravan was too far along for vehicles to catch up with it, and there was no way for him to contact anyone who could get Jasminda to safety. Panic threatened, but he beat it back through force of will.

He banged his fist on the table, and the young officer jumped. "Blast it! I would need wings to get to her now," Jack murmured, then stopped short. His gaze rose to the ceiling.

The airship.

Alariq's pride and joy. And the cause of his death.

It was still there on the roof of the palace. After the crash, technicians from Yaly had come to repair it. Jack had wanted the thing removed, but hadn't yet gotten around to ordering it.

The idea was risky, too risky to even be contemplating, but what was the alternative? Jasminda trapped in Lagrimar? Forced to work in the mines or the harems or worse. She could be killed. He could not save the hundreds of refugees, much as he wanted to, but one woman, the woman most precious to him, could he not even save her?

The airship was the only way to get to the border fast enough—maybe even beat the caravan that had left hours earlier. However, it was this precise situation, flying in a rainstorm, that had killed his brother. Jack had called Alariq foolish. . . . Who was the fool now?

He stalked out of the communications room and into the small office the army maintained in the palace.

"I need an airship pilot. Immediately," he told the soldier on duty.

"Sir, the army doesn't have any ships or pilots. The airship was a gift to Prince Alariq from—"

"Yes, I know all that. But there must be someone in this city who can pilot a bloody airship. Find the ambassador to Yaly. It's their invention, he must know someone."

The sergeant rushed to stand, confused but determined.

"Your Grace." A Guardsman appeared in the doorway. Jack whirled around to face him. "There's a woman here from the Sisterhood. She's been raising quite a ruckus for some time now, saying she needs to speak with you."

Jack sighed. "Now is not the time."

"Your Grace, she's saying it has to do with Miss Jasminda. I thought you might want to speak with her."

Jack peered more closely at the Guardsman. He was the same fellow who'd escorted Lizvette to questioning. Tension gripped Jack, and he nodded. "Take me to her."

They'd kept the woman in the main lobby of the palace, and Jack could hear her voice from two corridors away.

"I will not stand down, and you would do well to keep out of my way, sir. I refuse to leave this palace until I have seen Prince Jaqros!"

"Sister," Jack said as he approached. The woman startled and spun around, gracing him with the tiniest curtsey possible before rushing to his side. A Guardsman reached out to stop her approach, but Jack brushed him off. "What can I do for you?"

"You can stop a great miscarriage of justice, Your Grace. My niece, a citizen of Elsira, despite all appearances to the contrary, was chained and forcibly placed on a bus headed to Lagrimar with the refugees. She does not belong there, and I—"

"You are Aunt Vanesse," Jack said. The woman stopped, stunned. He should have recognized her at once, but his mind was scattered in a million directions. How many Sisters had burn scars on their faces? "Jasminda told me about you."

She looked confused, but the determination in her eyes burned bright.

"Please, come with me," he said, leading her toward his office. "I have been trying to rectify that situation, believe me. But I've been stymied at every turn."

Jack stopped at his secretary's desk. "Netta, I want you to check in with the palace regiment every five minutes for an update on their search for an airship pilot."

Netta nodded and picked up the phone.

"An airship pilot?" Vanesse said, squinting at him.

"Yes. I fear that is the only way to get to her before the caravan reaches the border. My brother had the only airship in Rosira, and pilots are in short supply."

"Your Grace, I have a . . . a friend, who can drive just about anything. She's competed in the Yaly Classic Air Race the past two years flying speed crafts. If there's anyone who can pilot it, she can."

Jack stared, speechless, before breaking into a grin. He picked up the startled woman and spun her around, only putting her down when her small fist began beating against his back.

CHAPTER FIFTY-TWO

On the occasion of their parents' deaths, Bobcat gathered his brothers and sisters. Let us put away petty things, he said, and rejoice in our kinship. For the day is not long off when our good-byes will multiply.

—COLLECTED FOLKTALES

The buses lurched to a stop where the paved road ended, just past the entrance to the Eastern Army Base. Beyond loomed the border, deceptive in its ordinariness. Grass of the foothills gave way to the Breach Valley, a nondescript stretch of rocky dirt. The hills on either side veered up sharply, transforming into jagged mountains towering overhead. All seven Mantle breaches had occurred here.

The only other visible indication that one country ended and another began were the hundreds of Elsiran troops and vehicles gathered with weapons drawn, pointing toward an equal number of Lagrimari troops on the other side. Bullets could not pierce the

Mantle until it was breached, but both sides were intent on their standoff.

The rain had ended sometime during the night. Perhaps the storm had done its work. The caldera was nearly back in Lagrimar, after all. Early morning sunshine broke through the gloom. The refugees filed off the buses silently to huddle together amidst a sea of soldiers.

On one side of Jasminda stood Osar; Rozyl was on the other. The only words the Keeper had spoken had been to ask whether Jasminda had the caldera on her. After she'd affirmed it, Rozyl had not left her side.

Across the border, rows of Lagrimari stood at attention. A familiar face at the front of the line made Jasminda's breath catch.

The soldier stepped forward, smiling broadly. "By order of His Majesty the True Father of the Republic of Lagrimar, I, Lieutenant Tensyn ol-Trador, do hereby declare this a day of peace. My brothers and sisters, I welcome you home."

Lieutenant? He'd had a promotion, then. Jasminda grew sick to her stomach to see the man's smug grin. She stood in the middle of the crowd of refugees, but hunched down anyway, hoping he wouldn't see her.

Tensyn raised both hands over his head and paused dramatically before clapping them together. An earsplitting crack rent the air. The ground shuddered, rolling and shaking, throwing everyone off-balance. From the direction of the army base, an alarm sounded.

"Breach!" shouted an Elsiran.

"Breach!"

"Breach!"

The word was repeated, the message passed along, as the Elsiran soldiers hunkered down.

The armies appeared evenly matched in numbers, though the

Lagrimari weaponry was visibly old. The soldiers bore muzzle-loaded, single-shot rifles at least fifty years out of date. Many had bayonets or swords as well. Jasminda eyed the Elsiran soldiers nearest her, noting the far more advanced automatic rifles with coils of ammunition at the ready. Tanks were spaced evenly along the border with smaller armored four-wheelers bearing giant rifles and larger weapons that looked like cannons or grenade launchers. The Lagrimari had no vehicles, but the barrels of huge wheeled cannons sat on the front lines. Elsira's superior economic power and technology was unquestionable. But the Lagrimari had one advantage the Elsirans couldn't buy.

The wind grew from a gentle breeze to a gale within the blink of an eye. Jasminda's hair whipped back, the force of the wind stinging her eyes. It died down after a few breaths. But thick clouds exploded into existence on the Elsiran side. They swirled and raged unnaturally, then shuddered as deadly sharp icicles shot down. The ice stopped in midair a hand's breadth from their heads, then crackled and fell apart, dusting the Elsirans and refugees in a layer of snow.

The army's Earthsingers were taunting them.

Movement at the top of the lower foothills drew Jasminda's attention. Lines of additional Lagrimari troops came into view from behind the hilltops on either side of the flatland of the breach area. They marched over the hills, descending across the border between the lands.

"They've done it," Jasminda whispered. "They've destroyed the whole thing. The Mantle is gone."

Within minutes, the number of Lagrimari soldiers more than doubled, vastly outnumbering the Elsirans. Jasminda spotted Tensyn leading his men across the former barrier. An Elsiran general marched forward to meet him.

"There is no need for losing life this day. I will address my brethren," Tensyn announced in broken Elsiran. The general reluctantly stood aside as the lieutenant approached.

"Listen close," Tensyn said in Lagrimari. This seemed to be a cue for all the refugees to sit down. Jasminda settled on the muddy ground with the others. "This day is a joyous one. The Mantle, which unfairly trapped us for so long, is now demolished."

A cheer went up among the Lagrimari soldiers. Tensyn drank in the applause, before raising a hand to silence the men. "I am pleased to welcome all of the lost souls back to the open arms of the Fatherland. Your presence will help us usher in a great peace. However, before your return, there is something His Majesty requires. One of you holds an artifact that has great significance to our blessed leader. A red stone, smaller than my palm." He raised his hand over his head. The Elsiran troops nearest him followed his movement with their rifles, but he paid them no mind.

"The stone must be returned before your homecoming may begin."

Jasminda's chest tightened. Though it must have been her imagination, the caldera in her pocket seemed to hum to life. She flexed her fingers, eager for a weapon of any kind, a way to fight through the terror and escape.

Tensyn paced the length of the tightly gathered crowd of refugees. "To underscore the importance of compliance with any and all beneficent requests of His Majesty's, I will return one of you to the World After every minute the artifact is not within my possession."

He pulled his pistol from the holster at his hip and pulled back the hammer. The general closest to Tensyn pulled his sidearm as well.

Tensyn chuckled. "I will harm no Elsiran. This is between me and my countrymen," he said in Elsiran. The general nodded but continued pointing his own gun at the lieutenant.

Tensyn produced a pocket watch from the pocket of his crisp uniform, and though Jasminda was at least three dozen paces away, she could feel each tick of the clock like a beat inside her chest.

The minute that passed felt like the longest of her life, until it ended and Tensyn grabbed a random refugee from the crowd. Gray hair, a stooped stature . . .

Gerda.

Jasminda gasped. When Tensyn lifted his pistol to the old woman's head, Jasminda hurtled into motion. Her body acted without thought, but she struggled against an immovable object while trying to rise and get closer to Gerda. She looked down to find hands wrapped around her waist, squeezing painfully, holding her in place. Wrenching her neck around, she stared into Rozyl's hard eyes, wet with unshed tears. But her face was implacable. Jasminda turned back around. Through the crowd, Gerda met her gaze and gave an almost imperceptible shake of her head. Jasminda slammed her eyes shut.

The shot rang out.

"No!" Jasminda's scream echoed in the wake of the gunshot, reverberating off the mountain peaks. Many things could be healed with Earthsong, but a close-range shot to the head was not one of them.

Rozyl didn't let go, tightening her hold and forcing Jasminda's head down.

"Someone has something to say? The location of the artifact perhaps?" Tensyn's voice was self-satisfied. Nausea swept over Jasminda. Her empty stomach heaved, but nothing came out. The Elsiran general looked horrified, but made no move to stop the executions.

The clock continued to tick, and Jasminda couldn't watch another person die. She couldn't be responsible for the death of one more innocent.

This time Tensyn pulled a young girl from the crowd, out of the arms of her shrieking mother. Jasminda slackened her body; Rozyl's grasp weakened slightly. Taking advantage, Jasminda broke out of the woman's arms and shot to her feet.

Tensyn's gaze landed on her, recognition widening his eyes. Jasminda opened her mouth to confess. Before she'd taken a breath, Rozyl shot up beside her.

Turwig was next, moving faster than a man of his age rightly should. One by one, the other Keepers she'd met in the cave and at the camp stood, and even Lyngar, a man she'd suspected of having no emotions whatsoever, had tears in his eyes as he looked at Gerda's lifeless form sprawled on the ground.

Tensyn blinked, peering from one Keeper to another. "The artifact. Who has it?"

"I have it," Rozyl called out, her voice strong and clear.

"I have it," Lyngar said.

The statement was repeated by every Keeper standing.

"I have it," young Timmyn said, taking to his feet. Other refugees, children and mothers, young and elderly all stood, claiming to have the caldera. Most of them had no idea what they were even admitting to, but Jasminda was moved all the same. She had thought she'd known misery and heartache since the loss of her family, but she had nothing on these people. She'd also thought she truly understood love, but the actions of the other refugees humbled her.

They were all in this together. This group of strangers were acting as one with her. Standing together in the face of almost certain death. Tears streamed down Jasminda's cheeks, and she swiped them away.

The lieutenant pursed his lips, searching the crowd until he found Jasminda. He looked ready to speak, when a ripple of movement behind him caused him to turn.

CHAPTER FIFTY-THREE

The Master of Spiders searched for his treasure throughout the land.
He found it not in the mountain, nor in the valley, nor by the sea.
After many years, he could no longer recall what he was looking for.

—COLLECTED FOLKTALES

The row of Lagrimari soldiers parted to reveal a solitary figure. Jasminda could only stare as dread cooled her skin.

Weak sunlight glittered off a jewel-encrusted mask covering the face of a man walking across the field. No holes for eyes, nose, or mouth were visible—just a covering of multicolored precious stones obscuring his entire head. A heavy tunic lined with even more jewels flowed nearly to his ankles. He walked across the ground as if laying claim to the land. As if he had already conquered everything he surveyed.

His approach was endless, his paces measured. The thousands gathered were silent; not even a bird call interrupted the quiet.

With a flick of his wrist, two dozen refugees before him went flying through the air and crashed in a heap on the ground. The Elsiran army appeared frozen in place. Jasminda was unable to tear her gaze from the force of nature that was the immortal king, but vaguely registered some barrier separating where she stood from the Elsirans around her.

Noise reached her ears slowly, as if muted. A jeweled glove jerked, and another swath of refugees went flying. A sickening crunch of bones accompanied them, and low moans rose.

Jasminda's lip quivered. Now, none stood between the True Father and her. Though she could not see his eyes, she felt his attention on her. He knew she carried the caldera.

He tilted his head to the side, regarding her. "What is this?" His voice was nothing like that of his younger self. Hollow and raspy, it was the sound of death.

Jasminda flinched.

"Yllis truly was innovative. He trapped his entire Song in the stone you carry, girl." The True Father laughed, a sandpapery sound that rippled down her spine. "So much power. A Song unmatched by any alive today. Give it to me and you *may* live."

Hot tears escaped Jasminda's eyes. Her body shook. A tunnel had been formed out of ice or wind or pure magic, perhaps all three, Jasminda couldn't be sure. On the other side of it the Elsirans raged, blurry and ineffectual. Their weapons fired into the swirling tunnel walls but did not penetrate.

She and the refugees, along with a handful of Lagrimari soldiers, were trapped in this cage with a madman. So this was his power, tainted and bitter.

"No." Her voice was soft amidst the immense twisting power surrounding them.

The True Father inclined his head. That was the only warning she had before she was ripped from the ground and tossed into the air. The earth came back to meet her; this time the crunch she heard was from her own bones. Pain was delayed for one blissful moment, then her entire body ignited.

The king's power lifted her again, only to smash her down just as cruelly. White-hot agony lanced her. Deafening screams rang in her ears. It took a moment to realize they were her own. Then, in a flash, she was healed and standing upright.

She wobbled on noodly legs, searching for support and finding none. The other refugees lay on the ground around her, many broken and bloodied, watching with wide eyes. Jasminda took a deep breath—not nearly enough to sustain her.

The True Father laughed again. "Who are you to defy me, girl? A child with barely enough power for me to take. An insignificant whelp, yet you dare utter the word 'no'?"

He turned in a circle as if to ensure everyone was watching. "Though perhaps I should thank you." He tilted his head to the side. "Your attempt to shore up the Mantle's cornerstone with your negligible power amused me. And there is so little left that I find entertaining."

Guilt shrank Jasminda's chest.

He drew closer. "You thought to use the stone you bear against me? Or do you wish to lash out with your feeble Song and do something to stop me?" He laughed—the brittle sound turned her blood to ice. "Now give me the stone, and you may die quickly."

Jasminda trembled. She could not stop him from taking the caldera, but she would rather die, as slowly as it took, than give it to him. "I know who you are, *Eero*," she said, fighting the quiver in her jaw.

The True Father froze. Once again, unseen eyes raked over her skin. "I have not heard that name in a long time."

This time, he dragged her into the air slowly. He stepped closer until he was directly beneath her, his head tilted up. "I think I would prefer to never hear it again."

Her skin constricted, squeezing tight against her muscles. The air surrounding her compressed, bearing down until her bones cracked, one by one. Her throat was crushed before she could scream. The pain went on and on. She lived inside it until she was certain she had passed out. But the impact of the ground on her shattered body rattled her. He'd dropped her.

Jasminda's skin was a bag of bone shards. She could not move. Drawing breath was nearly impossible. A whistling sound escaped her lips when she tried to fill her lungs. They must have been pierced with slivers of her ribs.

"Get the stone," the True Father's deathlike voice rasped. Apparently, he would not deign to get his bejeweled gloves dirty. She was vaguely aware of hands pawing her, and not gently. The pain on top of pain made little difference. She could not draw enough breath to cry out.

As the seeker mauled her, something brushed against her outstretched hand. Earthsong buzzed at the edges of her senses. Was this someone trying to heal her?

Somehow, she managed to agonizingly lift her eyelids, but closed them again immediately. She'd fallen next to Gerda's lifeless body. Jasminda forced herself to look upon the old woman. Gerda stared back sightlessly, her neck twisted at an impossible angle. Jasminda's vision blurred.

The Earthsong prickling at her was insistent. A link wanted to form. She could barely think but opened her Song to it—perhaps it would aid in the healing, though she knew in her heart it was too late. Even a strong Singer would need far more time than Jasminda had left in this world.

Whoever was searching her pockets stopped suddenly. The

warm presence of the stone left her. They'd found it. Now it was too late for everyone.

Gerda's blood pooled, inching towards Jasminda's face. Soon it would mix with her own. Had the old woman's sacrifice been in vain?

A memory tickled her mind. The spell Yllis had taught Oola in the last vision. A blood sacrifice.

The link opened between herself and whoever the persistent Earthsinger was—Osar, she recognized the feel of his Song belatedly. Some part of her skin must be in contact with him, though numbness had begun to erase her pain. He offered her control of the link and his powerful Song.

Jasminda startled at the feel of every heartbeat of every person nearby inside her body. She breathed with the breath of thousands. Insects burrowed deep under the ground came into crisp focus. Every blink of every eye was loud as a camera's shutter. She sensed the True Father's spell, the tunnel of wind and water separating the Elsirans from the Lagrimari. She could see how it was made, perhaps even copy it. She filed the knowledge away.

Instead, she centered her attention on the ground beneath her and reached for the memory of Yllis's spell. With her enhanced power, she could almost taste Gerda's blood mixed with the dirt and sand. Jasminda twisted the energy of Earthsong, mixing it with the woman's lifeblood.

Power swelled within her as she wove the threads of the differing energies together. The spell came to her as if channeled from another mind—in a way it had been. The complex fabric of intermingling energies was nothing she could explain, but she sang the spell as if possessed.

When she was done, her eyes blinked open again. Gerda's face was now peaceful before her. Underneath them, the ground had become glassy and smooth. Dark as midnight, it extended all around, like fast-spreading molasses. Though she couldn't see more than a few paces in front of her face, she could feel it. The earth beneath them had been transformed into the polished rock surface of the caldera. Just as in the caves.

The True Father's strange tunnel barrier died.

Osar's small face dropped between hers and Gerda's. The little boy watched her grimly.

The smooth surface beneath them echoed with the residue of magic that required death. There was something unnatural about it that made a shiver go up her ravaged spine.

The True Father roared. The sound was filled with anger, frustration, shock. Chaos erupted, and his scream cut off in a strangled cry. Emotions beat against her, but Jasminda's vision was narrow. She blocked it all out.

The ground is like the caves now? Osar asked in her mind. They were still linked, his mighty power under her control.

Yes, no one can sing. Jasminda wanted to laugh, but her entire body was numb. *No one but me.* She couldn't even feel her lips.

The caldera? she asked.

Osar's face disappeared, and the chaos surrounding her intensified. She sensed him motioning to Rozyl, communicating with gestures. Via the link, Jasminda watched through Osar's eyes as Rozyl rose from the ground and broke into a run. She leapt into the air to tackle a figure with his back to her. Tensyn.

Rozyl brought him down effortlessly and wrenched the stone from his grip. She walked back over to Jasminda and kneeled before her, placing it in her hand.

Though Jasminda could not feel the weight of the caldera, she didn't need to. The vision came anyway.

CHAPTER FIFTY-FOUR

This is good-bye. The last time I will see my brother.

We have given him everything he wanted. We stand at the border of what will now become two lands, two peoples. Songbearer and Silent, separated for all time.

Once Yllis's barrier spell falls into place, there will be no crossing—those were the terms of the treaty. That stipulation was put in by our side. Many Songbearers have grown weary of the fighting. It is against our nature. Some feel if they never see another Silent, it will be for the best.

Already I miss the way things were, but this was my decision and I must stand by it.

"Will you embrace me one last time, sister?"

The odd, smooth bracelets adorning Eero's wrists hold the magic of Yllis's binding spell. The blood magic that ensures Eero doesn't use whatever stolen Song may be left inside him. He can cause no further harm before the Mantle is erected.

His eyes shine, and I see the boy I once knew within them. One last time could not hurt.

I step closer. My arms wrap around him. We came into this world together, and I thought we would stay that way forever.

A sharp pain pierces my side. I pull back from him and stare at the dagger sticking out from between my ribs. I gasp up at him in horror, but Eero's face is a mask.

I reach for Earthsong, trying to knit the wound, but something is wrong. My Song is weakening, slipping out of my grasp like a wisp of smoke. I breathe in, and in some more, but the breath never makes it to my lungs. Eero whispers a string of foreign words, and I fall to the ground.

Everything goes black.

Voices call my name.

One voice.

Yllis.

"Oola! Oola! Please come back to me. My love, please."

He begs and pleads, apologizes and bargains.

I try to go to him but am locked in place. My breath is gone, and I am separated from my body.

Three archways loom before me. The widest leads back to my body. Another leads to the World After.

But the third calls to me, though narrow and ominous. I step through it, sealing my fate.

The World Between is a smoke-filled antechamber full of endless images of the living. Neither here nor there, it is vast and lonely, only grazed by the living in their dreams. Some believe all dreams take place here.

For me, it is a nightmare.

From here I bear witness to my body on the ground. Eero smashes the bespelled bracelets. He is full of my Song, stolen from my last breaths.

Yllis gives a great cry. He gathers a swell of Earthsong and sings the spell to create the barrier between the lands. The cornerstone engages, and I feel its power pulsing through the energy.

Eero steps away from his Silent followers, over to the band of aston-ished Songbearers. Yllis is too focused on his spell to notice. The barrier slams into place, leaving him holding my body on one side with the throng of Silent and Eero, bursting with my Song, on the other with the rest of the Songbearers.

This was his plan all along.

He never wanted to be shut up alongside the Silent forever. He merely wanted to have an inexhaustible supply of Songbearers to steal from.

Eero stands at the barrier, his expression smug. "Worry not, Yllis. She is not dead. She will awaken at any moment and live quite a fine life without her Song. She will know what it is like to be me."

Two archways still stand behind me, the one leading to the Living World pulsing brighter than the sun. Calling to me. Pleading with me. I am being given a choice.

Eero's look of triumph changes to a frown. "She will awaken," he says, a tremor invading his voice.

Yllis growls and pulls my body closer.

Eero tries to move forward, but the barrier stops him. He beats against the invisible wall with a fist. "Oola! Oola!" he screams.

Both archways dim and begin to fade. I must make my choice quickly.

If I go back to the Living World, I can resume a life without my heart. The World After holds no appeal, though Mother and Father are there. How can I face them with what I have done to Eero?

Here, in the World Between, I may watch. That will be my punish-ment.

Justice finally served for my crimes.

I will watch.

The archways fade and disappear.

I watch Yllis bear my body back to the city and cut a chamber into the mountains to house me. Above the chamber, the Silent construct a mag-nificent palace.

Yllis chooses a loyal Silent to rule. A young man of character and honor, Abdeen Alliaseen, to lead the people in the absence of their Queen.

Yllis makes Alliaseen promise to ensure that history is kind to me and bears no recollection of my fault in the start of the war. He spends weeks, months, years locked in his laboratory, scouring the libraries of the Cantors, searching for something. Doing what he does best, studying magic.

I watch on the day he finds what he has been seeking. He chants words in the ancient tongue of the Cavefolk, words I don't understand. He takes the pendant bearing my father's sigil, the one I always wore around my neck, and cuts himself, spilling his blood over it. He calls for Alliaseen, who, when asked, spills his own blood on the sigil without hesitation, binding the spell. The blood congeals and the magic grows, encasing the pendant in a bloodred stone.

Blood magic will do what Earthsong cannot.

Blood magic may be broken only by those who bear the blood.

Yllis journeys back to the barrier he created and crosses it, using another bit of magic.

He gathers those unafraid of standing against a now impossibly powerful Eero. Those who want to learn to fight. Songbearers are peaceful by nature, but these men and women have been broken. They become something new. He crafts the words of a promise to me, one these new soldiers vow to keep.

I watch as my beloved Yllis wages war on my beloved brother, and I watch when Yllis is slain. Eero is too strong, and the stolen Songs have twisted his mind and made him far more ruthless than even the broken Songbearers.

Yllis dies with the stone in his hand.

His final spell traps his own Song in the stone.

The Keepers of the Promise are supposed to take the stone, cross the border, and present it to the prince, whose touch will unlock the magic.

But the Keepers he commanded to hold back and stay safe, rush in seeking revenge. None survive the battle.

The stone sits where it lies. Yllis's gift to me, his whispered spell to bring me back to my body and gift me his own Song, lies under the rubble of the fallen city as his body turns to bones.

The archways are long gone now.

If they were here, perhaps I would pass into the World After to be with him. To thank him for trying to save me.

But being with Yllis is not punishment enough.

So I watch.

For a very long time.

Sometimes, a dream will find me and pierce the loneliness.

But more often, it is endless agony. Standing by watching while the centuries pass.

And now, Jasminda, you have heard my story. Judge me for my faults if you must. But you bear the only evidence of Yllis's love for me. His Song is in your hands.

Release it.

Release me.

It is time for me to end this.

CHAPTER FIFTY-FIVE

*Beseeched a new father to the Mistress of Eagles, Bless my baby,
for her mother died in childbirth.*

*Eagle replied, Your loss is like a volcano's flow which increases
the land. New worlds are born out of destruction.*

—COLLECTED FOLKTALES

Jack gripped the edge of the seat as the airship descended from the
clouds. What he saw on the ground below was mystifying. Judging
by the presence of Lagrimari troops, the Mantle had already been
destroyed. But where he'd expected a battle to be raging, there was
relative calm.

The Lagrimari sat in even rows on the ground with Jack's troops
maintaining the perimeter. Had they surrendered? Could that be
possible?

No enemy guns had been drawn, there were no environmental
disasters as in the Seventh Breach. What was going on?

Clove set the ship down at the edge of the gathered crowd.

"That was some bloody fine piloting, Clove," he said, clapping the woman on the back.

"Thank you, Your Grace!"

Flying through the vicious storm had been just as difficult as he'd imagined. They'd been bandied about by the wind and rain, and nearly struck by lightning twice. But Clove was unflappable, gripping the steering wheel with bloodless hands and navigating them safely through.

With a nod to Vanesse, who had insisted on coming as well, Jack opened the carriage door and tore across the ground, intent on finding Jasminda.

Several soldiers approached him. The base's high general, Verados, was in the lead. "Your Grace, the enemy has surrendered."

Jack looked on, incredulous. "How is this possible?"

"They laid down their weapons as soon as this witchcraft began." He tapped his foot and looked down. Jack peered at the strange, hardened ground.

"It's like the caves, Your Grace."

He turned toward the familiar voice to find Rozyl standing at the edge of the group of soldiers. He motioned her forward, and the men let her pass.

"No one can sing on it?" he asked.

She shook her head solemnly. "No one but Jasminda."

He opened his mouth to ask about her, but Verados cut him off. "The True Father has been captured. Once he was rendered powerless, his troops dropped their weapons. It was just a matter of bringing him into custody."

Jack's eyes widened. "Where is he?"

Verados motioned toward the base.

The king could wait. "Where is *she*?" he asked Rozyl. Her expression was grim. "Take me to her."

Rozyl turned on her heel and marched over to a group of refugees. They sat in a spiral around a prone figure in the middle. Jack's heart stuttered when he recognized Jasminda. He tore through the group to kneel at her side. "They can't heal her?"

"Osar is linking with her. She's controlling his Song but won't heal herself." Rozyl's voice was bitter. "She says she needs to save the power."

He turned back to Jasminda, his stomach clenching at her condition. All of her limbs were twisted at strange angles, and her eyes were barely open.

"Jasminda, my darling, I'm here. I'm going to get you off this blasted thing so they can heal you up, all right?"

She lay impossibly still, her eyelids the only movement. Osar sat by her head, stroking her hair. The boy looked up at him pleadingly, then looked to Rozyl.

"He says she wants you to stay with her."

Jack glanced at Osar, who'd never spoken a word. "Of course I will."

"She knows how to awaken the Queen. But there isn't much time."

Jack's pulse sped. "What do we have to do?"

"Take her hand."

Her hand lay palm up, and though her fingers were mangled, the caldera was held loosely in her grasp. He stared at the rock, the way it lay in her ravaged hand.

"Please." Rozyl's voice was a whisper.

Jack's heart broke. Jasminda was so weak. If this was what she wanted, he would do it. He whispered a kiss across her lips, not daring to press against her and cause more pain, then closed his hand over the caldera.

Searing pain shot through his body, as if he were being pulled apart one organ at a time. He might have screamed out loud, he wasn't sure, but the burning agony was like nothing he'd ever felt. His blood was on fire, burning bright and hot. Then it was gone.

Breath returned to his lungs. He was once again kneeling on the glossy surface of the unnatural ground, next to the woman he loved as she slipped further and further away.

An explosion of light above his head blinded him. He squinted against the small fireball, which rivaled the sun in sheer brilliance. It grew brighter, shining with a white-hot glare before disappearing.

In its place, a figure floated, wrapped in ivory fabric. Her skin shone gloriously. Dark, curling hair swirled around Her head, blown by a nonexistent breeze. She moved like liquid, spinning and stretching. She righted Herself and hovered before Jack, dark eyes piercing him with intensity.

He swallowed and lowered his head in deference.

The Queen had awoken.

CHAPTER FIFTY-SIX

Spider squabbled with his brothers and sisters over their parents'
inheritance.

I am most deserving, he said, for being the youngest, I had
them the least amount of time.

One by one, the others grew exhausted by the discord, leaving
Spider standing alone in a prison of victory.

—COLLECTED FOLKTALES

The normally tingling buzz of Earthsong was an earthquake against
Jasminda's consciousness. She was no longer linked with Osar, but
another Song shook her to the core. The swelling force pulled her
under, leaving her sputtering, coughing, gasping for breath.

She could now fill her lungs completely. Feeling came back to
her body. Her bones were in their proper places, her body whole
again.

A warm, solid hand rubbed her back in gentle circles. She
focused on the feeling, the comfort, and leaned into a familiar

embrace. Hands stroked her head, her face. Lips brushed her forehead. She wanted those lips someplace else, so she rose to meet
them.

Jack.

His kiss was like air to her. She breathed him in and held him
there inside her, never wanting to exhale. His arms tightened
around her, and he pulled his lips away. She whimpered, wanting
to keep kissing him. On his chuckle, she opened her eyes.

His smile undid her. She stared at him, drinking in the beauty
of his features.

"I thought I'd lost you," he whispered.

"I thought I'd lost me as well."

His expression shuttered, and he blinked back tears. He pressed
her to him again, wrapping his arms around her as she became
aware of her surroundings.

Shell-shocked refugees—healed of their injuries—rose from the
ground, staring in awe at a point behind her. She pulled away from
Jack, craned her neck around, and nearly fell backward.

Floating above them was Queen Oola, ethereal and beautiful,
fierce and overpowering. Jasminda gaped at the Queen's familiar
face. Looking at the woman was like looking into a mirror.

Something hard jabbed Jasminda's closed fist. She uncurled her
fingers to reveal a bronze pendant bearing the Queen's sigil attached
to a thin metal chain. The caldera surrounding the pendant was gone,
burned away by the awakening spell.

A hush of quiet descended. The refugees began to kneel. Jasminda climbed off Jack and kneeled as well, bowing her head.

"Jaqros Alliaseen. Jasminda ul-Sarifor." The Queen's voice rang
out, rich and thick as raw honey. "Rise."

Jasminda darted a glance at Jack; both of them stood on wobbly legs. Power surged along her skin as she and Jack were gently

lifted into the air and drifted over the heads of the awestruck crowd. The spell released her a handful of paces away from the Queen. The difference between Her power and the True Father's was night and day.

Queen Oola floated down until She was almost at eye level. The pendant in Jasminda's hand seemed to transfix Her. Jasminda held it out in offering. The chain lifted into the air and settled around Her neck, where it belonged.

Jasminda tugged at her mother's pendant, the same spidery sigil of snaking, curved lines around her own neck. The Queen's mark.

"I owe you gratitude for awakening me," the Queen said. "You must bow before no one."

Jasminda's Song flared to life. The slow trickle of her weak capacity for power enlarged, and she was engorged with a rush of Earthsong. She struggled to catch her breath as the sensation shot through her. It was like being in the link all over again: everything around her sharpened into focus. She gasped as pure energy pulsed inside her. Her Song expanded, stretched, changed. It grew larger and more powerful—a raging river, with white-capped waves shuttling over its banks.

This was different from what Oola had done for her brother, who'd had no Song to enlarge. This had the feel of permanence to it.

Jack caught hold of Jasminda's hand to steady her.

"Your Majesty," she said, inclining her head. "Why me?"

Queen Oola drew closer, Her dark gaze peering deep inside Jasminda as if seeing her very soul.

The power gushing within her made it hard to concentrate, but Jasminda stared at the pendant resting against Queen Oola's chest to bring her thoughts into focus. "Why was I the only one affected by the caldera? Why could no one else see the visions?"

Queen Oola's expression did not change, but Her eyes lightened and a breeze lifted Her hair. *Blood magic may be broken only by those who bear the blood.*

"Whose blood? Mine? I'm sorry, but I don't under—"

"Prince Jaqros," the Queen interrupted, out loud this time.

Jasminda wanted to push for answers, but Queen Oola had effectively ended her inquiry. She looked around. Every eye in every direction was glued to the Queen.

"You are the rightful ruler of this land." Oola turned to Jack.

He deepened his bow. "I rule only in your stead, Your Majesty."

"You are loyal and true, as is your beloved." She swept Her gaze to Jasminda, who still vibrated with her new, incredibly powerful Song and a head full of questions. "I will abdicate my throne to you. To both of you."

Gasps sounded. Jasminda's own heartbeat pulsed rapidly. She held onto Jack even tighter.

"My gift to Jasminda is the strength of Song she will need to be queen. Use it well. My wish is for you to unite the people as they once were. And rule. Well."

She ascended over the heads of the troops, toward the place where the two lands met. "This border is no more." Her voice carried, strong and clear. "Singer and Silent will live as one. So be it. See to it."

"Be it so," said Jasminda under her breath. She could barely think for the questions swirling around in her head. Could it really be true? She and Jack together as king and queen?

Oola rose higher into the air, surveying the land and the people. A disturbance among the Elsiran soldiers caught Her attention, and She hovered, staring at the sea of men.

"What is it?" Jasminda asked. Jack shook his head. They pushed forward through the gaping onlookers, following Oola as She floated closer to the buildings of the base.

Standing before one of the four-wheelers, surrounded by guards, was the True Father. Eero. His hands were bound before him and his mask was still in place, but his head was tilted up, clearly looking at his sister.

Jasminda tapped into the maelstrom of emotions surrounding her and struggled to parse them. The strongest by far were from Oola—pain, shame, anger, heartbreak, and finally, relief. Oddly, Jasminda could sense nothing from Eero. His emotions were a vast emptiness. Were he not standing directly on the caldera, she would have thought he was blocking her Song somehow, but perhaps he had no feelings left after centuries of tyranny.

Oola lowered Herself before Her twin until Her feet hovered over the ground. The Queen reached for him and ran a finger across his grotesque mask. Jasminda once again pushed forward, drawn toward the two as if by an invisible chain. Having spent so much time inside Oola's head, worry blossomed within her at the Queen's reaction.

"You have returned," Eero rasped.

Oola winced at this new voice of his. "I have come back for you," She said.

They spoke quietly, just for the two of them, but Jasminda made out their words.

"You came back to take from me what is mine," Eero said.

Oola dropped Her hand. Jasminda was now close enough to see the tears welling in the Queen's eyes. Her worry grew.

"I came back to right my wrong." One tear broke free and streamed down Oola's cheek. "What have you done, brother?"

She reached for his mask and pulled it off his face. A silent shudder went through those on both sides.

None alive had seen beneath the mask Eero had first donned centuries ago. Subjugation and misery had altered the collective memory, and the Lagrimari had forgotten their leader was not an Earthsinger like them. They'd forgotten why he preyed on them and stole their power.

The jeweled disguise fell from the Queen's fingertips. Beneath it, Eero's face was unchanged from the young man Jasminda had seen in Oola's memories. He looked Elsiran still, with haunting golden eyes and ginger hair.

The shock of the crowd was oppressive. It slammed into Jasminda, forcing her to throw up a shield against the assault. Murmurs filled the air as Lagrimari and Elsirans alike took in the two. The beloved Elsiran Queen and the hated Lagrimari dictator. Neither were what anyone had expected.

"Will you embrace me one last time, sister?" Eero's words echoed those he'd spoken before betraying his twin all those years ago. Jasminda froze.

Oola's emotions sharply changed. Guilt came to the forefront; Her resolve to right Her wrong was slipping away under the weight of the familiarity and love She still felt for Her brother. The metal band of his shackles snapped—the whisper of a spell from Oola.

Eero's amber eyes held a warmth that did not correspond to the emptiness inside him. Oola could not sense it, She had always been blinded to him, just as Yllis had said, and even now, *even now,* as Jasminda observed, She continued to be so.

Jasminda needed a way to get through to Oola, to make Her see Her brother for what he really was.

Your Majesty. Jasminda thought a message, the way she had with Osar, the way the Earthsingers of old had. *He is not the boy you knew any longer. You must not allow him to sway you.* If the message had gone through, if Oola had heard her plea, the Queen gave no acknowledgment. Instead, Her self-condemnation seemed to grow.

Jasminda trembled. History could not repeat itself. "We have to help Her," she whispered to Jack.

"Help *Her*?"

Jasminda never took her eyes off Oola. They'd thought Her a goddess, but She was a woman, a woman with a broken heart who had nothing left in this world. A woman caught in a vortex of pain.

"She can't do it. Even after everything . . ." Jasminda wrung her hands. She, too, knew heartbreak. She, too, knew loss. But somehow Oola had allowed those emotions to overtake Her resolve, and now She faltered when She needed to act.

"We have to stop him before he harms Her."

Jack's expression was incredulous, but he nodded. The True Father was now bound from using Earthsong by the caldera, and if Oola's feet touched the ground, She'd also become powerless. But in the final vision Jasminda had seen through Oola's eyes, Eero had then, too, been bound by Yllis's blood spell. The bracelets on Eero's wrists had been calderas with a similar spell against using Earthsong. But those bracelets had not stopped him from stealing his sister's Song. To do that he must have used pure blood magic, Jasminda surmised. And blood magic had allowed him to destroy the calderas.

If the True Father were to access Earthsong now, there was no telling the amount of damage he could do.

Jasminda strained to remember the words Eero had spoken after he'd stabbed his sister, words Oola had not understood, for they had been in the tongue of the Cavefolk. They invoked the blood spell, and if Eero used it, so could Jasminda.

She reached out to the soldier next to her and pulled the knife from his belt. The man looked up in surprise, but upon seeing the Prince Regent, held his tongue. Jack's gaze was questioning, but he made no move to stop her. Jasminda squeezed the knife's handle and moved closer to the standoff between the twins, with Jack on her heels.

Oola's face clouded in misery. Jasminda circled around Eero and approached him from behind. The king's shoulders stiffened, but he did not turn. Instead, he took a step closer to his sister and wiped the tears from Her face, then wrapped his arms around Her waist.

With a yell, Jasminda ran forward and plunged the knife into his back, then whispered the string of words that would bring him to the brink of death and release his Song.

The stolen Songs inside him catapulted at her, their attack violent. She kept a hand on the knife, but her knees buckled under the onslaught. The Songs were tainted; they battered ruthlessly. Her connection to Earthsong flared as her own Song fought back. Like a virus infecting her, the stolen Songs wore away at her shield, dragging her under. They were oily, slick with a layer of malevolence from their former host. Jasminda took them on, having no other option, but feared she would not survive the struggle.

Her knees hit the ground. Blackness swept over her vision.

Suddenly, another Song brushed against her consciousness. Oola was trying to link with her. Jasminda gladly gave up control of her Song, and the practiced strength of Oola's immense power took over. The Queen funneled the stolen Songs away from Jasminda. Her hand, still clutching the knife impaled in Eero's back, was covered by Oola's. Blood ran down Jasminda's arm.

Using the same spell Yllis had discovered to trap his Song in Her pendant and create the caldera, Oola manipulated the energy to force the stolen Songs into the knife before pulling the blade from Eero's back. The sickly taste of blood magic fled Jasminda's tongue as the Songs were imprisoned.

Oola pulled both their hands away, and the knife clattered to the ground, the blood on it spreading, hardening, transforming into the red stone of a caldera.

Oola released their link, and Jasminda fell back, gasping for breath. Jack was there behind her, propping her up, his arms like buoys in the whirling sea, keeping her afloat.

Eero crumpled to his knees screaming, his brittle shell pierced at last. Jasminda slammed her shield into place as the man's emotions sprang free of their bonds. She did not want to experience the suppressed feelings that five hundred years of ruthless brutality had forged.

Oola's tearstained face stared blankly at Her brother's weeping body. Her attention moved to Jasminda, eyes heavy but grateful. "It is done," She whispered, then shot into the air, soon becoming a dot against the sky.

CHAPTER FIFTY-SEVEN

Jackal stood at the edge of the world to watch the eclipse of the sun.
Though the light was obscured, it shined bright enough to blind.

—COLLECTED FOLKTALES

THE QUEEN HAS ARISEN

Week-Long Celebration Scheduled Across the Land
Elsira Enters New Age of Hope

The shortest Breach War in history ended only hours after its commencement, and the faith of thousands of Elsirans was renewed when our beloved Queen awakened from Her five centuries of slumber. Details are still coming in at this time, and we do not yet know what prompted this miraculous resurrection, but a source from within the Sisterhood stated that magic was almost certainly involved. . . .

QUEEN OF DECEPTION?

Reactions to Her Appearance Shock Many

[Continued from page A1]

One witness to the awakening, speaking on the grounds of anonymity, shared his displeasure with the revelation of the Queen's physical appearance. "To think, we were praying to a *grol* this whole time. I just can't believe it." Others call such statements blasphemy. Syllenne Nidos, High Priestess of the Sisterhood, decried the "false believers," saying, "Those whose faith was built on any assumption of the Queen's appearance must search their hearts and remember all of the blessings She has provided to so many. We must work together to heal the years of false thinking, both about magic and those who bear it."

Temple attendance has surged in the days following the Queen's awakening, though so has defection from the religion that many are now calling a cult. Attendance is rising at gatherings of Dominionists, a tradition which originated in Yaly and boasts a growing membership worldwide.

Jack tossed the newspaper aside and ran his hands through his hair. He rose to pace the floor of his office, his gaze skating back and forth to the clock on the wall. Finally, Usher pushed through the doors and closed them, leaning back.

The man was out of breath, and for a moment, Jack felt bad. Usher was not a young man, but there was no one Jack trusted more.

"Did you get them?"

Usher's expression was grim for a moment, before bursting into a smile. "Yes, both of them." He brought his arms from behind his back to reveal a velvet box in each hand. Jack was familiar with the long blue case in Usher's left hand. It held Jasminda's medal, reclaimed from the unscrupulous dealer who dared try to sell such a thing on the black market.

But the medal didn't concern Jack much. What he was really interested in was held in Usher's right hand. Jack snatched the smaller box and headed for the door.

"Thank you," he called over his shoulder in response to Usher's chuckle.

Jack slipped into the side corridor and over to the unused back passageways. He didn't want anyone stopping him in the hallways just now. His patience was paper thin, and he needed to get this done as quickly as possible.

The hidden paths he'd discovered as a child proved very useful. He slipped into the Blue Library unseen by all, including the room's sole occupant.

Jasminda sat amidst a heap of books, as was her way. She'd mentioned earlier that morning that she was researching the rules of succession for Elsiran monarchs. She took the prospect of being queen very seriously and was overwhelmed at all the knowledge she felt she needed to be a good ruler.

Jack wasn't worried about her, though. It would be a challenge to be sure, but one she was well suited for.

The days ahead would be difficult; the collective wounds on both sides were deep. But Queen Oola seemed confident the gap could be mended. They'd already taken the first baby steps.

The True Father was locked in the dungeon; Lizvette was under house arrest in her rooms, facing the possibility of exile; and her father, Nirall, had not been seen since the day of the breach. An arrest warrant had been issued for several counts of treason, but Jack did not expect the man to turn up anytime soon.

The monarchy had been secured in Jack and Jasminda's possession by Oola's word, but Jack needed to say a few words of his own.

He approached Jasminda from behind. She looked up, cocking her head to the side. With a burst of magic, she shot into the air and flew into his arms. The impact of her body against his was a little too hard.

"Oompf," she said, crashing into him. She smiled sheepishly as she clung to him. "I'm still getting used to this."

Jack chuckled, holding her tight before releasing her. Much as he always wanted her in his arms, he needed his hands free for this task.

"Do you forgive me for putting you in the dungeon?" he asked.

She pursed her lips as if thinking about it. He was afraid he would never hear the end of it and vowed to ask her once a day for forgiveness. "If you forgive me for trying to run away."

He dropped his head. Her leaving still caused a phantom pain in his heart, but he did forgive her. He kissed her to make sure she knew. And there was one thing he could do to ensure she'd never leave again.

He opened the velvet box he carried and dropped to one knee. Jasminda's eyes widened, and her lips began to tremble. He presented her with a traditional Elsiran engagement ring of two interlocking bands engraved with her name and his in curling script.

"Jasminda ul-Sarifor, will you marry me?" He brought her hands to his lips. "Will you love me? Honor and protect me? Rule with me? Be my queen? Repair the damage of the two lands with me? Grow old with me? Have children with me? Make this world a better place with me?"

She swallowed, and Jack held his breath. The moment stretched on until he wasn't sure he would be able to remember to breathe in this lifetime.

"Of course, Jack. Of course." Her smile was bright as she slipped the ring onto her finger.

Jack pulled her into his arms as they fell back onto the library floor. He vowed to never let her go again.

EPILOGUE

Spider, suspicious of the sun, kept to the shadows.

—COLLECTED FOLKTALES

The desert stretches out before me, bleak and brown. Lives have been scratched here into the dirt, but the misery of my people echoes. It reached me in the World Between, and it reaches me still.

The Elsiran soldiers have taken the capital city of Lagrimar. Their motorized transports cut across the country, inspiring awe and hope in those they pass. Word of my awakening has traveled with them. I ride upon the wind, crossing the vast distance in almost no time at all.

As I fly, dark heads tilt up and dark eyes rise to me. I block out their awe and fascination, their reverence and wonder. Block them out until I locate the one I seek.

He stands at the entrance to the city. His power is a brilliant star outshining a sea of flickering candles.

Your Majesty. His thoughts reach me cautiously. Not a smidgeon of awe can be found.

Darvyn. I smile internally, enjoying his wariness. Quite a lot of trouble could be avoided if people were more wary. Though for Darvyn, trouble is inevitable.

He has been through an ordeal these past weeks—one I did not foresee—and there are more tests to come. For I have need of him. Again.

You must go west, I tell him. He clenches his jaw. *You will aid the new king and queen, Jaqros and Jasminda.* I force myself to numb the sliver of jealousy slicing my heart when I think of them—their love, a living, breathing entity, taunts me. But I cannot begrudge these children their happiness.

No. I need to find her. His thoughts turn to his own tattered heart. To the woman who owns it.

Sympathy and sentimentality are like quicksand. I cannot allow them to pull him under as they did me.

Now is not the time for you and her. I owe the new queen a debt, and it must be paid. Family is all that matters now. And it is high time Jasminda's family came home.

His eyes bore into me coldly. I call the wind to me and rise into the air. He will help.

I will give him no other option.

ACKNOWLEDGMENTS

To the readers who rolled with me the first time around, you have my eternal gratitude! I hope this iteration of Jasminda and Jack's story makes the waiting more bearable.

This book was conceived after a weeklong writing workshop where my creative mind was torn apart and put back together again. The next year I went back with the opening chapter to have the process repeated. Huge thanks to Junot Díaz, Marjorie Liu, and both my VONA crews—your voices made me a better writer.

Thank you to my editor, Monique Patterson, for bringing me on this amazing journey. You offered me an unexpected detour that terrified me, but you have been the best possible guide. And immense thanks to everyone at St. Martin's Press for all the hard work that made this possible.

To the BCALA and the librarians who saw something relevant in my fantastical love story, I'm forever grateful.

Thanks to Danielle Poiesz, who first polished my words, and James T. Egan, who designed an amazing package for them to live in. To Quinn Heraty, my fabulous lawyer, thank you for shepherding me through unfamiliar terrain. To Kaia Danielle, the best signal booster ever, and Kara Stevens, who helped keep me accountable: y'all rock. And to everyone at the Muse Writers Center, thank you for lighting the match.

To Ines Johnson for being my favorite human, and Cerece Rennie Murphy for being relentlessly reliable.

To Paul, who's made of the same star stuff as me, only upside down and backward, thank you for carrying me across the finish line and supplying the missing pieces. To my father, who won't see this but I know is someplace where he can feel it, and my mother, who sees everything, thank you for always supporting my dreams.

And to Jared, thank you for believing in me and for lifting the heavy stuff to make space for me to write. I love you.